Francis Seymour Stevenson

Robert Grosseteste - Bishop of Lincoln

a contribution to the religious, political and intellectual history of the thirteenth

century

Francis Seymour Stevenson

Robert Grosseteste - Bishop of Lincoln
a contribution to the religious, political and intellectual history of the thirteenth century

ISBN/EAN: 9783337368920

Printed in Europe, USA, Canada, Australia, Japan

Cover: Foto ©Andreas Hilbeck / pixelio.de

More available books at **www.hansebooks.com**

ROBERT GROSSETESTE

BISHOP OF LINCOLN

A CONTRIBUTION TO THE RELIGIOUS, POLITICAL
AND INTELLECTUAL HISTORY OF THE
THIRTEENTH CENTURY

BY

FRANCIS SEYMOUR STEVENSON, M.P.

AUTHOR OF 'HISTORIC PERSONALITY,' ETC.

London
MACMILLAN AND CO., LIMITED
NEW YORK : THE MACMILLAN COMPANY
1899

PREFACE

THE contemporary authorities on which the present work is based are :—

(1) Grosseteste's own *Letters*, edited by Dr. Luard, Rolls Series, 1861.

(2) The first volume of the *Monumenta Franciscana*, edited by Dr. Brewer, Rolls Series, 1858. It includes, *inter alia*, Thomas Eccleston's *De Adventa Minorum*, and the *Letters* of Adam Marsh, a large number of which are addressed to Grosseteste.

(3) The *Historia Major*, for which Matthew Paris is partly responsible, as transcriber and corrector, for the period anterior to 1235, and solely responsible, as author, from that date onwards, edited by Dr. Luard, Rolls Series, 1872 *sqq.* The *Additamenta* in vol. vi. include several documents of importance relating to Grosseteste, and the admirable index in vol. vii. is of the utmost value in connection with the history of the times.

(4) The *Historia Anglorum*, or *Historia Minor* of Matthew Paris, edited by Sir F. Madden, Rolls Series, 1866 *sqq.* Although it is an abbreviation of the former work, it contains here and there some additional matter.

(5) The *Annales Monastici*, edited by Dr. Luard, Rolls Series, 1864 *sqq.* Even when transcribed by later hands, they may be regarded as essentially contemporary records. Those of Burton and of Dunstable are of most importance in their

bearing on Grosseteste's life, but those of Tewkesbury, Waverley, Osney, and Thomas Wykes are occasionally of use.

(6) The *Calendar of Papal Registers*, edited by Mr. Bliss, *Calendars of State Papers*. It describes numerous documents hitherto unknown, helps to fix the chronology with greater accuracy, and throws a new light upon several portions of Grosseteste's career, particularly upon the period which followed the Council of Lyons.

(7) The *Opus Tertium*, etc., of Roger Bacon, edited by Dr. Brewer, Rolls Series, 1859.

(8) Grosseteste's *Rolls*, of which I have consulted the copious extracts made by Matthew Hutton, Harl. MSS. 6950-51, British Museum.

(9) Various authorities, illustrating particular points, might also be mentioned in the same category, such as the letter of Giraldus Cambrensis to William de Vere, written in 1199 (*Giraldus Cambrensis*, vol. i., ed. Dr. Brewer, Rolls Series, 1861): some of the documents contained in the *Charters, etc., relating to the Diocese of Salisbury*, ed. Jones and Macray, Rolls Series, 1891: the *Register of St. Osmund*, ed. Jones, Rolls Series, 1883: the *Lettres de Jourdain de Saxe*, ed. Bayonne, Paris, 1865; and others, to which reference will be made in the notes.

Among authorities which are nearly contemporary, or based upon contemporary information, may be cited the following :—

(1) Trivet's *Annales*, edited by T. Hog, for the English Historical Society, 1845.

(2) Rishanger's *Chronicles*, including the one edited by J. O. Halliwell for the Camden Society in 1840, and the one edited by Mr. Riley among the *Chronica Monasterii Sancti Albani*, Rolls Series, 1863 *sqq*.

(3) The *Lives of the Bishops of Lincoln*, by John de Schalby, printed as an appendix to *Giraldus Cambrensis*, vol. vii., ed.

by Dimock, Rolls Series. Although written as late as 1330, or about that year, the narrative derives some importance from the fact that it purports to be founded upon the Lincoln Cathedral Registers. It does not, however, add materially to the fund of information to be obtained from other sources. The same volume also contains the will of Hugh de Wells and other documents relating to the Diocese of Lincoln.

(4) The *Flores Historiarum*, commonly known as "Matthew of Westminster," founded mainly upon Matthew Paris, for the period now under consideration, and edited by Dr. Luard, Rolls Series, 1890.

(5) The *Chronicon de Lancrcost*, edited by the Rev. J. Stevenson for the Bannatyne and Maitland Clubs, 1839.

(6) Various documents contained in the *Lincoln Cathedral Statutes*, edited by Bradshaw and Wordsworth, Cambridge, 1892-97.

The *Twelfth Report of the Historical Manuscripts Commission*, Appendix 9, gives some account of the papers concerning Grosseteste, which are preserved at Lincoln. They relate principally to the attempts to procure his canonisation, a subject on which the *Historical Papers and Letters from the Northern Registers* are also of use.

The scanty traditions preserved by Leland in his *Itinerary*, his *Collectanea*, and his *De Scriptoribus Britanniae*, with reference to Grosseteste's early life, are collected in Tanner's *Bibliotheca*, *s.v.* Grosthead. Owing to the loss of some of the sources of information to which Leland had access, his statements, even when unsupported, require serious consideration, though they must be treated with great caution. Still greater reserve is needed in regard to statements, based upon documents now lost, contained in Wood's *History of the University of Oxford* and in Du Boulay's *Histoire de l'Université de Paris*.

The metrical *Life of Grosseteste* by Richard, a monk of Bardney, written in 1503, and printed in Wharton's *Anglia Sacra*, together with certain other materials relating to Grosseteste, is a work of fiction, devoid of historical value.

A brief sketch of Grosseteste's life is prefixed to the edition of his *De Cessatione Legalium*, London, 1658. The appendix to Edward Brown's edition of the *Fasciculus* of Orthuinus Gratius, London, 1690, contains some of Grosseteste's sermons and *dicta*, as well as the memorandum which he caused to be read at Lyons in 1250 in the presence of the Pope and Cardinals. The letters printed in the *Fasciculus* are all included, with a corrected text, and with the addition of many others, in Dr. Luard's edition.

Among works written in the English language, Pegge's *Life of Grosseteste*, published in 1793, and Dr. Luard's preface to the *Letters*, published in 1861, are the most important contributions to the knowledge of the subject. The former is rather a collection of materials than a biography, and the progress of historical research has superseded much of its interest. It embodies, however, a large amount of useful labour, and contains some valuable appendices dealing with particular points, such as the origin of vicarages, etc. Owing, it is said, to a fire in the printing establishment, the book is unfortunately very scarce. Dr. Luard's preface sets at rest most of the chronological difficulties connected with Grosseteste's career. Its substance is reproduced in the article which he contributed to the *Dictionary of National Biography*.

Archdeacon Perry's interesting little work entitled *The Life and Times of Robert Grosseteste*, published in 1871 by the Society for the Promotion of Christian Knowledge, confines itself almost exclusively to his career as an ecclesiastical reformer. In regard to matters connected with the Diocese of Lincoln it possesses a special value, but its treatment of the larger questions at issue is somewhat unsatisfactory. I have availed myself here and there, of his paraphrases and translations. Among shorter studies relating to Grosseteste may be mentioned a lecture by Dr. Creighton, delivered in St. Paul's Cathedral on the 21st of November 1895, before he became Bishop of London, and briefly reported in the *Church Times* of the 29th of November; and a pamphlet by Mgr. W. Croke Robinson, published for the Catholic Truth Society in 1896.

In Germany Dr. Pauli issued as his Tübingen *Programm* in 1864 a brief dissertation on *Robert Grosseteste and Adam Marsh, a Contribution to the Earlier History of the University of Oxford.* In 1867 Dr. G. V. Lechler delivered before the University of Leipzig a lecture on Grosseteste, in commemoration of the 350th anniversary of the German Reformation. It appears in an English garb, with some variations, in vol. i. pp. 28 *sqq.* of his work on *John Wiclif and his English Precursors,* translated by Lorimer, London, 1878. In 1887 a fuller account of Grosseteste appeared from the pen of Dr. Joseph Felten, now Professor at the Faculty of Catholic Theology at Bonn University, and author of the *Life of Gregory the Ninth,* under the title of *Robert Grosseteste, Bischof von Lincoln ; ein Beitrag zur Kirchen- und Culturgeschichte des dreizehnten Jahrhunderts,* Freiburg, 1887.

M. Charles Jourdain's erudite, but rather fanciful essay, entitled *Doutes sur l'authenticité de quelques écrits contre la cour de Rome attribués à Robert Grosse-Tête, évêque de Lincoln,* which appeared originally in 1868, has been reprinted posthumously in his *Excursions historiques et philosophiques à travers le Moyen Age,* Paris, 1888. Dr. Felten discusses the question in an appendix. My views will be found on pp. 315, 316, 319 *sqq.*

Among the other works which I have found helpful in connection with the subject may be mentioned the Rev. H. Rashdall's *Universities of Europe during the Middle Ages ;* Mr.

Little's *Grey Friars at Oxford*, as well as certain other publications of the Oxford Historical Society; M. Émile Charles's *Roger Bacon*; M. Hauréau's *Histoire de la Philosophie scholastique*; Prof. Prantl's *Geschichte der Logik im Abendlande*; Dr. Ferdinand Kaltenbrunner's *Vorgeschichte der Gregorianischen Kalenderreform*; the Rev. Ed. Taunton's *Black Monks of St. Benedict*; some of Prof. Maitland's contributions to the *English Historical Review*; M. Sabatier's *Vie de St. François d'Assise*, and Canon Jessopp's essay on the *Coming of the Friars*. Bishop Stubbs's *Constitutional History* and his *Registrum Sacrum Anglicanum* have been frequently consulted. Although I have only dealt with Simon de Montfort within the limits indicated by his connection with Grosseteste, I have often turned to the pages of Dr. Pauli, Prof. Prothero, and M. Bémont.

With respect to the district in which Grosseteste was born I have consulted the Davy MSS. (Suffolk, Hoxne, and Hartismere Hundreds) in the British Museum, and have to thank Canon Raven, Vicar of Fressingfield-cum-Withersdale, and author of the *History of Suffolk* and other well-known works, for his replies to certain inquiries which I addressed to him thereon.

Although I have endeavoured to give some account of most of Grosseteste's writings, and have examined nearly all his printed works as well as several of the manuscripts, I have refrained from including a systematic bibliography, or *catalogue raisonné*. Lists, more or less accurate, are to be found in Boston of Bury, Leland, Bale, Pits, Oudin, Cave, Wharton, Tanner, Fabricius, Pegge, and the *Histoire Littéraire de la France*. Pegge's list extends to twenty-three quarto pages, but Tanner's is more useful for purposes of reference, as it gives, in the majority of instances, the name of the place where each MS. was at the time when he wrote. Dr. Luard, M. Brunet, Dr. Felten, Bishop Lightfoot (in his Introduction to the Epistles of

St. Ignatius), and others provide supplementary information, and the notes to the present volume contain sundry additions and corrections which may, perhaps, be of use to the future bibliographer.

Anxious as I am that the present work should come to be regarded as the standard Life of Grosseteste, I am nevertheless fully conscious of the possibility that the discovery of fresh materials may throw a new light upon certain aspects of the earlier part of his career. As far, however, as the period which followed his accession to the See of Lincoln is concerned—with the partial exception of the interval from the end of January 1251 to the middle of March 1253, during which the Papal Registers do not supplement the information obtainable elsewhere—it may be affirmed that the existing materials are now sufficient to enable a definite and final judgment to be pronounced, and that any future additions they may receive are only likely to affect the consideration of details. May I add that, although there is much in Grosseteste's life, and in the great movements he directed, or with which he was otherwise associated, that lends itself to controversial treatment, I have endeavoured to approach the questions at issue singly with a view to historic truth. The preparation of this volume has necessarily involved a considerable amount of research, undertaken in the midst of other work. If it succeeds in inspiring the reader with a true conception of Grosseteste's place in history, it will not have been written in vain.

FRANCIS SEYMOUR STEVENSON.

PLAYFORD MOUNT,
NEAR WOODBRIDGE, *July* 1899.

CONTENTS

CHAPTER I

CHAPTER II

CHAPTER III

CHAPTER IV

CHAPTER V

CHAPTER VI

CHAPTER VII

CHAPTER VIII

CHAPTER IX

CHAPTER XIV

CHAPTER XV

CHAPTER I

THE importance of the place occupied by Robert Grosseteste in the life and thought of the thirteenth century, and the remarkable and, in certain respects, dominant character of the influence which he exercised over the revival of religion, the revival of learning, and the revival of the national spirit in this country, not only during his own times, but for several generations that ensued, render all the more regrettable the scantiness of materials relating to his early years. Concerning the locality in which he was born, however, no serious doubt can be raised, as Matthew Paris, Trivet, and Capgrave are at one in declaring that he owed his origin to the county of Suffolk, whilst the compiler of the *Flores Historiarum*, formerly known as Matthew of Westminster, adds that the actual place of his birth was Stradbroke.[1] That county, which originally derived, from the number of its churches and from the strength and simplicity of its faith, the epithets of "holy" and "silly," in the obsolete sense of the term, by which it became known in early times, has, indeed, justified its ecclesiastical reputation by producing a long array of distinguished prelates, amongst whom Wolsey in

[1] *Hist. Anglorum*, ed. Madden, iii. 148; Trivet, ed. Hog, p. 242; Capgrave's *Chron. of England*, ed. Hingeston, p. 156; *Matthew of Westminster*, Frankfort edition, 1601, p. 354. The sentence appears to have dropped accidentally in Luard's edition of the *Flores Historiarum*. It ought to occur either on page 388 or on page 392 of vol. ii. The insertion of an interpolation from one of the manuscripts doubtless led to the omission. Luard refers to the passage on p. 31 of his Introduction to the *Letters*.

the sixteenth and Sancroft in the seventeenth centuries are, after Grosseteste himself, the most conspicuous figures. Hardly anything is known as to his parentage and early training. That he was of humble origin is proved by the united testimony of several chroniclers,[1] and by the fact that the canons of Lincoln, at the time of his dispute with the dean and chapter of that cathedral, are stated to have resented the appointment of a Bishop of such lowly birth to rule over them, and to have expressed their discontent even in his presence.[2] In all likelihood his father was a small farmer. Howell, the historiographer, in one of his *Epistolae Ho-Elianae*, written in the seventeenth century, mentions, on the authority of some old tradition incorporated in a lost work, that Grosseteste had a brother, to whom he once said, " A husbandman you are, and a husbandman you will remain." [3] Of his relatives, however, there is no trace to be found in his correspondence beyond the fact that he had a sister named Juetta, who took the veil in a nunnery near Oxford, probably at Godstow, and to whom he communicated his doubts and difficulties in the year 1232, in which, under the stress of bodily suffering, he resigned the offices he held in the Church, with the exception of his Lincoln prebend.[4] Her death is mentioned in one of Adam Marsh's letters.[5] Reference is also to be found there to two of Grosseteste's kinsmen, who were in poor circumstances, and whom he was asked to befriend and support in connection with their University studies.[6] That brief enumera-

<hr>

[1] *Hist. Anglorum*, l.c. ; *Chronicon de Lanercost*, ed. J. Stevenson, where he is described as *genere infimus*. Trivet uses the words *de ima gente Suthfolchiae*.

[2] *Historia Major* (ed. Luard), iii. 528.

[3] Howell, *Epistolae Ho-Elianae*, p. 420 (ed. of 1754). " I have read a tale of Robert Grosthead, Bishop of Lincoln, that being come to his greatness, he had a brother who was a husbandman, and expected great things from him in point of preferment; but the Bishop told him that if he wanted money to mend his plough or his cart, or to buy tacklings for his horses, with other things belonging to his husbandry, he should not want what was fitting ; but wished him to aim no higher, for a husbandman he found him, and a husbandman he will leave him."

[4] Letter 8.

[5] *Monumenta Franciscana* (ed. Brewer), pp. 95, 164.

[6] *Ibid.* p. 137.

tion exhausts, however, what is known with regard to his family. It is even uncertain whether the name of Grosthead, or Greathead, or Grosseteste was one which he inherited from his father, or whether it was a surname given to him by reason of some physical or other peculiarity. The former view is in harmony with the fact that among his contemporaries there were at least two who bore the name of Grosseteste, one of whom was at Oxford in 1238, whilst the other was rector of Wissenden, in the county of Rutland, in 1245.[1] It is also borne out by the form of signature which he used before he became Archdeacon.[2] On the other hand, both Matthew Paris and Trivet speak of his " cognomen " of Grosseteste in terms which imply that it was given to him personally,[3] possibly for the reason suggested by Fuller that " he got his surname from the greatness of his head, having large stowage to receive, and store of brains to fill it." [4] The variations in the spelling of his name are almost as numerous as those which occur in that of Shakespeare. It was sometimes latinised into *Capito*, but Robert of Lincoln, *Lincolniensis*, and St. Robert are the designations by which he was best known during the two following centuries to the readers of his works.

Few as are the materials which throw light upon the history of Grosseteste's early years, even the glimmer they cast has been, to some extent, darkened by two documents of no historic value, which have served merely to perplex successive biographers. The first is a genealogy of the year 1666, on the strength of which Thoresby, in his *History of Leeds*, was induced to connect him with the Yorkshire family of Copley, one of whom was

---

[1] See Pegge's first Appendix, pp. 292-296.

[2] Dugdale's *Monasticon*, v. p. 191, where he witnesses, as " Master Robert Grosseteste," without any addition, a confirmation by Hugh de Wells, Bishop of Lincoln, of all the benefactions made to the priory of St. Andrew's at Northampton.

[3] Matthew Paris speaks of " Roberto cognomento Grosseteste," and of " Roberto dicto Grossum Caput." Trivet says that he " nominatus est a pluribus Grossum Caput." " His to-name is Grosseteste," says Robert de Brunne in the poem to be mentioned later, p. 334.

[4] Fuller's *Church History*, iii. p. 65.

alleged to have married the daughter of Sir Richard Walsingham of Suffolk, and to have been the father of the future Bishop of Lincoln. It is, no doubt, possible that a branch of the Copleys may have settled in Suffolk, and that Grosseteste may even have owed to them his origin and his name, which he may have exchanged for the one by which he became known; but the authority for the statement is so slender, and its probability so infinitesimal, that it may safely be disregarded in the absence of confirmatory evidence, and it is hardly conceivable that a contemporary chronicler would have described a grandson of Sir Richard Walsingham, in the language used by Matthew Paris, as being *ex humillima stirpe procreatus*.[1] The other delusive document is the metrical life of Grosseteste by Richard, a monk of Bardney, who wrote in 1503. It must be regarded as a work of fiction, destitute of serious importance, and the majority of the statements which it embodies are devoid of all foundation. The place of his birth is wrongly given as Stow, and he is represented as knocking in a ragged condition at the door of the Mayor of Lincoln, and refusing to accept alms on the condition that he would undertake never to be Bishop of that See. Both the pedigree and the poem, however, have been sufficiently discussed and discredited by Pegge and by Dr. Luard.[2]

Although the precise date of Grosseteste's birth is uncertain, the year 1175 is approximately indicated by the fact that Giraldus Cambrensis, in the letter in which in 1199 he recommends Grosseteste to the attention and protection of William de Vere, Bishop of Hereford, speaks of him as a *magister* or regent of arts, implying that he must have been, in all likelihood, not less than twenty-four years of age at the time.[3] As he died in 1253, the age of seventy-eight, to which he would, on that supposition, have attained, renders intelligible the language said

---

[1] *Hist. Anglorum*, ii. 376.

[2] Pegge, Appendix II. pp. 297-302; Luard, Introd. to Grosseteste's *Letters*, p. xxxi. Richard of Bardney's metrical life of Grosseteste is given in Wharton's *Anglia Sacra*.

[3] Giraldus Cambrensis, ed. Brewer, i. 249.

by Matthew Paris to have been used with regard to him shortly before his death by Pope Innocent IV., and also the tribute paid by Roger Bacon to the length of his days.[1]

Stradbroke was, in relation to the circumstances of the time, a place of greater importance than it is now. It was to receive from Henry III., rather more than half a century later, a grant of market rights,[2] and the large and stately church, which stands on the site of an earlier edifice, and was supplemented by a *libera capella* in another part of the parish, bears witness to what must have been the existence of a considerable resident population. Several manors were included in the parish,[3] of which the largest was granted in the days of Stephen to Ernald, son of Roger Rufus, or Rous, in the hands of whose descendants it remained for several generations. If, as is probable, Grosseteste's father was what would now be termed a tenant of the Rufus family, it is possible that the Giles de Rous, or Rufus, who was appointed in 1246 by the Bishop of Lincoln to the archdeaconry of Northampton,[4] may have owed his introduction to the Bishop's notice to some connection with his native place. The principal manor of Stradbroke formed part of the royal honour of Eye, as was also the case with the soke and advowson of the church. The latter was also intimately connected with the Benedictine priory of Eye, which was dependent upon the famous abbey of Bernay in Normandy; and as it was situated within a distance of about six miles from Stradbroke, it is not unlikely that Grosseteste may have acquired from some monk attached to that priory the rudiments both of Latin and of French. The supposition, however, is hardly confirmed by the appearance of the name of Robert, Bishop of Lincoln, in the manu-

[1] Roger Bacon, *Compendium Studii*, ed. Brewer, p. 472, "solus dominus Robertus, propter longitudinem vitae et vias mirabiles quibus usus est, prae aliis hominibus scivit scientias." Dr. Luard thinks that the date 1175 cannot be far wrong. See p. 313.

[2] Granted in 1227 to Hugh Rufus. Another grant appears to have been made about two years earlier, *Rot. Lit. Claus.* ed. Hardy, p. 68.

[3] Not merely two, as stated in Kirby's *Suffolk*. See vol. xv. of the Davy MSS. collections relating to Suffolk (Hoxne Hundred) in the British Museum.

[4] Willis, p. 110 ; Grosseteste's Roll. Possibly his pupil Adam Rufus (see p. 20) may also have belonged to the same family.

script register of that priory[1] in the list of its benefactors, a fact which might be thought to indicate that in the days of his subsequent greatness he was not unmindful of the aid rendered to him in ascending the first rungs of the ladder; for the two undated charters which bear that name may be assigned, with far greater likelihood, to one of the two Roberts who presided over the see of Lincoln in the course of the twelfth century, as is shown, almost conclusively, not only by the position in which they stand in the cartulary, but also by the nature of their contents.[2] It may, perhaps, be supposed that the agricultural knowledge exhibited at a later date in the rules which he framed for the guidance of the Countess of Lincoln with regard to the management of her estate, and the share which he is believed to have taken in the translation of Walter of Henley's treatise on husbandry into English, may have been due, in some measure, to his recollection of the methods and practice in the important corn-growing district of which Stradbroke was the centre, and of the practical experience he had acquired on his father's holding. It is not necessary, however, to adopt Richard of Bardney's statement that Grosseteste, in his boyhood, tended swine, like the Felice Peretti who subsequently became Pope Sixtus the Fifth, although in a letter addressed to the convent of Missenden, the Bishop shows incidentally a remarkable acquaintance with the qualities needed in a swineherd, whose

---

[1] Taylor's *Index Monasticus;* Davy MSS. Suffolk (Hartismere Hundred), vol. xiii. pp. 197 *sqq.*

[2] There was also a small Benedictine priory at Hoxne, even nearer to Stradbroke, founded by Herbert de Losinga, Bishop of Norwich, as a cell to Norwich. Canon Raven, in his *History of Suffolk*, suggests that, as the Bishops of Norwich frequently stayed at Hoxne, Grosseteste may in his boyhood have come under the notice of John of Oxford, who was Bishop of Norwich from 1175 to 1200, and who was a patron of men of letters. Daniel de Morley was assisted by him.

It is unlikely that there was a school at Hoxne at that time. The monks, who previously inhabited the Bishop's palace at Hoxne, do not appear to have removed to the priory until some date subsequent to the consecration of Thomas de Blunville as Bishop of Norwich in 1226. The school at which two poor boys were educated gratis, in addition to others, can hardly have been founded before the completion of the cell, and probably belongs to a much later date. The latter stood near the chapel which commemorated the site of the martyrdom of St. Edmund. See Davy MSS.

calling he introduces into his argument by way of illustration.[1]

An anecdote related in the *Lancrcost Chronicle*, if correct, throws some light upon the class of life from which Grosseteste sprang, and also upon the nature of his early training.[2] Richard de Clare, Earl of Gloucester, whilst on a visit to the Bishop of Lincoln, with whom he was on terms of intimacy, expressed surprise at the unfailing courtesy and courtliness of his dispensation of hospitality, in view of the humility of his origin and the slender opportunities he had enjoyed in early life of obtaining the requisite knowledge of the world. Grosseteste replied that it was quite true that his father and mother were in lowly life, but that from his earliest years he had studied the characters of the best men in the Scriptures, and had endeavoured to conform his actions to theirs. Whatever advantages he may have derived from the proximity of the priory of Eye, it is clear that he must, like every other man who has risen to greatness, have derived more from himself than from any teachers. There is, indeed, no evidence of historical value with respect to his early career. Leland, who bases his assertions on the testimony of authorities no longer extant and of traditions the exact value of which can no longer be measured at this distance of time, states that he received his early education in Suffolk, and that he displayed such remarkable powers, such natural facility of expression, and so acute a

---

[1] Letter 85, ed. Luard, p. 269. Richard of Bardney's lines run thus (Wharton, ii. p. 336) :—

Porcorum custos ascendit culmina Cleri ;
  Praesulis officium rusticus aggreditur.

[2] *Chron. de Lancrcost*, p. 44. The immediate occasion for the remark was this : It was a fish-day on which it was customary to eat choice sea-wolves. The larger fish was placed before Grosseteste, and the smaller one before the Earl, who sat on his right. "Take that fish away," said the Bishop to the seneschal, "or give one of equal size to the Earl." The servants replied that they could not find another so large. "Then," said the Bishop, "set aside the whole of this for alms, and give me a smaller one like the rest." A somewhat similar story is related by Selden (pref. to the *Titles of Honour*, ed. Wilkins, iii. part i. p. 96), with the difference that Henry the Third is represented as the questioner, and not the Earl of Gloucester. Selden gives as his authority John de Athona's notes on the Constitutions of Ottoboni, tit. de Bonis Intestat. *s.v.* Baronum.

judgment in proportion to his years, that he was sent by his kinsmen,[1] as soon as they were able to do so, to the University of Oxford, which was then in a most flourishing condition. If that statement be trustworthy, it disposes of the supposition, suggested by Richard of Bardney's lines, that Grosseteste may have spent some time at the school of Lincoln previous to his arrival at Oxford. The possibility, however, must not be left altogether out of sight; for the Lincoln school was one of no mean order, as is shown by the fact that Giraldus Cambrensis, when nearly fifty years of age, thought fit to spend some years there, from 1196 to 1199, whilst engaged in the study of theology, and it is not inconceivable that it was in that manner that Grosseteste made his acquaintance and obtained through him his introduction to the Bishop of Hereford. It may also be inferred that a lower-grade school was in existence in the city of Lincoln.[2] The probability, however, is that Grosseteste must have reached Oxford some years before 1196, as otherwise he would not have had time to become a " magister " by 1199; and consequently, Leland's account is, in the absence of further evidence, the one best entitled to belief. If, however, the date of the visit of Giraldus Cambrensis [3] to Lincoln could be assigned to 1192 instead of 1196—and there is some doubt as to the chronology of that portion of his life—the hypothesis that Grosseteste himself studied at that school by way of

[1] " A propinquis," an expression which might, however, mean his neighbours and not his kinsmen. Leland's *Collectanea*. The passage is given at length in Tanner's *Bibliotheca*.

[2] Cp. Mr. A. F. Leach's paper on the History of Endowed Schools, vol. v. p. 65 of the *Report of the Royal Commission on Secondary Education*. Also his *English Schools at the Reformation*, p. 8, etc.

[3] Giraldus Cambrensis, ed. Brewer, vol. i. 93, 109, 110, 294. It was owing to the outbreak of hostilities between England and France that Giraldus went to Lincoln and not to Paris to study theology. See also vol. v. ed. Dimock, Introd. p. 53, note 2. Wharton, who is followed by Sir R. Colt Hoare (*Life of Giraldus Cambrensis*, London, 1806, p. 55) and by Dr. Brewer (Introd. to vol. i. of Giraldus Cambrensis, p. 56), was of opinion that 1192 was the date when he went to Lincoln. Mr. Dimock, however, in the passage cited, shows almost conclusively that the duration of his stay at Lincoln must have been from 1196, and not from 1192 to 1199. See also vol. iv., preface, p. 37. The outbreak of war was in 1196. On William de Monte and the Lincoln school see p. 16.

preparation for his University career, after he had left Stradbroke, would receive additional and perhaps preponderating support.

Whether or not Grosseteste used one of the Lincoln schools as an intermediate stage between his native place and the University which he was destined to adorn, the contrast between the calm of the former and the activity of the latter must have appealed with special force to one who had already learnt to be a keen observer of men and of things. The Oxford of that day was not, as has been sometimes supposed, a semi-monastic organisation removed from the turbulence of the outer world. It was, on the contrary, a microcosm in which might be discerned the tendencies of the age, and in which almost every aspect of life was represented. The city itself ranked in wealth and population among the foremost in the kingdom; it was a fortress of considerable importance; its Jewry was one of the largest in the country, and its merchants carried on their trade and their intercourse, not only with the capital and the inland districts of England, but with the lands beyond the sea. Alike in the days of Canute and in those of Stephen, it had witnessed the meeting of great national assemblies, and, within a comparatively brief span of years, it was to play an even more important part in the Parliamentary history of the realm.[1]

The University was rapidly advancing in importance at the close of the twelfth century, probably as the result of a migration which had taken place from Paris in 1167, and which had led to the almost immediate development of Oxford into a *studium generale*,[2] and had enormously increased the reputation it derived from the existence of its earlier schools. It possessed an extensive book trade, as is shown by the fact that one document relating to a transfer of property in Cat Street shortly after 1180 contains, among its parties or witnesses, no fewer than three illuminators, one bookbinder, one writer, and two parchmenters of that immediate neighbourhood.[3] Students

---

[1] See Green's *Stray Studies.*

[2] Rashdall's *Universities of Europe in the Middle Ages,* ii. 329-332 and 340.

[3] Rashdall, ii. p. 343, and the facsimile at the commencement of vol. ii. part ii.

flocked in from various parts of the world, and in 1192 Richard of Devizes speaks of the clerks of Oxford as so numerous that the city could hardly feed them,[1] and the members may be estimated roughly—though they doubtless varied greatly from year to year—from the contemporary statement that the academic population amounted in 1209 to at least three thousand souls.[2] It is interesting to note that in 1197, as Jocelyn de Brakelond relates, the celebrated Abbot Samson of Bury St. Edmunds, whilst serving on a commission together with Hubert, Archbishop of Canterbury, and St. Hugh, Bishop of Lincoln, for the purpose of restoring the expelled Coventry monks, entertained in his Oxford lodgings a large party of Oxford Masters and others ; and it may perhaps be surmised that Grosseteste, in view of his position in the University and his connection with the Abbot's county, was one of the guests on that occasion.[3]

The most important reference, however, to the Oxford of that time is contained in the celebrated description given by Giraldus Cambrensis of the manner in which he had read in public his *Topography of Ireland ;* and it is not a matter for surprise that, in view of the place which he must, according to that account, have filled in the eyes of all for several ensuing years, Grosseteste should have turned to him for a letter of recommendation, even if he was not previously acquainted with him at Lincoln. The following is the description, in which Giraldus, following the example of Cæsar and anticipating that of Moltke, speaks of himself in the third person. " Wishing," he writes, " not to hide the candle he had lighted under a bushel, but to place it on a candlestick, so that it might give light, he arranged to read his work aloud before a large audience in Oxford, where the clergy were more flourishing than elsewhere in England,

<hr>

[1] Rashdall, ii. p. 347 ; Richard of Devizes, ed. J. Stevenson, p. 61.

[2] *Hist. Maj.* ii. 526.

[3] Jocelyn of Brakelond, ed. Camden Society. Also in Arnold's *Memorials of St. Edmund's Bury,* i. 295. The entertainment was given at Oxford, and not, as one writer supposes, at Bury St. Edmunds.

and excelled in the knowledge appertaining to a clerk.   There were three parts to his book, of which he recited one each day, so that the recitation lasted three successive days.   And on the first day he invited for the purpose all the poor (that is, the poor scholars) of the whole city, and entertained them hospitably and publicly.   On the following day he entertained all the doctors of the various faculties and their better-known and more distinguished pupils, and on the third day the rest of the scholars, together with many knights, townsmen, and burgesses.   It was indeed a costly and a noble function, for it was, in a way, a renewal of the genuine old times of the poets, and neither during the present age nor in the days of old has England witnessed such a spectacle." [1]

Of the opportunities afforded by his stay at Oxford, it is evident that Grosseteste must have made abundant use.   The details, indeed, of his University career during that period of his life are unknown to us: it would be interesting, for instance, if some memorial had been preserved of the sequence and precise nature of his studies, of the means of information to which he had access, of the lecturers whose courses he attended, and of the mode by which he was able to maintain himself, in spite of his poverty, during the years which preceded his admission into the household of the Bishop of Hereford.   The collegiate system, as need hardly be observed, had not yet come into existence.   Of the colleges which now exist, the three oldest, Balliol, Merton, and University, were not called into being until the second half of the thirteenth century, and the students resided either in private lodgings or in small hostels, which were not replaced by, or merged into the larger institutions until a later date, and the lectures were delivered in the various schools, of which a considerable number had already sprung up.   Only a small percentage of students, in all likelihood, lodged in the monasteries of St. Frideswyde's and

---

[1] Giraldus Cambrensis, *De Rebus a se Gestis*, ii. p. 73.   This was in 1186, or almost immediately afterwards.

Osney. It is possible that Edmund Rich of Abingdon, better known in after years as St. Edmund of Canterbury, may have taught at Oxford for some time previous to the year 1200, in which case the tradition which mentions Grosseteste among his pupils may refer to that period. It is more probable, however, that Grosseteste, in common with several other distinguished men, such as Robert Bacon and Richard Fishacre, attended these lectures at a considerably later date, some years after he had taken his degree. On the other hand, it is by no means unlikely that he may have derived from the teaching of Thomas de Marleberge, afterwards Abbot of Evesham, some of the knowledge of canon and of civil law which he undoubtedly acquired.[1]

Although the details, however, are obscure, the general results of his Oxford training are clear. The following letter, addressed, in all likelihood, in 1199 by Giraldus Cambrensis to William de Vere, Bishop of Hereford, affords some indication of what they were. "In the words of Symmachus," writes that celebrated chronicler, "'he who intervenes on behalf of good men appears to commend his own judgment in no less a degree than he conduces to their advantage.' Hence it is that I only ask on behalf of Master Robert Grosseteste, whom you have recently welcomed, as I have learnt with gratification, into your household and your intimacy, that his rewards should equal his merits. I am indeed aware that his assistance in your various affairs and in your determination of causes, as well as in the task of securing and preserving your bodily health, in all of which matters he is signally proficient, will soon be doubly, or rather I should say manifoldly, necessary to you. In his case those faculties which in our days are above all others profitable in temporal affairs, have been built upon the sure foundation of the liberal arts and an abundant knowledge of literature, and are illuminated and adorned by the praiseworthy excellence of his character ; for, whilst it often happens that those who are

---

[1] On Thomas de Marleberge see Dugdale's *Monasticon*, vol. ii. p. 5 ; Rashdall ii. p. 347.

skilled in the aforesaid faculties are vacillating in their good faith, you will perceive that he is conspicuous by his good faith and by his fidelity, in addition to his other virtues and the endowments of his mind. In short, to crown all, he possesses such natural gifts and so much industry, that you will find in him, if I am not mistaken, a man after your own heart, and one in whom your spirit will find itself most at ease." [1]

The foregoing letter, which is obviously one of recommendation, and not of introduction to the Bishop of Hereford, into whose household Grosseteste had just entered, may have been preceded by an earlier letter from the same writer, the record of which has been lost. It indicates a close acquaintance on the part of Giraldus with the attainments and the character of Grosseteste. It also shows that, in addition to the seven liberal arts included in the "trivium" and the "quadrivium," [2] of which the former embraced grammar, rhetoric, and logic, while the latter consisted of arithmetic, geometry, music, and astronomy, he must have advanced considerably beyond the limits of that curriculum. The references to "the preservation of health" and "the determination of causes" point to the knowledge of medicine, and to that of canon, if not of civil law. He certainly shows in his correspondence that he was skilled in both those branches. To what extent, however, he had applied himself at that stage to the three subjects which chiefly engrossed his attention, namely, theology, physical science, and the study of ancient languages, is a question which the letter of Giraldus leaves unsolved. "John, Abbot of Peterborough," following, probably, the statement of Matthew Paris, mentions that he was deeply versed in the seven liberal arts, [3] and Leland has preserved the tradition that, within a few years of his arrival at Oxford,

---

[1] Giraldus Cambrensis, ed. Brewer, i. p. 249. The letter is also given in Wharton's *Anglia Sacra*, ii. p. 344.

[2] In the *Historia Anglorum*, ed. Madden, Matthew Paris states that Grosseteste was "eleganter tam in trivio quam in quadrivio eruditus," ii. 376, and again as "vir in Latino et Graeco peritissimus," ii. 467.

[3] "John, Abbas Petriburg." p. 107, in Sparke's Collection (London, 1723).

he had earned the reputation of being most acute in dialectics and in philosophy supreme.[1]

The fact that Grosseteste should have turned to Giraldus Cambrensis for a letter of recommendation, and the tone in which that letter is couched, are creditable alike to the learned and versatile chronicler whose work and whose merits had received their recognition in the century then about to expire, and to the earnest and brilliant scholar whose career forms part of the history of the next fifty years, and whose influence extended over many succeeding generations. Any hopes of advancement, however, which Grosseteste may have entertained in connection with his admission into the Bishop of Hereford's household were doomed to speedy disappointment, as William de Vere died in December of 1199. It is probable that the loss of that opportunity must have appeared to Grosseteste at that time as a serious blow to the aspirations he cherished. In the light of subsequent experience it must have appeared as a blessing in disguise. Had he become dependent upon one man, however excellent and however eminent, he would have been deprived of many of the advantages of which he was able to avail himself when thrown back upon his own resources. His time would have been occupied with the performance of duties which others would have been equally competent to fulfil. He would have been debarred, in a large measure, from access to the sources of information open to him at Oxford, and have been thereby prevented from broadening and deepening the knowledge to which he had already attained ; he would not have been able to teach and to influence the ablest intellects of the country ; and he would not have been brought into that intimate connection with the Mendicant Orders which was, in later years, at one and the same time the result of his insight and, to a certain extent, the secret of his power.

> Es bildet ein Talent sich in der Stille,
>   Sich ein Character in dem Strom der Welt,

---

[1] Leland, *ap.* Tanner's *Bibliotheca*, s.v. Grosthead.

says Goethe. If Grosseteste had remained in the service of the Bishop, he would, on the one hand, have lost the opportunity afforded by quiet study for further intellectual improvement, and, on the other hand, he would have been stranded at some point short of the channel in which flowed the main current of national life and of national activity.

It was probably on the death of the Bishop of Hereford that Grosseteste proceeded to Paris for the purpose of continuing his studies. There is, it is true, no contemporary evidence relating to his visit, but Du Boulay (Bulaeus), in his history of that University, which is largely based upon documents no longer in existence, states that he studied there for several years, and took the Master's degrees, and in another passage he speaks of him as having been formerly an illustrious professor in the University of Paris.[1] Although Bulaeus is often inaccurate, his statement is in accord with inherent probability as well as with tradition. It was a constant occurrence for scholars to proceed from Oxford to Paris with the object of perfecting themselves in certain branches of knowledge; the migrating habits of students in the Middle Ages were a conspicuous feature in the University life of that period; and Grosseteste, in taking the course which he adopted, was following in the footsteps of many distinguished men, including John of Salisbury, St. Thomas of Canterbury, Stephen Langton, Daniel de Morley, Giraldus Cambrensis, and Edmund Rich, the last of whom defrayed the expenses of his journey and of his maintenance by asking alms, in accordance with a practice common to the poorer students. Grosseteste's intimate acquaintance with such men as William de Cerda and William Arvernus, Bishop of Paris, his familiarity with the details of the theological course

---

[1] Bulaeus, vol. iii. pp. 260, 709. "Diu in hac Academia litteris operam dedit, in qua Gradus omnes Magisterii consecutus est." Bulaeus also emphasises the words of Cardinal Egidius, as recorded by Matthew Paris: "novit hoc gallicana et anglicana cleri universitas," *i.e.* the whole body of the French and of the English clergy. Cp. *Hist. Litt. de la France*, vol. xviii. pp. 437 *sqq.* Pits, *Relationes Historicae de Rebus Anglicis*, Paris, 1619, p. 965, mentions Grosseteste amongst the *alumni* of the University of Paris.

of studies pursued there, as shown in his letter to the Regents in theology at Oxford, and the references of Cardinal Egidius to his fame throughout the whole body of the French and of the English clergy, all tend to confirm the view expressed by Bulaeus. The date of his visit, however, is open to doubt. It is not likely to have taken place before the letter of recommendation sent by Giraldus Cambrensis, as in that case it would, in all probability, have been mentioned by that writer as an additional qualification for the post, and it is better, therefore, to assign it to the years which immediately followed the Bishop of Hereford's death. The account given by Bulaeus, however, is compatible with the occurrence of a second visit, and it is quite possible that, as will be mentioned at a later stage, he spent some of the years covered by the Great Interdict, during which next to nothing could be done at Oxford, or, indeed, in England, in the task of teaching the students who in 1209 migrated from the English to the French University, as well as others who wished to attend his lectures, and at the same time of completing some of his studies.

Although the Paris schools were not formally incorporated as a " university " until the early part of the thirteenth century, they had attained to the highest reputation under William of Champeaux, Abelard, and other distinguished teachers of the twelfth, and had nearly developed in practice the organisation which was definitely crystallised some years later.[1] The celebrated school on Mont St. Geneviève had, however, fallen from its high estate and sunk into a position of subsidiary importance;[2] if Grosseteste really went to Lincoln before he proceeded to Oxford, he might have listened there to one of the last of the eminent teachers who had taught theology at "the Mount," and had, indeed, derived from it his appellation of William de Monte;[3] and it was the old Cathedral school which was at once

---

[1] Rashdall, i. pp. 293-321.

[2] *Ibid.* p. 279.

[3] Giraldus Cambrensis, ed. Brewer, i. p. 93. It was of him that Alexander Neckam wrote in his *De Laudibus Divinae Sapientiae*, ed. Wright, Rolls Series, line 845 :

Transiit ad montem Montanus monte relicto.

the basis and the nucleus of the University. The division into four distinct "nations," the French, the Normans, the Picards, and the English, a classification according to which the French embraced all the Latin races, whilst the English included the Germans and other inhabitants of Northern and Eastern Europe,[1] had not yet come into definite existence, and it may therefore be assumed that there was at that time closer intercourse and more frequent interchange of ideas between the students belonging to various nationalities than was possible after they were sorted and penned up in separate groups, as appears to have been the case after 1219[2] for a few months, and permanently after 1231.

The principal object of Grosseteste's visit to Paris was probably the study of theology. According to Leland's account, founded either on earlier documents or on tradition, " he there read with great accuracy almost all the theologians, and thereby became himself one who would have been acclaimed as such even by the most learned period of early Christianity." Little can be surmised either as to the date or as to the length of his sojourn. It is, however, in accordance with probability that he also devoted himself, whilst there, to philosophical studies, and that he found better opportunities than at Oxford for extending his knowledge of Greek and of Hebrew, the former of which, and possibly the latter, he had already commenced to learn in a rudimentary fashion,[3] thus setting a noble example in a direction which lay altogether outside of the beaten track. Grosseteste's degree in divinity was undoubtedly taken at Oxford,[4] and it must therefore be supposed that he graduated in that faculty in his old University after his return from Paris, though the precise date cannot be fixed. If, however, the statement of Bulacus is to be harmonised with the other accounts, it would appear that Grosseteste graduated in arts at Oxford in or

---

[1] Rashdall, i. p. 320.

[2] *Ibid.* i. p. 316.

[3] Leland, *apud* Tanner.

[4] See Hearne's note to the *Dunstable Annals*, i. p. 299 ; Luard's Introd. to Grosseteste's *Letters*, p. xxxiii.

before 1199, at Paris in the same faculty after that date, and again at Oxford in divinity after his return.

Although, in the absence of further materials, it has been impossible to follow the details of Grosseteste's studies and of his career at the two universities, the general results of the training he acquired are sufficiently clear. In spite of the extraordinary proficiency to which he attained both in theology and in dialectics, his mental bias was in favour of keeping those studies as far as possible distinct one from another, and not intermingling them in the manner which had become fashionable during the twelfth century. The important place assigned to logic and cognate studies in the Oxford, as well as in the Paris curriculum, was, no doubt, intended to promote the development of the reasoning faculties, as distinguished from the mere cultivation of the memory. The effect, however, of paying excessive attention to logic was that the abler intellects of the twelfth century were diverted from the consideration of the facts of human experience, past and present, to that of abstract questions of the kind which divided the Realists from the Nominalists, whilst the Aristotelian doctrines which formed the basis of the teaching, acquired an artificial abstruseness and unreality by reason of the circumstance that they were studied not in the original Greek, but in Latin versions of Boëthius. The ingenuity was sharpened, but the mind was not directed to the search after truth. The system, indeed, was one which enabled a man possessing Abelard's depth of insight and lucidity of thought to achieve great philosophical triumphs, but in the case of the ordinary student it had a tendency to make him look to the soundness of the syllogism as the sole test, and to neglect to inquire into the accuracy or inaccuracy of the premises. When the mental process thus acquired came to be applied to theology, it was apt to lead to the neglect of the positive sources of knowledge. The Scriptures and the early Fathers were comparatively little read, and the main object appeared to be to prove or to disprove on abstract grounds

certain theological propositions, the test of success being found
in the consonance of the argument with the accepted rules of
dialectic. Similarly, when the process was applied to other
branches of knowledge, it resulted in a disregard of original
authorities, a neglect of the study of languages, and a disinclination to spend time in the observation of physical phenomena.

The *Sentences* of Peter Lombard, which became before
the close of the twelfth century the standard text-book in the
theological schools, may be regarded as constituting, in a sense,
a reaction against the excessive admixture of logic with theology,
and, from another point of view, an attempt to reconcile reason
with authority, rather than authority with reason. The object
of the work was to collect under the heads of the various theological questions which had been propounded, the statements
contained in the Scriptures and in the Fathers which bore, or
were thought to bear, upon the solution of the points at issue.
It was based, to some extent, upon a similar work written by
Robert Pullen, who had lectured at Oxford in 1133.[1] Although
it was intended, however, to supply a final solution of many
of the difficulties which had presented themselves, it became
the starting-point of an entirely new set of commentaries, of
which Pits enumerates no fewer than one hundred and sixty
composed in England alone, without counting other countries,
by an equal number of writers.[2]

Grosseteste's point of view approximated rather to the
positive than to the scholastic system of theology, and his
training in that respect appears to have been largely guided by
the *Sentences*. At the same time he perceived that the work
was in danger of being treated as an authority in itself, instead
of serving merely as a stepping-stone to the study of the original
texts on which it was based, and it was doubtless the recollection
of the inadequate mental diet thus afforded which dictated, in
later years, his celebrated letter to the Regents of theology at

---

[1] *Ann. Monast.* (Osney), ed. Luard,
iv. p. 19. See Rashdall, iii. p. 335.

[2] Pits, *Relationes Historicae de Rebus
Anglicis*, Paris, 1619, p. 947.

Oxford.   His early manner and the influence of Peter Lombard may be discerned in Grosseteste's treatment of the question "Deus est prima forma et forma omnium," and his brief essay on the nature of angels, both of which are combined into one letter, which occupies the first place in Dr. Luard's collection,[1] and is addressed to his pupil,[2] master Adam Rufus.   It must have been written before Grosseteste obtained his first preferment, and probably at a much earlier date.   Its structure and its method of reasoning suggest the *Sentences*.   It forbears to cite Aristotle, though it is imbued with Aristotelianism, but appeals to the authority of the Scriptures, introduces numerous quotations from the writings of St. Augustine and of St. Ambrose, and strengthens arguments founded upon authority by means of arguments derived from analogy.   Some of his illustrations are singularly apposite, and perhaps original, as, for instance, that of the silver seal supposed to be endowed with life, intellect, and will.[3]

As in theology, so in the other departments of intellectual activity the principles which Grosseteste took for his guidance during his University career, and endeavoured to carry out in his writings and in his life, were (1) the desirability for resorting, whenever possible, to what lawyers would call "the book at large," that is the actual text, and not a translation or abridgment of it; (2) the consequent necessity for acquiring the Greek and Hebrew languages; (3) the value and importance of physical science and mathematics, and (4) the need for a better classification of the departments of knowledge.   In the next chapter it will be possible to show the practical outcome of the first, third, and fourth of those propositions.   At this stage it will be sufficient to touch briefly upon his efforts during the early part of his life to learn the two languages mentioned in the second.

---

[1] Letter 1.   Peter Lombard's influence does not extend, however, beyond the method of treatment.   Grosseteste's leading principles of philosophy are akin to realism rather than to nominalism.   See pp. 42, 43.   Prantl, *Geschichte der Logik*, iii. 85 *sqq.*

[2] See Letter 38.

[3] Letter 1, pp. 4, 5.

How remarkable that effort must have been is indicated by the fact that at that time hardly any even of the most learned scholars of the West were acquainted with Greek, whilst Hebrew was studied only by a few who had been brought into special relations with the Jewish communities. With the exception of John of Salisbury, it is almost impossible to name any Englishman of the twelfth century who was acquainted with that language, a contrast to the days in which the Venerable Bede could write that there were many scholars of Theodore, Archbishop of Canterbury, who knew Greek as well as their mother tongue. In France, however, several learned men, foremost among whom was Macaire, Abbot of Fleury, addicted themselves to its study,[1] and it is stated that both Abelard and Héloise had some knowledge of it, though no one in that country appears to have done as much towards its encouragement as was effected in Italy by Bourgoudion, chief magistrate of Pisa, who, about the year 1150, translated from Greek into Latin the works of St. Chrysostom, of St. Gregory of Nyssa, and of John of Damascus. Grosseteste, in approaching the subject, appears to have had the advantage of the assistance given by a certain Greek named Nicholas, who may have been a contemporary of his, though slightly junior, both at Oxford and at Paris. The tradition, however, so far as the early connection is concerned, is doubtful, and rests mainly on the authority of a document cited by Wood, which has now been lost; but there is no doubt whatsoever with regard to the friendly relations which subsisted in later years between Grosseteste and Nicholas, and the help which he derived from his co-operation in the work of translation. Nicholas was a clerk connected with the Abbey of St. Albans, and was presented by that body to the living of Datchet in Buckinghamshire. When, some years after the commencement of his episcopate, Grosseteste directed his attention once more to the study of Greek, and determined to arrange for the translation of certain of the writers in that

---

[1] *Hist. Littéraire de la France,* xiii. 313 *sqq.* (new edition) ; cp. ix. 151, 152.

language, it was to Nicholas as well as to John of Basingstoke that he turned for the purpose of enabling him to carry out his task, and to supply him with fresh material.[1] The probability is, on the whole, that Grosseteste must have been acquainted with Nicholas during his University days, as otherwise it would have been practically impossible for him to have made a beginning, in the almost entire absence of Greek manuscripts from England,[2] though the difficulty would not have been as great if the foundations of his knowledge were laid whilst he was studying at Paris ; and it must be remembered that several years elapsed after the Latin conquest of Constantinople in 1204 before any of the literary treasures found in that city were brought to the West.

In view of the large number of Jewries then in existence, it is strange that the knowledge of Hebrew had not become more widely spread than appears actually to have been the case. The Jewish medical schools, too, were to be found in many cities of Europe. Perhaps the feeling that dictated the Cistercian prohibition which forbade the monks of that order to seek the aid of the Jews for the purpose of learning Eastern languages, and which led to a monk of Poblet in Catalonia being punished for that offence, may have been a symptom of a prevailing prejudice, and may account for the general ignorance of Hebrew. There were, however, exceptions, amongst which Héloise is, as usual, reckoned.[3] It is possible that Grosseteste may have had recourse to the precise method which the Cistercians condemned, and have sat at the feet, for that particular purpose, of some Gamaliel connected with the Oxford Jewry.[4] The proceeding does not appear to have been uncommon, but to have been discountenanced through fear of the

---

[1] *Hist. Major*, iv. 233. See pp. 224 *sqq.* The Nicholas Gre . . . who was canon of Lincoln in 1278, and whom Mr. Wordsworth (*Tracts of Clement Maydeston*, ed. for the Henry Bradshaw Society, p. 168) supposes to have been NicholasGraecus, may have been a name-sake ; or, perhaps, "Gre . . ." stands for "Gretton." As Roger Bacon says, Grosseteste sent for numerous Greeks.

[2] See Pegge's Appendix 10, pp. 345, 346.

[3] *Hist. Litt. de la France*, xii. p. 630.

[4] Wood, p. 46. See note on p. 98.

effect which intercourse with Jews might produce upon the Christian's faith: in 1222 a deacon was hanged at Oxford for becoming a Jew.[1] It would not be surprising if Grosseteste's subsequent interest in the conversion of Jews, as shown in his writings, especially in his work on *The Ceasing of the Law* and his translation of the *Testament of the Twelve Patriarchs*, as well as the feeling, more kindly than was at that time entertained in ecclesiastical circles, which he expresses in his letter to the Countess of Winchester,[2] could be traced to his earlier relations with some learned member of that community. The question, what progress Grosseteste effected in his Hebrew studies, is one which cannot well be answered. Roger Bacon, who testifies that both he and Adam Marsh used the Hebrew text, also affirms that his knowledge of Greek and of Hebrew was not sufficient to enable him to effect his translations without the assistance of others.[3] Trivet and Boston of Bury both state that he extracted much from the " glosses " of the Hebrews.[4] It was by efforts of that description in a virtually new field that Grosseteste added to the stores of learning which were the wonder of his own and of the following generations. His great merit, however, in that respect consisted not so much in his own contributions, important as they were, to the advancement of linguistic attainments, as in the stimulus which he gave to the desire to search for knowledge at the fountain-head. In his view the study of Greek and of Hebrew formed part of a comprehensive and all-embracing system, which included the whole of knowledge then known. In the domain of intellectual activity Grosseteste must, as will be shown, be regarded as the founder and inspirer of what may be termed the encyclopaedic school of the thirteenth century, imparting to it a unity of purpose and a loftiness of conception to which those who followed him hardly ever attained, although in particular branches and on specific subjects they advanced beyond his teaching.

---

[1] *Hist. Maj.* iii. 71.   [2] Letter 5.
[3] Roger Bacon, ed. Brewer, pp. 330, 472.   [4] Trivet, ed. Hog, p. 243.

CHAPTER II

WHATEVER may have been the precise date of Grosseteste's return from Paris to Oxford, it is evident that he brought with him an enhanced reputation as a scholar, a wider circle of acquaintances and friends, and a determination to devote his best efforts to the task of increasing the usefulness and the renown of the English University. Some time after he had taken his degree in divinity he was appointed to the post which was commonly called that of Chancellor, but which Hugh de Wells, Bishop of Lincoln, and in that capacity diocesan of the University, preferred to call that of Master of the Schools, or of the Scholars. In the register of Oliver Sutton,[1] who was Bishop of Lincoln in 1294, it is stated that Grosseteste, " who filled the office (of Chancellor) at the time when he was Regent at the said University, declared, just after he had been made Bishop, that his immediate predecessor in that see had not allowed him to be called Chancellor, but *Magister Scholarum* or *Scholarium*." Hugh de Wells presided over the see of Lincoln from 1209 to 1235 ; and although it is possible that Grosseteste had been appointed to the office before 1209, and that the question of the precise designation by which he should be called was still in abeyance at that time, it is more probable that his appointment belongs to a period subsequent to

---

[1] Twyne, xii. p. 7, quoted by Wood, Pegge, Luard, and Rashdall.

that year, though the exact date cannot be fixed. The first
formal mention of " the Chancellor whom the Bishop of Lincoln
shall set over the scholars " is to be found in the Legatine
Ordinance of 1214, the earliest Charter of the University, and it
may perhaps be inferred that Grosseteste, who was undoubtedly
the first Chancellor of the University, only occupied that position after the date named.[1]

The chronology, indeed, of the period of about thirty years
which elapsed between Grosseteste's return from Paris and the
year 1235, when he became Bishop of Lincoln, is somewhat
obscure. In 1209 his name appears, without any addition, in
the list of witnesses of the deed by which Hugh de Wells confirmed the donations and benefactions made to the priory of
St. Andrew's, Northampton, and it was probably about that time
that he was brought into close personal contact with the new
Bishop, who had been installed in that very year, and whom
he was destined to succeed twenty-six years later. His first
ecclesiastical preferment, according to the doubtful authority
of Richard de Bardney, was to the prebend of Clifton in the
Cathedral of Lincoln. In 1210 he appears to have become
Archdeacon of Chester,[2] though there is some doubt with regard
to the matter. In 1214 he probably exchanged that office for
the archdeaconry of Wilts. His name appears in the Salisbury
registers in that capacity in 1214 and in 1220,[3] and he also held

---

[1] See Rashdall, ii. p. 351. Mr.
Rashdall also mentions (p. 355 and
Appendix 21) that a papal Bull
addressed to the Chancellor of Oxford
in 1221 remained unexecuted on the
ground that no Chancellor of Oxford
was then in existence, but that in 1225
there is a record of a definite act having
been performed by that official in connection with a tithe suit, Rot. Claus.
9, Hen. III. m. 8. It is tempting,
therefore, to infer that Grosseteste
may have become Chancellor between
those two dates. On the other hand,
the vacancy in 1221 may have been of
a merely temporary character. A
letter from the convent of Eynsham,
printed in the *Lincoln Cathedral
Statutes*, ed. by Bradshaw and Wordsworth, part ii. (Cambridge, 1897),
Introd. p. 67, and referring to the
" Cancellarius " of Oxford, appears to
have been written not long after
1209.

[2] Whitelocke, quoted by Wharton,
Anglia Sacra, i. p. 457. See Luard,
Introd. to Grosseteste's *Letters*, p.
xxxiv.; Pegge, pp. 20 *sqq.* See p. 231.

[3] *Register of St. Osmund*, ed. Jones,
Rolls Series, 1883, i. 380, ii. 16, and
ii. 133. In 1214 he was present at
the framing of the *nova constitutio*, at

the living of Calne, in which connection he was brought in contact with Fulk Basset, rector of Winterbourn Bassett, subsequently Bishop of London, and his lifelong friend. He had an amicable dispute with him at that time with respect to the tithes of Berwick Bassett. During the latter portion of his residence in the Sarum diocese he came under the influence of Richard Poore, who became Bishop in 1217, and whose importance in relation to the liturgical history of England during the Middle Ages can hardly be over-estimated. It is also worthy of note that Edmund Rich, afterwards Archbishop of Canterbury, and in or about 1219 Treasurer of Salisbury, was Grosseteste's successor as Rector of Calne.[1] In 1221 or 1222 he gave up his connection with the diocese of Salisbury and became Archdeacon of Northampton, holding at the same time the prebend of Empingham in Lincoln Cathedral. Lastly, he exchanged the archdeaconry of Northampton for that of Leicester, which he retained until 1232, when he resigned all his preferments with the exception of his Lincoln prebend.[2] In 1225 he was collated to the church of Alboldesley, or Abbotsley, in Huntingdonshire, and he also held the rectory of St. Margaret's, Leicester, probably at the same time as the archdeaconry of that name. More will be said at a later stage with regard to some of those preferments.

It will be observed that the portion of that period with respect to the chronology of which there is most doubt is that

the time when the removal from Old Sarum to the new Cathedral at Salisbury was in immediate prospect. In 1220 he acted as scrutineer of the votes in the election of W. de Wanda as Dean of Sarum. In the third passage we find that he presented to the Cathedral some vestments. He had ceased, however, to be Archdeacon of Wilts some time before the first service which was held in the new Cathedral in 1225. His name generally appears as "Ricardus" in the Salisbury registers.

[1] *Charters and Documents relating to Salisbury*, ed. by Jones and Macray, Rolls Series, 1891, pp. 111-113. The decision relating to the Berwick Bassett tithes is dated August 18, 1221. Possibly "Ricardus" mentioned on page 121 as Archdeacon of Wilts (January 17 1222) may also be Robert Grosseteste.

[2] The words "R. fuit tunc Archidiac. Leircest." in the Rolls of Hugh de Wells, *ann.* 12, refer to Grosseteste. The years are reckoned from the commencement of the Rolls in 1217, not from that of the episcopate.

which extends from 1209 to 1214. The interval almost exactly coincides and synchronises with the duration of the Great Interdict.[1] That formidable weapon, employed by the growing power of the Papacy for the humiliation of the temporal power, had been brought into requisition on three occasions since the date of Grosseteste's birth, first against Scotland in 1180, secondly against Normandy in 1196, and thirdly against France in 1198, but it was in the case of England that it was put in force with the greatest rigour. It is probable that chroniclers like Ralph of Coggeshall have to some extent exaggerated the ecclesiastical stagnation produced by the Interdict, but even if more work was actually done by the parish priests during that time than has been sometimes represented, the absence of almost every bishop from these shores must have brought to a standstill the greater part of the administration and organisation of affairs within the Church.[2] The see of Coventry, in which diocese was included the archdeaconry of Chester, was vacant, so that if Grosseteste obtained that post in 1210, it must have been by the action of the chapters of Coventry and Lichfield, which were guardians of the spiritualities during the vacancy.[3] It is possible that the appointment may, in the special circumstances of the case, have been of an almost nominal character, and have involved few duties. Hugh de Wells was consecrated abroad,[4] but may have appointed Grosseteste to the Clifton prebend in Lincoln Cathedral between

[1] *Hist. Maj.* ii. 522, 575.

[2] R. de Wendover's words are : "Cessarunt in Anglia omnia ecclesiastica sacramenta, praeter confessionem et viaticum in ultima necessitate et baptisma parvulorum." The usual form, however, was to pronounce "sacrorum et divinorum omnium officiorum interdictionem, excepto baptismate parvulorum et poenitentia morientium." See the comments of Cujacius (*Opera*, Naples, 1758), vol. vi. p. 1064, on Tit. I. book iv. ch. ii. of Gregory the Ninth's *Decretals*, with special reference to the form of words used by Pope Alexander III. The rules of Hugh de Wells as to the observance of the Interdict in his diocese are in a MS. of Lincoln Cathedral, *Twelfth Report of the Historical MSS. Commission*, App. 9, p. 565. The form used by Innocent III. is given in Martene and Durand's *Thesaurus Novus Anecdotorum* (1717), vol. i. col. 812.

[3] See Pegge, p. 20.

[4] *Hist. Maj.* ii. 528 ; Stubbs, *Reg. Sacrum Anglicanum*, p. 54.

the date of his election and that of his consecration, just in the same way as he exercised his episcopal functions with respect to the priory of St. Andrew's, Northampton, and other matters.

In addition, however, to the general Interdict which affected the whole country, special conditions had arisen at Oxford, also in consequence of the tyranny of King John, who in 1209, after a "town and gown" riot, ordered the execution of two or, according to another account, three scholars who had been imprisoned for an offence which had really, we are assured, been committed by others who had sought safety in flight.[1] The result was a rapid dispersion of masters and of students, some of whom migrated to Reading, some to Cambridge, and some to Paris. In view of the statements previously quoted from Bulaeus, which suggest that Grosseteste may have been twice to the University of Paris, first as scholar and then as teacher, and considering the state of affairs which then prevailed both in England as a whole and at Oxford in particular, it is by no means unlikely that he may have been one of those who found their way in 1209 from the Isis to the Seine. The reasons which may have rendered his absence from England desirable ceased to exist in 1214, when King John's submission to the Pope was followed by that of the citizens of Oxford to the legate, Nicholas of Tusculum, and the first charter which placed upon a definite basis the organisation of the University was embodied in the Legatine Ordinance of that year.[2] There is no valid ground for supposing that Grosseteste cannot have held the office of Chancellor during a portion, at any rate, of the period from 1214 to 1232, during which he was successively Archdeacon of Wilts, Northampton, and Leicester; for the practice of continuous residence enforced in the case of the Chancellor in later years may not have come into operation at that period, and it is clear that in 1224, and during the following years, he was able to combine his lectures to the Franciscans, to

---

[1] *Hist. Maj.* ii. 525, 526, 569; *Chron. de Lanercost,* p. 4. Other authorities are mentioned by Rashdall, ii. p. 348.

[2] *Ibid.* ii. 569; Anstey's *Munimenta Academica,* p. 1.

which reference will be made later on, with his tenure of the last of the above-mentioned archdeaconries.

If, then, we examine Grosseteste's life, in the light of such materials as are available, from December of 1199, when his patron, William de Vere, Bishop of Hereford, passed away, down to the commencement of 1232, when he was compelled by ill-health to resign all his preferments with one exception, it will be found that it divides itself roughly during that period into three portions, during the first of which (from 1200 to 1209) he was enabled to devote himself unreservedly to academic studies, whilst during part of the second (1210 to 1214) he may have lectured in Paris, though holding what were perhaps nominal appointments in England, and during the third (from 1214 to 1232) he combined the active discharge of important pastoral duties with the care of the University of Oxford, where, besides the lectures which he gave on various subjects to all who chose to attend, and in addition to his organising work as Chancellor, he became in 1224 in a special sense reader in theology to the Franciscans; and although, as has been pointed out, the exact number of years during which he filled the Chancellorship is unknown, there can be no doubt that, whether in an official or an unofficial capacity, he devoted much of his time and of his energy to the advancement of learning and the promotion of the best interests of the University, which in later years he continued to further in other ways. The most salient feature, however, of the thirty-two years is that they constitute the period of Grosseteste's greatest intellectual activity, to which the majority of his writings are probably to be assigned. Again and again, during the latter portion of his life, he found renewed and ever-increasing interest in literary work, but the pressure of other duties prevented him from bestowing upon it as much time as he might have desired.[1]

It may be well to endeavour at this stage to classify, as far as possible, the works which Grosseteste may be supposed to

---

[1] See, for instance, Letter 77, p. 173.

have written during the years of his life now under consideration. It is impossible, however, to assign precise dates, or even
to indicate the probable order of composition. In so doing it is
necessary to eliminate for the present certain works which
unquestionably belong to a later period, such as the treatise
De Cessatione Legalium, written either in 1232 or in 1233, the
sermons which he preached whilst Bishop of Lincoln, the
numerous pamphlets issued during his episcopal days,[1] the
translations from the Greek which he carried out with the
assistance of others during his last ten or twelve years,[2] and his
Rules of Estate Management and similar writings,[3] as well as the
vast majority of the letters which have been preserved. It is
also needful to leave out of sight his postillation of the Psalms,
which, as the *Lancrcost Chronicle* and Gascoigne [4] inform us, was
effected continuously as far as the 100th Psalm, and was
interrupted only by the prelate's death, thus clearly belonging
to his later and not, as has been thought, to his earlier years.
His interest in the *Nicomachean Ethics* of Aristotle may also
be referred, for reasons stated in another chapter,[5] to the latter
part of his career, though he was certainly acquainted during
his Oxford days with the *Eudemian Ethics*. It is also well to
bear in mind that some works have been erroneously attributed
to Grosseteste by those who have attempted to compile a
bibliography; for instance, as Dr. Luard shows,[6] the *Oculus*

---

[1] For instance, his pamphlets concerning the attacks on the liberties of
the Church (Letter 72), and concerning
the episcopal right of visitation (Letter
127), both of which are printed in Dr.
Luard's Collection, the so-called sermon
delivered at Lyons in 1250 in the
presence of the Pope and Cardinals,
and the pamphlet entitled "De
Principatu Regni et Tyrannidis,"
mentioned by Adam Marsh (*Mon.
Francisc.* p. 110). See pp. 31, 270.

[2] See pp. 223 *sqq.*

[3] See pp. 229 *sqq.*

[4] Gascoigne's *Liber Veritatis, s.v.*
"Christus." He wrote, however, an
earlier commentary on the Psalms, in
addition to his later postillation. Cp.
Rogers's edition of Gascoigne, pp. 126-
128, with p. 177. " Vidi ego, Thomas
Gascoigne, hoc scriptum suum super
Psalterium propria manu sua scriptum,
et est Oxoniae inter fratres minores, et
registratur ille liber Epistolae Pauli A.
Et scripsit idem doctor super Psalterium usque ad Psalmum centesimum
inclusive," etc. On p. 177 Gascoigne
refers to a commentary not written in
Grosseteste's own hand.

[5] See p. 247.

[6] Introd. p. xi.

Moralis of Archbishop Peccham and the *Stimulus Conscientiae* of Richard Rolle of Hampole, both of which belong to a later date, and the *Parvus Cato*, written in the twelfth century, have been wrongly assigned to him. The treatise *De Summa Justitiae* was probably the work of John Wallensis,[1] and the tract *De Dignitate Conditionis Humanae*, which Grosseteste himself quotes as if from St. Augustine, has been included by mistake in some lists of his works.[2] On the other hand, the bibliographies of his writings are by no means complete, as may be inferred from the fact that none of them mentions the treatise on "The Principle of a Kingdom and of a Tyranny," which he wrote for the instruction of Simon de Montfort, and to which Adam Marsh refers in one of his letters.[3] And it is only of recent years that Bishop Ussher's hypothesis, which pointed to Grosseteste as the author of the Latin version of what is known as the *Middle Recension of the Epistles of St. Ignatius*, has been definitely confirmed by the researches of scholars.[4] All due allowance being made for unwarranted insertions, the extraordinary range and profundity of his powers, as exhibited in the works which are unquestionably his, entitle him to a place in the history of intellectual progress even more important than that which has been usually assigned to him, whilst the evidences of his multifarious activity excite wonder and admiration. Without attempting, therefore, to arrange in chronological sequence the works belonging to that period of Grosseteste's life, or to give an exhaustive list of them, it may be convenient to group them under certain heads.

In theology he was one of the most prolific writers of the Middle Ages.[5] The bibliographers mention the titles of between

---

[1] Dr. Felten, p. 80.

[2] Letter 1, p. 10; Luard's Introd. p. xi.

[3] *Mon. Francisc.* p. 110.

[4] See p. 223; Lightfoot's *Apostolic Fathers*, part ii. (2nd ed. 1889), vol. i. pp. 76 *sqq.*

[5] Cp. Gascoigne, *Liber Veritatis, s.v.* "Deus" and "Infernus," pp. 12 and 176 of Rogers's edition. "Ego Thomas Gascoigne saepe vidi et credo firmiter, quod opera quae dominus Lincolniensis doctor Robertus Grosseteste edidit et propria manu sua scripsit, quae opera ego saepe vidi, extendunt se in quantitate scripti ultra quantitatem doctoris Nicholai de Lyra supra scripturam sacram."

two and three hundred of his sermons, more than sixty of his longer treatises, and a collection of 147 *Dicta*,[1] or short discourses on particular points of Christian doctrine and Scriptural interpretation. Whilst many of the sermons clearly belong to the time when he was Bishop of Lincoln, others may have been preached by him in his archdeaconries, and some, as, for instance, the one in praise of poverty,[2] at Oxford. The importance of the spoken word was emphasised by him on every possible occasion. He wrote more than one treatise on the art of preaching, encouraged, as will be seen, the Friars Preachers, and set the example himself with a force and a fervour which were the marvel of his generation. Towards the end of his episcopal career he frequently preached in English, but his practice during the earlier portion of his episcopate was to preach in Latin to the clergy, and to instruct them to use the English language in their sermons to their congregations, in order that they might address themselves to the largest possible number in the language best understood.[3] The reason why few or none of his English sermons have been preserved[4] is doubtless due to the fact that they were preached extempore, whilst his Latin sermons were committed to writing. In encouraging and occasionally using the English language for that purpose, he was following the example set in his native county by Abbot Samson, who, according to Jocelyn of Brakelond, had caused a pulpit to be erected in the Abbey Church of Bury St. Edmunds, from which he and others preached in the vernacular.[5] There can be no doubt, however, that Grosseteste's sermons during the period of his connection with the University and his four archdeaconries were in Latin, with the probable exception of those which he preached in the parishes of which he was at various times incumbent. His sermons were not based, as a rule, upon texts, but he was in the

---

[1] Nineteen, however, of the 147 *Dicta* are properly sermons.

[2] *Mon. Francisc.* i. p. 69.

[3] See p. 296. Grosseteste's *Constitutions*, Letter 52 *, p. 155, etc.

[4] Wharton, *Anglia Sacra*, ii. pp. 344 *sqq.*, mentions some English sermons, but they may have been translations from Latin originals.

[5] *Memorials of St. Edmund's Abbey*, ed. T. Arnold, i. p. 245.

habit of choosing some definite subject, and developing it and illustrating it by arguments and quotations derived from Scripture.

The relation between the sermons and the *dicta* is indicated in a note appended to two of the manuscript collections of his *Dicta Theologica:* "In this volume are contained 147 chapters, some of which are short 'sayings' which I wrote down briefly whilst I still lectured in the schools. They were composed to assist the memory, and they deal with different subjects and are not continuous. I have given to them titles in order to enable the reader to find them with greater ease. Some, however, are sermons, which I addressed at the same time to the clergy or to the people."[1] Out of the 147 chapters which form the collection, 19 are sermons and 128 are *dicta*. The foregoing note, however, hardly does justice to the merit of the latter; for although they have neither the arrangement nor the length of a sermon or of an essay, they generally comprise within narrow limits a clear statement of the subject with which they deal, and a survey of its most salient features, accompanied by apposite reflections and terse and often luminous definitions. One of their most noteworthy characteristics is to be found in their constant appeal to the authority of Scripture, and in the writer's extraordinary familiarity with its contents. Dr. Luard's observation [2] that Grosseteste's "wonderful knowledge of Scripture might perhaps be the object of remark in our day, though in his own it was probably not more than was possessed by almost all theological students, at least by such as at all approached to his stamp," may be thought to overrate the familiarity exhibited in the thirteenth century with the text of the Bible, and is not altogether borne out by the words of Roger Bacon, written in 1267, about thirty years later, in his *Opus Minus*,[3] to the effect that "at Paris," where, be it remembered, the theological teaching was, according to Grosseteste, superior in some respects to that

---

[1] Cotton MSS. Otho, D. x., and the Merton MS. quoted by Tanner and by Pegge, pp. 272, 273.

[2] Introd. p. 90.

[3] Roger Bacon, ed. Brewer, pp. 328, 329.

at Oxford, "the bachelor who reads the text is sacrificed to the one who reads the *Sentences*," and that "elsewhere the one who reads the *Sentences* takes part in disputations, and is accounted a master, whilst the one who reads the text is unable to take part in them, as has been shown at Bologna and in several other places"; and he proceeds to contrast the state of things then in existence with the practice adopted by Grosseteste, Adam Marsh, and other teachers of the greatest calibre, who only used the original texts. It is evident, therefore, that Grosseteste must have been one of a comparatively small band of men who had recourse to the fountain-head,[1] instead of satisfying themselves with second-hand extracts, passages taken out of their context, and skeleton outlines. At the same time a certain familiarity with the passages quoted is doubtless assumed to exist in the minds of the hearers or readers. Great as was the debt which Grosseteste probably owed to the writings of Peter Lombard, he had never regarded them as a substitute for the study of the original Scriptures, but simply as a help to their comprehension; and Dr. Luard is absolutely correct in his remark that "Grosseteste's reverence for Scripture as the ultimate appeal in all controversies is unbounded"; and he not only speaks of the "auctoritas irrefragabilis Scripturae,"[2] but acts upon that principle throughout his life. His skill in the interpretation of the Bible excites, in the following century, the unqualified admiration of Tyssington, who says that "to compare him to the modern doctors is as the comparison of the sun to the moon when the latter is eclipsed."[3]

Twelve of the *Dicta* are printed in Edward Brown's appendix to his edition of the *Fasciculus* of Ortuinus Gratius.[4] He transcribed them from a manuscript in Trinity College, Cambridge. Their titles are (1) concerning Faith; (2) on Grace, which is

---

[1] "Ut dulcius ex ipso fonte biberentur aquae," Roger Bacon, ed. Brewer, p. 330. The view here expressed must, however, be qualified by the consideration that in the passage quoted Bacon mixes up two different questions, that of the study of the Hebrew and Greek original, and that of the study of the Latin "text at large."

[2] Letter 2, p. 18.

[3] *Fasciculi Zizaniorum*, ed. Shirley, p. 135.　　[4] London, 1690.

defined as " bona voluntas Dei," and Justification ; (3) and (4) on Praying and on Prayer ; (5) on Pride ; (6) on Detraction and its evils ; (7), (8), and (9) on Humility ; (10) on Patience ; (11) on the Mercy and Justice of God, and (12) concerning true and false prophets.[1] The clearness of the definitions which they contain, and the remarkable appropriateness of some of the similes employed for the purpose of illustrating the arguments, help to explain the reputation which he acquired as a lecturer in theology at Oxford, and the influence he obtained over the Franciscans. It is impossible, by snatching a sentence here or there out of its context, to convey an accurate impression of the style and purport of the *Dicta*, but one or two sentences may, perhaps, be quoted. Pride is defined as " an inordinate fondness of one's own excelling," envy as " an inordinate fondness of the depression of others," humility as " the love of remaining firmly in the state of life fitted to one under all conditions," patience as " the inflexibility of the soul as respects troubles."[2] In another place Grosseteste speaks of humility as " the virtue which enables a man to know himself," but that " the more it is consciously sought, the less is it likely to be attained." His view of the relation between the Divine grace and the operation of the human will is stated in the following manner : " Everything which is in us is from the grace of God, for there is no good thing which He does not wish to be, and His will is the cause of being. There is no good thing, therefore, which He does not make. The aversion of the will from evil, its conversion to good, its perseverance in good, He makes. Nevertheless these same things our free will also makes, just as a grain of corn germinates by a kind of germinative power which is exterior to it, by the heat of the sun and the moisture of the earth. For if we could not turn ourselves away from evil and

<hr>

[1] A few passages from the *Dicta* are translated into English by Canon Perry, pp. 47-50, and into German by Dr. Felten, pp. 77-79. It is time that some competent theological editor should do for the MSS. of the *Dicta* what Dr. Luard did for those of the *Letters*.

[2] Brown's *Fasciculus*, ii. pp. 284, 288, 290, 293 ; Perry.

turn ourselves to good, we should not deserve praise for this,
nor in Scripture should we be enjoined so to do. And if we
could do this without grace, God would not need to be prayed
for this, nor would His will be the doing of it."[1] His methods
of illustration may be gauged by the following passage relating
to the subject of united prayer: "As many heavy things when
bound together descend the quicker, and many light things
when united ascend with greater velocity, inasmuch as the
inclination of each of the separate things has a general effect
upon the combined aggregate; so many individuals joined
together by the bond of love and prayer are moved upwards
more easily and more swiftly, as the prayer of each one of them
has its influence upon that of each of the others. For as polished
objects, when placed close together and illuminated by the power
of the sun, in proportion to their number, shine with greater
brightness on account of the multitude of the reflections of the
light's rays, so too the more souls that are illuminated by the rays
of the sun of righteousness, the more they shine by reason of
the reflection of their mutual love." No fair idea can, however,
be formed of the *Dicta* from brief extracts of that description.[2]

In addition to sermons and *Dicta* must be mentioned the
numerous tracts, treatises, and commentaries which Grosseteste
wrote on theological subjects, principally during his pre-episcopal
days. They devote, as a general rule, more attention to the
practical, pastoral, and ethical side of Christianity than to its
purely doctrinal aspects; in fact, the more abstruse doctrines are
generally introduced for the purpose of enforcing moral precepts,
or explaining and emphasising the personal application to the
reader. The writer never succumbs to the temptation, to which
most contemporary theologians were prone, of writing religious
treatises in the spirit and after the manner of dialectical dis-

[1] Brown's *Fasciculus*, ii. p. 282.
[2] Capgrave, *Chronicle of England*, ed. Hingeston, p. 153, speaking of Grosseteste's election by the canons of Lincoln, says: "They chose to her Bischop Maister Robert Grostede, which man we clepe in Schole 'Lincolniensis.' For he wrot much thing upon Philosophye; he made eke a noble book they clepe his Dictes."

quisitions ; and he dwelt rather, if the phrase may be permitted, upon the dynamics than upon the statics of theology. At the same time it must not be imagined that he deviated in any degree from the received faith of the Church because he accentuates certain features in its teaching more than others ; and, indeed, the contrary might easily be proved by reference to his works ; but it was precisely the practical bent of his teaching which tended most, as will be seen, to create a close bond of union between him and the early Franciscans.

The titles of some of his more important theological tracts or treatises [1] are (1) on Truth ; (2) on the Divine Names ; (3) on the Seven Sacraments ; (4) on Confession ; (5) on the seven deadly sins ; (6) meditations on the words and actions of St. Anselm ; (7) moral expositions concerning the works of the seven days ; (8) on free will ; (9) on the knowledge and will of God ; (10) on God as the Formative Principle of all things, a treatise possibly identical with the first part of the letter to Adam Rufus, previously quoted ; (11) on the order and efficiency of the Divine causation ; (12) on the reparation for the fall ; (13) on wisdom and knowledge ; (14) on the articles of faith and the priestly office—a work which was translated at a later date from Latin into French ; (15) on the Ten Commandments ; (16) on assiduity in prayer—apparently different from the *dictum* with a similar name ; (16) on man ; (17) a summary of St. Augustine's *De Civitate Dei* ; [2] (18) notes on the Epistles of St. Paul, especially on those to the Corinthians and to the Galatians ; [3] (19) meditations or moral comments on the four Gospels, in 297

---

[1] Pegge, pp. 267-278 ; T. Gascoigne, *Liber Veritatis*, ed. Rogers, pp. 12, 102, 126-129, 140, 142 ; Tanner, *Bibliotheca, s.v.* "Grosthead."

[2] The vol. of St. Augustine's *De Civitate Dei* (Bodleian MSS. 198) once belonged to Grosseteste, and is full of his marginal annotations. See Rogers, Introd. to T. Gascoigne, p. 7.

[3] It is doubtful whether Gascoigne's reference (*Dict. Theol.* "liber Veritatis" *s.v.* "Fides") to the "expositio Domini Lincolniensis in epistolam Pauli ad Corinthos, et super omnes epistolas Pauli, sparsim manu propria in margine communis glossae ; et liber ille est Oxoniae inter Fratres Minores in Libraria Conventus, sed non est in libraria scholarum, quoniam ibi sunt duae librariae," relates to this work or to some notes which he made in later life.

short chapters ; (20) on the tongue and the heart ; (21) on repentance, with additional notes written at later dates ; (22) a collection
of homilies, distinct from the sermons ; (23) on the Cross ; (24)
on the humility of Christ ; (25) on the proper pronunciation of
Biblical names ; (26) on prophecy ; and (27) on sacrilege.   He
also wrote commentaries on Genesis, on Job, and on Jeremiah.
In addition to his moral comments on the four Gospels, he
appears to have written more elaborate dissertations on the one
according to St. Luke and on the one according to St. John ;
and it is possible that his commentary on the Psalms may be
distinct from the postillation of the Psalms which he had not
completed at the time of his death.[1]   The treatises on the
pastoral power and on the duties of a Bishop clearly belong to
the episcopal portion of his life.

Of the two principal French works of a theological or semi-
theological character which have been ascribed to Grosseteste,
the *Chasteau d'Amour*, commencing with the words " Ki ben
pense, ben peut dire," is the only one which can be attributed
to him with any degree of certainty.   It is a kind of religious
romance, dealing with the fundamental articles of Christian
belief under the guise of a romaunt of chivalry,—a pious *Roman
de la Rose*, as M. Jusserand puts it,—which was widely read
in the thirteenth and fourteenth centuries, and was translated
into English in the early part of the latter, probably in the
reign of Edward I., by a writer whom Warton[2] conjectures

[1] *Chron. de Lanercost*, Trivet.   But
Richard Taverner's translation of
Capito's *Prayers on the Psalms* (London,
1539) is not from Grosseteste, but from
Wolfgang Capito.

[2] Warton's *English Poetry*, i. 79-88 ;
Pegge, p. 286.   The French original
is printed in Cooke's *Carmina Anglo-
Normannica*, Caxton Society, 1852.
For the various English versions see
the *Castle of Love*, ed. by Halliwell,
1849 ;   the   minor   poems   of   the
Vernon MS., ed. by Horstmann and

Furnivall, Early English Text Society,
1892 ; and the *Castell of Love*, an Early
English translation of an old French
poem by Robert Grosseteste, Philological Society, 1864.   See M. Jusserand, *Hist. litt. du peuple anglais*, p.
217, and Mr. W. J. Courthope's
History of English Poetry, p. 139.
See also Morris's edition of the
Cursor Mundi for the Early English
Text Society.   Dr. Felten is inclined
to think that Grosseteste inspired the
theme, but was not the actual writer
of the verses, pp. 87, 88.

to be Robert Mannyng de Brunne, whose Lincolnshire origin attracted him to the Bishop's works, though the likelihood is that the version is due to another. It is composed after the fashion of the songs of the troubadours, and is sometimes called the "Roman des Romans." It might have been called "Paradise Lost" and "Paradise Regained," as far as the subject matter is concerned, as it is a rudimentary attempt to produce, within the compass of about 1750 lines, the sort of poetic narrative for which Milton found fit expression four centuries later. The Latin preface, evidently written by another hand, states that "although the French language has not the savour of sweetness in the estimation of clerks, the work is intended for laymen, who have less knowledge; and the wise reader, who knows how to extract honey from a rock, and oil from the hardest stone, will find the little work full of pleasantness, as in it are contained all the articles of the Faith, relating to the Divine as well as to the human nature." In the following century the translation of the work into English makes a similar apology for the use of the latter language.[1] Other English versions also exist. The *Pricke of Conscience*, composed by Richard Rolle of Hampole in the fourteenth century, and erroneously ascribed to Grosseteste, is based partly upon his *Chasteau d'Amour* and partly upon some of his *Dicta*, as well as upon other foundations, though it is apparently a version of a Latin piece called the *Stimulus Conscientiae*, which may have been by Richard Rolle himself.[2] The other French work of the same order as the *Chasteau d'Amour*

---

[1] Warton's *English Poetry*, i. p. 80. The English version of the *Chasteau d'Amour* contained in the Vernon MS., fol. 292 (Bodleian Library), says :—

> Her begynnet a tretise
> That is ycleped Castel of Love,
> That bishop Grostest made ywis,
> For lewd mens behove.

Ritson's *Bibliographia Poetica* (London, 1802).

Similarly Robert de Brunne's *Pricke of Conscience* contains the lines

> For lewed men I undyrtoke
> In Englyshe tonge to make this boke.

[2] Pegge, p. 287. See the *Pricke of Conscience*, ed. by Morris, Philological Society, 1863. The translator's title runs: "Here begynneth the boke that men clepyn in Frenshe Manuel Peche, the which boke made yn Frenshe Robert Groosteste byshop of Lyncoln." Lydgate says (Bochas, f. 217b) that—

> Richard hermite, contemplative of
>   sentence,
> Drough in Englishe "the prick of
>   conscience."

with which Grosseteste has been credited is the *Manuel des Péchés* or *des Pechiez*, sometimes called the *Enchiridion*, which was translated into English verse by Robert Mannyng de Brunne, under the title *Handlyng Synne;*[1] but the reference which it contains to the great prelate shows that it cannot have been written by Grosseteste, though it may have been based in part upon his treatise on the seven deadly sins, as well as upon the *Liber Floreti* ascribed to Jean de Garlande.[2] The actual writer appears to have been William de Widdindune or Wadington. The author was evidently conscious of his imperfect mastery of French, as is indicated in the lines

> De le français ni del rimer
> Ne me doit nul hom blamer,
> Car en Angleterre fus né
> Et nourri, ordiné et élevé,

lines which could not have been written by Grosseteste, who enjoyed ample opportunities of attaining to proficiency in the language. With respect to the English theological works ascribed to Grosseteste,[3] it is possible that he may have written some which have not survived; but the two which have been specially identified with him, namely, the above-named *Pricke of Conscience*, commencing with the words "The might of the Fader in Heaven," and a short tract on the Lord's Prayer, are precisely the two the authenticity of which is most open to dispute; and both of them may be assigned, with far greater probability, to Richard Rolle of Hampole.[4] The statement of the author of the preface to the 1658 edition of the *De Cessatione Legalium*, that Grosseteste wrote verse *patrio sermone*, cannot,

---

[1] *Handlyng Synne*, ed. for the Roxburghe Club by Furnivall, 1862. See Pegge, p. 286; Jusserand, p. 216; Warton's *English Poetry*, i. 59.

[2] W. J. Courthope's *Hist. of English Poetry*, p. 141.

[3] Wharton's *Anglia Sacra*.

[4] Pegge, p. 287. Several of the poems by William de Shorcham, vicar of Chart by Leeds, Kent, written in the Kentish dialect of the fourteenth century (ed. Wright, vol. xxviii. of the Percy Society publications, 1849), are based on Grosseteste's theological writings. One of them (p. 134) has at the end: "Oretis pro anima Domini Roberti Grosseteyte, quondam episcopi Lincolniae."

therefore, be sustained by any manuscript hitherto discovered; and as his French writings appear to be limited to the *Chasteau d'Amour* and the *Reules Seynt Roberd*,[1] whilst his work in the English language is confined (as far as has been definitely ascertained) to a certain number of extemporary sermons, and possibly to the translation of Walter of Henley's *Treatise on Husbandry*,[2] it is clear that an overwhelming proportion of what he wrote was composed in Latin.

From Grosseteste's theological works it is necessary to pass to his contributions to philosophy, mathematics, and natural science, as it was upon them, even more than upon his other achievements, that his reputation chiefly rested during the generations which immediately followed. In spite of Roger Bacon's reference to Grosseteste's neglect of Aristotle,[3] a reference which obviously relates partly to his disregard of the third-hand and inaccurate versions of that philosopher derived from the Arabic manuals of Averroës and Avicenna, and partly to his dissatisfaction with the physical treatises, it is evident that, at any rate during his career at Oxford, and possibly also at Paris, he devoted much attention to the Stagirite. In that respect Oxford at that time had the advantage over the French University, inasmuch as at the latter rigid measures were adopted, in 1210 and 1215,[4] to prevent the study of " the books of Aristotle upon Natural Philosophy and his Commentaries," and several years elapsed before the prohibition was removed. The logical works of Aristotle had, of course, been long familiar, but the *Categories*, the *De Interpretatione*, and the *Organon* alone appear to have been made the subjects of lectures. According to Roger Bacon,[5] Edmund Rich was the first who read the *Sophistici Elenchi* at Oxford. Grosseteste shortly

---

[1] See p. 230.

[2] See pp. 229 *sqq.*

[3] *Compendium Studii*, ed. Brewer, p. 469.

[4] Rashdall, i. pp. 356, 357.

[5] *Compendium Studii Theologiae*, quoted by Rashdall, ii. p. 754. Wood, i. p. 279, thinks that it must have been about 1227. His opinion is based upon the statement of Roger Bacon in the *Opus Tertium*, written in 1267, relating to the condemnation of certain books of Aristotle at Paris " about forty years before."

afterwards wrote a commentary on that work, and also on the *Predicaments*, the *Prior Analytics*, and the *Posterior Analytics*;[1] the last-named commentary was frequently issued after the invention of the printing press.[2] His influence was distinctly on the side of Realism, as against Nominalism;[3] but it was a realism which differed widely from the crude system of thought with which William de Champeaux had been identified, and which ascribed to universal notions an objective reality. In the eyes of Grosseteste universals are *ante rem*, *in re*, or *post rem*, according to the point of view; pure thought perceives them to be principles of being, whereas thought which falls short of that standard regards them as merely principles of cognition; and they exist *ante rem* in the mind of the Creator, are expressed *in re* in the phenomenal world, and can be reconstructed *post rem* in the mind of the thinker by induction and abstraction, following upon observation and experiment, but pure thought views them from the Creator's standpoint.[4]

The impulse given to the revival of Aristotelian studies by the Latin versions of Arabic translations affected, however, in the main, the physical treatises of that philosopher, rather than those which related to logic. It would be interesting to know

[1] Prantl (*Geschichte der Logik*, iii. p. 121) attributes to Grosseteste the *Syncategorematica fratris Roberti*, the word *fratris* being assumed to have been inserted by mistake. Grosseteste in his *De veritate propositionis* shows some acquaintance with Byzantine logic, and it was his friend William of Shirewood (p. 247 of this work) who first adapted Psellus.

[2] It was printed at Venice in 1494, and again in 1497, 1504, 1514, 1537, and 1552. Bound up with the British Museum copy of the 1494 edition of Grosseteste's commentary on the *Posterior Analytics* are the "Ruberti Lincoliensis bonarum artium optimi interpretis opuscula dignissima nunc primum in lucem edita et accuratissime emendata," published at Venice in 1514. They include the treatises (1) de artibus liberalibus, (2) de generatione sonorum, (3) de calore solis, (4) de generatione stellarum, (5) de coloribus, (6) de statu causarum, (7) de veritate propositionis, (8) de unica forma omnium, (9) de intelligentiis, (10) de veritate, (11) de impressionibus elementorum, (12) de motu corporali et luce, (13) de finitate motus, (14) de angulis et figuris, (15) de natura locorum, (16) de inchoatione formarum, (17) an homo sit minor mundus, (18) de motu supercoelestium, and (19) de differentiis localibus.

[3] See Hauréau, *Hist. de la philosophie scholastique*, i. pt. ii. p. 178; Prantl, *Geschichte der Logik*, iii. pp. 85 *sqq.*

[4] *Comment. in Poster. Arist.* i. 7, 14; *De Artibus Liberalibus*, fol. 2. The former passage comments on Plato's "ideas."

what was the exact date of Grosseteste's summary of the eight
books of Aristotle's *Physics*, accompanied by a commentary, but
it may be assigned, in all likelihood, to the latter portion of his
life at Oxford, within a few years of his appointment to the See
of Lincoln. The *Summa Roberti Lincolniensis super VIII Libros
Physicorum* was frequently printed in later centuries, sometimes
in connection with the commentaries of St. Thomas Aquinas
on the same subject.[1] In regard to the physical sciences, however, Grosseteste found it necessary to depart from the teaching
of Aristotle: "the lord Robert," says Roger Bacon, " neglected
altogether the books of Aristotle and their methods, and by
his own experiments, and with the aid of other authors, and by
means of other sciences, employed himself in the scientific questions which Aristotle had treated; and he knew and described
the questions with which the books of Aristotle deal a hundred
thousand times better than they can be understood from the
perverse translations of that author."[2] Bacon's reference is
doubtless to Grosseteste's numerous treatises on scientific
subjects, such as those on meteorology, on comets, on the rainbow, on light, on colour, on optics, and, above all, to his *Compendium Scientiae*, about which something will be said later on.
The value of scientific works necessarily becomes less from year
to year in proportion as they are supplemented or superseded
by new discoveries and new inventions; but the importance of
Grosseteste's contributions to physical science consisted not
merely in the additions which he made to the existing stocks of
knowledge, but in the fact that he gave to experiment the same
place in scientific method which it holds in the writings of Roger
Bacon, and to which it was not again restored until after the
lapse of several centuries.

Although there are but few indications that Grosseteste was
closely acquainted with Aristotle's *Metaphysics*,[3] and a short

---

[1] It was printed at Venice in 1498
and 1500, and at Paris in 1538.

[2] *Compendium Studii*, ed. Brewer,
p. 469.

[3] And yet William le Breton says
that Aristotle's *Metaphysics* were read
at Paris in 1209, having just been
brought from Constantinople, and

treatise which he wrote on the subject has been lost,[1] a large portion of the *Physics*, as well as of the *Posterior Analytics*, is in reality devoted to metaphysical questions, and supplies the commentator with a text for inquiries of that nature. Some glimpses into Grosseteste's notion of "forms" has been already given in the reference to the letter addressed to Adam Rufus, in which he gives reasons for asserting the proposition that God is "the First Form of all things."[2] In the commentary on the *Physics* he defines "form" as that which is the cause of being—*quod dat esse rei*. He distinguishes three kinds of "forms," namely (1) that which is immanent in matter, which constitutes the subject of natural science; (2) that which is rendered abstract by the operation of reason, a "form" with which the mathematical branches of knowledge are concerned; and (3) the immaterial form, with which metaphysics deal. By immaterial forms are meant "spiritual substances," such as God, the soul, and so forth. Further light is thrown upon Grosseteste's metaphysical views by the statement of Roger Bacon with reference to the question whether the *intellectus agens*—that is, Aristotle's νοῦς ποιητικός—does or does not form part of the soul, that both Grosseteste and Adam Marsh answered the question in the affirmative, whereas he had heard William Arvernus, formerly Bishop of Paris, maintain the contrary.[3] The psychological side of metaphysics was perhaps of greater interest to Grosseteste than the ontological.

It has been seen that in the domain of theology Grosseteste

---

translated from Greek into Latin. Bouquet, t. xvii. p. 84, quoted by Rashdall, i. p. 354.

[1] Among the books belonging to Durham College, Oxford, in 1315, were Grosseteste's work on the *Posterior Analytics*, and his "Exposicio super metaphisica, ex procuracione ciusdem." *Durham College Rolls*, ed. Blakiston, Oxford Hist. Society's *Collectanea*, vol. iii. p. 37.

[2] Letter 1.

[3] *Opus Tertium*, ed. Brewer, p. 74, 75. William Arvernus was an esteemed correspondent of Grosseteste. See Letter 78. Some of Grosseteste's minor philosophical disquisitions on causes, on the freedom of the will, on the nature of the soul, etc., are printed in a volume of *Opuscula varia philosophica*, Venice, 1574. In letter 1, p. 11, Grosseteste writes : "Sicut Deus simul totus est ubique in universo, ita anima simul tota est ubique in corpore animato."

was more intent upon Christian ethics than upon Christian dialectics. In the domain of general philosophy he also devoted greater attention to the more practical than to the more theoretical divisions of knowledge. To the *Ethics* of Aristotle he paid close attention, both in his University days and during the latter portion of his episcopal. There are reasons, however, for thinking that during the former period the work which he studied was the *Eudemian Ethics*, whereas in later years it was the *Nicomachean Ethics*.[1] The translation of the latter work, with which he is credited, and which he probably carried out with the assistance of others, belongs to the last ten years of his life, and will be noticed in that connection. Some notes, however, on questions connected with Aristotle's *Ethics* belong to his academic days, and he also commented on the *Consolation of Philosophy* by Boëthius.[2] Some of the works assigned to him under this, as under other heads, are possibly notes of his lectures, put into shape by his pupils, with or without revision by himself; but their value and importance are not greatly diminished by that consideration, as they serve in any case to indicate the progress which he effected in the methods of thought and of teaching, and to illustrate his steadfast adherence to the rule never to depend upon a translation, or a summary, or a paraphrase when you can go back to the original, and always to verify your premises by practical experiment when the nature of the subject is such as to admit of its possibility. If Trivet's statement be correct that Grosseteste wrote his commentary on the *Posterior Analytics* whilst he was a Master of Arts,[3] and if, on the other hand, it be true, as M. Hauréau[4]

---

[1] See p. 247, where the reasons are given.

[2] Ch. Jourdain, *Études historiques et philosophiques*, pp. 54, 55, traces certain passages which occur, in almost identical terms, in Trivet's commentary on the *Consolations* of Boëthius, and in that which is ascribed to St. Thomas Aquinas, to a commentator who must have lived later than Guillaume de Conches and before them. I venture to infer, from the language and from the sentiments of the passages quoted, that the commentator in question may have been Grosseteste. Grosseteste's glosses on Boëthius are in MS. 14,380 of the Bibliothèque Nationale, Paris.

[3] Trivet, p. 243.

[4] *Hist. de la philosophie scholastique*, i. pt. ii. p. 176; Dr. Felten, p. 73.

thinks, that his commentary on the *Physics* shows traces of Gregory the Ninth's declaration in 1231 that Aristotle's works should be studied in expurgated editions,[1] it may, perhaps, be inferred that the former work must be assigned to a still earlier period in Grosseteste's life, whereas the latter would belong to the three years which elapsed between the resignation of his preferments in 1232 and his elevation to the See of Lincoln in 1235, in which case the ethical notes occupy an intermediate position. On the whole, however, it is more probable that they cannot be arranged in precise chronological order, and that he was engaged simultaneously in the various branches of study, though additions were doubtless made, as time went on, to the materials at his disposal.

According to the Dominican chronicler Trivet, Grosseteste's treatises on "the Sphere" and on "Art" were amongst those which did most to increase his fame. The former work is cited again and again by writers of the thirteenth and following centuries, especially by Roger Bacon, as one which marks an important advance in astronomical research. It appears to have been anterior to the treatise on the same subject by John Holywood (*Johannes de Sacro Bosco*), by which it was superseded, for educational purposes, during the remainder of the Middle Ages, but it is doubtful in what relation it stands to the notes which Michael Scot is generally stated in the manuscripts to have written on John Holywood's *De Sphaera*, though a comparison of dates would seem to indicate that what Michael Scot wrote

---

[1] The first, however, is doubtful. As Mr. Rashdall shows (i. p. 358), William Arvernus, who was Bishop of Paris from 1228 to 1248, made free use of the suspected books, and the New Aristotle had triumphed by the middle of the century. Michael Scot's translations, made at Toledo, appeared in Northern Europe before 1230, but the only version made by him on which Grosseteste appears to have commented (and it may possibly have been on another version) is the treatise *De Generatione et Conceptione*. As Prantl, however, shows (*Geschichte der Logik*, iii. p. 85), Grosseteste had access to other translations of the *Posterior Analytics* besides that of Boëthius, and was also acquainted with the commentary of Themistius. He says, i. 10 : "Littera aliarum translationum et sententia Themistii neutri praedictarum sententiarum videtur concordari."

was really an independent work, which was subsequently appended to the longer treatise. Michael Scot, at any rate, died in or about the year 1235, whilst John Holywood probably survived Grosseteste by three years, and died in 1256.[1] The subject, however, requires further elucidation. It would also be of interest and importance if the relation in which Grosseteste stands, in that respect, to Arabic writers, such as Alphraganus, could be defined or approximately surmised, as well as the extent of his acquaintance with their writings.[2] There can be no doubt, however, that, whatever the sources of his inspiration may have been, Grosseteste did more than any one else to give a strong impulse to the study of astronomy and of mathematics in the thirteenth century.[3] The other treatise mentioned by Trivet, entitled "On Art," is probably identical with the one known as the *De utilitate artium*, and has been erroneously described as the *De arte computandi.*[4]

Grosseteste also wrote various mathematical treatises, on "lines and figures," on "angles," on "numerical notation," and on "practical geometry." A *Computus* and a *Computus Ecclesiasticus* may both be ascribed to him. Both in his work on "the Sphere" and in his *Computus Ecclesiasticus* he anticipates Roger Bacon's views as to the errors of the unreformed Julian calendar, and as to the necessity for the changes which were ultimately introduced in the sixteenth century through the medium of the Gregorian calendar, and which were not adopted in this country until the eighteenth.[5] The same subject

---

[1] On Michael Scot's works see the Rev. J. Wood Browne's *Life and Legend of Michael Scot*, Edinburgh, 1897.

[2] Prantl, *Geschichte der Logik*, iii. pp. 88, 89, discusses the question briefly of Grosseteste's logical and metaphysical indebtedness to the Arabs.

[3] Episcopi Roberti Lincolniensis, *Sphaerae Compendium*, Venice, 1518.

[4] Archdeacon Perry, p. 37, quotes the passage from Trivet from the *Spicilegium* of Dacher, which makes it appear as if the treatise were "de arte computandi," whereas in Hog's edition of Trivet it is called simply "de arte." Probably the word *Computandi* was inserted by some copyist who knew of Grosseteste's *Computus* and confused the two works. Pierre d'Ailly speaks of Grosseteste's work on the years and months of the Arabs "de quibus Lincolniensis diffuse tractavit." F. Kaltenbrunner, *Die Vorgeschichte der Gregorianischen Kalenderreform* (Vienna, 1876), p. 47.

[5] See Bacon's *Opus Tertium*, pp. 221

was treated almost simultaneously by Roger Bacon and by Campano :[1] the former work was written in 1263, the latter probably a year or two before or after that date. Grosseteste's *Computus* is therefore anterior to both by many years, and may doubtless be regarded as the foundation upon which they built. In the sixteenth century Maurolycus cites as his authorities on that subject Robert of Lincoln, John Holywood, and Campano.[2] Grosseteste does not appear, however, to have been convinced of the hopelessness of squaring the circle, if any inference may be drawn from the title of the Bodleian manuscript *De quadratura circuli per lineas* reputed to be his. The extent to which he was prepared to apply mathematical principles, or, in other words, to assert the existence of the reign of law, in the domain of science is shown in his little treatise, *De physicis lineis angulis et figuris per quas omnes actiones naturales complentur.*[3]

The treatise called by the name of *Tractatus Domini Lincolniensis de artibus liberalibus* may or may not be identical with the work " on art " mentioned by Trivet, to which reference has previously been made; but it appears to be the same as the first of the nineteen tracts, entitled " On the Utility of Arts," printed at Venice in 1514, and it is possible, therefore, that the title of the part was given to the whole.[4] That particular tract also forms part of the so-called *Summa Philosophiae* of Grosseteste, a somewhat miscellaneous collection mentioned by Leland, con-

---

sqq. ; Charles, *Roger Bacon,* p. 275. Cp. F. Kaltenbrunner, *Die Vorgeschichte der Gregorianischen Kalenderreform,* pp. 18-21, 44, 46, 47, 69. Dr. Kaltenbrunner shows clearly the indebtedness both of Roger Bacon and of Pierre d'Ailly to Grosseteste's *Computus.* See also the " Notitia de Kalendario Linconiensis " printed on p. 125 from the Vienna MS. 5508, fol. 205a.

[1] Campano died in 1267. His *Computus* was printed at Venice in 1518, in the same year as Grosseteste's work.

[2] Maurolycus, *Opuscula Mathematica,* Venice, 1578.

[3] Printed at Nuremberg in 1503, and described by Mr. Boole in the vol. of the Archaeological Institute for 1850, p. 139. Among the MSS. in Pembroke College, Cambridge, are Grosseteste's " Computus," " Dicta, cum Tabula," " De Lingua," and " De Literas Componendi forma." Grosseteste's *Computus* is in the Harl. MS. (British Museum), 7402, his *De Sphaera* in Harl. MS. 4350.

[4] See p. 42, note 2.

taining essays on forms, light, colours, the rainbow, and comets, as well as on the utility of the liberal arts. Amongst other writings of Grosseteste of a scientific or philosophic character which have been printed at Venice in 1514 may be enumerated treatises on the origin of sounds, on the heat of the sun, on the origin of stars, on the colours, on the nature of causes, on truth, on the impressions of the elements, on the movements of the body, on the finite character of time and motion, on the nature of places, and on man as a microcosm, in addition to some of the minor treatises previously mentioned.

The most important, however, of Grosseteste's works, from the point of view of the history of the advance of knowledge, and of his relations with his predecessors and with his pupils, amongst whom Roger Bacon must certainly be classed, was the *Compendium Scientiarum*, in which he attempts a classification of all the departments of knowledge then known. The manuscript was seen by Tanner in the last century.[1] The headings furnish some clue to the general arrangement which he adopted, and to the nature of the system he employed. They are (1) the divisions of philosophy, (2) a compendium of natural philosophy, (3) mathematics, (4) metaphysics, (5) grammar, (6) rhetoric, (7) logic, (8) the art of medicine, (9) arithmetic, (10) music, (11) geometry, (12) astronomy, (13) optics, (14) astrology, (15) astronomy, (16) mathematical sciences in general, (17) politics, (18) economics, (19) ethics, (20) on the unity and simplicity of knowledge. Truly Grosseteste was one of the great encyclopaedic thinkers of the world, and one who, in view of the limited opportunities then afforded for the acquisition and diffusion of learning, and the difficulty of procuring the materials of study, must be ranked among the foremost who have sought to reduce

---

[1] It used to be in the University Library at Cambridge, IIh. iv. 13. Hauréau was unable, however, to find it there, i. part ii. p. 174. The MS. Ji. iii. 19, however, which I have seen in that Library, entitled *Summa Philosophic Lincolnicnsis*, and not to be confused with the *Summa Philosophiae* mentioned by Leland (p. 48), contains twenty chapters which are identical with those of the *Compendium Scientiarum*, with the addition of Poetry and Mechanics, and the omission of Metaphysics and Astronomy (12).

diversity to unity, and to survey the whole extent of what is knowable, with the aid of observation and experiment, and in the light of all-embracing principles.

Roger Bacon's estimate of Grosseteste's achievements in the domain of science derives special value not only from the range of the writer's own attainments, but also from the fact that he was not inclined, as a general rule, to praise either his immediate predecessors or his contemporaries. It is well, therefore, to compare and to contrast that estimate with the opinion he formed and repeatedly expressed with regard to the three most widely read writers of his own age, Alexander de Hales, Albertus Magnus, and Thomas Aquinas. Of Alexander, the *Doctor Irrefragabilis* of the Franciscans, whose *Summa* was on one occasion proclaimed by an assembly of seventy doctors to be infallible, Bacon declares that the *Summa* in question, though it was as heavy as the weight of a horse, was full of errors, and displayed ignorance of physics, of metaphysics, and even of logic.[1]   Of Albertus Magnus, the *Doctor Universalis* of the Dominicans, he writes that what is useful in his works might be summed up in a treatise twenty times as short as they are.[2]   Thirdly, in speaking of Thomas Aquinas, who, it is true, had not attained at the time when Roger Bacon wrote to the commanding position of authority which was afterwards accorded to him in the schools, he couples him with Albertus Magnus, and says that they both became teachers before they had been adequately taught, and lectured on a philosophy and a theology which they had imperfectly learned. Without adopting the somewhat harsh judgment passed upon those great men by Roger Bacon, whose disregard for authority led him to be

> Nullius addictus jurare in verba magistri,

---

[1] *Opus Minus*, ed. Brewer, pp. 325-327 ; *Opus Tertium*, p. 30.

[2] *Opus Tertium*, p. 30.   I have followed É. Charles (p. 107) in the supposition that the passage refers to Albertus Magnus.   See also *Opus Minus*, p. 327.   The Order is that of the Dominicans, and not (as the marginal note says) that of the Franciscans.

and whose disappointments in his career were apt to embitter his feelings with respect to those whose success was recognised in their own generation, it is evident that the very independence of his judgment and the keenness of his critical faculty impart additional importance to his estimate of Grosseteste.

What, then, was that estimate?   The expressions of his views on the subject are to be found scattered throughout his works, and are invariably marked by a profound admiration of the great teacher's genius.   One passage has already been quoted.[1]   In another he states that "one man alone had really known the sciences, namely, Robert, Bishop of Lincoln,"[2] and again, that whilst Boëthius was the only translator who had an adequate knowledge of languages, "the Lord Robert alone, on account of his long life and the wonderful methods which he employed, excelled all men in his knowledge of the sciences."[3] In his work on mathematics, Roger Bacon says: "Nobody can attain to proficiency in that science by the method hitherto known, unless he devotes to its study thirty or forty years, as is evident from the case of those who have flourished in those departments of knowledge, such as the Lord Robert of holy memory, sometime Bishop of Lincoln, and Friar Adam Marsh, and Master John Hendover, and the like, and that is the reason why so few study that science."[4]   On the same subject he says, in the *Opus Majus*, in a passage of which the reading and the meaning are somewhat obscure, that "there were found some famous men, such as Robert, Bishop of Lincoln, and Adam Marsh, and several others, who were aware that the power of mathematics is capable of unfolding the causes of all things, and of giving a sufficient explanation of human and divine phenomena; and the assurance of this fact is to be found in the writings of those great men, as, for instance, in their

---

[1] *Compendium Studii Philosophiae*, p. 469.   See p. 43.

[2] *Opus Tertium*, p. 33.   Cp. *Opus Majus*, ed. Jebb, p. 45; ed. Bridges, i. p. 67.

[3] *Compendium Studii Philosophiae*, p. 472.

[4] Quoted by Wood, i. p. 82. Cp. *Opus Tertium*, p. 472.

works on the impressions, on the rainbow and the comets, on the generation of heat, on the investigation of geography, on the sphere, and on other questions appertaining both to theology and to natural philosophy."[1]　If by "the power of mathematics" Bacon means something akin to what would now be termed the "reign of law," ample recognition of that principle is to be found in Grosseteste's writings, without the addition of the fanciful comparisons by the aid of which Bacon expresses theological and moral truths in terms of mathematical phraseology.[2] Grosseteste and Adam Marsh, says Bacon in the *Opus Tertium*,[3] "rank among the greatest of the clergy the world has produced: they were perfect in divine and human wisdom."　In another passage he repeats that thought with even greater emphasis :[4] "Few have attained to consummate wisdom in the perfection of philosophy: Solomon attained to it, and Aristotle in relation to his times, and in a later age Avicenna, and in our own days the recently deceased Robert, Bishop of Lincoln, and Adam Marsh."

Lastly, in a passage, to which brief reference has already been made, relating to the translation of ancient authors,[5] Roger Bacon, after commending Boëthius for his knowledge of languages, says: "No one really knew the sciences except the Lord Robert, Bishop of Lincoln, by reason of his length of life and experience, as well as of his studiousness and zeal.　He knew mathematics and perspective,[6] and there was nothing which he was unable to know ; and at the same time he was

---

[1] *Opus Majus*, ed. Jebb, p. 64 ; ed. Bridges, i. p. 108.

[2] For instance, Bacon compares the Trinity to an equilateral triangle, argues that the divine light of grace reaches the good in a direct perpendicular ray, the weak in a refracted ray, and the bad in a reflected ray, and compares the virtues to the rational numbers, and the passions to the irrational, etc.　Grosseteste, however, is also fond of illustrations taken from optics.　For instance he says (*Comment. in Poster. Arist.* i. 17) that just as the light of the sun irradiates the organ of vision and things visible, enabling the former to see and the latter to be seen, so too the irradiation of a spiritual light brings the mind into relation with that which is intelligible.　Cp. his *De Veritate*, fol. 3 ; Prantl's *Geschichte der Logik*, iii. p. 87.

[3] *Opus Tertium*, p. 75.

[4] *Ibid.* p. 70.

[5] *Ibid.* p. 91.

[6] Perspective included optics.　See Part V. of the *Opus Majus*.

sufficiently acquainted with languages to be able to understand the saints and the philosophers and the wise men of antiquity; but his knowledge of languages was not such as to enable him to effect translations until the latter portion of his life, when he summoned Greeks, and caused books on Greek grammar to be brought together from Greece and other countries." And although the translations thus carried out were few in number, they compare favourably, adds Bacon, "with the numberless ones which were made by Gerard of Cremona, Michael Scot, Alfred of England, the translator employed by Manfred,[1] and others who knew neither the languages nor the sciences." The last portion of the statement relating to Grosseteste must be taken with certain reservations, as it is probable that he had commenced his studies of Greek and of Hebrew during his academic days, and indeed there is nothing in the passage to contradict either that supposition or the tradition that he was acquainted with Nicholas, the Greek, at that period of his life, and he may have had the advantage of his assistance then, as in later years; but the words of Bacon must be understood to refer specially to the mission of John of Basingstoke to Athens and elsewhere in search of Greek manuscripts, and to the translations which Grosseteste commenced in 1241 or 1242 with the aid of Nicholas and others.[2] In one place Bacon suggests that in order to increase the knowledge of Greek, some should journey to Italy, in some portions of which—for example, in Apulia—the clergy and the people were really Greeks, and that Bishops, Archbishops, rich men and old men should follow the example set by Grosseteste, and send to those parts in search of

[1] Manfred, son of Frederick II., was killed in 1266 at the battle of Benevento, where he was defeated by Charles of Anjou. Hence Roger Bacon, in the passage above quoted, written in 1267, speaks of him as "nuper a rege Carolo devicti." Mr. Archer, in reviewing the Rev. J. Wood Browne's *Life and Legend of Michael Scot*, Edinburgh, 1897, in the *English Historical Review* for April 1898, suggests that the Scot MS. which declares that one of Scot's treatises was written for Frederick's son Manfred in 1256, may have mistaken the "translator Manfredi" for Michael Scot.

[2] See pp. 223 *sqq.*, "Habuit multos adjutores," *Comp. Studii Philosophiae*, p. 472.

books as well as of persons acquainted with Greek; and he adds that several of the persons for whom he had thus sent were still in England at the time when he wrote.[1]   Concerning Grosseteste's efforts, however, to revive the study of Greek during the latter part of his life more will have to be said in a subsequent chapter.

In one important respect, and in one only, does Roger Bacon appear to have had the advantage over his teacher.   His knowledge of Arabic brought him into direct contact with the thoughts and writings of Avicenna and Averroës and others of the school of Cordova, while Grosseteste was obliged, in studying them, to rely upon inferior Latin translations or summaries, and to depart to that extent from the principle which he so often advocated, that recourse should be had to the original text.   To what extent the manuals at his disposal enabled him to appreciate the results at which they had arrived is a question beset with difficulties; but it may be safely assumed that, in whatever form they may have reached his hands, they facilitated his endeavours to work out for himself, by means of his own experiments and observations, the questions to which they had applied themselves, and stimulated, even if they did not direct, his efforts in particular departments of knowledge.   Their importance, however, from the point of view of their effect upon the development of the European intellect, consisted not so much in their own achievements as in the fact that they served as the channel through which the majority of the writings of Aristotle other than those which dealt with logic found their way into Europe; and as Grosseteste's life synchronised not only with the influx of Latin versions of the Arabic commentators and translators of Aristotle, but also with the facilities afforded by the Crusades, and more especially by the Latin conquest of Constantinople for the acquisition of Greek manuscripts, he was able to avail himself of both movements, and, within certain limits, to correct and supplement the one by means of the

<hr>

[1] *Compendium Studii Philosophiae*, p. 434.

other. His impulse to the study of mathematics and physical science was derived principally from the former, his impulse to the study of ethics chiefly from the latter. What Grosseteste does is to collect the scattered threads. He thinks out for himself the various problems, combines the solutions in the light of certain general principles, the truth of which he tests by observation and experiment, and endeavours to regard knowledge as a whole and to classify its component elements. He stands forth as the first and, in some respects, as the greatest of the encyclopædic thinkers of the thirteenth century. If, on the one hand, his teaching gives an impetus to the successive generations of schoolmen who, with increased material at their command, though with less boldness, perhaps, than had been exhibited in the twelfth century, devote themselves to the task of reconciling reason with faith, on the other hand he lays the foundations of the systematisation of universal knowledge attempted, on various principles, in various ways and with varying results, by Roger Bacon, Albertus Magnus, and Thomas Aquinas. Of the three, Roger Bacon is the one whose methods and whose range of studies are most akin to those of Grosseteste; there are indeed few of the leading ideas to be found in the writings of the Franciscan friar which may not be traced to the teaching of "Robert of holy memory"; and although the filiation of the two great Dominican writers is less direct, there can be no doubt that, not only at the University of Paris, through William Arvernus and others, they were able to become acquainted with his works, but also that Jordan of Saxony,[1] the second general of the order, John de St. Giles, and other prominent Dominicans who were intimate friends of Grosseteste even before he had been raised to the episcopal see, were instrumental in making his opinions and his researches known.[2]

---

[1] See pp. 66, 67.

[2] Albertus Magnus seldom quotes living writers by name, but a comparison of his commentary on the *Posterior Analytics* with the earlier one by Grosseteste shows the nature of the debt he owed. Prantl, *Geschichte der Logik*, iii. pp. 89, 107, assumes that they both derived simultaneously from the Arabic the distinction between

In Grosseteste's writings may be found the germ of at least two of the scholastic controversies which agitated Oxford and Paris during the latter part of the thirteenth century, that of the unity or plurality of forms, and that which concerned the principle of individuation. It is a testimony to the true greatness of his intellect that his influence should be traceable in two writers such as Roger Bacon and Thomas Aquinas, who at first sight appear to belong to entirely different types of thought; but the former was more than a scientist, and the latter was more than a schoolman.

"Friar Bungay," writes an ecclesiastical historian,[1] "had a profound knowledge of mathematics, which he owed either to the inspiration of the demon or to the teachings of Roger Bacon." It is not a matter of surprise that in an age in which the vast majority of the laity were steeped in ignorance, and the studies of the clergy were confined, with comparatively few exceptions, to narrow and well-beaten tracks, the men who rose head and shoulders above their contemporaries in the range of their knowledge and the breadth of their views should have been supposed by popular imagination to owe their intellectual superiority to fictitious advantages derived from the use of magic. It is worthy of note, however, that the legends embodying those fancies clustered exclusively round those who devoted most attention to the pursuit of mathematics and of natural science. The old dislike of mathematics, which finds expression in the prohibitions contained in the Theodosian code, was of long continuance. Grosseteste's reputation did not escape from the charge, and before long he, Albertus Magnus, Roger Bacon,

---

definitio formalis and *definitio materialis;* but it seems more likely to have come to Albertus through Grosseteste. M. Charles Jourdain's excellent *Philosophie de St. Thomas d'Aquin* (Paris, 1858) was written before he had turned his attention to Grosseteste, and he failed to realise that the latter had probably written before William Arvernus,

whose influence he traces in St. Thomas. Cp. the passages quoted from St. Thomas in vol. i. pp. 170 *sqq.* of his work with those which Prantl quotes from Grosseteste, *Geschichte der Logik*, iii. pp. 85 *sqq.*

[1] *Hist. Eccles. Magdeburgensis*, t. iii., quoted in Charles's *Bacon.*

Thomas of Bungay, and several others had been invested by the credulity of a subsequent generation with the possession of supernatural powers. John Gower, in his *Confessio Amantis*,[1] says :—

> For of the grete clerk Grostest
> I rede how redy that he was
> Upon clergy an hede of brass
> To make and forge it for to telle
> Of such thyngs as befelle ;
> And seven yeres besinesse
> He layde but for the lacknesse
> Of half a mynute of an houre,
> For fyrst that he began laboure
> He lost all that he had to do.

The making of the brazen head is in most story-books ascribed to Roger Bacon, and in the Elizabethan age the idea was worked out by Robert Greene in his *Historie of Friar Bacon and Friar Bungay*, a play of which the scene is placed in the very district in which Grosseteste was born,[2] a coincidence which suggests that the identity of the legends may have led to a confusion between the persons to whom they relate. In Greene's play Friar Bacon misses the critical moment, much in the same way as Grosseteste misses it in Gower's poem, and allows the brazen head to utter the words, " Time is " and " Time was," before its third utterance, " Time is past," tells him that the opportunity of obtaining an insight into the hidden nature of things has gone for ever. In Greene's play, again, Friar Bacon's wish is to " circle England round with brass," just as Marlowe's Dr. Faustus seeks to

> Circle Germany with walls of brass,

and the legends connected with Dr. Faustus in the sixteenth

---

[1] Book iv. Richard de Bardney writes of an infernal horse, named Beal, which conveyed Grosseteste in one night from England to Rome, to enable him to officiate there on behalf of the Bishop of Salisbury, who was old and infirm. Similarly in the " Volksbuch," published by Spies at Frankfort in 1587 under the title of *Historie von Dr. Johann Fausten*, Dr. Faust is made to ride to Rome upon Mephistopheles, who has transformed himself into a horse with " the wings of a dromedary."

[2] Fressingfield is within four miles of Stradbroke.

century have much in common with those which are associated in the thirteenth with the name of Albertus Magnus, who, like Grosseteste and Roger Bacon, was credited with a " brazen head." Similar stories had been told in the tenth century of Gerbert, the learned mathematician and scholar, who became Pope Sylvester II. It has been seen that Grosseteste wrote a short treatise on astrology, which forms part of his *Compendium Scientiae*, and if it be true that he also wrote on the philosopher's stone and on the astrolabe, it must be confessed that he did not take such precautions as were needed in that age to prevent the growth of imputations of that character. It is probable, however, that those two works, if he was their author, were really treatises on chemistry, as then understood, and on astronomy, and were a part of his scheme for dealing in a systematic way with the whole of science at the stage which it had reached ; and, after all, as Emile Charles observes in his *Life of Roger Bacon*, legends of that description represent merely the homage paid by ignorance to knowledge.

Enough has, perhaps, been said in this chapter to show that Grosseteste is entitled to a place of no mean order amongst the encyclopædic thinkers whom the world has produced. He had, indeed, become possessed of a secret more precious than that of the philosopher's stone : he had grasped the essential idea of the unity of knowledge, the interconnection and interdependence of all that relates to nature and to man.

CHAPTER III

BEFORE passing to the circumstances which induced Grosseteste at the end of 1231 or beginning of 1232 to relinquish most of his ecclesiastical duties and to restrict in a large measure the sphere of his activity, it is necessary to give some account of his relations with the two orders of Friars which, making their appearance on these shores a few years previous to that date, had begun to rouse England out of the moral and spiritual lethargy into which she had been plunged at the time of the Great Interdict, to appeal to new social strata barely touched by existing organisations, and to teach men that religion was as compatible with a life of activity as with a life of contemplation. It is among Grosseteste's merits that he was one of the first to divine the new ideas thus presented to the world, and to encourage and guide the new forces thus called into existence.

The first Dominicans landed in England in 1220, the first Franciscans in 1224; and in view of the fact that they both sought Grosseteste's protection and advice, and that to both he remained a firm and faithful friend, though specially associated with the latter as the earliest reader to their school at Oxford, it is desirable to refer briefly to the origin and importance of the two orders, as well as to their introduction into this country and their settlement at the University in which he was the foremost scholar.

The Dominicans and the Franciscans were imbued alike with the missionary spirit which aims at the salvation of souls. The methods, however, by which they sought to attain to that object differed as widely as did the character and temperament of their respective founders. The followers of the Castilian St. Dominic were essentially an order of preachers, whilst the followers of St. Francis of Assisi were essentially an order of workers. The former took pride in their severe and even fanatical orthodoxy, and relied mainly on the eloquence of the spoken word for the furtherance of their efforts; the latter relied mainly on the eloquence of practical example, and looked for their ideal to the teaching of the Sermon on the Mount. The Black Friars appealed rather to the feeling of fear, the Grey Friars to that of love. They both, as distinguished from the old monastic orders, found scope for their work in the towns rather than in the country, and addressed themselves to the masses rather than to the few. St. Francis had "taken poverty as his bride," and had imposed the same vow upon his disciples, an example which was followed by St. Dominic, who had not originally intended to include it in his rule. In comparison with them the great Benedictine monasteries, with their wealth, their culture, and their relative exclusiveness, stood at a disadvantage when the question was how to reach the people's ear. The Dominicans suited their style of speech to their hearers, addressing the learned with arguments which derived their strength from the subtlety and ingenuity of their dialectic, whilst they spoke to the unlearned in language which aroused in turn their hopes and their apprehensions. The Franciscans, without disdaining the merits of a persuasive utterance, paid more attention to the practical works of charity, nursing the sick, and especially those who were afflicted with the more loathsome forms of disease, such as leprosy, which had at that time acquired a strong hold in Europe, and extending their care not only to their human brethren, but also to dumb animals, in emulation of their founder, who had preached a sermon to birds, and had declared on one occasion, "If I could only be presented to the Emperor, I would pray him to issue an edict prohibiting any one from catching or imprisoning my sisters, the larks, and ordering that all who have oxen or asses should at Christmas feed them particularly well."

The extraordinarily rapid advance effected in the course of a few years by the new orders, and the hold which they obtained over men's minds, were due in part to the fact that they supplied a moral and spiritual want which had long been felt, and with which existing religious bodies were either unable or unwilling to cope. The age, moreover, was one of intellectual ferment, and was favourable to the growth of generous enthusiasm and fervent emotion, which generally assumed a religious form, though in other cases it partook of a different character. The feelings which had brought about the Crusades had not yet been extinguished, although the fall of Jerusalem in 1187 had produced a widespread sense of gloom and consternation. Contact between East and West had familiarised Europe with other modes of thought. In Southern and Central Italy the Cathari, a corrupt offshoot of the strict and even puritanical sect of the Patarenes,[1] threatened, with their Manichaeism, their revival of old-world ceremonies, and their abolition of marriage, to sap the foundations of society at the centre of Christendom. In the north of the peninsula, apart from the Patarenes, who were to be found chiefly in and about Milan, the Waldenses, striving after a purer form of faith, gradually withdrew from communion with the rest of their compatriots. In the centre of what is now France the "poor men of Lyons," to whom the Waldenses owed their inspiration, and probably their origin, had formed themselves into a guild of charity, bound by solemn vows, of which the vow of poverty was one. In Gascony the Albigenses, who, like the Patarenes, had derived their ideas from Eastern sources, at first hand from the adherents of the Bogomilian sect in Bosnia, and

---

[1] For the precise distinction between the Patarenes and the Cathari see F. Tocco's *Eresia nel medio evo*, Florence, 1884.

at second hand from the Paulicians of Armenia, adopted a form
of belief for which they paid a terrible penalty at the hands of
the fourth Simon de Montfort, whose name is as infamous in
the annals of repression as the name of his greater son is illustrious in the history of freedom.[1]   In Germany the year
1213 had witnessed the extraordinary outburst known as the
children's crusade,[2] and a few years later the sect of the Catini,
or Städinger, was subjected to wholesale massacre.[3]   On the
other hand scepticism, also derived in part from contact with
the East, was making its appearance in high places.   Philip
Augustus threatened to become a Mahometan when the Interdict was used as a weapon against him; King John of England
was said to be so indifferent to the responsibilities of Christian
kingship that he offered at one time to place himself under the
suzerainty of the Moorish Khalif, and, not many years later,
similar stories were current concerning the Holy Roman
Emperor himself, Frederick the Second of Germany, and were
thought to receive some countenance from the conciliatory disposition which he manifested towards the Saracens in Sicily and
in the Holy Land.   The Almarician heresy, which came to the
front at the University of Paris, was rigorously suppressed in
1210.[4]   In England, almost alone among nations, heresy had
obtained no footing.

Such were the conditions which prevailed at the time when
the mendicant orders sprang into existence.   From the first the
Dominicans were the faithful servants of the Roman see; no
question was raised as to their willingness to obey implicitly

---

[1] In the *Hist. Maj.* iii. 78 it is stated
that the Pope of the Albigenses and of
the Patarenes resided "between the
confines of Bulgaria, Croatia, and Dal-
matia," *i.e.* in Bosnia.   The filiation
of the Albigenses and Patarenes to the
Bogomiles, and through them to the
Paulicians, is explained by Mr. Arthur
Evans in the historic sketch prefixed
to his *Through Bosnia and Herzegovina* (London, 1876), and the authorities are there quoted. Adherents of the
Bogomilian doctrines are still to be
found in some of the remoter valleys
of the Herzegovina.   Large numbers
of them were massacred in 1238 by
Koloman, brother of the King of
Hungary.

[2] *Hist. Maj.* ii. 558.   It was headed
by a French (? Franconian) boy.

[3] *Ibid.* iii. 267.

[4] Rashdall, ii. 355-357.

the orders which they received. The case of the Franciscans
was somewhat different, and it is impossible to read the account
of their founder's life without coming to the conclusion that,
had it not been for the tact and good management of Cardinal
Ugolino,[1] he and his followers would have drifted away from
the main body of the Church, and have become a separate sect,
much in the same way as the Waldenses. A comparison has
often been drawn between the Franciscans and the Wesleyans.
As Canon Jessopp puts it, "St. Francis was the John Wesley of
the thirteenth century, whom the Church did not cast out."[2]   Dr.
Kuenen compares the relation of the Franciscans to the Church
with that of the Buddhists to Brahmanism, adding that the
connection with the parent tree was retained in the one case
and lost in the other.

Comparatively little is known with regard to the first settlement of the Dominicans in England. In 1221,[3] the very year
after the chapter held at Bologna, at which they virtually
transformed themselves from an order of Austin canons into
one of mendicant friars by the adoption of constitutions framed
in imitation of those of St. Francis, the first party of Black
Friars, twelve in number, in addition to Gilbert de Fraxineto, or
de Fresnoy, under whose leadership they were placed, landed on
these shores, were well received by Stephen Langton, Archbishop of Canterbury, preached in London on the 10th of
August, and reached Oxford on the 15th of that month. Almost
immediately after their arrival they established a friary, with
church and schools attached, though it must be remembered
that the Dominican church of St. Nicholas, which was destroyed
during the reign of Henry the Eighth, was not dedicated until
1262, that is to say, more than forty years after their arrival,
and it is known that they occupied in the meantime a

---

[1] The Cardinal failed, however, in
his endeavour to bring about an
amalgamation between the two orders.
See Sabatier.

[2] *The Coming of the Friars.*

[3] Trivet, p. 209.

[4] Wood, *City of Oxford*, ed. Clark,
ii. p. 321.

temporary habitation.[1]   Leland says that two schools were connected with their friary, one for divinity in the chapter-house, and one for philosophy in the cloisters.   Robert Grosseteste was among the first to welcome them, and it is by no means unlikely, in view of the attitude towards them exhibited in his letters, that they came to Oxford at his suggestion and invitation.   If, as is possible, he was Chancellor of the University at that time, it was natural that their earliest communications should be addressed to him.   His views as to the importance of preaching were in harmony with theirs.   Three of his most intimate and distinguished friends joined the order at an early date, namely, John de St. Giles, Robert Bacon, and Richard Fishacre.

John de St. Giles, in the middle of a sermon in which he was commending the vow of poverty, determined to put his principles into practice and to resign his worldly wealth, descended from the pulpit, assumed the black garb of the Friars Preachers, and then returned and finished his discourse.[2]   He is believed to have been the first Englishman who joined the Dominicans.   The incident is related by Trivet under the year 1222, and took place apparently at Paris; but it is evident from the fact that the pulpit was in the Dominican Church that John de St. Giles must have been in previous sympathy with the order, if not an actual member, and it was in 1218 that he had presented to them the Hôpital de St. Jacques, probably out of the funds which he had accumulated as first physician to Philip Augustus.   It was doubtless by reason of

---

[1] See *Ann. Monast.* (Worcester), iv. 413.   The older schools, according to Leland, stood "infra locum quem nunc habitant."   The early settlement was in the heart of the Jewry, where the church of St. Edward was handed over to them by the Countess of Oxford and the Bishop of Carlisle.   Rashdall, ii. p. 376; Wood, *City of Oxford*, ed. Clark, Oxford Historical Society, ii. pp. 312 *sqq.*   They entered their new house in the parish of St. Edward's in 1245.   *Ann Monast.* (T. Wykes), iv. 94.

[2] Trivet.   See Mr. Kingsford's article on John de St. Giles in the *Dict. of Nat. Biography* and Denifle's "Quellen zur Gelehrtengeschichte des Predigerordens im 13ten. und 14ten, Jahrhundert," in the *Archiv für Litteratur und Kirchengeschichte des Mittelalters*, ii. p. 165.

earlier friendship, formed in all likelihood at Paris, that Grosseteste invited him in 1235 [1] to come and preach in his own
country. He accepted the invitation as soon as he was able
to return from his attendance in Germany on the Princess
Isabella, who had now become the wife of the Emperor Frederick II.,[2] and he became the head of the Dominican School at
Oxford. His friendship with Grosseteste continued to the end.
He was presented by the Bishop to the prebend of Leighton
and the archdeaconry of Oxford, but soon asked to be released
from these preferments for reasons of health.[3] In 1239 he was
Chancellor of the diocese of Lincoln.[4] He was repeatedly an
inmate of Grosseteste's palace, as a friend whose counsel was
eagerly sought, though not always implicitly followed, and also
as a physician whose skill was called into requisition on more
than one occasion during the Bishop's life, and more particularly
during his last illness.[5]

Of the other two prominent friends of Grosseteste who
joined the order about that time, Robert Bacon, probably uncle
of Roger Bacon, the Franciscan, is said to have become a Friar
Preacher in his old age, and in the height of his reputation
as a scholar and a theologian, and to have continued for several
years his lectures at St. Edward's Schools, as the schools
attached to the Dominican friary were then called.[6] With
him were always associated in his own and in the following
generations the name and the memory of Richard Fishacre,
best known as a commentator on Peter Lombard's *Sentences*
and a postillator of the Psalms. Although Fishacre's name is
not mentioned in Grosseteste's correspondence, the tradition
with respect to their intimacy is in harmony with the statements of Matthew Paris and of Trivet that Robert Bacon and
he were inseparable companions, lectured in the same schools,
and were as undivided in their death as in their life, both dying

---

[1] Letter 16. See also Letters 14, 15.

[2] *Hist. Maj.* iii. 324.

[3] *Mon. Francisc.* pp. 132, 172.

[4] Le Neve, *Fasti*, ii. 91.

[5] *Hist. Maj.* v. 705, 400, 401.

[6] Trivet, pp. 229, 230 ; *Hist. Maj.* v. 16 ; Leland.

in 1248.[1] It may therefore be assumed that the friends of the first must also have been the friends of the second. About Grosseteste's relations with Robert Bacon there can be no doubt. Their two names are associated, together with that of the Chancellor of the University, in a mandate issued by Henry the Third at Oxford in June 1234, in which the mayor and bailiffs are instructed to take steps for the expulsion of women of bad repute from the city, with the stipulation that if any should remain there after eight days, they might be seized by order of the Chancellor, or of Master Robert Grosseteste, or of Friar Robert Bacon, and detained until the King's further pleasure should be made known.[2] It was shortly before that date that Robert Bacon advised the King publicly in a sermon that he would never enjoy peace until Peter des Roches, Bishop of Winchester, and Peter de Rievaulx were driven from the kingdom.[3] It was on the same occasion that a certain clerk, who is stated to have been Roger Bacon, asked the King the riddle, "Wherein lies the greatest danger to those who are crossing the straits?"—the reply to which, suggested by the propounder himself, was "Petris et Rupibus," a punning allusion to the Latin name of Henry's evil counsellor. With the views thus expressed Grosseteste, as the friend of the Marshalls,[4] must have been in thorough accord. A reference occurs in one of the Bishop's letters of the year 1235 to Robert Bacon, whose name appears in the manuscript, probably owing to some error, as Roger. Another connecting link between them was, in all likelihood, the regard felt by Robert Bacon for St. Edmund of Canterbury, who was his teacher or, according to other accounts, his pupil, and probably both, and whose life he subsequently wrote.[5]

In 1230 the head of the Dominican order, Friar Jordan of

---

[1] Trivet, pp. 229, 230; *Hist. Maj.* v. 16.

[2] Pegge, p. 34 ; Kennett's *Parochial Antiquities*, i. 306, 307 ; Dodsworth MSS. (Bodleian), vol. ciii. fol. 168.

[3] *Hist. Maj.* iii. 244, 245.

[4] See pp. 93, 108.

[5] *Hist. Maj.* v. 369. Eccleston (*Mon. Francisc.* p. 56) refers to the entry of Robert Bacon into the Dominican order at an advanced age.

Saxony, who had succeeded to St. Dominic in the office of general, came to Oxford.[1] An anecdote of his visit to England is related by Eccleston.[2] Seven years later Grosseteste wrote to him in affectionate terms, recalling the pleasant intercourse he had enjoyed with him at Oxford, praising the work of the Friars Preachers, and expressing the hope that John de St. Giles, among other members of that body, might be permitted to remain at his side, in order to assist him in the task of dealing with the requirements of so vast a diocese as that of Lincoln.[3] " I hope," writes Grosseteste, " that he may remain with me to strengthen my weakness, to supplement my insufficiency, to stir me up when I am too easy-going, to sustain me when I stagger, to push me forward when I hesitate, and to comfort me in the days of tribulation." At an earlier date, in 1235, immediately after his appointment to the bishopric, he had addressed a similar request to Friar Alard, provincial prior of the order in England, then holding a chapter at York, and had asked him to send not only John de St. Giles, but also Geoffrey de Clive, together with a third skilled in canon and civil law.[4] From another letter written apparently in 1242 [5] to Friar Matthew, who was then provincial prior, it seems that the Pope had granted to Grosseteste a privilege allowing him always to have two Dominicans with him ; and he expresses the hope that they may be changed less frequently. Other testimonies might

---

[1] *Lettres de Jourdain de Saxe*, ed. Bayonne (Paris, 1865), pp. 122 *sqq.*, 134. " Apud studium Oxoniense, ubi ad praesens eram, spem bonae capturae Dominus nobis dedit." And, again, " sanus ante Purificationem B. Virginis de Anglia vobis scripsi." The letters are addressed to Diana, foundress of the convent of St. Agnes at Bologna, and give an account of the " conversions " the writer was able to effect at Paris, Padua, Vercelli, Bologna, and other Universities. Matthew Paris mentions his death by drowning. *Hist. Maj.* iii. 390-391.

[2] *Mon. Francisc.* p. 11.

[3] Letter 40. The letter was written in 1237.

[4] Letters 14, 15.

[5] Letter 100. There is no complete list of the provincial priors of the Dominican order in England, as there is of the provincial ministers of the Franciscans. Mr. A. G. Little, in the *English Historical Review* for July 1893, attempts to supply the names and the dates from various sources. Gilbert de Fresnoy was provincial prior in 1221, Alard in 1235, Henry in 1240, and Matthew from 1245 to 1254.

be quoted from his correspondence, pointing to the regard he entertained for them, and to the value he attached to their help, and showing that the relations commenced at Oxford continued throughout his life. In a letter written in 1236 to Alexander de Stavensby, Bishop of Coventry and Lichfield, Grosseteste, referring to trustworthy reports which had reached his ears to the effect that his correspondent had spoken ill of the Franciscans at Chester, on the ground that they desired to settle there in company with the Dominicans, speaks of the zeal and usefulness of both orders, and adds that their simultaneous presence in a city, far from injuring each other's efforts, had the effect of rendering their work more abundant and more effective by the stimulus of friendly rivalry.[1] It was natural that Grosseteste should take an interest in a matter affecting a city where he had once been Archdeacon, though it may only have been for a short time,[2] and should be anxious to assist in effecting an arrangement. There can, however, be no doubt that the Dominicans made less progress in England than was the case with the Franciscans, and that the latter obtained over men's minds a hold which the former were unable to secure.

Close as were the relations which Grosseteste maintained with the Friars Preachers, it was with the Friars Minors that he was most in sympathy, as might, indeed, have been expected in one whose mind dwelt more on the moral and practical aspects of Christianity than on those which were of a purely doctrinal character. The coming of the Franciscans to England has been so fully told by Eccleston, and so often retold since the publication of Brewer's edition of that manuscript, that it is unnecessary to deal with it here at any length. Grey Friars they were often called from their garb, and also "Fratres Minores," or Minorites, a designation which they originally adopted partly out of humility, and partly, in all likelihood, with indirect reference to the democratic party at Assisi, which had long been known as that of the "minores," as distinguished

<hr>

[1] Letter 31. See *post*, p. 78.   [2] See p. 25.

from the "majores," as the city oligarchs were termed. On the 11th of September 1224, two years after the arrival of the Dominicans, and two years before the death of St. Francis, their first band landed penniless at Dover, having been conveyed across the Channel as an act of charity through the care of monks of Fécamp. They consisted of four clerks, of whom, however, only one, a Norfolk man named Richard of Ingworth, was in priest's orders, and of five laymen, under the guidance of Friar Agnellus of Pisa, whom their founder had intended for the post of first provincial minister of the order in England. Eccleston has related in touching terms the narrative of the hardships they encountered, of the simple faith by which they were sustained, and of the zeal and fearlessness with which they performed what might have appeared a well-nigh impossible task.[1] Within five years they had established themselves in every important city in England. In a little more than thirty years the members of the order had increased from 9 to 1242, had settled in no fewer than forty-nine different localities, and had covered the whole country with a network of organisation directed to the furtherance of their founder's principles. They betook themselves, as a rule, to the suburbs of the towns, in the midst of the poorest of the population amongst whom they laboured. We are told how in London, after they had been entertained by the Dominicans on the simplest fare for the space of a fortnight, they succeeded in securing a house in the Cornhill, where they constructed separate cells, stopping the interstices with dry grass. In November two of them, Richard of Ingworth and Richard of Devonshire, proceeded to Oxford, where they were hospitably received by the Black Friars, and established a settlement in the parish of St. Ebbe's, "where was sown a grain of mustard seed, which grew to be greater than all the trees." It is interesting to note that the first town to which, in the summer of the following year, they travelled from Oxford was Northampton,[2] with which

---

[1] *Mon. Francisc.* pp. 5 *sqq.*   [2] *Ibid.* pp. 9, 10.

Grosseteste had been connected shortly before in his capacity of Archdeacon, and that they afterwards built themselves at Cambridge a small wooden chapel, erected by a carpenter in one day from fourteen couple of planks, doubtless with the help of clay.[1] To describe, however, how they passed from town to town. making converts wherever they went, and meeting with a specially warm response at Lynn, Yarmouth, Norwich, and other places in the eastern counties, would lie outside the scope of this work.

Of their early settlement at Oxford several particulars are recorded by Eccleston, who himself studied in the school which they there established.[2] William of Esseby, a novice, was invested with the garb of the order, and made their first warden, As their numbers increased, and "as Oxford was the principal place of study in England, where the whole body of scholars was wont to congregate, Friar Agnellus caused a school of sufficiently decent appearance to be built on the site on which the Friars had settled, and induced Robert Grosseteste of holy memory to lecture to them there; and under him they made extraordinary progress in sermons as well as in subtle moral themes suitable for preaching," and continued to do so until " he was transferred by Divine Providence from the professorial chair to the episcopal see."[3] It is not quite clear whether Grosseteste began to lecture to the Franciscans immediately after their arrival at Oxford, or whether a short interval elapsed. At any rate, he was the first who undertook the discharge of those duties, and it is probable, therefore, that his work began before the rapid extension of their property and of their buildings. It must have been about twenty years before they had added to their holding in the parish of St. Ebbe's the marshy strip of ground outside the town wall, where they afterwards resided.[4] Grosseteste, indeed, appears to have warned

---

[1] *Mon. Francisc.* p. 18.

[2] *Ibid.* pp. 10, 18, 27, 28, 31, 37-39, etc.

[3] *Ibid.* p. 37.

[4] *Grey Friars at Oxford*, pp. 12 *sqq.*, 22 *sqq.*

them, on sanitary grounds, not to build their houses too near the water's edge,[1] but they probably paid little attention to advice which seemed to derogate from their self-sacrificing enthusiasm. The school cannot have been of imposing proportions if it resembled the hospital which they also constructed at Oxford, and of which Eccleston says that it was so low that the walls barely reached beyond the stature of a man.[2] The humility of their dwellings was akin to the simplicity of their habits ; for several years the Oxford Franciscans slept without pillows, and never used shoes except in cases of illness, when special permission had to be obtained ; and yet we are told that many bachelors of arts and many nobles entered the order.[3] It is added by Eccleston that readers were also appointed, apparently somewhat later, at Hereford, Leicester, Bristol, and Cambridge, as well as at Oxford, and that "the gift of wisdom so overflowed in the province of England, that before the deposition of William of Nottingham [4] there were as many as thirty lecturers in England, in addition to four who lectured without 'disputations.' A regular succession of them was provided in the universities." [5]

It is not known whether Grosseteste had any acquaintance with the Franciscans previous to their arrival at Oxford. He had doubtless heard much concerning them from his Dominican friends, and from his correspondents in Paris, and possibly in Italy. Although Adam Marsh does not appear to have become a Franciscan until the year 1226,[6] or shortly afterwards, when

---

[1] *Mon. Francisc.* p. 66.

[2] Of their first house "fuit area brevis et arcta nimis," p. 17. Eccleston calls the school "satis honestam."

[3] *Mon. Francisc.* pp. 17, 28.

[4] Probably in 1251. See Mr. Little's article on the succession of the provincial ministers of the Friars Minors in England in the *English Historical Review* for October 1891, and his *Grey Friars at Oxford*, p. 184. But see also *Mon. Francisc.* p. 551, according-

ing to which the date would be 1254.

[5] *Mon. Francisc.* p. 38 ; Brewer's preface, p. 48.

[6] *Mon. Francisc.* pp. 15, 16. Dr. Brewer's statement (p. 79) in the preface that he assumed the habit at Worcester "during the wardenship of Agnellus, that is, between 1236 and 1239," is clearly a slip. Agnellus of Pisa was provincial minister from 1224 to 1235. The Bishop of London

he entered the order at Worcester, following the example set by Adam of Oxford, he appears to have been in sympathy with their views at an earlier period of his life; and it is possible that he may have written to Grosseteste on the subject from Padua, where, according to one account of doubtful authenticity, though inherent probability, he was studying at that time, and where St. Anthony of Padua, one of St. Francis' disciples, is said to have been amongst his friends.[1] More probably Richard of Ingworth, as an East Anglian, may have been acquainted with Grosseteste in earlier days. And in this connection it is not unimportant to emphasise the preponderance of the East Anglian element among the pioneers of the movement, a fact which may possibly account in part for its rapid spread in that part of England, whilst, on the other hand, there must have been something in the attitude of the Minorites which appealed in a special degree to the East Anglian mind, much in the same way as the religious movements of the fourteenth, fifteenth, sixteenth, and seventeenth centuries found most favour there. Perhaps Milman's saying that Franciscanism was "the democracy of Christianity," affords some explanation of the friendly reception with which it met in a district in which similar tendencies of thought have often manifested themselves. Canon Jessopp well observes that "of the first eighteen masters of the Franciscan school at Cambridge at least ten were Norfolk men, whilst of the first five Divinity readers at Oxford whose names have been

inadvertently adopts Dr. Brewer's statement in his article on Adam Marsh in the *Dict. of National Biography*, and says that Adam Marsh entered the order about 1237. It was Albert of Pisa who was minister from 1236 to 1239.

[1] If Adam Marsh studied at Padua, it can hardly have been before 1222, as no regular lectures appear to have been delivered there until that year, when a migration of students took place from Bologna, Rashdall, ii. p. 11. See Wadding's *Annales Minorum*, ii. 48, 240. It is possible that he may have been both to Bologna and to Padua. Wadding's account may, however, be based upon a confusion with his alleged visit to Italy in 1230, when he is said to have accompanied St. Anthony of Padua to Rome in opposition to the minister Helias. According to another account, also mentioned by Wadding, it was at Vercelli that he studied. See Mr. Little's *Grey Friars at Oxford*, p. 135. See also note 4, p. 76, of the present work.

recorded, after [and including] those of Grosseteste and of Roger de Weseham, four were unmistakably East Anglians."[1]

What was Grosseteste's main object in encouraging the settlement of the Grey Friars at Oxford, and in undertaking the task of becoming their first lecturer? In the position which he then occupied as former, or possibly actual, Chancellor of the University, as its leading scholar, as regent in arts and doctor of theology, and with the reputation of being *summus philosophus*, it must have required a certain amount of moral courage on his part to identify himself so prominently with a body of men whose views and whose practice were little in harmony with received notions. Representing as they did to a great extent the admixture of the laity in religious affairs—for most of them were laymen, at any rate at first—they could not be expected to be received with heartiness by the secular clergy. Embodying as they did the voluntary principle, they were certain to incur sooner or later the hostility of the monastic orders, which depended mainly upon endowments. As independent of class distinctions, they afforded a contrast alike to the ideas inseparable from the feudal system, and to the aristocratic exclusiveness of the monks. Oxford, however, was not monastic in its nature or in its tendencies, except so far as St. Frideswyde's and Osney were able to exercise any influence ; it had as yet no endowments of any consequence, and it had already on various occasions shown signs of the exercise of independent judgment on ecclesiastical as well as on political matters. Moreover, Grosseteste's force of character, and the weight he carried in the University, were such as to enable him to overcome prejudices and obstacles of that description. Doubtless he felt deeply the charm and freshness of the movement, and admired the unselfish devotion of its leaders. His object, however, in helping to bring about and in strengthening their connection with the University must have been twofold. He desired to promote the revival

---

[1] Dr. Jessopp's *Coming of the Friars.* A certain Peter, afterwards Bishop in Scotland, intervened between Grosse- teste and Roger de Wescham, *Mon. Francisc.* pp. 37, 38.

of learning, and also the revival of religion. His action furthered
both ends. It brought the University into touch with a great
spiritual and moral influence which was calculated and qualified to appeal to the people as a whole, whilst at the same time
it imparted to the friars a culture to which they would not
otherwise have attained. Every friar who passed from the
Franciscan school at Oxford to do his duty in the world in
accordance with his calling, would thus carry with him, and be
able to convey to others, some of the learning he had acquired,
or at any rate its spirit; and, in turn, every friar who came to
the University would help to raise the tone of the studies,
and to direct them to the worthiest purposes.

Such was, in all probability, the ideal which Grosseteste had
in view. It differed, however, from the ideal of St. Francis,
who "had set his face against learning, and would have his
followers like the poor, not in dress only, but in understanding."[1]
"I am afraid," he once said, when he heard that a great doctor
of Paris, possibly Alexander of Hales, had been received into the
order, greatly to the joy of the clergy and of the city, "I am
afraid that such doctors will be the destruction of my vineyard.
They are the true doctors who, with the meekness of wisdom,
exhibit good works for the improvement and edification of their
neighbours. A man has no more knowledge than he works, and
he is a wise man only in the degree in which he loves God and
his neighbour." On another occasion he severely rebuked one
of his provincial ministers, Peter Stacia, for having organised
some kind of Franciscan school at Bologna.[2] It is easier, however, for those who have tasted of the sweets of knowledge to
part with riches than to part with learning, and it was at
Bologna that most of his early successors studied, such as
Peter of Catagna, John Parenti, Helias, Albert of Pisa, Haymo
of Faversham, and Crescentius.[3]

<hr>

[1] Brewer's preface to the *Mon.
Francisc.* p. 29. For anecdotes relating to Grosseteste's career as a
lecturer at Oxford see *Mon. Francisc.*
pp. 64-66, and pp. 332, 333 of the present work.

[2] Sabatier, *Vie de St. François
d'Assise,* chapter xvi.   [3] *Ibid.*

In view of the subsequent history of the Franciscan school at Oxford, and of the influence exercised by the order in England, as compared with other countries, it cannot be denied that Grosseteste's attempt to combine the revival of learning with the revival of religion was largely justified by its results. Nowhere has the Franciscan order done so much as in England for the advancement and dissemination of knowledge, nowhere has it furnished so long a list of distinguished names, and nowhere has it presented so clear and so clean a record of useful work. With few exceptions every really great man of learning belonging to the order came from these islands. It was from the very school at which Grosseteste was the first lecturer, and at which Adam Marsh, his most intimate friend, subsequently read, that proceeded Richard of Coventry, Roger Bacon, John Wallensis,[1] Thomas Dockyng, Thomas of Bungay, Archbishop Peccham, Richard Middleton, Duns Scotus, Occham, and Burley. As Dr. Brewer observes, "Lyons, Paris, and Cologne were indebted for their first professors to the English Franciscans at Oxford. Repeated applications were made from Ireland, Denmark, France, and Germany for English friars; foreigners were sent to the English school as superior to all others. It enjoyed a reputation throughout the world for adhering the most conscientiously and strictly to the poverty and severity of the order; and for the first time since its existence as a University, Oxford rose to a position second not even to Paris itself. The three schoolmen of the most original and profound genius, Roger Bacon, Duns Scotus, and Occham, were trained within its walls."[2] Among the Dominicans Germany produced Albertus Magnus, and Italy St. Thomas Aquinas; among the Franciscans Italy had its St. Bonaventura, and Spain its Raymond Lully; but "no nation can show three schoolmen like the English, each unrivalled in his way, and each working with equal ability in opposite directions.

---

[1] Not to be confused with Thomas Wallensis, who succeeded Roger de Weseham as reader at the same Franciscan school, and who became Archdeacon of Lincoln in 1238, and Bishop of St. David's in 1248.

[2] Brewer, pref. to the *Mon. Francisc.* p. 81.

The influence of the English school was consequently more profound, more brilliant the reputation of its teachers." To Grosseteste, more than to any other man, must the credit be accorded.

One of the most important effects, so far as Grosseteste's own life was concerned, of the part he took in furthering the Franciscan movement was to cement the bonds of friendship between himself and Adam Marsh.[1] That learned man, whose name is constantly coupled with his by Roger Bacon and others, and the trend of whose theological and mathematical studies lay in the same direction, is stated by Trivet to have been a native of the diocese of Bath, was educated at Oxford, where he was a pupil of Grosseteste,[2] and held, according to the *Lancrcost Chronicle*, a living at Wearmouth, in the diocese of Durham, previous to his admission into the order. His uncle, Richard de Marisco, who was Bishop of Durham from 1217 to 1226, bequeathed to him his library in the latter year.[3] The traditions relating to his studies in Italy rest upon somewhat vague foundations, but derive some support from the internal evidence afforded by his letters.[4] He was the first Franciscan who

---

[1] M. Charles Jourdain (*Excursions Historiques*, p. 133) suggests, with more fancifulness than probability, that Adam Marsh may have been a native, not of Somerset, but of Ponts et Marais, formerly called de Marisco, near Eu in Normandy, on the ground that he was a correspondent of the Archbishop of Rouen, that a certain Peter of Pontoise was among his friends, and that he communicated indirectly with Blanche of Castile, Queen of France. It may be replied (1) that he may have made the acquaintance of Odo, who became Archbishop of Rouen in 1248, on his way back from the Council of Lyons in 1245, before Odo, who was a Minorite, had been appointed to that office; (2) that Pierre de Pontoise was in the service of Simon de Montfort (*Mon. Francisc.* p. 261); and (3) that his letter to the Archbishop of Rouen (p. 80) and his indirect communication with Blanche de Castile (p. 381) both relate to Simon de Montfort's business. In view, therefore, of Adam Marsh's relations to that great man, no further explanation is required of his acquaintance with the correspondents in question. Fuller in his *Worthies* (*s.v.* Somerset) suggests Brent Marsh as the place of his nativity. Trivet's statement, which M. Jourdain appears to have overlooked, may be accepted as conclusive that he was born in the diocese of Bath. Leland mentions Somerset in this connection.

[2] Roger Bacon (*Opus Tertium*, p. 187) speaks of Grosseteste as Adam's master.

[3] Close Roll, 10 Henry III. m. 6. See the biographical notice of Adam Marsh in Mr. Little's *Grey Friars at Oxford*, pp. 134-139.

[4] E.g. *Mon. Franciscana*, p. 206, where he speaks of his old friendship

lectured at Oxford,[1] where the variety of his attainments and the lucidity of his teaching earned him the name of *doctor mirabilis*. His entry into the Franciscan order took place at Worcester shortly after 1226, and not, as has been erroneously supposed, about the year 1237.[2] Between him and Grosseteste there was constant intercourse during the remainder of their lives, as well as constant interchange of thoughts concerning the welfare of the University and of the Minorites, the need for ecclesiastical reform, and the social and political condition of the times. Nor was Adam Marsh the only member of his family with whom Grosseteste was on friendly terms. In later years Robert Marsh, who appears to have been his brother, was collated by the Bishop of Lincoln soon after 1245 to the living of Aylesbury,[3] and in 1248 to the archdeaconry of Oxford, accompanied him to Lyons in 1250, acted as his official in the latter days of his life,[4] and became Dean of Lincoln in 1258, five years after the death of his friend and patron. Their intimacy may be inferred from the fact that in one letter Adam Marsh notes that Grosseteste had expressed a desire to be present at his brother's inception at Oxford, and to preside at the ceremony,[5] whilst in another he requests that Robert may be admitted to the priesthood by the imposition of the Bishop's hands.[6] Two of his kinsmen appear to have been in Grosseteste's service ; one of them, William, was bailiff of Buckden,[7] and the other, Thomas, was at one time attached to his household.[8]

Of Adam Marsh's letters which have been printed in the

---

with the Abbot of Vercelli, and, p. 306, where he writes to St. Bonaventura. The evidence, however, is not of value *per se*, but only in so far as it helps to confirm the traditional account. A certain John de Vercelli was a Lincoln prebendary and a Buckinghamshire rector ; Bliss, *Calendar*, i. 181. See also p. 72, note 1.

[1] *Mon. Francisc.* pp. 38, 542, 549. He was a doctor of divinity before he entered.

[2] See pp. 71, 72 of the present work and Little's *Grey Friars at Oxford*, p. 135. His readership, of course, belongs to a later date.

[3] *Hist. Maj.* iv. 425.

[4] *Ibid.* v. 186.

[5] *Mon. Francisc.* p. 135.

[6] *Ibid.* p. 132. Cp. Brewer's preface, pp. 77, 78.

[7] *Mon. Francisc.* p. 252.

[8] *Ibid.* pp. 95, 223, etc.

Monumenta Franciscana, more than sixty are addressed to Grosseteste, whilst of the letters written by the latter and edited by Dr. Luard, only two are addressed to Adam Marsh.[1] The earlier of them belongs either to the end of 1232 or to the beginning of the following year, and the second to the year 1236. Although Adam Marsh's own letters are not arranged in chronological order, the vast majority of them clearly belong to the last few years of Grosseteste's life, and it is a matter of deep regret that no trace should have been preserved of the Bishop's own letters to which they reply. The two collections, however, notwithstanding their manifest deficiencies, constitute a record of unique importance, and throw a flood of light not only upon the lives of the writers themselves, but also upon the history and social and intellectual condition of the times. Upon many of the topics to which they refer it will be necessary to comment in subsequent chapters. Here it will be sufficient to point to a few of the passages which illustrate the sustained interest which Grosseteste continued to take, after his elevation to the see of Lincoln, in the affairs of the Grey Friars whom he had befriended in his academic days.

One of Grosseteste's early letters, written probably in 1225 or soon after, whilst he was Archdeacon of Leicester,[2] is addressed to Friar Agnellus of Pisa, provincial minister of the Friars Minors in England, and the convent of St. Ebbe's, for the purpose of consoling them on the occasion of the departure of Friar Adam of Oxford, who was about to preach to the Saracens, and who, according to Eccleston, became famous throughout the world.[3] Grosseteste speaks in high terms of his noble qualities, of the importance and value of his resolve, and of his eminent fitness for missionary work,[4] and adds that he had assumed a Friar's garb for the special purpose of being able to carry out that duty with greater efficiency. In his episcopal days he

---

[1] Letters 9, 20.   [2] Letter 2.

[3] *Mon. Francisc.* pp. 15, 16.

[4] Lumen scientiae ejus tam fulgens est, ut merito ibi maxime collocetur, ubi densissimas infidelitatis tenebras dissipet. Fervor quoque ejus tantus, ut corda lapidea et congelata divino adjutorio liquefaciat et accendat.

again and again commends the zeal, the piety, and the usefulness
of the Minorites. A letter to Adam Marsh in 1236 indicates
that one Friar Garinus had been at his side, but had been recalled, and he now wishes for the assistance of some Franciscans, as their presence is of the utmost value both to him and
to the Church.[1] In 1237 he sends to Friar Helias, Minister-
General of the Franciscans, a letter,[2] similar in character to that
which he addresses at the same time to Friar Jordan of Saxony,
Prior-General of the Dominicans, requesting him to interest
himself in the affairs of the Lincoln diocese. In writing to Pope
Gregory the Ninth, about the year 1238, he bears testimony in
the following terms to the excellence of the Friars:[3] " Your
Holiness may be assured that in England inestimable benefits
have been produced by the friars; for they illuminate the whole
country with the light of their preaching and learning. Their
holy conversation excites vehemently to contempt of the world
and to voluntary poverty, to the practice of humility in the
highest ranks, to obedience to the prelates and head of the
Church, to patience in tribulation, abstinence in plenty, and, in
a word, to the exercise of all virtues. If your Holiness could
see with what devotion and humility the people run to hear the
word of life from them, for confession and instruction in daily
life, and how much improvement the clergy and the regulars
have obtained by imitating them, you would indeed say that
' upon them that dwell in the light of the shadow of death hath
the light shined.' " So, too, in the letter previously quoted,[4]
addressed to the Bishop of Coventry and Lichfield with reference
to the settlement of the Franciscans at Chester alongside of the
Dominicans, he emphasises the usefulness of the Friars Minors
to the people among whom they dwell, " since both by the word
of preaching and the example of a holy and heavenly conversation, and the devotion of continual prayer, they are indefatigable in causing peace and in illuminating the country ; and in

---

[1] Letter 20, p. 71.   [3] Letter 58 ; Luard's preface, p. 22.
[2] Letter 41.   [4] Page 67 ; Letter 34.

this part," he adds, with what is perhaps a humorous turn of phrase, seeing that it is addressed to an episcopal correspondent, "they supply in great measure the defect of the prelates."

One of the results of Grosseteste's views as to the necessity for combining missionary work with culture is that he interposes repeatedly for the purpose of endeavouring to secure such relaxation of the strict rules of the order, in the case of particular individuals, as will enable them to obtain special books and other means of study. Roger Bacon relates, not many years later, how difficult it was for him to obtain ink and parchment. Under the influence of Adam Marsh, prompted by Grosseteste, every effort was made to facilitate special studies on the part of this or that friar. It must be remembered, however, that writing materials were very expensive, that the price of books was virtually prohibitive,[1] and consequently that it was impossible for men who had taken the vow of poverty to effect much in that direction by their own unaided efforts. The care taken of the volumes is indicated by Adam Marsh's request[2] that the copy of St. Gregory's *Moralia*, which he had left at Reading, as well as that of Rabanus's *De Natura Rerum*, and other works, may be forwarded to him at Lyons, "packed neatly in a waxed cloth with the wooden covers removed."[3] In some cases he asks for books for this or that friar; in another he expresses a wish for parchment and vellum of calf's skin to be sent to him for writing purposes at the earliest opportunity.[4] It may be noted that

---

[1] On the system which prevailed at the Universities of letting out books on hire to scholars see Rashdall, i. pp. 191 *sqq.*, 415 *sqq.* In the Countess of Leicester's Household Roll of 1265, pp. 9, 24 (Bannatyne Club, 1841), it is stated that in order to make her pocket breviary, twelve dozen of fine vellum were purchased at the price of ten shillings. The writing, executed at Oxford, cost fourteen shillings. It must be remembered that one shilling then would purchase as much as fifteen shillings now. See Sir T. D. Hardy's Introd. to the Close Rolls, pp. 45 *sqq.* Bartholomew of Pisa, in his *Liber Conformitatum* (Milan, 1510), p. 79, says that Friar Agnellus sent ten pounds sterling to the Curia for a copy of the Decretals, in order that the Oxford Friars might study them. *Mon. Francisc.* p. 634.

[2] In 1245, *Mon. Francisc.* p. 378. See p. 247.

[3] Bene, si placet, faciatis componi libros praenominatos, ablatis asseribus, in panno cerato.

[4] *Mon. Francisc.* p. 391.

requests made to Grosseteste's generosity on behalf of poor students as well as for other purposes meet with ready response. In one of his letters Adam Marsh mentions that the Bishop of Lincoln had contributed twenty-four shillings, no small sum in those days, towards the expenses of the Minorites in their late chapter at Gloucester,[1] that is, to an object which could have but little relation to his own diocese. Of his benefactions within that diocese, and more especially in connection with Oxford, there are numerous evidences.[2]

If the wide range of Grosseteste's interests, and the extent to which his counsel was sought and followed by men of all ranks and all conditions,[3] are illustrated in the correspondence of Adam Marsh, a side-light is also thrown upon the apparent facility with which, in spite of the existing difficulties of communication, the friars passed from place to place and from country to country. Grosseteste frequently made use of them for the purpose of conveying or receiving messages of importance, and his hand may be traced in the decision taken by those of the bishops who met in 1241, under the presidency of the Archbishop of York, to send a mission of friars to the Emperor Frederick II. for the purpose of urging him to give breathing time to the Church.[4] The reason for their selection on that occasion was embodied in the quotation from Juvenal :

"Cantabit vacuus coram latrone viator,"

a line which Grosseteste is said to have cited also in one of his death-bed conversations with reference to the friars, though with a different application.[5] The activity and ubiquity of the friars are exemplified in the case of Adam Marsh himself, who, in addition to his Oxford lectures and all the work he was obliged to perform in connection with the University as a whole

---

[1] *Mon. Francisc.* p. 242.

[2] For instance, on one occasion he sends 13 shs. towards the maintenance of poor scholars, *Mon. Francisc.* p. 135.

[3] Cp. the *Lanercost Chronicle*, p. 45, for the way in which the Friars asked for Grosseteste's advice on various questions as they arose, and also Eccleston's anecdotes, *Mon. Francisc.* pp. 64-66. See also p. 332 of the present work.

[4] *Hist. Maj.* iv. 173.

[5] See p. 321 ; *Hist. Maj.* v. 401.

and the administration of the Franciscan school, was in constant consultation or communication with Grosseteste himself at Lincoln, at Buckden, and elsewhere.[1] At one time we hear of him in France, at another at Rome, at another he is asked to go over to Ireland. He is said to journey in 1230 to Rome with St. Anthony of Padua in opposition to the policy which Helias was endeavouring to impose upon the Franciscan organisation;[2] in 1245 he accompanies Grosseteste, as will be seen, to the Council of Lyons; he acts as adviser to the King and to the Queen, to the Archbishop of Canterbury, and also to the Earl and Countess of Leicester; attends Parliament at Grosseteste's desire; preaches a crusade; serves on more than one commission relating to ecclesiastical disputes, and is able at the same time to maintain his reputation as a scholar, a theologian, and a mathematician, as well as his general interest in literary questions.[3] That he was able to combine so much is a tribute to the well-ordered economy of his intellect, and to his unlimited capacity for work. Neither did the performance of those various duties interfere with the attention which he paid to the needs of the numerous persons in humble life who came within the scope of his charitable endeavours, concerning whom he often appeals to Grosseteste's ever open purse, and writes to others who are able and willing to assist their special requirements. In all these departments of activity he and the Bishop of Lincoln assist and supplement one another, but it is easy to discern in the correspondence that Grosseteste's is the stronger will, his the spirit which impresses itself upon the age, his the mind which moulds other minds in accordance with his own.[4]

It must not be supposed that because Grosseteste helped the friars and discerned their merits, he was blind to their imperfec-

<hr>

[1] On one occasion Grosseteste endeavoured to bring about a mission of Franciscans to Denmark (Dacia), *Mon. Francisc.* p. 91; Luard's pref. to Grosseteste's *Letters*, p. 23.

[2] Wadding, ii. 240. But see Little's *Grey Friars at Oxford*, p. 135.

[3] See Brewer's preface to the *Mon. Francisc.* pp. 82-85.

[4] It will be necessary in later chapters to revert to the relations between Grosseteste and Adam Marsh.

tions. Although at a chapter held at Oxford he preached a sermon in praise of poverty and mendicancy, he told William of Nottingham in private that there was a rung of the heavenward ladder which stood even higher, and that was that a man should live by his own labour; and on that account he commended the newly founded sisterhood of the Beguines, who recognised the principle, and did not burden the world with their exactions.[1] It would, no doubt, be a serious error to ascribe to the mendicant orders, in the early stage of their existence, any of the corruptions which subjected them, in the following century, to the fierce invective of the author of *Piers the Plowman*, the good-natured satire of Chaucer, and the lash applied to them by Wycliffe during the last few years of his life. Yet even at that time they manifested some of the tendencies which in later years brought them into disfavour. As long as Grosseteste lived he was able to prevent them from having any serious quarrel with the University, but it was with the utmost difficulty that he smoothed over disputes in which they became engaged by reason of their invasion of monastic territories, or their encroachments on the rights of the parish clergy. As early as the year 1235 Matthew Paris makes himself the mouthpiece of the feeling prevailing on the subject in the Benedictine monasteries when he writes: " At this time some of the Minorite brethren, as well as some of the order of Preachers, unmindful of their profession and the restrictions of their order, impudently entered the territories of some noble monasteries, under the pretence of fulfilling their duties of preaching, as if intending, after having done so, to depart on the following day. On the ground of illness, or on some such pretext, however, they remained, and, constructing an altar of wood,

---

[1] *Mon. Francisc.* p. 69. Wadding, *Annales Minorum*, i. 364, mentions two sermons which Grosseteste bequeathed to the Oxford Franciscans, one being *de laude paupertatis*, and one *de scala paupertatis*. The former was originally preached on the feast of St. Martin, and contains the words, " sumusque in loco paupertatis et inter professores paupertatis." Little's *Grey Friars at Oxford*, pp. 58, 69.

they placed on it a consecrated stone altar which they had brought with them, and clandestinely and in a low voice celebrated mass, and even received the confessions of many of the parishioners, to the prejudice of the priests."[1] Allowance must, no doubt, be made for the jealousy with which the monks and the parochial clergy looked upon the new orders, as the necessary consequence of the not unnatural antagonism between endowments and voluntaryism, and between the parochial system and the non-parochial. It is evident, however, that Grosseteste, whilst giving to the friars all the assistance in his power, was anxious that they should avoid, as far as possible, conflict with the existing religious organisations, and should confine their activity to places where it was really needed. His attitude may be illustrated by his letter, written about 1244, to the abbot of the Cistercian convent at Scarborough, who was desirous of getting rid of the Franciscans who had settled in that town, and of obtaining the demolition of their house.[2] Grosseteste reviews briefly the legal arguments which had been urged for two days before the official appointed on his behalf and on the third day in his own presence, and mentions that on the latter occasion the proctor who represented the friars acknowledged that the law was on the side of the Cistercian contention, but maintained that " ordinary law and right must give place to the salvation of souls." In view, however, of the fact that "their profession was the Gospel, which bids us offer the right cheek to the smiter, they were willing freely to recede from their moral right, and abandon the place which had given rise to the dispute." Grosseteste comes to the conclusion that, as the friars are prepared to act in such a spirit of Christian humility, it would not be wise, in the interest of the Cistercians themselves, that the abbot should press his advantage. There is evidence in the letter that he must have brought considerable personal influence to bear on

<hr>

[1] *Hist. Maj.* iii. 332. *Francisc.* pp. 406, 642 ; *Hist. Maj.*
[2] Letter 109. See also *Mon.* iv. 291.

both sides with the object of bringing about an amicable arrangement.

It was, perhaps, the absence of some such diplomacy which led to the unfortunate dispute at Bury St. Edmunds between the Benedictine abbey and the Grey Friars. The quarrel, which lasted from 1257 to 1263, ended in the temporary discomfiture of the latter, who were compelled by an order from Pope Urban IV. to remove to Babwell, beyond the precincts of the liberty of St. Edmund. It may be noted that, according to the *Dunstable Annals*, the Franciscans attempted to settle at Bury as far back as 1233,[1] but that the dispute did not take a definite shape until twenty-four years later, that is to say, four years after Grosseteste's death, and about the same time, in all likelihood, as that of Adam Marsh ;[2] and it may be more than a mere coincidence that the outbreak of that dispute occurred when the two men who had exercised so strengthening and, at the same time, so restraining an influence upon those who were responsible for the central administration of the Franciscans in England, had been removed from the earthly scene.[3]

Moreover, as long as Grosseteste lived, he made a point of concentrating the energies of the Grey Friars on the evangelising work assigned to them by their founder, whilst endeavouring at the same time, as has been shown, to utilise their services for the revival of learning as well as for that of religion. In after years it often happened that the friars were regarded merely as

[1] *Ann. Monast.* (Dunstable), iii. 134. The monastic chronicle, however, given in the *Memorials of St. Edmund's Bury*, ed. by T. Arnold (Rolls Series), ii. 264, endeavours to make out that the Franciscans had only been at Bury for five and a half years previous to 1257, and that an earlier settlement of 1238 had been futile. It does not refer to the attempted settlement of 1233. The Dunstable Annals are hardly likely to be mistaken on a point of that kind.

[2] Adam Marsh probably died on the 18th day of November 1258. W. of Worcester's *Itinerary*, p. 81 ; Little's *Grey Friars at Oxford*, p. 138. The *Lancrcost Chronicle* is mistaken in assigning 1253 as the date.

[3] Cp. his indignation, as recorded by Matthew Paris, with the methods of Friar John, provincial minister of the Franciscans in Provence, who had been sent to England by Innocent IV. for the purpose of collecting money. See p. 260 : *Hist. Maj.* iv. 599.

papal agents, and earned additional unpopularity on that
account. In the early part of the thirteenth century such a
description would certainly not have been applicable to the
Franciscans as a body, and only with certain reservations to the
Dominicans. In after years, too, the simplicity of the Minorite
rule yielded place to a less exalted standard, and the voluntaryism which had been their strength became to them an
occasion of stumbling and a rock of offence. Even in his own
lifetime Matthew Paris thought he had occasion to contrast the
growing luxury of their buildings with the humility of their
profession.[1] It would be altogether outside the present purpose
to follow the subsequent fortunes of the Franciscans in this
country; but it may perhaps be noted as a strange instance of
the irony of fate that the body of men upon whom the first blow
fell in the reign of Henry the Eighth, when the Reformation
was imposed from without, should have been the very one
which, three centuries earlier, in the reign of Henry the Third,
had attempted a Reformation from within.

In his friendship with Adam Marsh and his goodwill to the
Franciscans Grosseteste was faithful to the last. It will be seen
how in his will he bequeathed his books to their convent at
Oxford.[2] It was there that Thomas Gascoigne was able
frequently to consult them in the fifteenth century. He calls
attention to the notes written in the Bishop's own hand in the
margin of St. Paul's Epistles, and observes that the volume was
in the library of the convent, but not in that of the students, for
the Friars Minors have two libraries.[3] He also possessed
Grosseteste's copy of St. Augustine's *De Civitate Dei*, full of his
marginal annotations. It had been given to him by the Friars
under their seal in 1433, or shortly before, and was afterwards
bestowed by him upon Durham College, from which, after
various vicissitudes, it passed to the Bodleian Library, where it

---

[1] *Hist. Maj.* iv. 279.

[2] Trivet, p. 243; *Mon. Francisc.* p. 185.

[3] Gascoigne's *Dict. Theol.* (*Liber Veritatis*) art. Fides; Wood's *History of the University of Oxford*, p. 78.

now rests.[1] Other works, too, composed, translated, or annotated by Grosseteste, were seen in the convent library by Boston of Bury and by Thomas Netter of Walden, as well as by Gascoigne.[2] The books, however, were inadequately cared for, and were gradually dispersed, some being given to Durham College,[3] and some being sent, it is said,[4] to Durham. If the latter statement be correct, the removal of these volumes may perhaps be attributed to Richard de Bury, Bishop of Durham, and author of the *Philobiblon*, who was an indefatigable and (on his own showing) a somewhat unscrupulous book-collector,[5] though his object was to rescue valuable manuscripts from destruction. At any rate when Leland, the celebrated antiquarian, visited the convent in 1535,[6] he found that the books which remained had fallen a prey to moths and to dust, and that those which had been of most value had long since been removed.

---

[1] Bodleian MSS. No. 198. See Hearne's *Collections*, printed for the Oxford Historical Society, vol. iv. (1898), pp. 325, 326.

[2] Little's *Grey Friars at Oxford*, pp. 57-59.

[3] See note on p. 43, *Durham College Rolls*, ed. Blakiston, Oxford Historical Society's *Collectanea*, vol. iii. p. 37.

[4] Brown's *Fasciculus*, ii. p. 329; Pegge, p. 231. For the list of Grosseteste's works at Durham see the *Catalogues of the Library of Durham Cathedral*, ed. Botfield (Surtees Society, vol. vii.), pp. 27, 36, 43, 82, 83, 104, 129. On p. 24 it is stated that in 1391 the monks had a copy of Grosseteste's *Distinctiones de Virtutibus*, in uno quaterno; but on p. 100 (1416) a marginal note, probably by John Fyshborne, says that the work in question was by a certain Dominican, and not by Grosseteste.

[5] *Philobiblon*, chapter viii.

[6] Leland, *Script. Brit.* p. 286, quoted in Tanner's *Bibliotheca*.

CHAPTER IV

It has been necessary, in the foregoing chapter, to anticipate in some measure the subsequent march of events, in order to give a more connected view than would otherwise be possible of Grosseteste's relations with the Mendicant Orders. It is now possible to turn to the consideration of certain incidents which occurred in 1231, and in the years which immediately followed, and which constitute a turning-point in his career. In 1231 Grosseteste, besides being divinity lecturer to the Franciscans, may still have been (though there is no direct evidence on the subject) Chancellor of the University. In addition to his Oxford work, he was also engaged in duties of a pastoral character. He was Archdeacon of Leicester, and held the Lincoln prebend of Empingham, which included the impropriation of the Rectory of Empingham, in the county of Rutland, and the advowson of the Vicarage.[1] He was also Rector of St. Margaret's, Leicester.[2] Moreover, in May 1225 he had been collated by Hugh de Wells, Bishop of Lincoln, to the church of Alboldesley, or Abbotsley,[3]

---

[1] Pegge, p. 22. In 1221 Grosseteste had presented a certain clerk to the Vicarage of Empingham. Brown Willis, p. 181. It is evident that Grosseteste did not reside at Empingham.

[2] Luard's Introduction, p. 34.

[3] In Baroness de Paravicini's *Early History of Balliol College* (London, 1891) several interesting documents relating to Alboldesley are printed from the Balliol College archives. A grant of about 1256 from Ralph Riddell to the Abbot of Jeddeworth (Jedburgh)

in Huntingdonshire, which had been vacant since November of the previous year, and to which the Bishop was consequently entitled to present by virtue of a decree of the fourth Lateran Council of 1215, which gave to the immediate superior the right of presentation to churches which had been vacant for more than three months. At a time when pluralities were in vogue there was nothing unusual in the number of ecclesiastical offices which he held. His conscience, however, reproached him on the subject; and an interesting piece of autobiography, which throws light upon that portion of his career, is contained in the letter which Grosseteste, when Bishop of Lincoln, addressed, probably in 1239, to the Cardinal Legate Otho, who had requested a Lincoln prebend for his clerk Atto. In his reply Grosseteste observes, among other things, that he is not disposed to give a cure of souls to Atto, as he himself, who once held a prebend of that description and a parish simultaneously, resigned the latter after consulting the Pope. "It is true," he says, "that many are of opinion that it is possible for a prebend with a cure of souls and a parish church to be held together lawfully; but, for my part, I am still in doubt on the point, as there was a time when I held the two simultaneously; but as my conscience pricked me, I consulted the Pope through the medium of a wise and God-fearing man, who brought back the reply (which he

of the advowson of Abboldesley, with a confirmation by Malcolm, King of Scotland, would appear to indicate that by that time the Abbey of Reading had ceased to be concerned in its fortunes. In 1340 the Abbot and convent of Jedburgh granted to Sir William Felton, for his life and that of his heir, an annual pension of three marks which they had from the parish church of Abbodesley, with the right of patronage. There is also a grant by Edward the Third to Sir William Felton, dated April the 12th, in the 14th year of his reign, of the advowson of the church, which had come into his hands by the forfeiture of the Abbot of Jedburgh's rights, with permission to Sir William to give it to the master and scholars of Balliol notwithstanding the Statute of Mortmain. Sir William Felton bestowed upon Balliol College the Rectory and various fruits, rents. and revenues arising out of the parish, and the appropriation was confirmed by Pope Clement VI. The gift was for the purpose of helping scholars of that College after they had become Masters in Arts. It thus happened that revenues arising out of the parish of which Grosseteste had been rector were used ultimately for an object of which he would certainly have approved. See p. 237.

was unable, however, to obtain in writing) that I could not lawfully combine a prebend of this particular kind with a parish."[1]   It will be seen that towards the end of 1232, after a severe attack of illness, which was probably brought on by the physical and mental strain involved in the discharge of so large a number of duties, he decided to resign all his ecclesiastical preferments with the exception of his Lincoln prebend.[2]   The passage above quoted appears, however, to refer to some other step of a definite and specific character which he took, but the precise nature of which is not altogether clear.

Archdeacon Perry[3] is of opinion that the journey to Rome which Grosseteste contemplated in the latter months of 1231, and on which he intended to start on the 6th of January 1232, was probably connected with the qualms of conscience felt by him on the subject of his preferments.   The letter which has already been cited shows, however, that he actually consulted the Pope through an intermediary and obtained a verbal answer.   That being so, there was no reason why he should on that account alone have thought of travelling all the way to Rome, on what was after all a personal matter of comparatively small importance.   It is clear, partly from an indirect reference contained in a letter he wrote to the Abbot and convent of Reading on the subject of a troublesome claim which they had made for arrears of rent-charge, said to be due from Alboldesley,[4] and partly from the mention of the distinguished prelates who interested themselves in his plans, that the errand on which he desired to go was one of deeper moment.   In the letter he states that he had been unable to meet the representatives of the Abbot and convent at Durham before Christmas (1231) by reason of the pressing urgency of the occupations in which he was engaged.[5]   He had made arrangements to start on his journey to Rome immediately after the feast of the Epiphany

---

[1] Letter 71.

[2] See p. 105.

[3] Page 63.

[4] Letter 4.

[5] Pro negotiorum arctius urgentium occupatione.

1232, and says : "My witnesses in this matter are men most worthy of credence, and to whom no exception can possibly be taken," and adds that, as his departure has now been postponed, he is willing to refer the question at issue with regard to the Alboldesley rent-charge to the arbitration of the Bishop of Durham, and to meet the convent when and where they pleased. In another letter, written a few days earlier, to the Dean and Chapter of Lincoln,[1] Grosseteste says : "My reason for delaying my journey is this : I was fully equipped for my departure, when I went to our venerable father, the Lord Bishop of Lincoln,[2] to bid farewell, as was meet, to him whose license had previously been obtained through your good offices. A discussion took place about my journey, in the presence of the Bishop of Bath,[3] as well as of the Archdeacons of Lincoln, Huntingdon, Northampton, and Bedford, and many other discreet and far-sighted men, who, in the sincere affection which they bore me, were not a little anxious concerning my safety. In accordance with their unanimous advice the Bishop strictly prohibited my proposed journey, and asked me to wait until more was known about the disturbances which had arisen owing to the plunder and capture of certain Romans and, according to rumour, the murder of some of them. It was feared that if I were to fall into the hands of the Romans at a time when, owing to their recent injuries, they are still craving for revenge, I might incur grave peril, or at any rate some serious loss. I accordingly resolved to abide by the friendly advice of men so numerous and so wise, as, if I were to disregard it and consequently fall into danger through want of foresight, I should not only expose myself to the well-deserved indignation of so many eminent friends, but also be stigmatised as contumacious and presumptuous. I hope, however, that the Lord, according to whom,[4] in matters of this kind, there should be no long tarrying, will not impute to me this delay." And he proceeds to express the hope

<hr>

[1] Letter 3.

[2] Hugh de Wells.

[3] Jocelyn de Wells, brother of the Bishop of Lincoln.

[4] Eccles. xxxi. 27.

that he will not be numbered with those who are described in the Epistle to the Ephesians as "tossed about with every wind of doctrine," or with the swimmers of whom Seneca says that they are carried along by the current, and quotes St. Augustine as an authority in favour of the view that action should have some relation to time and circumstance, and that a right decision should not be unduly pressed when the time is inopportune, but rather that its execution should be postponed to a more suitable occasion.

The wording of the foregoing letter would appear to indicate that the matter concerning which Grosseteste was desirous of going to Rome was one about which he felt deeply and keenly, and one which was of greater consequence than any relating merely to the exact number of his parochial livings. Perhaps it may be permissible to suggest, as more probable one of the two following explanations of Grosseteste's project. He may have been asked by Adam Marsh, who is said to have been at Rome only a few months before, in 1230,[1] to go there for the purpose of emphasising, with his well-known eloquence and with all the weight which he derived from his reputation as a scholar and a divine, the usefulness of the Franciscans in England, and at the same time of using his influence as an *amicus curiae* to help in the task of hindering the efforts of Friar Helias to turn the Order from its founder's purpose. Certainly no man was better qualified than Grosseteste to explain the efficiency of the Minorite work in England, and the necessity for its continuance, and no man was more likely to be acceptable as a mediator. The successive deposition and restoration of Helias, followed a few years later by a second deposition,[2] placed a severe strain upon the Franciscan organisation. The supposition that Grosseteste was asked to take some part in the controversy as a peacemaker derives some countenance from the affectionate terms in which Grosseteste writes to Father Helias in 1236 and 1237,[3] whilst

---

[1] Wadding, ii. 240.   [2] *Mon. Francisc.* p. 44; Sabatier.
[3] Letters 31 and 41.

Adam Marsh must certainly have submitted to him the other side of the case. Or again, it is possible that Grosseteste's projected visit may have been connected with the desirability of placing before the Pope certain considerations relating to the existing state of the English Church. As the friend and adviser of Richard Marshall, Earl of Pembroke, to whom he addresses in 1231 two letters of spiritual counsel,[1] and who was about to become the head of a party in the State in antagonism to the foreign influence represented by Peter des Roches and in support of the principles with which Stephen Langton used to be identified, Grosseteste may have had special reasons for wishing to explain to the Pope in person the new situation which was arising, and to urge upon him the need for redressing the grievances due to the encroachments of the Italian clergy. Just as in later years Grosseteste, as will be seen, endeavoured to imbue Simon de Montfort with a sense of the necessity for co-operation between those who desired to reform and strengthen the Church and those who desired to reform and strengthen the State, so it is possible that he had at that time conceived the plan of finding in Richard Marshall a fit instrument for the execution of a design fraught with possibilities beneficial to the ecclesiastical as well as to the political organism. In order, however, that there might be co-operation between the two forces, it was necessary, on the one hand, that the friends of civil liberty should help to defend the liberties of the Church, and, on the other hand, that the champions of the latter should

---

[1] Letters 6 and 7. Although they both deal apparently with spiritual matters only, they contain one or two passages which are susceptible of a twofold interpretation. *E.g.* on page 40 Grosseteste writes: "Quia non decet tantum virum, militiae cingulo praecinctum, hanc viam quae ducit ad patriam segniter super pedes incedere, ascendatis equum sancti et caelestis desiderii, cujus frenum sit discretio, sella circumspectio," etc. Richard Marshall was killed in Ireland in 1234. Grosseteste was also a friend of Richard Syward. See Letter 29. It is also worthy of note that in December 1233 it was Agnellus, Provincial Minister of the Franciscans in England, and the very one who had invited Grosseteste to become the *lector* at the Franciscan school at Oxford, who offered his services as peacemaker between the King and Richard Marshall. *Mon. Francisc.* p. 52 : Little's *Grey Friars at Oxford*, pp. 7, 177.

do their best to remove all obstacles which impaired its popularity and its efficiency. It so happened that the year 1231 witnessed the outbreak of the anti-Roman tumults to which Grosseteste refers in his letter to the Dean and Chapter of Lincoln ; and as the existence of the specific grievances against which they were directed was one of the principal obstacles which stood in the way of harmonious action, it may have been among the objects which he had in view to impress upon Gregory the Ninth the desirability for the spontaneous introduction of the required reforms.

In order to understand the nature of those tumults of 1231, it is necessary to glance briefly at the history of the previous years. Since the days of the Great Interdict, the Papacy had increased its hold yet further upon these islands, first by virtue of the feudal homage paid by King John, and secondly owing to the fact that, during the minority of Henry the Third, Pope Honorius the Third had been able, as guardian, to impose his will, through his legates, in no small degree upon the direction of public affairs, besides earning the young King's gratitude for the support accorded to him against the French.[1] At a time, however, when, partly owing to the loss of Normandy in King John's time, and partly owing to other causes, England was becoming more isolated and insulated, and a healthier national feeling was coming into existence, the claim of the Pope to dispose of ecclesiastical revenues without regard to the special conditions and requirements of the country encountered a spirit of resistance which found expression in the rejection in 1226 of his demand for two prebends from every cathedral and a corresponding contribution from every monastery. Two years later followed the death of Stephen Langton, Archbishop of Canterbury, whose influence had been exercised on the side of the maintenance both of national and of ecclesiastical rights ; and almost immediately afterwards, in 1229, Gregory the Ninth

---

[1] See Henry the Third's conversation on that subject with Grosseteste, Letter 117, which shows that in 1245 he was not unmindful of his obligations.

endeavoured to levy a tenth of all property in the realm.[1] The laity resisted, but the clergy, being unable to offer successful opposition, agreed to the demand. In addition, therefore, to the recognised collection of Peter's pence, and to the thousand marks a year promised by King John, an additional source of revenue, of a more important character, was thus secured for the papal coffers. Moreover, the practice of filling English benefices with foreigners was rapidly increasing, to the annoyance alike of the clergy, whose chances of promotion were thus curtailed, and who in other respects sympathised with their countrymen's feelings, and of the laity, whose money was handed over to persons ignorant of the language and neglectful of their duties.

The growing feeling manifested itself in 1231 in a remarkable movement organised by laymen. A secret society was formed, the members of which despatched in all directions letters sealed with a new seal, on which were engraved two swords.[2] The letters were addressed to Bishops and to chapters in the name of "the whole community of those who would rather die than be put to shame by the Romans," and after setting forth the nature of the grievances of which they complained, asserted their determination "to rescue the Church as well as the King and the kingdom from the yoke of such oppressive slavery," and warned the recipients not to interfere with the condign punishment which would be meted out to the Romans, under penalty of sharing their fate. Similar letters were sent to those who held churches in farm from the Italian beneficiaries, ordering them not to pay to the Romans the rent of the lands which they held from them, but to pay the money to agents of the society on the Sunday on which is chanted the psalm "Let Jerusalem rejoice."[3] The "plan of campaign" thus sketched out was not

---

[1] *Hist. Maj.* iii. 102.

[2] *Ibid.* iii. 210 *sqq.*, 217, 218 ; *Ann. Monast.* (Dunstable), iii. 129. Orders were issued in the name of "William Wither," and the members of the society called themselves "Lewy-thiel." See Pegge, Appendix 18, pp. 364-368 ; Perry, pp. 249 *sqq.* ; Stubbs, *Constitutional History*, ii. 43 ; Dr. Felten, *Papst. Gregor. IX.*, pp. 187 *sqq.*

[3] Mid-Lent.

confined to words. At Wingham, on Christmas Day 1231, a fortnight before the date of Grosseteste's proposed departure, masked men plundered the barns belonging to a Roman ecclesiastic, put the sheriff's men off the scent by exhibiting to them forged letters purporting to come from the King, and sold the corn cheap, or distributed it gratuitously to the poor, in order to enlist their sympathy on behalf of the movement. Similar tactics were adopted elsewhere, bands of armed and masked men appearing suddenly in various parts of England and seizing the property of the foreign clergy. Cincio, an Italian canon of St. Paul's, was captured on his way from St. Albans to London, and John de Ferentino,[1] Archdeacon of Norwich, narrowly escaped a similar fate. It was ascertained afterwards that the principal organiser of the society was a certain Sir Robert de Twenge, of Lytham, in Lancashire, who held various manors in Yorkshire and in Westmoreland, and who had a special grievance of his own, as a living in his gift had been seized twice consecutively in order to be given to a Roman. Hubert de Burgh was suspected, but apparently on insufficient grounds, of connivance in the movement. It is unnecessary to relate how subsequently Sir Robert de Twenge went to Rome, made his peace with the Pope, and brought back to those who had sent him a conciliatory letter from Gregory the Ninth, declaring that it was not his wish to interfere with rights of presentation enjoyed by the laity in England.[2] The bearing of the incidents upon Grosseteste's life is that the disturbances thus caused were the occasion of the postponement of his journey to Rome; that the movement of which they were the outcome was likely, if unchecked, to render co-operation between the friends of the Church and the friends of the State difficult, and

---

[1] John de Ferentino was a friend and correspondent to whom Grosseteste addressed two letters (43 and 66) probably in 1238, when he was at Rome as the Pope's chamberlain. Grosseteste thanks him for having silenced his detractors and forwarded his business. Roger de Wendover speaks of him incorrectly as Florentinus, but the error is corrected by Matthew Paris.

[2] *Hist. Maj.* iii. 609-613.

thus to undo the beneficial effects of Stephen Langton's influence ; and that, as it was clearly in the interest both of the Church itself and of those who, on political grounds, were opposed to the policy of Peter des Roches, to obtain from the Pope a speedy removal of the objectionable " Provisions," Grosseteste may have thought, in the first instance, that a personal interview with Gregory the Ninth would help to effect the desired end. It must not, indeed, be supposed that he had at that time definitely assumed the attitude which he adopted in the course of his episcopal career towards the papal Provisions. It is clear, however, from the anxiety displayed by Hugh de Wells and his other friends on his behalf, that he was believed even then to be antagonistic to the intrusion of foreign beneficiaries, and on that account in danger of being subjected to retaliatory proceedings if he went to Italy. In any case the occurrences of that year must have made a deep impression upon Grosseteste, and have contributed towards the development of the views which he subsequently expressed with so much courage and energy.

The question of the position and prospects of the Jews was exciting at that time widespread attention, and appears to have exercised a special fascination over Grosseteste's mind. He had in various ways been brought in contact with members of that race. In his early years in Suffolk he had doubtless heard much talk concerning the massacre of Jews which took place at Bury St. Edmunds in 1190,[1] after the coronation of Richard I., and the subsequent expulsion by Abbot Samson of those who remained. In the discharge of his ecclesiastical duties connected with his various archdeaconries he must have had frequent occasion to take into account their financial relations with the clergy and with the monastic houses, of which Jocelyn of Brakelond has left so curious a description.[2] In his Hebrew studies he probably derived assistance, as tradition affirms, from

---

[1] *Hist. Maj.* ii. 358 ; *Memorials of St. Edmund's Abbey*, ed. Arnold, ii. 5, 6.

[2] *Memorials of St. Edmund's Abbey*, ed. Arnold, i. 210.

one of the Rabbis connected with the Oxford Jewry,[1] and, as Chancellor, he was doubtless obliged to concern himself, as he did in later years when Bishop of Lincoln, in questions affecting loans advanced to students by members of that community. At Paris he must have had other opportunities of becoming acquainted with the educational advances which they had effected ; for they had their academies not only there, but also at Narbonne, Beaucaire, Arles, Marseilles, Lunel, and several other cities.   Until the advent of the Friars they almost monopolised the art of medicine ; but the most learned Jew of that period, Maimonides, though a native and a student of Cordova, and though he died at Cairo as early as 1204, does not appear to have been known by name to Grosseteste, and hardly comes within the European orbit.[2]

In England, in spite of the existence of their schools at Oxford and in London, they do not seem to have played so prominent a part as an intellectual force as they did in France. Here they were chiefly known in their financial aspect.   Sir Walter Scott's picture of Isaac of York in *Ivanhoe*, though probably in accordance with historic truth as far as the period was concerned which immediately followed the massacre of 1189-90, and which extended into the reign of King John,[3] can hardly be regarded as a faithful representation of the general condition of the Jews ; for although they were subject to the King's exactions, they also enjoyed the King's protection, and the excellence of their stone houses, some of which may still be seen at Lincoln, Bury St. Edmunds, and elsewhere, must of itself have placed their leading members in a

---

[1] See Tovey, *Anglia Judaica*, pp. 244 *sqq.* Mr. Neubauer, who denies that the Oxford, or, indeed, the English Jews generally possessed much secular learning, fully admits that students were able to learn Hebrew from the Jews in Oxford. *Collectanea* of the Oxford Hist. Society, vol. ii. (1890), p. 287.

[2] A translation of his *Moreh*, or *Doctor Perplexorum*, came into use in the course of the thirteenth century. See Friedländer's pref. to his German translation of that work.   An English edition was published for the English and Foreign Philosophical Library (London, 1885).

[3] See, for instance, *Hist. Maj.* ii. 528, 531.

position of advantage, when compared with the mud hovels and wooden structures by which they were surrounded. Stone architecture was, in fact, confined to ecclesiastical buildings, castles, and the private houses of the Jews. They had, moreover, privileges of their own and a special jurisdiction.[1] Nevertheless the popular feeling against them had not died out, and found expression in the eagerness with which the accusations to which they were exposed were received ;[2] it rendered possible Henry's sale of the Jews in 1255 to his brother Richard, Earl of Cornwall, in order, as Matthew Paris says, that the Earl might disembowel those whom the King had skinned ;[3] and it ultimately led, in 1280, to the passing of the Act of Parliament which expelled them altogether from the kingdom, a statute which remained in operation until 1655, when Oliver Cromwell recalled them to England at the suggestion of Manasseh ben Israel.

In 1231 two proposals relating to the Jews were attracting attention. The first, the outcome apparently of the individual initiative of certain great landowners, was that the Jews who were expelled from certain estates should be collected together, as far as possible, on other estates, where they would be encouraged to work with their hands. The second, which appears to have been inspired by the clergy, though the King took the leading steps in the matter and the Exchequer provided the funds, was that a determined effort should be made to bring about a wholesale conversion of the Jews to Christianity by the methods of persuasion. As a means to that end a "Domus Conversorum" was established in that year in London, and an annual pension of seven hundred marks was issued out of the Exchequer towards its maintenance, until such time as the King could endow it more amply. In later years Edward the First assigned to it the deodands all over England.[4] It was

---

[1] See, for instance, Shirley's *Royal Letters of Henry III.* vol. ii. Letter 451, and Madox, *Hist. of the Exchequer*, ii. p. 3 ; see also *Hist. Maj.* iii. 369, etc.

[2] *Hist. Maj.* iii. 305, 543 ; iv. 30, 377; v. 516, 519 *sqq.*

[3] *Ibid.* v. 488. Earl Richard, however, seems to have treated them with more consideration.

[4] See also Hall's *Red Book of the Exchequer*, Introd. i. p. 139.

known in recent times as the Rolls Chapel in Chancery Lane.[1]
A "Domus Conversorum" was also built at Oxford; and in
other cities, too, similar fabrics were erected, with the same
object in view, but on a humbler scale.

On both proposals Grosseteste had something to say. His
views with regard to the first are contained in a letter which
he addressed, whilst Archdeacon of Leicester, to Margaret de
Quincy, widow of the Earl of Winchester, and sister of Robert
Fitz Parnell, Earl of Leicester.[2] Out of the goodness of her
heart she had conceived the plan of sheltering on her property
the Jews whom Simon de Montfort had expelled from the town
of Leicester,[3] "in order that they might no longer oppress the
Christians who resided there unmercifully with usury."[4] The
purport of Grosseteste's letter has been somewhat misunder-
stood. It must not be construed as objecting altogether to the
plan, but as putting forward certain reservations and qualifications. After a brief review of the history of the Jews since the
dispersion, as well as of the causes which brought it about, and
after some reference to the fulfilment of Scriptural pro-

[1] *Hist. Maj.* iii. 262. It was begun
in 1231, and opened in 1233. Pegge,
p. 30, note.

[2] Letter 5 ; Luard's note, p. 453.

[3] Municipium.

[4] Page 33. Dr. Pauli (*Simon de
Montfort*, Tübingen, 1867, p. 39) was
under the impression that the
" dominus Leircestriensis " here mentioned was Ranulf, Earl of Chester,
and not Simon de Montfort. But M.
Bémont (*Simon de Montfort*, pp. 4, 5,
Paris, 1884) shows that Ranulf gave
up, at any rate, his moiety of the honour
of Leicester and a good deal else in 1231
to Simon. See *Excerpta e rotulis finium*,
August 1231, vol. i. p. 217 ; Shirley's
Royal Letters, i. p. 401 ; Mrs. Green's
Lives of the Princesses, vol. ii. pp. 65, 66.
The lands, consisting of the town of
Leicester and the moiety of the Earldom, with the office of seneschal, were
delivered in 1231. In the following

year Simon received, for a consideration, a formal cession of his rights from
his elder brother, Amaury. Shortly
after the death of Ranulf, Earl of
Chester, in October 1232 (*Hist. Maj.*
iii. 229), Henry III. confirmed to Earl
Simon his moiety of the honour of
Leicester. A copy, dated January 24,
1236, now in the possession of the
Leicester Corporation, is printed on
pp. 35-37 of Miss Bateson's *Records of
the Borough of Leicester* (London, 1899).
The other moiety belonged to the Earl
of Winchester. *Ibid.* p. 37. For Simon
de Montfort's subsequent charter of
1253 for the complete banishment of
the Jews from Leicester, see Thompson's
English Municipal History, p. 62 ;
Mr. Leonard's paper on the " Expul-
sion of the Jews by Edward I." in the
*Transactions of the Royal Historical
Society* for 1891, and M. Bémont's
Simon de Montfort, p. 62.

phecies, he lays down the two following propositions. Firstly, with the recollection of the massacre of 1189-90 still vivid in his mind, he protests against the notion that they should be injured, still less exterminated ; for (*a*) it was to them that the Law and the Prophets were given, and consequently they bear unconscious testimony to the truth of Christianity, and (*b*) it must be expected that they will ultimately embrace the Christian faith. In the meantime they were undergoing a second captivity, in which it was their lot to be subservient to princes, and their duty to work with their hands in order to maintain their existence. The second proposition is that, if their punishment should not be increased, neither should it be diminished ; and they should not be encouraged by Christian princes to oppress Christians with usury and live in luxury on the proceeds, the first duty of Christian rulers being to their Christian subjects. Princes who act on a contrary principle, and give to the Jews special facilities for lending money to Christians at an exorbitant rate of interest, must be regarded as their accomplices, and ought to share their punishment. Worst of all are the princes who act thus in order that they may derive their share of profit from the moneys which the Jews are able to extort from the Christians. " Take heed, therefore, dearest lady, not to be polluted by becoming a party to the offences of such (rulers), or to incur the penalties of the kind to which a strict judgment would render them liable."

It is evident that Grosseteste's object is not so much to deter the Countess from the execution of her plan, as to warn her not to encourage the settlers in usurious practices, and still less to derive any indirect benefit from them herself, but rather to induce them to earn their livelihood by manual labour instead of money-lending. The letter, which shows a kindlier feeling towards the Jews than was then customary, may also be regarded as containing an attack upon the methods by which the King enriched the Exchequer. Grosseteste's hatred of usury

was by no means confined to its practice by members of the
Jewish race, though it was excusable to use language of strong
condemnation in regard to men who advanced money to monks
at 43 per cent interest,[1] and to students at the rate of more than
43⅓ per cent,[2] and exacted the uttermost farthing. One of his
last utterances,[3] if one may trust the death-bed conversations
attributed to him by Matthew Paris, was directed against the
Caursins or Christian usurers, of whom the St. Albans historian
declares [4] in 1235 that " there was hardly any one in all England,
especially among the Bishops, who was not caught in their
net, and the King himself was indebted to them in an incalcul-
able sum of money, and that they circumvented the needy in
their necessities, cloaking their usury under the show of trade."
In spite of the fact that Matthew Paris describes them elsewhere as " transalpine usurers," that they undoubtedly acted as
agents for the Roman court for the purpose of collecting and
transmitting funds, and that some of them came from Siena, it
is a mistake to confuse them with the Italian financiers, chiefly
from Lombardy and Florence, who, later on, during the hundred
years' war, provided the moneys needed for the English cam-
paigns in France. The Caursins derived their name not, as has
sometimes been supposed, from the Florentine family of the
Corsini, but from the city of Cahors, in Aquitaine, which was at
that time a commercial and financial centre. It was with
reference to them that Dante, in his hatred of usury, says

E però lo minor giron suggella
Del segno suo e Sodoma e Caorsa,[5]

---

[1] Jocelyn of Brakelond.

[2] Luard's Introd. to the *Letters*, p.
69. That was fixed as the maximum
in 1248, and must therefore have
been exceeded before that date.

[3] *Hist. Maj.* v. 404, 405.

[4] *Ibid.* iii. 328 *sqq.*

[5] Dante's *Inferno*, cant. xi. line 50.
Muratori's sixteenth dissertation in
his *Antiquitates Italicae Medii Aevi,*
vol. i., contains a letter of Pope
Gregory IX. to certain merchants of
Siena concerning the accounts of their
receipts and expenditure in England,
France, the Papal States, and elsewhere. Muratori proceeds to quote
several documents relating to the
Caursins. An edict of Philip, son of
St. Louis, differentiates the Caursins
from the Lombards, the former term
being applied to those from Gaul, and
the latter to those from Italy.

coupling Cahors with Sodom in the intensity of his poetic wrath. From Matthew Paris's account it appears that they charged interest on loans which were not paid off by a certain date at the rate of ten per cent for two months, or sixty per cent per annum, in addition to certain incidental charges which included, among other things, the travelling expenses of one merchant, with one horse and one servant, wherever the merchant might be, until the full repayment of the money advanced, together with the aforesaid interest. Grosseteste's words on the subject, according to the account of his last conversations given in the *Historia Major*,[1] denounce the Caursins, "whom in our time the holy fathers and teachers have driven out of France by their preaching, but who are protected by the Pope in England, which did not formerly suffer from the pestilence which they bring with them; but if any one complains or rebukes them, he exposes himself to difficulties and to loss, as has been shown in the case of Roger, Bishop of London." And he then proceeds to point out that usury is contrary to the teaching of the Old and the New Testaments, and that the terms exacted by those pests of society are even worse than those imposed by the Jews. "When you return to a Jew," he says, "the money he has lent you, he will receive it with good grace, and with interest commensurate only with the time during which the money has been advanced; but the Caursin, on the other hand, lends you, say, one hundred marks,[2] in return for which you sign an acknowledgment that you owe him one hundred pounds,[3] to be paid at the year's end; and if you wish to pay him back within a month, or some such shorter period, he makes no allowance, but exacts the full sum of one hundred pounds." There are reasons for thinking that the Caursins were by no means strangers to the outcry which was raised against the Jews throughout England in 1255, two years after

---

[1] *Hist. Maj.* v. 404, 405.

[2] One mark = thirteen shillings and fourpence sterling.

[3] At twenty shillings to the pound.

Grosseteste's death, on account of the supposed murder by them of a boy named Hugh at Lincoln ;[1] and it is interesting to note that, at a moment when the members of that persecuted race were exposed to an outbreak of popular fury, it was Grosseteste's beloved Franciscans who intervened to save certain of them from punishment and the danger of massacre.[2]

With respect to the second proposal which has been mentioned as having been put forward in 1231 in regard to the conversion of the Jews, it was probably in that year[3] that Grosseteste wrote his celebrated treatise, *De Cessatione Legalium*, on "The Ceasing of the Law," which was widely circulated in his own and in the succeeding generations, and which was printed for the first time three centuries and a quarter later, in the days of the Commonwealth.[4] The primary

---

[1] See especially *Hist. Maj.* v. 519. For the incident itself see *Hist. Maj.* v. 516, the recent work of Mr. Jacobs on the subject, and also Canon Jessopp's *Life of St. William of Norwich.*

[2] *Hist. Maj.* v. 546. In the *Lanercost Chronicle*, p. 24, it is stated with regard to Adam Marsh, presumably in connection with the episodes of 1255, that "when the Jews had transgressed against the peace of the kingdom, so that both by the judgment of the King and the princes of the land they were judged worthy of death, he alone resisted their arguments and forbade that they should be put to death." Little's *Grey Friars at Oxford*, p. 137. According to the Burton Annals the Dominicans also tried to save the Jews on that occasion. *Ann. Monast.* (Burton), i. 346-348.

[3] Pegge, pp. 31, 269 ; Luard's Introduction, p. 36.

[4] *Liber de Cessatione Legalium*, printed at Lyons in 1652, and in London in 1658. The preface to the latter edition says incidentally : "Episcopi nomen, per saecula augustum, ipsique religioni Christianae coaevum, jam-

pridem sorduit ; quidquid Romanum est, etiam ipsa lingua Romana, superstitionis damnatur ; eo usque, ut non desint nonnulli adeo suis furiis agitati ut Italiam fere ipsam exterminandam putent, quia Papae subsit, et vix amni Tiberi ignoscant, quia Romam praeterfluat." It is only a portion of the treatise which was printed. See Brown's *Fasciculus*, ii. pp. 246 *sqq.* ; Dr. Felten, p. 76. Of the MSS. in the British Museum, the fullest is *Bibl. Reg.* 7 F. ii. fol. 121 : "De Cessatione Legalium, in tribus particulis." The MS. *Bibl. Reg.* 5 C. iii. fol. 264 is an abbreviation. Several copies of both are in existence. In his treatise, "De Anno Civili Veterum Judaeorum," vol. i. pt. i. p. 59 of his works, ed. Wilkins, Selden says of the subject "de cessatione legalium" : "Egregius de ea re extat liber Roberti Capitonis (Grosseteste vocitant) Lincolniensis olim episcopi nondum typis editus, qui luce sane dignissimus." Selden's opinion of Grosseteste's learning is expressed in his epigram, vol. ii. pt. ii. p. 1717 :—

Robertus an tu
Perdoctus Capito? etc.

object of the work is evidently to supply, in a connected and closely reasoned form, materials and arguments which may be used in controversy with the Jews, for the purpose of bringing about their conversion to Christianity, and is intended to refute the notion of the permanence of the Mosaic law, as well as to trace and to explain the various points of difference between the old dispensation and the new.   It might be described as a thirteenth-century Epistle to the Hebrews.   It appears to have inspired the treatise by John Baconthorpe and also the one ascribed in error to Wycliffe, which bear the same title : and among those who in a later age derived most benefit from its perusal must be cited Selden, and also Sir John Eliot, the resolute friend of freedom in the reign of Charles I.   The latter appears to have drawn from its manuscript pages, which he doubtless found in the Cotton library, some of the arguments which he applies, in his *Monarchy of Man*, to the task of proving the need for replacing the old system of government by one more in accordance with the requirements of the people, and for substituting the law of love for the law of fear.[1] Grosseteste's treatise on the Ten Commandments,[2] which is a sequel of the *De Cessatione Legalium*, would seem to have been written shortly afterwards, possibly during the three years of relative leisure to which it will now be necessary to refer ; and it may be noted that the subject continued to be in his thoughts for several years, as may be inferred from the statement of Matthew Paris that his translation of the *Testament of the Twelve Patriarchs*, which he effected with the assistance of Nicholas the Greek in 1242,[3] was intended for the refutation of the Jews.[4]

It is not surprising that the strain involved in Grosseteste's devotion to his pastoral and to his educational duties, as well as in his literary activity and extensive correspondence, should have brought on, just before November of 1232, a sharp attack of illness, which acted as a warning to him not to overtax his

---

[1] Sir John Eliot's treatise was printed in 1879 by Dr. Grosart.   With regard to Selden, see the passage previously quoted.

[2] A fragment is printed in Brown's *Fasciculus*, ii. p. 308.

[3] See pp. 222 *sqq.*

[4] *Hist. Maj.* v. 285.

strength, and induced him to resign all his preferments, or at any rate his fixed sources of income, with the exception of his Lincoln prebend.[1] Two letters written at this crisis in his life, both showing signs of physical depression consequent upon his illness, though the intellect which inspires them is as keen as ever, have been preserved. The first is addressed to his sister Juetta, who was a nun in a convent near Oxford, probably at Godstow, and who had exhibited some anxiety lest the decision at which he had arrived should injuriously affect his subsequent career. The second is written to Adam Marsh. "As you are anxious," he writes to his sister, "to know how I am, and are, as you express it, greedy to hear the latest news in a letter from me, let me say briefly that before the feast of All Saints I was seized with a sharp attack of fever, but by the blessing of Divine Providence have been restored to my former and usual health. I have resigned all my fixed sources of income, with the exception of the prebend I hold in the Church of Lincoln. You, who wear a nun's garb, and have uttered the vows of religion, must not be affected or saddened if I have of my own accord become poorer in order that I may become richer in virtues; if I am of less importance in the world in order that I may become more acceptable to the denizens of Heaven; and if on account of the merit of obedience I have given up certain temporal advantages, seeing that no virtue can obtain its celestial reward save through obedience. The good which you cherish in yourself you ought to cherish in me also, and with all the more ardour by reason of our close relationship. True religion renounces the world, in accordance with the word of truth which declares that 'Whosoever forsaketh not all that he hath cannot be My disciple.' Considering, therefore, that you, who

---

[1] Letter 8. "Omnes reditus quos habui, resignavi, praeter praebendam quam habeo in ecclesia Lincolniensi." Archdeacon Perry, p. 64, conjectures that Grosseteste may have retained his archdeaconry, as there was no *reditus* from that, but only the payment of fees. In the will of Bishop Hugh de Wells, however, which is dated 1st June 1233 (see p. 109), his name does not appear in that connection.

have made a profession of religion, value in yourself these and other blessings which it confers, do not, I pray you, grudge me my effort, feeble though it may be, to attain to them ; bear with equanimity that I have laid aside the heavier part of the burden which oppressed me, and rejoice from the bottom of your heart that which, were I not free from it, would grievously weigh me down."

The tone of the foregoing letter, and the religious fervour which it displays, confirm the statement of Matthew Paris that, at one period of his life, he conceived the plan of taking the vow of poverty and joining the Franciscans, much in the same way as Robert Bacon joined the Dominicans in spite of his advancing years.[1] He does not appear, however, to have received any encouragement from Adam Marsh, who, as his most intimate friend, and as virtually the foremost Franciscan at that time in England, might have been expected to exercise over him a special influence in that direction. Perhaps Adam Marsh understood the bent of his mind more clearly than he did himself, and foresaw that he would be more useful to the cause which the Minorites had at heart if he retained his independence, and was enabled to attain to a position in which he could find fitting scope for the exercise of his administrative abilities. It is evident, from Grosseteste's letter written to him at this juncture,[2] that Adam Marsh had conveyed his congratulations, and had expressed his sympathy with him in the decision at which he had arrived, a sympathy which was all the more welcome by reason of its contrast with the contempt felt by some of his so-called friends for his act of self-sacrifice, and with the abuse hurled at him by others, probably pluralists who thought that the step he had taken cast a reflection upon them, as well as with the well-meaning but unappreciative counsels of injudicious friends who told him that he was injuring his own interests. There is, however, nothing to show that Adam Marsh

---

[1] *Hist. Maj.* iv. 579. Semper ordinis aemulator et amator singularis, adeo ut ad ordinem eorum propositum habu- erit convolandi, exstiterat.

[2] Letter 9.

had made any overtures to him with the object of inducing him
to become a Minorite. In the course of his reply Grosseteste
writes : " I know that the perils of an exalted station are neither
few nor inconsiderable. I know its pitfalls, how hard it is to
repress pride, how rare is the sense of one's own weakness, how
easy it is to feel contempt for others, how difficult to adapt one-
self to the needs of the weaker brethren : it is the shadow of
power, and the reality of servitude. I know also from experience, and still suffer from the knowledge, how many thorns
there are in riches, how many occasions they afford for acting
wrongly, how often they are misused, how true it is that they
impoverish instead of enriching their possessors, and how those
same possessors, who are really themselves owned by the wealth
of which they are the reputed owners, find their intellects
blinded and rendered torpid and dormant." With reference to
the charge brought by some that he had abandoned the pastoral
office, he replies : " I was urged to take the course I adopted,
on the one hand, by my utter inability to discharge the duties
which, with too little circumspection and too much boldness,
I had undertaken, and, on the other, by the obedience which I
owe to the constitutions of the Apostolic See. It is, however,
true that a pastoral charge, once undertaken, should not be
given up," except under certain conditions which he proceeds to
enumerate. He concludes by asking for the aid of his friend's
prayers, in order that, if what he has done has been wrong, it
may be forgiven, and that if, as he hopes, it has been right, God
may cleanse away the blemishes which circumstances may have
wrought in this and any other good thing that he may have
done.

The intensity of Grosseteste's religious fervour at that time
may be inferred, not only from the correspondence here indicated, as well as from the two letters, of which mention has
already been made, which he addressed to the Earl of Pembroke
in 1231,[1] one of which relates to " the glory and riches of

<hr>

[1] Letters 6, 7.

Heaven," while the other has for its thesis the difference between "the wisdom of the just" and "the wisdom of the world," but also from a letter[1] which he wrote not long after his illness, that is to say, at the end of 1232 or early in 1233, to a clergyman whom he describes as older than himself, who had long been his friend, but who had fallen away from a high standard of conduct into luxurious and licentious habits. The scathing severity of its denunciations and the persuasiveness of its exhortations to repentance have rarely been equalled. It reveals the secret of Grosseteste's moral force, which enabled him to exercise so profound an influence over his generation.

Little is known with respect to Grosseteste's actions during the period which elapsed between the date of his illness at the end of 1232 and that of his appointment to the see of Lincoln in 1235. Apart from his Lincoln prebend, he does not appear to have held any ecclesiastical appointment during that interval, and the suggestion that he retained his archdeaconry of Leicester is sufficiently refuted by the fact that in the will of Bishop Hugh de Wells, dated June 1, 1233, his name does not appear in that connection.[2] Richard of Bardney's statement that he acted as the King's private secretary, and subsequently became guardian of the privy seal, is the invention of a later age, is based upon no historical foundation, and is contrary alike to intrinsic probability and to contemporary evidence.[3] It is probable that part of his comparative leisure was employed in the composition or completion of some of the works enumerated in an earlier chapter, and it is certain that he was engaged, at any rate at one time, in the dis-

---

[1] Letter 10.

[2] The will of Hugh de Wells is printed in the Appendix to Giraldus Cambrensis, vol. vii. pp. 223-231. "Robert, Archdeacon of Lincoln," p. 228, is Robert de Hayles, and "Robert my chaplain" is another person.

[3] Richard of Bardney's lines, in Wharton's *Anglia Sacra*, ii. p. 334, are:

In Regis mensa prior inter Regis amicos
Ellicitur. Probitas emerat illud ei.
Secretarius hic Regi, Custosque Sigilli
Postea Privati, Rege jubente, fuit.

Matthew Paris, on the other hand, says (*Hist. Anglorum*, ii. 376): "Praesentari regi nolens, singularis erat conversationis, et propriae sectator voluntatis, suae innitens prudentiae, quod perspicue postea manifestavit."

charge of administrative duties connected with the University of Oxford, though he had ceased to act as Chancellor. The King's mandate of 1234, to which reference has previously been made, imposes upon him and upon Friar Robert Bacon, as well as upon the Chancellor, certain duties of a disciplinary character.[1] That being so, it is by no means unlikely that he resided at Oxford during the greater part of the time, and was present in 1233 at the celebrated protest which Robert Bacon uttered, in the presence of Henry III., against the continued presence of Peter des Roches in England.[2] In view of his relations with Richard Marshall, Grosseteste must have sympathised deeply with that protest, and have followed with special anxiety the course of events which led to his friend's temporary triumph in 1233, in conjunction with Hubert de Burgh, and to his murder in Ireland in the following year. Eccleston's account, moreover, implies that Grosseteste continued to lecture in the Franciscan school until his elevation to the episcopate,[3] and a similar view is embodied in the *Lancrcost Chronicle*.[4] It may therefore be assumed that, whatever may have been the occupations which he found it necessary to abandon, his practical interest in the welfare of the University, and more especially of the Franciscans, was sustained and unabated throughout those years.

---

[1] Page 66. Kennett's *Parochial Antiquities*, i. p. 307 ; Dodsworth MSS. vol. ciii. p. 168.

[2] If the document printed in the *Collectanea* of the Oxford Historical Society (1885, vol. i. pp. 39-47, ed. Fletcher), which describes Grosseteste's election to the office of *rex natalicius*, and his confirmation by the genius of Christmas, be genuine, it may perhaps be referred to one of these years. It is certainly in complete harmony with the spirit of Robert Bacon's protest. The MS. seems to have been written by a Franciscan student, and the fact that Grosseteste is described as "Magister" indicates apparently that he was not yet a Bishop. It is possible, however, that the document may merely be a political skit of a later date, and that Grosseteste's name is used to attract attention.

[3] *Mon. Francisc.* p. 37. Ipso igitur a cathedra magisteriali in cathedram pontificalem providentia divina translato, etc.

[4] *Chron. de Lancrcost*, p. 45.

CHAPTER V

THE year 1235, which witnessed Grosseteste's appointment to the see of Lincoln, forms the principal landmark in his life. Already he had reached what must have been the age of sixty, and he was now called upon to commence a practically new career at a time when other men, endowed with less vigour of mind, might have been deemed entitled to well-earned repose. If, however, his promotion had been so long postponed, the delay was due to the disadvantage under which the man who depends solely upon the weight of his own character and abilities labours in comparison with the one who receives at birth the fairy gifts of fortune. If Grosseteste had been of an envious disposition, he might, in after days, have contrasted the slowness of his own advancement with the rapidity with which, only a few years later, Boniface of Savoy was raised to the office of Archbishop of Canterbury merely because he was the Queen's uncle ; and among the prelates of his own acquaintance more than one owed their position not to their own merits, but to favour of the powerful or to the power of the purse. No such thoughts, however, seem to have entered Grosseteste's mind. Behind him lay a long period of activity, in the course of which he had achieved more than any man of his generation. He had mastered and systematised the learning of his time, grasped the idea of the unity of knowledge, enriched literature with works of permanent value, and pointed the way to new avenues of thought. He had welcomed, encouraged, and guided the two orders of Friars which were seeking to bring about a revival of religion in this country, and had himself been in a special sense the teacher of the Franciscans, and had, moreover, endeavoured to unite the movement which aimed at the revival of religion with the movement which aimed at the revival of learning. As the first Chancellor of Oxford, he had taken a leading part in the organisation of the University. As Archdeacon of four successive archdeaconries, he had obtained an intimate acquaintance with the practical aspects of ecclesiastical work which were most likely to be of use to him in his new position. Before him, on the other hand, lay a new period of his life, during which he would, indeed, have ample opportunities for turning to good account the experience gained in his previous career, whilst his knowledge, his eloquence, his high character, his strength of will, and his power of organisation would all help to ensure the efficiency of his administration; but his course was, as will be shown, beset, owing to the circumstances of the times, with difficulties and even with dangers, and imposed upon him in an eminent degree the necessity for the active exercise of those qualities of judgment, presence of mind, foresight, and energy which are sometimes attributed to statesmen. He entered upon the discharge of his new duties with a high sense of the importance of the episcopal office, and with an unflinching determination to shirk no responsibilities, but to right the wrong wherever it lay in his power in the vast diocese committed to his charge.

Hugh de Wells, Grosseteste's predecessor, to whom he probably owed the advice to the Dean and Chapter which ensured his selection, and to whom he had unquestionably been indebted for six out of his eight previous preferments, one of which would seem to have been the very first which it was in that prelate's power to confer, died on the 7th or 8th of February 1235.[1] Owing to the intimate relations which subsisted between the Bishop of Lincoln on the one hand and Oxford and its University on the other, he had been brought into frequent contact, in that connection as well as in other capacities, with Grosseteste, who speaks of him in terms of great affection and respect,[2] and who must have appreciated in him the qualities which caused him to be described by Roger de Wendover and Matthew Paris as "omnium virorum religiosorum inimicissimus,"[3] a phrase signifying that he attempted to make the monks amenable to discipline, and which may be illustrated by the "Articles of Inquiry" he had issued in his diocese.[4] The words do not represent any real hostility on his part to the monastic orders, as is shown by the provisions contained in his will[5] in favour of numerous religious houses, including, among others, those of Caldwell, Missenden, St. Neot's, Torksey, and Bourne, together with sundry additional bequests to those of them that were the poorest. Among them, as well as among poor lepers, the masters and scholars of Oxford, converts from Judaism in the diocese, and the poor residing on his manors, was the residue of his estate to be divided.[6] No mention is made of Grosseteste in the will among the Archdeacons, for the simple reason that it was made in June 1233, when he held no preferment of any kind with the exception of his Lincoln prebend ; but Hugh de Wells leaves to his successor, for purposes connected with the cultivation of his manors, 208 oxen,[7] and it is also interesting to note that vineyards are mentioned among the episcopal possessions in the diocese.

---

[1] Pegge, p. 35.

[2] Letters 44, 68.

[3] *Hist. Maj.* iii. 306. Matthew Paris adopts the phrase from Roger de Wendover. See Luard's Introd. to the *Letters*, p. 37.

[4] Printed in the first vol. of Wilkins's *Concilia*.

[5] Printed in the Appendix to Giraldus Cambrensis, vol. vii. pp. 223-231.

[6] Giraldus Cambrensis, App., vol. vii. pp. 227 *sqq.*

[7] Such is Mr. Dimock's interpretation of the phrase "26 carucatas boum," vol. vii. Glossary, p. 252. According to him one "carucata boum" means eight oxen.

They are more likely to have been situated near Henley on Thames than near Barton on Humber.[1]

The *congé d'élire* was issued on February 19,[2] and the provisions of the Great Charter which were intended to ensure freedom of election appear to have been carefully respected on that occasion. In accordance with what had probably been their late Bishop's wish, the Dean and Chapter proceeded, on March 27, to elect Grosseteste, who had long been a member of their body, and whose unquestioned pre-eminence marked him out for the position. The story that Giraldus Cambrensis was mentioned as an alternative candidate[3] arises clearly from a confusion between the vacancy which occurred on the death of Hugh de Wells and that which had taken place in 1200 on the death of St. Hugh of Avalon. The choice was unanimous.[4] On April 5 the King's approval was given, and was conveyed by letter to the Archbishop, who confirmed the election. On the 16th of that month the temporalities were restored, and on May 14 he received from Henry the Third what was probably the customary present of ten bucks.[5] Some difficulty arose, however, with regard to the place of his consecration. The monks of Christ Church, Canterbury, claimed as an ancient right that he and all other Bishops of the province should be consecrated in their cathedral. St. Edmund of Abingdon, the new Archbishop, had reasons of his own for taking a different view. He was involved at that time in a dispute with his Chapter, and was not inclined to pay undue deference to their wishes, and was also probably of opinion, on general grounds and in the public interest, that it was not desirable that one

---

[1] See preface to vol. vii. p. 93.

[2] Pegge, p. 35 ; Luard's Introd. to the *Letters*, p. 37.

[3] Cited in Brewer's preface to vol. i. of Giraldus Cambrensis. If Giraldus was alive in 1235 — and it is more likely that he died about 1220 — he would have reached at that time the age of nearly ninety.

[4] In the *Historia Anglorum*, ed. Madden, ii. 376, Matthew Paris says that although the choice was unanimous, it was only so "post multas inter canonicos contentiones," and "contra omnium opinionem, licet, ut dicebatur, Ordini Minori obligaretur."

[5] Le Neve's *Fasti*, ed. Hardy, ii. 10.

Cathedral Chapter should enjoy a monopoly of consecration fees. Grosseteste paid a visit to Canterbury, together with some members of the Lincoln Chapter, in connection with the matter, and afterwards wrote a letter[1] to the Archbishop in which he expresses the hope that, for the sake of peace, he will not adhere to his resolution, but give way to the desire of the monks. "In regard to nothing that is in itself indifferent," he writes, "ought we to place a rock of offence or an occasion for stumbling in the way of one of our brethren. In view of the fact that, as I truly believe, the monks of Canterbury cannot be induced on any consideration to agree of their own good will that I shall be consecrated elsewhere than in their church ; and as it is probable that, if I am consecrated elsewhere against their will, they, being offended at this matter, in itself indifferent, will fall into the pit of anger, rancour, and hatred, and, by appealing against your action, will give rise to difficult and expensive litigation ; and as, moreover, 'the servants of God ought not to strive,' and 'it is utterly a fault if ye go to law one with another' 'lest we offend them,' 'destroying,' as I trust may not be the case, 'some weak one for whom Christ died, and not walking charitably' ; inasmuch as consecration can be given to me without sin or offence or scandal at Canterbury, I most humbly and earnestly entreat you to agree to consecrate me in the Church of Canterbury ; for it is better to be consecrated there, however great an expenditure of this world's goods may be thereby incurred, than that the ceremony should take place elsewhere, at less cost, but in such a way as to cause offence to the weaker brethren. I trust that this argument may be deemed sufficient, unless it be that for some reason of which I am not cognisant, my consecration cannot take place at Canterbury without sin. With respect," he adds, "to the report you heard to the effect that one of those who accompanied me to Canterbury spoke harshly to the monks, and threatened them, that, whether they agreed or not, I should be consecrated

---

[1] Letter 12.

elsewhere, I am sure that the story is without the slightest foundation ; for my companions were men of an eminently peaceful and discreet disposition, and the requests which they addressed to the monks were couched in humble and respectful terms."

The Archbishop, however, thought it necessary to be firm, in order not to admit what might be a troublesome claim, and the monks, on the understanding that no precedent was to be created, agreed that the consecration should take place elsewhere. In June—according to one account on the 3rd, according to another on the 17th of that month [1]—he was consecrated in the Abbey Church of Reading, at the same time as Hugh, Bishop of St. Asaph, by the Archbishop of Canterbury, who was assisted by the Bishops of Bath, of Salisbury, of London, of Ely, and of Hereford. It is not known on what special grounds Reading was selected for the purpose. Probably the convenience of its situation, the fact that it was often chosen for Council and other meetings,[2] and the magnificence of its Abbey afforded reasons sufficient to justify the choice. On subsequent

---

[1] *Hist. Maj.* iii. 306, gives the former, while the *Winchester Annals* and Wykes give the latter date. St. Michael's Day (Sept. 29) mentioned by the *Lanercost Chronicle* is out of the question. Of the days named in 1235 only the 3rd and 17th of June are possible, as the others do not fall on Sundays. Bishop Stubbs (*Episcopal Succession*) prefers the 17th, while Luard (Introd. to the *Letters*, p. 37) and Dimock (note on John de Schalby, App. to vol. vii. of Giraldus Cambrensis, p. 204) prefer the 3rd. For the other dates mentioned by various writers see Pegge, p. 35, note. That Bishops could only be consecrated on Sundays is shown by the Rubric in the English Pontifical, cited in Maskell's *Monumenta Ritualia*, iii. 212. See Dimock's pref. to the *Magna Vita S. Hugonis Lincolniensis*, p. 28.

[2] It was at Reading that King John, with the Legate, met the Archbishop and Bishops in 1213 to arrange about the restoration of the confiscated property (*Hist. Maj.* ii. 570), and it was there that, in 1240, another Legate, Cardinal Otho, conveyed to the assembled dignitaries of the Church the papal message (*Hist. Maj.* iv. 10). In the *Calendar of Papal Registers* (Bliss, vol. i. p. 149) is mentioned an Indult to the prior and convent of Canterbury, that their right to have all the bishops of the province consecrated in their Church shall not be prejudiced by their having permitted the Archbishop to consecrate the Bishop of Lincoln at Reading. Dated Viterbo, 12 Kal. Dec. 1235. In 1238 (page 167) the Pope sent a confirmation to the prior and convent of Canterbury of the ancient concession that the suffragans of the see should not be consecrated elsewhere without the consent of the chapter.

occasions the same Archbishop consecrated various bishops elsewhere than at Canterbury, but that was in consequence of the suspension he had inflicted upon his Chapter.   For example, he consecrated William de Raleigh, Bishop of Norwich, at St. Paul's, London ;[1] Hugh de Pateshull, Bishop of Coventry and Lichfield, at the priory of Newark, near Guildford ;[2] Peter d'Aigueblanche, Bishop of Hereford, at St. Paul's, London,[3] and Howel, Bishop of St. Asaph, at Boxgrave.[4]   In the last-named instance, however, the monks of Canterbury addressed a protest in writing to the Legate and to the Archbishop of York, as well as to the other prelates and nobles who were present.   The precise motives which guided St. Edmund's action with respect to the place of Grosseteste's consecration are by no means clear, but it is possible that, acting under the influence of Simon Langton, Archdeacon of Canterbury, he was desirous of bringing the dispute with his Chapter to a head, in order to settle it once and for all.   In February of the following year Grosseteste was solemnly enthroned in Lincoln Cathedral.

During the months which elapsed between the date of his election and the fulfilment of the requisite ceremonies, Grosse-teste had not been inactive.   He had devoted his energies to the task of mastering the affairs of his diocese, and in preparing the measures which he proposed to take, with a view to their reorganisation and reform.   One incident which occurred during that interval throws light on the intense earnestness with which he approached his new duties.   A certain monk had brought to him, for institution to a benefice, one who was not even in priest's orders, being only a deacon, and whom Grosseteste describes as wearing clothes of scarlet and rings on his fingers, more like a dandy layman or a knight in appearance, and practically of no education, as could be gathered from his replies to questions.[5]   The Bishop-elect addressed the monk in

<hr>

[1] *Hist. Maj.* iii. 617.   See Pegge, p. 36.   [4] Haddan and Stubbs, *Councils,* i. 405.
[2] *Ibid.* iv. 31.   [3] *Ibid.* iv. 75.   [5] Letter 11.

language of fierce rebuke : "How can you," he exclaimed, "who call yourself a monk, and who by your habit and your vow make profession of saintliness, and are thereby bound to mortify your carnal life for the salvation of souls,—how dare you present to a cure of souls one who by his bearing and his garb shows himself more fitted to slay those souls than to heal them ? Our Lord Jesus Christ gave His precious blood, yea, His very life, to a most bitter and shameful death, to save and give life to each individual soul ; and you are trying to hand over so large a number of souls to one who by his bad example will betray and destroy them. You, who would not give up to the wolf one single sheep which you had bought for twelve pence, do not hesitate to hand over to the destroyer the soul which Christ has purchased with His blood, which is a price incomparably greater than the whole of Creation. Is it not clear that you, by dishonouring that great sacrifice, are on your way to perdition ? " The monk and the deacon left his presence, and complained afterwards of the strength and, as they deemed it, the injustice of his language. He received what appears to have been an anonymous letter couched in terms of abuse, and a friend of his, Michael Beleth, who occupied a prominent position at the Court,[1] conveyed to him in writing the expression of his opinion that he had been unduly severe. To the latter Grosseteste replies[2] at some length, giving an accurate account of the incident and of the words he had used, and explaining their justice and their necessity. He feels that if he did not speak strongly with regard to such matters, he would himself be a participator in the offence. Without objecting to criticism, he wishes that his critics, instead of blaming him, would think of the wrong done to the parishioners by the institution of an incumbent of that description, and would join with him in trying to rescue the sheep from the wolves. "If they would do

---

[1] He was chief butler at the marriage of Henry III. *Hist. Maj.* iii. 338. He was the founder of Wroxton Priory. Luard's note, *Letters*, p. 449. See also Hall's *Red Book of the Exchequer* (Rolls Series), i. p. 758, where he is spoken of as "Magister."

[2] Letter 11, p. 52.

so," he concludes, "I have no doubt that they would succeed where my isolated efforts fail.   If, on the other hand, instead of helping, they place impediments in the way of the little I am able to effect, they are in danger of being adjudged guilty of the destruction of those sheep.   I leave it to your discretion to decide whether, in the sight of God and of those who are zealous for the welfare of souls, my severity is as reprehensible as is thought."

That Grosseteste's action in the case of that particular deacon was not an isolated specimen of the firmness he displayed in that respect may be gathered from the numerous instances in which he refuses improper presentations.[1] Within the next few months, indeed, at least two of the letters which he wrote bear upon the subject.   In one of them he explains to William de Raleigh, Treasurer of Exeter,[2] that he is obliged to refuse to institute his nominee, a certain William de Grana, on the ground that he is a minor, imperfectly educated, still in his Ovid, and one whose institution would be contrary to the interests of the cure of souls, to the injunctions of Scripture, and to the canons of the Church.   Grosseteste knew, however, how to temper severity with generosity; and, in view of the special circumstances of the case, he expresses his willingness to pay William de Grana ten marks a year out of his private purse, until he is fit to be appointed to a living, and adds that he has mentioned the matter to Friars Robert Bacon[3] and Adam Marsh, as well as to Masters Robert Marsh, Thomas Wallensis, and John de Basingstoke, Archdeacon of Leicester.   The other letter[4] is addressed to John Blundus, Chancellor of York, one of whose relatives Grosseteste refuses to admit to a living on

---

[1] See, for instance, Letters 17, 19, 26, 30, 49, 52, 72, 74, 87, 124, 126, and 128.

[2] Letter 17. William de Raleigh was afterwards Bishop, first of Lichfield and Coventry, then of Norwich, and then of Winchester.

[3] The MS. says "Roger." Dr. Luard, in the Index, assumes that "Roger" is a mistake for "Robert," as is probably the case.

[4] Letter 19. It was John Blundus who in 1232 had been elected Archbishop of Canterbury, but had been rejected by the Pope. *Hist. Maj.* iii. 223, 243, and v. 41.

account of his ignorance. In later years, as will be seen, the Bishop of Lincoln had to deal with similar requests put forward by personages far more powerful than the Treasurer of Exeter or the Chancellor of York. It is also in the same spirit of devotion to the advancement of religion that he entreats Hugh de Pateshull, King's clerk and treasurer, and afterwards Bishop of Coventry and Lichfield,[1] not to take a larger benefice, on the ground that, owing to his secular engagements, he neglects the one already committed to his care.

Almost immediately after his consecration, Grosseteste appears to have taken the steps already mentioned [2] to secure the presence and assistance in his diocese of John de St. Giles and Geoffrey de Clive, as well as of a third Dominican skilled in canon and civil law. John de St. Giles, however, was at that time in Germany, where he had accompanied the Princess Isabella, now the wife of the Emperor Frederick II., and he was only able to accept Grosseteste's invitation at a later date. At the end of 1235 or the beginning of 1236 the Bishop writes to Adam Marsh [3] to the effect that, since the recall of a certain Garinus, he has had none of Friars Preachers or of the Friars Minors with him, and requests that some of the latter may be sent to him. He expresses, however, special anxiety for the help of Adam Marsh himself, particularly with regard to communications with the Roman Court : [4] " for several new things have come to light, about which it would take me too long to write, and also other things which I cannot safely make known to more than a few persons. There are, moreover, several other matters with regard to which I stand in need of your assistance." "I have found in you," he adds, "and in you alone, a truthful

---

[1] Letter 25. The letter clearly belongs, as Luard supposes, to 1236, as is shown by the papal mandate to the Bishop of Lincoln, dated May of that year, to allow Hugh de Pateshull to let his benefices in the Lincoln diocese, provided that arrangements are made for them to be properly served. Bliss, *Calendar of Papal Registers*, i. p. 154.

[2] Letters 14-16, 20.

[3] Letter 20.

[4] " In petitionibus et consultationibus ad curiam transmittendis." The context shows that " curia" here means the Roman and not the English Court.

friend, a faithful counsellor, one who looks to the reality and not to the outward appearance, and who rests on a firm and solid foundation, not on a hollow and fragile reed." He also invited William de Cerda, who was at that time engaged in lecturing at the University of Paris, to undertake certain duties in the diocese of Lincoln.[1] William de Cerda excused himself, for the time being, on the twofold ground that he must finish his course of theological lectures, and that he did not feel capable of undertaking the particular office suggested to him. Grosseteste, in reply, writes in terms of praise and commendation of his zeal as a teacher, and trusts that it may be of value to many. At the same time he reminds him that "Our Lord said to the chief of the Apostles, 'If thou lovest Me, feed My sheep,' not, 'If thou lovest Me, lecture from the professor's chair to the shepherds of My sheep.' The pastoral office is of more importance than the professorial"—an utterance which appears somewhat strange on the part of one who had probably effected more *ex cathedra* than any of his contemporaries, though it is in complete harmony with the views which he expresses elsewhere. He concludes with the promise that he will keep the post vacant for another six months or a year, in order to enable William de Cerda to complete his course of lectures in the meantime, and that he will arrange, during the interval, for the duties connected with it to be performed by a Friar Preacher, as far as preaching is concerned. Whether William de Cerda ultimately agreed is not known. Two years later, however, Grosseteste was able to enlist out of the professorial into the pastoral office a still more important recruit in the person of Thomas Wallensis, who had succeeded Roger de Weseham as reader to the Franciscan school at Oxford, and to whom he gave the archdeaconry of Lincoln in 1238.[2]

In the letters which he addressed in 1237 to the respective heads of the Franciscans and of the Dominicans, asking for their assistance, as well as in a more elaborate memorandum

which he forwarded through his proctor to the Pope, after sub-
mitting it to the celebrated Dominican canonist Raymond de
Penaforte, in order to obtain the advantage of his criticisms,
Grosseteste dwells upon the size and population of his diocese.[1]
The diocese of Lincoln was, in fact, at that time by far the
largest and the most populous in the country. It included
the archdeaconries of Lincoln, Leicester, Stow, Buckingham,
Huntingdon, Northampton, Oxford, and Bedford, and extended
from the Thames to the Humber. It had been formed by the
union of the bishopric of Lindisse, or Sidnacester, originally
connected with Northumbria, with that of Leicester, originally
Mercian, of which the see had been removed to Dorchester.[2]
Remi, or Remigius, the first Bishop of the united diocese appointed by William the Conqueror in 1067, resolved to transfer
his principal seat to Lincolnshire, as that county was no longer
suffering from the troubles to which it had been exposed at the
time of the Danish invasions ; and, in accordance with the
policy which found favour with the Council of London in 1072,
which decided that episcopal sees should be transferred, when
necessary, from smaller places to the more populous walled
cities, he appears to have anticipated the decrees of that
Council by choosing the important and fortified city of Lincoln
instead of the time-honoured but insignificant site of Lindisse.
A few years later, in 1081, Remigius dropped the title of Bishop
of Dorchester and used the appellation of Bishop of Lindisse,
which had been that of his earliest predecessors. He refrained,
however, from calling himself Bishop of Lincoln, as there was
still in existence a Bishop suffragan known by that name [3] who
lived until about 1088, when any difficulty which might have

---

[1] Letters 40, 41, 37. A map showing the extent of the diocese of Lincoln
as it then was and as it now is, is
prefixed to the *Diocesan History of
Lincoln*, by Canon Venables and Archdeacon Perry.

[2] *Ann. Monast.* (Dunstable), iii. 11 ;
Stark's *History of the Diocese of Lincoln*, pp. 419 *sqq.* See John de
Schalby's Lives of the Bishops of
Lincoln, App. to Giraldus Cambrensis,
vol. vii. pp. 193 *sqq.*, with Mr. Dimock's notes, as well as the *Life of St.
Remigius* by Giraldus Cambrensis himself, also contained in vol. vii.

[3] Stark, pp. 475, 476.

been felt with regard to the assumption of that designation by the Bishop of the entire diocese came to an end. The building of the principal part of the great Minster, begun under the auspices of St. Remigius, is said, according to one account, to have occupied only four years; but although its founder and inspirer lived to witness the completion of the most necessary portions, he died a few days before the date appointed for its consecration in 1092. Two years later a dispute between the Archbishops of York and of Canterbury, the former of whom claimed supremacy over the northern portion of the diocese, while the latter claimed supremacy over the southern, was brought to a friendly solution by means of an agreement arrived at with the sanction of William Rufus, and signed by himself, St. Anselm· of Canterbury, Thomas, Archbishop of York, and the Bishops of Durham, Winchester, and Rochester, with the result that the cathedral was consecrated in that year, during Robert Bloet's tenure of the episcopal office.

When Grosseteste became Bishop nearly a century and a half later, in 1235, nothing, in all likelihood, remained of the massive Norman structure of St. Remigius, with the exception of the magnificent central portion of the west front, the grandeur of which still excites the admiration of the spectator. Fire had destroyed the roof in 1141, and in 1185 a great earthquake had, in the words which Roger de Hoveden quotes from Benedict, Abbot of Peterborough, split the church in two from top to bottom.[1] In the following year St. Hugh of Avalon, better known as St. Hugh of Lincoln, the Carthusian monk who had come to England from the Grande Chartreuse at the invitation of Henry the Second, was raised to the see. He determined to rebuild the cathedral, and employed for the purpose a certain Geoffrey de Noyers, whose designs, executed partly during the lifetime of the Bishop, and partly during that of his successors, brought into existence the

---

[1] Roger de Hoveden, ed. Stubbs, ii. 303; *Ann. Monast.* (Dunstable), iii. 23.

first and, in the opinion of many, the noblest product of Early English architecture. It departs, according to M. Viollet-le-Duc,[1] in every essential respect, as well as in the details of its ornamentation, from the French school of the twelfth century, as exemplified in the cathedrals of Paris, Noyon, Senlis, Chartres, Sens, and even Rouen. "The construction," he says, "is English, the profiles of the mouldings are English, the ornaments are English, and the execution of the work belongs to the English school of workmen of the beginning of the thirteenth century." By the time Hugh de Wells, Grosseteste's immediate predecessor, had completed his life's work, it is probable, notwithstanding the damage done by the victorious troops after the battle and capture of Lincoln in 1217,[2] that, in addition to St. Hugh's choir and eastern transept, the nave and the great transept had been nearly completed, as well as the wings of the west front, the Galilee porch, and the chapter house.

Such, then, was the diocese and such the cathedral entrusted to Grosseteste's care. Concerning his administration of the first the following pages will speak. Of the work he carried out in connection with the second there is comparatively little to relate. He completed those portions of the nave and of the great transept which had been left unfinished by his predecessor, and raised the rood tower as high as the lower level of the upper windows, it being afterwards raised to its final elevation by Bishop Dalderby.[3] He also built the great hall in connection with the episcopal palace.[4] Matthew Paris repeats a story to the effect that, during the early stages of the dispute with the Dean and Chapter, one of the canons was preaching to the people in the body of the church, and, in denunciation of the Bishop's action, used the words, "If I should not speak, the very stones would cry out," whereupon the stone work of the new tower fell down and caused much damage, and the co-

---

[1] See the *Gentleman's Magazine* for May 1861, partly reprinted in Murray's *Handbook to the Cathedrals of England, s.v.* Lincoln.

[2] *Hist. Maj.* iii. 23.

[3] See Pegge, p. 217.

[4] *Lanercost Chronicle*, p. 43.

incidence was regarded as a prodigy in the Chapter's favour.[1] As the Peterborough chronicle, however, points out, the accident was really due to a flaw in the workmanship,[2] and the *Dunstable Annals* indicate that the part which fell was not a portion of the tower, but of the wall near the choir behind the Dean's stall.[3] Three persons were killed by the accident. Grosseteste caused the defects to be promptly repaired, and continued the task of completing the edifice in the spirit and after the designs adopted by St. Hugh and his intervening predecessors. His true greatness, however, is to be found in the fact that he erected monuments more enduring than any built of stone.

[1] *Hist. Maj.* iii. 520, 638. It was in 1239.

[2] Chron. of "John, Abbot of Peterborough," p. 107.

[3] *Ann. Monast.* (Dunstable), iii. 149.

See also *Ann. Monast.* (Tewkesbury), i. 113. After the accident the choir "celebravit ante majus altare officium diurnum et nocturnum, donec circumquaque columnae et arcus firmarentur."

CHAPTER VI

GROSSETESTE'S first thought was to make an earnest and fearless
attempt to remedy the abuses which prevailed in his vast
diocese. Some five years before the death of Hugh de Wells,
that prelate had issued certain questions or articles of inquiry,
probably the earliest framed in this country, asking whether
any rectors or vicars were scandalously illiterate, and seeking
for information with regard to certain evils which injuriously
affected the ecclesiastical administration and the moral condition of the clergy.[1] Grosseteste, who, as Archdeacon of
Leicester, had doubtless helped to ascertain the particulars, and
who, as prebendary of Lincoln and an intimate friend of the
Bishop, may have been the one who actually suggested the
plan, was now enabled, owing to his succession to the see, to
adopt further measures of greater stringency and efficacy, first,
by addressing a letter to all the Archdeacons, containing specific
injunctions against the various abuses, and pointing out how
they were to be rectified, and, secondly, by embarking upon
what was then the unprecedented task of a personal and
thorough visitation of his diocese.

The letter to the Archdeacons, written in 1236 shortly after

---

[1] Printed in Wilkins's *Concilia*, i. 627 *sqq.* ; Sir Hy. Spelman's *Councils*, ii. p. 192.

his enthronement, relates principally to the clergy, though also in part to the laity.[1] The first duty to which he calls their attention is that of combating drunkenness amongst those with whom they come in contact, on the ground that strong drink "deprives man made in the image of God of the use of his reason, brings on the worst diseases, shortens his life, is a stepping-stone to apostasy, and engenders other innumerable evils"; and with that object in view he instructs them to put an end to the "scotales," or drinking bouts, which appear, from the description given of them in the Constitutions of St. Edmund,[2] to have resembled in some respects the drinking competitions still practised by certain students' corps in the German Universities. He next turns to the subject of games, and objects altogether to those in which two contending parties placed wooden rams on wheels, and charged at each other, sometimes with fatal results, and generally to the destruction of the peace of their parish.[3] Against games, however, which are not dangerous and which do not promote discord he has nothing to urge, though he considers that they should be discouraged on Holy Days, and agrees with St. Augustine that it would be better if on such occasions men were to plough and women to spin, inasmuch as necessary and useful labour is less out of harmony with the sanctity of the day than frivolous occupations.[4] Vigils and funeral feasts, he regrets to learn, have often been converted into scandalous orgies, which ought to be stopped. Games of any description in churches or churchyards should be strictly prohibited, and "the house of prayer" must not be turned into "a den of thieves." The clergy should take frequent opportunities of warning mothers and

---

[1] Letter 22.

[2] Wilkins, i. 635.

[3] Kennett, in his *Parochial Anti-quities*, i. p. 29, identifies the *arietum levatio* with the "quintan."

[4] In Letter 84, written in 1240, Grosseteste rebukes Robert de Lexington and other justices itinerant at Lincoln for punishing the "dean of Christianity" at Lincoln, because he had denounced them for trying causes, and especially capital causes, on Sunday.

nurses against the danger of overlaying infants. Private marriages should be absolutely forbidden. Parish processions on the occasion of the Archdeacon's annual visitation should not be allowed, partly because they are unnecessary, and partly because it sometimes happens that rival processions from different parishes, with their banners, come into conflict with one another, and give rise to disturbances which are a discredit to the Church. He then protests against the practice which has grown up, whereby the parishioners present their customary Easter offering to the parish priest at the time of the celebration of the Mass, and says that the priest should be prohibited from receiving it at that time, and punished if he continues to do so ; on the ground that anything of the nature of a monetary transaction is out of keeping with the solemnity of the service, and that an erroneous impression may be created to the effect that those who fail to bring an offering are not entitled to partake of the Sacrament, whereas exactly the reverse is asserted by the general as well as by the provincial Councils,[1] both of which have declared that in no case should the payment of a fee be a condition precedent.

In a similar spirit, and about the same time, Grosseteste also wrote to the Archdeacons[2] to the effect that no goods should, under any pretext, be exposed for sale in sacred places, and mentioned that the King had consented to sanction, in the case of the fair at Northampton, regulations forbidding any buying or selling in the church or cemetery of All Saints. In another letter,[3] addressed to the Dean and Chapter of Lincoln, he demands the immediate abolition of a species of festivity which used to be celebrated in Lincoln Cathedral and in some other churches on the 1st of January under the name of the Feast of Fools, and which, however innocent its origin may have been, had long since degenerated into a grotesque,

---

[1] That is, by the Lateran Council of 1179 and the Council of Oxford of 1222, ch. 26. Wilkins, i. p. 589.

[2] Letter 21.

[3] Letter 32.

irreverent, and licentious carnival, which he denounces as worthy
of execration. It must not be confused with the so-called
Feast of Asses, which appears to have been celebrated at
Beauvais on the 14th of January 1223, as well as in some
other French cathedrals. The Feast of Fools was of extreme
antiquity, though more honoured in the breach than the
observance, whilst the Feast of Asses was a comparatively late
innovation. The latter was not finally abolished, at any rate in
Sens Cathedral, until the sixteenth century, though its most
obnoxious features had previously been eliminated. The Feast
of Fools, on the other hand, survived to a later, as it had
originated at an earlier date, in spite of all efforts of Popes and
Councils to bring it to an end.[1]

The circular letter to the Archdeacons was accompanied, in
all probability, by the issue of Articles of Inquiry similar to
those issued by Grosseteste's predecessor,[2] and was followed by
the altogether novel experiment of a personal visitation. That
the latter created, and did not follow a precedent may be inferred
partly from his own words, and partly from the fact that when
Roger de Weseham, Bishop of Coventry and Lichfield, and
sometime Dean of Lincoln, issued in 1252 Articles of Inquiry
for the use of his diocese, and also effected a personal visitation,
the chronicler[3] states that he acted in accordance with the
example set by Robert Grosseteste. The Bishops of Lincoln
had, indeed, been in the habit of paying from time to time
visits to the religious houses in their diocese, and of receiving
from them procurations on those occasions;[4] but even those

---

[1] Innocent III. refers to the Feast
of Fools, *Decretals*, book iii. tit. i.
See Pegge's note, p. 320. The Rev.
S. R. Maitland, in *The Dark Ages*,
pp. 149-157, refutes some of the statements on the subject, and shows clearly
the difference between the Feast of
Fools and the Feast of Asses. The
account of the latter given by the
editors of Ducange, from what Mr.
Maitland considers untrustworthy
sources, is to be found in Collet's *Relics
of Literature*, pp. 136-139, Lond. 1823.
See Ducange (Benedictine edition), *s.v.*
Festum Asinorum.

[2] *Ann. Monast.* (Burton). See
Pegge, p. 312, and the same author's
Life of Roger de Weseham, p. 34.

[3] *Ann. Monast.* (Burton), i. 296.

[4] *Ibid.*

visits had never been conducted systematically or with a view to the requirements of the diocese as a whole, and the parochial clergy had been left entirely to the Archdeacons, most of whom left the performance of their duties in the hands of the rural deans, while the latter, in their turn, made use of the *bedelli*, or " sompnours," for the purpose of preserving discipline. On what principle the last named carried on their work may be seen in the satirical poems, attributed to Walter de Mapes, written towards the close of the twelfth or the beginning of the thirteenth century, and, at the end of the fourteenth, in Chaucer's account of the sompnour in the Prologue to the *Canterbury Tales*. Grosseteste's object was to include within the scope of his visitation both the monastic houses and the parochial clergy, to reform their defects and raise their tone, and to secure the unity and harmony, as well as the efficiency, of the whole of the religious work performed within the diocese. In his " Propositio de visitatione diocesis suae "[1] Grosseteste, describing his " new and unaccustomed proceedings," says : " As soon as I was made Bishop I considered myself to be the overseer and pastor of souls, and therefore I held it necessary, lest the blood of the sheep should be required at my hands at the last judgment, to visit the sheep committed to me with diligence, as the Scripture orders and commands. Wherefore, at the commencement of my episcopate, I began to go round through the several archdeaconries, and in them through the several rural deaneries, causing the clergy of each deanery to be called together on a certain day and in a certain place, and the people to be warned that, at the same time, they should be present with the children to be confirmed and in order to hear the word of God and to confess. When clergy and people were assembled, I myself was accustomed to preach the word of God to the clergy, and some friar, either Preacher or Minor, to the people. Four friars

---

[1] Wharton's *Anglia Sacra*, ii. pp. 317 *sqq.* Some of the passages are translated by Archdeacon Perry, p. 86. The " Propositio " really forms part of the *sermo* which he caused to be read before Innocent IV. in 1250.

were employed at the same time in hearing confessions and enjoining penances;[1] and when the children had been confirmed, on that and the following day, I and my clerks gave our attention to inquiries, corrections, and reformations, such as belong to the office of inquiry. In my first circuit of this kind, some came to me to find fault with these proceedings, saying, ' My Lord, you are doing a new and unaccustomed thing.' To whom I answered, ' Every new thing which instructs and advances a man is a new thing fraught with blessing '; nor could I suppose at that time that on account of this my visitation any mischief would afterwards befall those placed under me." The visitations were repeated at frequent intervals during his tenure of the episcopal office, and are often recorded by Matthew Paris as well as by the Burton and Dunstable chroniclers.

The severity and the thoroughness of Grosseteste's first visitation may be illustrated by the fact that in 1236 he removed from their offices the abbots of Leicester, Owston, Torrington, Nutley, Bourne, Dorchester, and Missenden, and the priors of St. Frideswyde, Cold Norton, Bradwell, and De la Land, and replaced them by others.[2] In cases in which the priors were removed on the ground of age or infirmity and for no fault of their own, they were allowed a retiring pension of thirty-five marks a year, and similar arrangements were doubtless made with respect to the abbots.[3] The prior of St. Frideswyde, however, was removed for an actual offence, and considerable difficulties were placed in the way of the Bishop's firm action, as is shown in a papal mandate of the following year, addressed to the legate Otho, ordering him to annul the sentence passed by the prior of Bolton and his fellow judges against Grosseteste in connection with the removal of that

---

[1] In Addit. MSS. (British Museum), 6716, fol. 63, is the " Modus sive forma confitendi secundum Dominum Robertum Lincolniensem." Bound up with it is his " De Poenitentia." The former is identical with the " De modo confitendi," Harl. MSS. 211, fol. 102.

[2] *Ann. Monast.* (Dunstable), iii. 143.

[3] See Pegge's note, p. 48.

prior.[1] The judges, who had condemned the Bishop in costs amounting to 140 marks, were cited to appear before the Pope. It was probably on the occasion of his visit to St. Frideswyde's that he took the opportunity, at the King's request, of allaying a quarrel which had broken out at Oxford between the members of the University and the townsmen.[2] The strictness with which Grosseteste carried out what he deemed to be his duty with respect to the monastic houses gave rise to grave perturbation within their walls, and laid the foundation of the obstacles which he subsequently encountered when he proceeded to apply the same principles to his own Chapter.

One of the practical results of the great Council of the English Church held in St. Paul's, London, under the presidency of the Cardinal legate Otho in November of 1237, an event to which it will be necessary to refer at a later stage,[3] was the issue, by the Archbishop of Canterbury and by some of the Bishops, of "Constitutions" embodying certain of its decisions, which were themselves partly based upon the canons of the Lateran Councils of 1179 and 1215, as well as other matters affecting the order and discipline of the various dioceses. The Constitutions of St. Edmund differ in several respects from those of Grosseteste and from those of Alexander de Stavensby, but agree in the inclusion of many of the injunctions contained in the Bishop of Lincoln's letter to his Archdeacons in the previous year.[4] The inference may therefore be drawn that, even if Grosseteste did not take a prominent part in the deliberations of the Council of London, he must at any rate have been in communication with the leading prelates on the subject of the necessary reforms, and have suggested to them the points which were of most practical importance. It may also be assumed

---

[1] Bliss, *Calendar of the Papal Registers*, i. p. 163. The mandate is dated 10 Kal. Jul. 1237.

[2] Wood's *Hist. and Antiq. of the University of Oxford*, i. p. 220 ; Luard's Introd. to the *Letters*, p. 38.

[3] See pp. 177 *sqq.*

[4] P. 126, Letter 22. The Constitutions of St. Edmund were intended for his diocese, and not for his province, though they are published by Lyndwood as provincial Constitutions.

that the communications which he had addressed to the Pope with regard to the condition of affairs in his own diocese must have had some influence upon the selection of topics enumerated in what would now be called the agenda paper of the Council, and afterwards embodied in its canons.

It is hardly needful to give more than a brief summary of the Constitutions he addressed to "the rectors, vicars, and parish priests" of his diocese,[1] partly because several of the injunctions which they contain have already been mentioned in connection with his earlier letter to his Archdeacons,[2] and partly on account of the resemblance they bear to the Constitutions issued by certain contemporary prelates, notably by St. Edmund of Canterbury, though they also include much that is peculiar to themselves, and though the arguments by which they are maintained, and the illustrations used in their support, are distinctly Grosseteste's. They throw light, however, upon the condition of the clergy at the time, and upon the imperative need for the reforms which Grosseteste was seeking to introduce. They are also of special interest in their bearing upon the history of religious observances.

1. In the first of the forty-five articles into which the Constitutions are divided, he begins by reminding the clergy that they must have sufficient knowledge to be able to instruct their parishioners in the ten Commandments, to inculcate the duty of avoiding the seven deadly sins, to explain in simple language the nature and meaning of the seven Sacraments, and to set forth the general principles of the Christian faith, as contained in the three Creeds. In teaching laymen they should use the vernacular—that is, the English tongue. The above are the only doctrines to which he refers. He then admonishes them

2. that they should themselves observe, and urge upon others the necessity for the observance of, a reverent demeanour during the celebration of the Eucharist, and also when the

---

[1] Letter 52, pp. 154-166. The table of contents is on pp. 164-166.
[2] P. 126, Letter 22.

3. reserved Sacrament is conveyed to the sick. Priests should always be ready to attend members of their flocks, in case of illness, by night as well as by day, for the purpose of hearing their dying confession and administering the last communion

4. and the extreme unction. The super-altars—that is to say, the pieces of wood or stone fixed in the wood of the altars— should not be taken out and used for grinding colours or similar

5. irrelevant and irreverent purposes. Chrism-cloths used at baptisms should not be turned to common uses. In per-

6. forming the divine service the priests should utter their words distinctly and think of what they are saying; this applies to lessons, hymns, psalms, and, in fact, to every part of

7. the service. They are to be diligent in prayer and in reading of the Scriptures, in order that they may thereby be enabled to give to inquirers rational answers on matters affecting their hopes and their faith. Children should learn

8. the Lord's Prayer, the Creed,[1] the Salutation of the Virgin,[2] and the sign of the Cross ;[3] and the same should be the case with persons of riper years, who have not previously been taught.

Next follow a series of injunctions relating to morality.
9. The lives of the clergy are to be pure. They are not to

10. be married—a stipulation which shows that the celibacy of the clergy imposed by the laws of the Western Church was not

26. universally practised at that time, as is also indicated by the further provision that sons who have succeeded to their fathers' livings must forthwith resign them. Evidence is afforded from several sources that a determined and concerted effort was in progress in the first half of the thirteenth century to put an end, once and for all, to the continued existence of a

---

[1] When "symbolus" is used without any defining adjective, it means the Apostles' Creed. Of the three Creeds mentioned in article 1, the "major" is the Nicene, the "minor" the Apostles', and the "Quicunque vult" the Athanasian.

[2] St. Luke i. 28.

[3] In the table of contents (p. 164) the passage runs, "quod instruant subditos in oratione Dominica et symbolo," the following words being left out.

practice which Giraldus Cambrensis had bitterly denounced, and which the stringent decrees issued in the previous century

11. had not completely succeeded in extirpating.[1] They are

12. not to visit nunneries without valid reason, or to allow in their houses even a kinswoman whose presence may give rise

13. to injurious reports. They are not to frequent taverns or give way to drunkenness, but to be sober and abstemious, ever remembering the sacred character of their calling. No

14. clerk in holy orders should engage in trade or usury.

15. Grosseteste then passes to the existence of certain evils connected mainly with defects of organisation. Churches and matters appertaining to churches must neither be put out or taken to farm, except in the special cases in which exceptions are

16. allowed by the Councils. Neither should the clergy occupy in the civil administration of the country offices for the discharge of which they would have to be responsible to the

17. secular authorities. No arrangement can be sanctioned by virtue of which the rector assigns to the one who performs

18. the duty on his behalf, an insufficient stipend ; for a priest is entitled to receive such salary as will provide him with

19. an adequate and an honourable livelihood. The farming of Church property[2] to laymen is forbidden except in special

20. cases ; and ecclesiastical funds shall not be applied to the purpose of erecting buildings on land not belonging to the

21. Church, nor shall the infeudation of tithes to laymen be permitted.[3] Contributions from laymen ear-marked for definite

[1] See, for instance, Giraldus Cambrensis, *Gemma Ecclesiastica*, vol. ii. chapters xxii. and xxiii. He refers, no doubt, principally to the state of things in Wales, but the practice existed in England also, though to a less extent. Cp. Stephen Langton's decree, *Hist. Maj.* iii. 95, and numerous instances can be adduced from the Cal. of entries in the *Papal Registers*, Bliss, vol. i. The laity seem to have been strongly in favour of the celibacy of the clergy. In the Cotton MSS. Cleopatra E, iv.

81, John Tyrrel reports that the vicar of Mendlesham, Suffolk, has brought home his wife and children, which was most abominable to the lay people in the neighbourhood. June 12, 1246. St. Edmund, in canon iv. of his Constitutions, requires that the "concubines" of the clergy shall either marry laymen or go into cloisters.

[2] "Liberae terrae de dominiis ecclesiarum."

[3] This last provision must have been adopted *pro forma* from the canons of

services or pious functions should not be diverted to other
23. objects. The clergy should not spend their time in wit-
nessing the performances of mimes, jesters, and actors, or in
24. playing at dice. They must not bear arms, and must
have the tonsure to distinguish them from those who are not in
25. holy orders. Pluralities are forbidden, except where a dis-
27. pensation is granted by the Apostolic See. No money
must ever be received for the administration of the Sacraments,
28. and priests must not impose penances for the sake of any
29. gains which may accrue to themselves. Priests alone,
and not deacons, have the right of hearing confessions[1] and of
administering the Sacraments, and consequently incumbents
30. must not delegate those duties to deacons; and it follows
that all who are instituted to a benefice must take the requisite
31. orders, if they have not done so already. They must
32. reside in their parishes, unless they have obtained special
dispensation. In all churches in which sufficient funds are
available for the purpose, there should be a deacon and, if
necessary, a sub-deacon in addition to the priest; whilst in
others the services of one priest are adequate, provided that
he possesses the requisite qualifications. They must see that
34. churchyards are properly fenced, that the churches are
kept in proper repair, that the ornaments and sacred vessels are
kept in safe keeping, and not handed over to laymen for custody,
36. except in cases of reasonable and evident necessity. The
wine used for the Eucharist must not be sour wine ("acetum").
37. The beneficed clergy must not devote themselves to
the study or the teaching of the secular—that is, the civil
and the common—law in schools, not because there is anything
to condemn in that pursuit, but because their primary duty is
the fit discharge of their pastoral functions, for which reason

the Lateran Council, reproduced by
the Council of London. It can hardly
have had any practical application in
England at that time.

[1] For the conditions under which

Franciscans could obtain episcopal
license to hear confessions see Eccleston,
Mon. Francisc. p. 41; Little's *Grey
Friars at Oxford*, pp. 63, 74.

38. they should refrain from occupations likely to absorb and divert their energies.[1] The canon of the Mass shall be duly corrected; a reference, probably, to the carelessness of the

44. scribes who copied out the service books for each church.[2] Laymen ought not to remain in the chancel during the performance of divine service, but an exception to the rule may be made in favour of the patron of the church. The remain-

33, 35, 39-43. ing injunctions contained in the Constitutions are the same as those which he had communicated to his Arch-

45. deacons in 1236.[3] He concludes with a direction that the excommunications pronounced by the Council of Oxford in 1222 should be read once a year in every church, in order to strike terror into the hearts of evil-doers.

---

[1] See Mr. Rashdall's remarks, i. p. 323, on the bull issued by Honorius III. in 1219 with reference to the study of civil law.

[2] Luard's Introd. to the *Letters*, p. 39. It is possible, however, that the reference may be to the "consuetudines et officia," which appear to have been drawn up about 1236 or 1237, and which form part of what is described in the preface to the *Book of Common Prayer* as the "Lincoln use." *Twelfth Report of the Historical MSS. Commission*, Appendix 9, p. 561. What was the precise relation of those "consuetudines et officia," which must have been drawn up under Grosseteste's supervision, to earlier and existing "uses" is a question of interest in its bearing on liturgical history. See the *Lincoln Cathedral Statutes*, ed. by Bradshaw and Wordsworth, i. pp. 50 *sqq.*, 57, 58; ii. pp. 45 *sqq.*, 824 *sqq.* The "Consuetudinarium de Divinis Officiis" of 1265 was compiled by the seniors of the Lincoln Chapter in the time of Richard de Gravesend, and it may, perhaps, be assumed that the documents of 1236-37 were prepared in a similar manner. Richard Poore, in his Salisbury Constitutions, had said: "Et praecipimus quod omnes sacerdotes habeant canonem missae secundum consuetudinem Sarum correctum, et quod verba canonis in missa rotunde dicantur et distincte," etc., *Sarum Charters*, pp. 128 *sqq.*; *Lincoln Cathedral Statutes*, p. 833. Richard Poore, after he became Bishop of Durham in 1228, also issued for that see Constitutions of a similar character. It is probable, especially in view of Grosseteste's earlier connection with Richard Poore, that he may have had the same object in view. Although the Lincoln use comprised variations, introduced by St. Hugh, in the order of reading the Psalms, and numerous special customs and ordinances, some of which were communicated to Moray Cathedral in Scotland in 1212, in the time of Hugh de Wells, there appears to be no sufficient reason for thinking that the canon of the Mass was different from that in use at Salisbury. York, Lincoln, and Salisbury are the three cathedrals which play the most important part in the development of the liturgy in England. See also the *Tracts* of Clement Maydeston, ed. by Wordsworth for the Henry Bradshaw Society, p. 208 (London, 1894).

[3] Letter 22.

It will be perceived from the fifteenth article of the foregoing Constitutions that, among the evils to which Grosseteste's attention was directed, were the abuses connected with the system of farming churches, by which was meant that an absentee rector made a compact, generally with a religious house, whereby the latter undertook, on the one hand, to pay him a fixed annual sum, and, on the other, to make its own arrangements with some one else who was to do the actual work. In earlier days the usual practice had been for a monastery, in a case of that kind, to utilise the services of one of its own members for the purpose; but it had not been found desirable to make a rule of keeping a monk away from his monastic home for any length of time in order to carry out what were really the functions of the parish clergy, and consequently it was thought best to obtain the assistance of secular priests who were willing to undertake the duty on behalf of the religious house. A similar principle applied to "appropriations," that is, to cases in which benefices were assigned in perpetuity either to monasteries or to other ecclesiastical corporations, which thereby became responsible for the discharge of the duties—a term which must not, of course, be confused with the "impropriations" which denoted then in France and Italy, as they afterwards did in this country, assignments of ecclesiastical titles to laymen. How numerous those appropriations had become may be inferred from the fact that, early in the twelfth century, more than two-thirds of the parish churches in England were already in the hands of monasteries. And, just as it was found desirable to obtain the help of the secular clergy rather than to divert the monks from their proper sphere of occupation, so also it became expedient that permanent, instead of temporary arrangements should be made for the due performance of the parochial work, and the remedy was sought in the devotion of some portion of the revenues of the living to the endowment of a resident parish priest. Hence the origin of vicarages.

In Grosseteste's time all these methods of dealing with benefices were in operation.   Apart, that is to say, from parishes in which dwelt resident rectors, who received the whole of the proceeds and carried out the duties themselves, and apart also from those in which a rector, compelled for special reasons to be absent, made his own arrangements for the presence of a deputy for the time being, there were, roughly speaking, three kinds of parishes which did not fall within either category : first, those in which the rector put the living out to be farmed either, as was generally the case, by a monastery or, as sometimes happened, by an individual ; secondly, those in which the church was appropriated to a monastery, or to a chapter, or to some other religious foundation, and in which the services were performed by persons temporarily appointed for the purpose by those bodies ; and thirdly, the appropriated churches in which vicarages had been established.   With all three systems Grosseteste was brought in contact.   To the farming of churches to monasteries he was altogether opposed, as is shown not only in his Constitutions, but also in his letter[1] to John Romanus, Sub-Dean of York, in which he says that he has received a communication from Boetius, the Pope's nuncio, requesting him to give to the said John Romanus free disposition of his church at Chalgrave ; but " to put a church to farm," declares Grosseteste, " is not freely to dispose of it, but rather to reduce the free faith of Christ to a servile condition ; and the necessity," he adds, " of residing elsewhere does not prevent you from having a faithful deputy. When the Oxford Council laid down (in 1222) the rule that a church may only be farmed by 'an individual who must be honourable and in holy orders,' it evidently intended by that definition to exclude religious corporations." Grosseteste concludes by saying that, although the nuncio has threatened him, he fears not the threats of man.   The accounts of his visitations also indicate clearly the line which he pursued in that respect. On one occasion the Abbot of Tewkesbury consulted Grosseteste

---

[1] Letter 18.   Written probably in 1236.

as to the best way of converting the church of Great Marlow to the use of the abbey.[1] The Bishop replied by a severe rebuke, and refused to sanction an appropriation. The Abbot then suggested that he should appoint a certain Gilbert de Clare,[2] who would have been ready to let the church on farm to the abbey. Grosseteste also declined to accede to that request, but agreed to a compromise, by virtue of which the abbey should appoint a qualified priest, and should reserve out of the revenues of the benefice an annual pension to be paid to Gilbert de Clare until he was provided with another benefice. The custom of farming churches was, in fact, so widely prevalent that it could not be abolished all of a sudden, and it was often necessary to effect compromises. The *Dunstable Annals* relate that the monks had great difficulty in obtaining from Grosseteste the churches which they held at farm for three years.[3]

As between the second and the third of the systems previously enumerated, both of which existed in the case of the appropriated churches, Grosseteste strongly favoured the establishment of vicarages, placed on a definite and stable basis, as contrasted with temporary arrangements, which he considered unfair to the parishioners, upon whom were thus foisted men who were badly paid, of little or no education, and in other respects unfit for the cure of souls, whilst the system promoted the growth of a grasping disposition on the part of the monastic bodies. In the course which he pursued in that respect the Bishop was in full accord with the Canon of the Lateran Council of 1179, which required religious houses to establish vicars in their churches, as well as with similar enactments of the Council of Westminster in 1200[4] and of the Council of Oxford in 1222.[5] In the latter year Stephen Langton had

---

[1] *Ann. Monast.* (Tewkesbury), i. 122.

[2] Presumably this is the same as the Gilbert de Clare, a clerk in the diocese of Worcester, who is mentioned in the Papal Registers (Bliss, *Calendar*, i. p. 207) in 1244 as a *protégé* of Richard Earl of Cornwall.

[3] *Ann. Monast.* (Dunstable), iii. 147.

[4] Wilkins, i. pp. 509, 510.

[5] *Ibid.* i. p. 596.

devoted several articles of his Constitutions to the subject of vicarages, and had required, among other things, that "churches not worth above five marks a year should be given to none but such as would reside in person and minister in such churches," and that "those who failed to do so should be deprived by the diocesan, after due admonition."[1] The term "vicar" had, no doubt, been in frequent use in previous centuries; but endowed vicarages, in the strict sense of the word, date from the end of the twelfth or the beginning of the thirteenth. Hugh de Wells, Grosseteste's predecessor, had already created several hundred vicarages in the diocese of Lincoln, and the same policy was continued and extended by Grosseteste himself.[2] What he endeavoured to secure was that the vicar should be resident in the parish, and in an independent position, so that he should not merely be the servant of the monastery, but stand, as nearly as possible, in the place of the rector in all respects, except as far as the salary was concerned; though, as is well known, the vicar's insecurity of tenure continued for more than a century and a half longer, in spite of various attempts to improve his status.[3] It was in view of the fact that the vicar was liable to dismissal—a liability which placed in the hands of those who employed him a lever for keeping his salary low—that Grosseteste and other prelates who desired to increase the efficiency of the parochial clergy and to promote the welfare of the parishioners laid so much

[1] Archbishop Langton's *Canons*, 1222, art. 15; see also articles 12, 13, 14, 16.

[2] See Pegge, p. 327, and the whole of Appendix vii. pp. 322-333, on the Origin of Vicarages. On the establishment of about 300 vicarages by Hugh de Wells see A. Gibbons, *Liber Antiquus de Ordinationibus Vicariarum tempore Hugonis Wells Lincolniensis Episcopi*, 1209-1235 (Lincoln, 1888), with preface by Archdeacon Perry. As the Archdeaconry of Leicester is not included, the number of vicarages must have been even larger. Mr. Herbert Thurston, in his *Life of St. Hugh of Lincoln*, London, 1898, pp. 319-325, gives reasons for assigning a somewhat earlier date to the introduction of perpetual vicarages into England. He quotes four established by St. Hugh—at Chesterton, Swinford, Shillingdon, and Hemingford. The name of the vicar in the last instance was Master Aristotle (*Ramsey Cartulary*, ii. p. 176). Other instances might also be given, but the system did not become prevalent until the time of Hugh de Wells. St. Hugh favoured appropriations to religious houses.

[3] See the Act of 1402 (4 Henry IV., ch. 12).

stress upon the need for fixed financial arrangements for their proper maintenance.

The question of the amount of the quota generally assigned to vicars is one of considerable difficulty, as it appears to have depended rather upon the special circumstances of each case than upon a fixed principle. It would seem, however, from various entries relating to the vicarages established by Hugh de Wells that the sum of five marks was usually, and on an average, considered a fair payment for a vicar.[1] A comparison of some of these entries with a certain number of those which are to be found in his successor's rolls, seems to show that the latter assigned, wherever he could, a somewhat higher stipend. It is, however, difficult to form even a rough estimate of the amount actually received by the vicar, as in some cases the value of the parsonage-house has to be deducted. For instance, the vicarage of Totternhoe established by Hugh de Wells is stated in the *Dunstable Annals*[2] to have been worth five marks, while the whole church was worth twelve ; but the sum of five marks was arrived at by adding together "the altar dues of the said church, the rent of tenpence from the land of a certain Richard Godwer, the parsonage-house, and the half of the tithe of hay from the whole parish." The tendency, however, as far as tithes were concerned, was to assign to the vicar one-third, and to leave to the monastery the remaining two-thirds, in accordance with the old canonical principle that one-third of the tithes should go for the support of the Church, one-third for the poor, and one-third for the priest. That principle had been embodied in England in the sixth article of the so-called Church Grith law of 1014, passed by Ethelred II. with the consent of his Witan,[3] but it is doubtful how far that ordinance was carried into effect even at the time when it was promulgated, and there is certainly no evidence that it was in legislative operation after

---

[1] *Ann. Monast.* (Dunstable), iii. 59. See Archdeacon Perry, p. 97.

[2] *Loco citato.*

[3] Thorpe, *Anglo-Saxon Laws*, i. p. 342.

the Norman Conquest.   The principle, however, was repeatedly stated and upheld, as being what Professor Freeman calls a "counsel of perfection."[1]   In the words, for instance, addressed by the rectors of Berkshire in 1240 to the papal legate, as recorded by Matthew Paris,[2] "by the authority of the holy fathers the revenues of the churches are devoted to certain uses, to wit, the use of the church, that of the ministers, and that of the poor."   Rectors, therefore, including all appropriators, whether corporations aggregate or corporations sole, were under a canonical and moral obligation to act as trustees of the funds they thus received for the benefit of those three objects.   The well-administered monasteries were not only alive to those responsibilities, but endeavoured faithfully to carry them out by making the requisite provision for the relief of the poor and the repair of the fabric, which they had in many instances built at their own cost.   Other monasteries, however, disregarded their duty in the matter, or were remiss in its performance.

The uncertainty, too, of the revenue from tithes had to be taken into account.   The rectors of Berkshire, in the address previously quoted, state, among the reasons which they give for their inability to contribute to the funds which the Pope was trying to raise in order to assist him against the Emperor, that their churches are hardly sufficient to provide daily food for the clerks, by reason of their small amount, that famine sometimes assails the country when the crops fail, and also that so large a number of poor people and travellers come to them, some of whom they have seen die for want of nourishment.   It may well be imagined that, in cases in which the bulk of the revenues of a living went to absentee rectors in other parts of England, or found its way out of the country into alien hands, the im-

---

[1] In a letter addressed to the Rev. Morris Fuller, quoted in the *Nat. Review* for November 1886.

[2] *Hist. Maj.* iv. 40.   Cp., on the one hand, Lord Selborne's *Ancient Facts and Fictions Concerning Churches and Tithes*, p. 180, and, on the other, Clarke's *History of Tithes*, s.v. Church Grith Law.

poverishment of the parish clergy, and the consequent injury to the parishioners, must have been even more conspicuous and even more lamentable. In the case of vicars a stipend of five marks a year, with the value of the parsonage-house deducted, can hardly have been sufficient, even when all due allowance is made for the difference in the value of money, to attract men of education and character from the ranks of the secular clergy, who had to live by their profession ; though doubtless to a monk who had his home in his monastery, and enjoyed means of support in connection with it, and who was called upon to take the duty in a particular parish, an even smaller sum would have appeared adequate, whilst to a friar who had taken the vow of poverty it may have appeared excessive.[1]

During the greater part of his episcopal career Grosseteste was repeatedly brought in contact with the question, and as the method pursued was generally the same in most instances, it is unnecessary to deal with them in detail.[2] His strenuous opposition to new appropriations, and his insistence that, in the case of existing appropriations, adequate financial arrangements should be made by the establishment of vicarages, earned him the hostility of the monastic bodies, even more than any other action he took in the course of his lifetime. It may, perhaps, be permissible to anticipate here what occurred in 1249. In that year Grosseteste, having previously obtained authority from the Pope to prohibit the religious houses from appropriating tithes without the consent of himself and his chapter, " caused all the monks who held benefices in the diocese of Lincoln to be summoned, first at Stamford, secondly at Leicester, and thirdly at Oxford, to appear before him for the purpose of

---

[1] It must be borne in mind that the vicars had their burdens. Matthew Paris, in his *Vita Abbatum*, p. 131, describes the " onera " of the vicars as " parochialia, synodalia, archidiaconalia, ordinaria et consueta." Cp. Pegge, p. 332.

[2] The method of procedure described in the *Dunstable Annals* (*Ann. Monast.* iii. 59) is typical of that adopted in other cases. The inquiry was made in the chapters of the rural deans, who sent in their reports to the Bishop. He then made any modifications he chose, and his decision was entered in the registers.

exhibiting the charters of their founders, the confirmations of bishops, and the papal privileges. And these being exhibited, he retained a copy of them all for his own use, and said that he would consult the Pope about them."[1] It was in the following year that he obtained from Pope Innocent IV. a bull enabling him to make better provision for the endowment of vicarages,[2] in spite of the fact that the *Dunstable Annals* say that he did not, after all, speak to the Pope at Lyons about that particular matter.[3]

St. Bernard had once exclaimed, in the previous century, " It is no longer true that the priests are as bad as the people, for the priests are worse than the people." The condition of things had no doubt improved since those days. As far as England was concerned there had been a distinct improvement since the time when John of Salisbury wrote, and even since the days when Giraldus Cambrensis penned his *Gemma Ecclesiastica*. Grosseteste, however, refers repeatedly in his letters to the low standard of conduct which prevailed among the secular clergy, and especially to "the multiplicity of evils from which the people are suffering, and the errors and sins into which they are led, owing to the negligence of their rectors, the carelessness of their pastors, and often (a subject for tears rather than for a letter) the bad example and open wickedness of those who ought to be their spiritual guides."[4] In order to mitigate and, if possible, to destroy those evils, Grosseteste applied himself to the task of removing their causes. Rebukes, admonitions, exhortations, and penances were only partial palliatives and temporary expedients. The real remedy, he clearly perceived, was

---

[1] *Hist. Maj.* v. 96 ; *Ann. Monast.* (Dunstable), iii. 180.

[2] *Hist. Maj.* vi. 152.

[3] " De praedictis nihil fecit," *l.c.* The bull is dated 25th September 1251, *Hist. Maj.* vi. 152. See also *Hist. Anglorum*, iii. 68, 69. In the *Hist. Anglorum*, iii. 120, Matthew Paris begins to see the *rationale* of Grosseteste's support of the vicars : " Epis-

copus Lincolniensis R. portiones vicariorum, in dampnum rectorum, adauget, considerans quoniam ipsi fervores diei sustinent et labores."

[4] Letter 130, p. 440 ; Luard's Introd. p. 24. Cp. *Hist. Anglorum*, ed. Madden, iii. 113, on the way in which Grosseteste endeavoured to enforce strict morality in his clergy.

to impart to the clergy a higher sense of the nobility of their
calling, to improve their education, to direct their attention to
the duty of teaching and of preaching, to attract into their
ranks a better class of men, and, by placing their means of livelihood upon a more stable basis, to make them independent of
the necessity for pursuing other and less worthy avocations.
He took every opportunity of promoting the increase of their
knowledge, with the object of augmenting their efficiency, and
was not averse to an incumbent being allowed, on fitting occasions and within due limits, to leave the care of his parish for
a certain time to a deputy, whilst he pursued a course of theological studies with the object of improving the value of his
teaching.   In one case, for example, he obtained from the Pope
permission to pay to Robert de Melkeley, rector of Clahaule, the
proceeds of that church during the time he attended the schools
of the theological faculty, provided that he was teachable and
apt to study;[1] and in another he procured a similar privilege
for a more important personage, the Archdeacon of Buckingham.[2]
Neither was his encouragement of the Franciscans and of the
Dominicans unconnected with his desire to reform the parochial
clergy, and to induce them to emulate the zeal of the Friars, and
to be taught by their example.

[1] Bliss, *Calendar of the Papal Registers*, i. p. 238 (1247).
[2] *Ibid.* i. p. 241 (1247).

CHAPTER VII

IT has already been pointed out that it was Grosseteste's endeavour to secure the harmony and efficiency of the whole of the religious work within his diocese, that with that object in view he included both the religious houses and the parish priests in his visitations, and that in 1236 he removed from office no fewer than seven abbots and four priors.[1] In dealing with the monks he was brought in contact with a very different class of men from that which formed the bulk of the secular clergy. If the latter were steeped to a great extent in ignorance, and displayed a low standard of moral conduct, the failing of the former was relatively indolence. Grosseteste frequently inveighs against the character of the parish priests, but never against that of the monks, with the exception of those who belonged to the convent of Minting, a foreign cell connected with the abbey of Fleury;[2] and the only instance in which he is known to have deposed the head of a monastic establishment for a breach of the moral law is in the case of the prior of St. Frideswyde's.[3] When he finds fault with the monks, it is not so much on account of what they do, as of what they leave undone. His complaint is that they do not adhere to the strictness of their rule, and that, owing to their dislike of the parochial clergy and their jealousy of the

---

[1] P. 131.

[2] Letters 54 and 108.

[3] P. 131; Bliss, *Calendar of the Papal Registers*, i. p. 163.

friars, they fail to give the active assistance in the diocesan work which it would be in their power to render, and he insists more particularly upon their neglect of the duty of preaching.

The early part of the thirteenth century was, indeed, as it has been called by more than one writer, the golden age of English monachism. It has also been called the golden age of English churchmanship;[1] but while the latter phrase is true of the brilliant array of distinguished prelates and other dignitaries of the Church who rendered that age memorable, it does not hold good with regard to the bulk of the parish clergy; the former may be said to apply, with few reservations, to the general body of those to whom it refers. The growth of the reforming spirit, which coincided with the introduction of the Cluniac monks into England shortly after the Conquest, and which found a more complete expression in the twelfth century in the establishment of the Cistercian order, had also exercised its influence upon the older foundations which adhered to the Benedictine rule, and had led to important improvements in their methods of administration as well as in their general tone. At the same time the Benedictines, while striving to approach more nearly to the spirit of the founder of their rule, had avoided the narrowness of view which was inseparable from their stricter and straiter offshoots. The extent of popularity of the monks at that time may be judged not only by the number of monasteries founded since the Conquest, but also from the many symptoms of good-will shown towards them, as indicated in contemporary records. If the friars brought with them increased attention to medicine, natural science, and philosophy, the monks, especially the Benedictines, were the pioneers of literary culture and historic study. In their "scriptoria" were written the chronicles of the times. Through their transcribers the writings of previous ages were preserved. They founded schools, distributed relief to the poor, and dispensed hospitality to all sorts and conditions of men, from the

---

[1] Stubbs, *Constitutional History*, ii. p. 299.

King with his retinue to the neediest wayfarer. As landowners they set an example, rarely followed under the feudal system, of respect for the duties as well as the rights of property, and, as agriculturists, they introduced and applied improved methods to the cultivation of the soil.

It has been estimated that, towards the commencement of the reign of Henry III., there were in existence in England about 560 religious houses, of which 130, including the largest and the wealthiest, had been founded before the Conquest, and the remaining 430 during the period of only one century and a half which had elapsed since that event.[1] In view of the vast extent of the Lincoln diocese it may well be imagined how large a proportion of those houses was to be found within its borders. The Cistercians, indeed, were specially exempted by the Pope from episcopal visitations, and Grosseteste was unable, therefore, to control the numerous houses belonging to that order which were situated in his diocese, such as Woburn, Wardon, Bittlesden, Saltrey, Kirkstead, Louth, Revesby, Swineshead, Vaudey, Pipewell, and Thame, and the same exemption applied to the Cistercian nunnery of Stykeswold. Of the older Benedictine abbeys, however, St. Albans was the only one within his purview which enjoyed a similar immunity in common with four others in different parts of England, namely, Canterbury, Evesham, Bury St. Edmunds, and St. Augustine's, Westminster.[2] Over the remaining Benedictine abbeys and priories he possessed and exercised visitatorial rights; and the importance of the great monasteries with which he was thus brought in contact may be judged by the historical associations connected with such names as Croyland, Bardney, Ramsey, Spalding, Peterborough, Eynsham, and Hertford, not to mention several other smaller houses, as well as a few Benedictine nunneries, prominent among which

---

[1] Tanner's figures, in his *Notitia Monastica*, bring the total up to 610, but they include about 50 houses which were founded before 1066, and subsequently re-founded.

[2] On the exemption of St. Albans from visitation see *Hist. Maj.* v. p. 381.

was that of Godstow. The Carthusians do not appear to have made much headway either there or elsewhere in England, in spite of the fact that they had given a bishop to the See of Lincoln in the person of St. Hugh of Avalon; Eppworth had not been founded in Grosseteste's time. The Austin Canons, in proportion to their importance, gave him more trouble than the Benedictines. The houses at Caldwell, Dunstable, Newenham, Missenden, Huntingdon, Kirkby, Leicester, Bourne, Markby, Thornton, Osney, Thornholm, Northampton, Canons Ashby, Dorchester, Wroxton, and several others belonged to that order, and their names occur repeatedly in Grosseteste's letters, in his rolls, and in the register of papal letters addressed to him. With the exception of the alien priories at North-ampton, Daventry, and Tykeford, the Cluniacs had hardly any footing in the diocese. The Gilbertines, on the other hand, had their original home at Sempringham, where St. Gilbert had instituted the order in the previous century, and Grosseteste was frequently called upon to intervene in their affairs; and on one occasion he was obliged to obtain from the Pope a special mandate to the legate Otho to compel the master and brethren of Sempringham to pay due obedience to their diocesan.[1] They also had houses at Lincoln, Alvingham, and Bullington. It was in the Lincoln diocese, too, that the Premonstratensian Canons had first taken up their abode when they came over from Normandy. Their settlement at Newhouse had been followed by others at Barlings, Croxton, Salby, and else-where. The diocese also contained numerous establishments of Templars and Hospitallers, as well as colleges of secular canons.[2]

---

[1] Bliss, *Cal. of the Papal Registers*, i. p. 189 (1240). In March 1253 Innocent IV. sent a mandate to Grosse-teste not to molest the master, prior, and convent of Sempringham touch-ing the taxation by the late Bishop Hugh de Wells of the perpetual vicar-ages of churches appropriated to them. Bliss, *Calendar*, i. p. 284.

[2] A fuller sketch of the religious houses in the diocese of Lincoln will be found in the *Diocesan History of Lin-coln*, by Canon Venables and Arch-deacon Perry (London, 1897), pp. 226-241. It is based, like the present account, upon Tanner, but includes houses founded after Grosseteste's time.

In spite of the priceless services which the Benedictines had rendered in the past, increase of wealth had brought with it a laxer interpretation of their rule, for example in regard to the use of meat, and an increasing tendency to a life of ease. They were what Dr. Johnson would have called "very clubbable men," and the advantages which the monastery presented as a social home often obscured the higher objects for which it had been instituted. The renewed growth of monasticism in England after the Conquest favoured the newer foundations, such as those of the Cluniacs, the revived Austin Canons, the Premonstratensians, and the Gilbertines, rather than the older establishments which followed the rule of St. Benedict. The latter, however, still held a dominant position by reason of their antiquity, their wealth, their culture, and their refinement, and were consequently the protagonists in the defence of all monastic institutions against what were deemed to be episcopal invasions of their rights. When Matthew Paris complains that Grosseteste "came down upon the monks like a hammer, and was a great persecutor of them," and again that "the same Robert was wont to thunder terribly against the monks, and even more terribly against the nuns, with plenty of well-meant zeal, but not, perhaps, according to knowledge," it is evident that the historian of the great and wealthy abbey of St. Albans is writing under the influence of the *esprit de corps* which resented all outside interference with monastic management, rather than by reason of any objections which could justly be urged against the Bishop's action in particular cases, and that he also has in his mind the numerous instances in which Grosseteste tried to secure good terms for the vicars. About the strictness and severity of his visitations there is, however, no doubt; and although the accounts given by Matthew Paris cannot be regarded as absolutely trustworthy in all their details, as he was necessarily biassed by his surroundings, and had often to depend for his information upon the narratives given by the very men who thought themselves aggrieved, there is no need to dispute the fact that Grosseteste showed want of tact and impatience of opposition on several of those occasions. Matthew Paris, however, qualifies his statement by paying a tribute to the excellence of Grosseteste's intentions, and by comparing his impulsiveness to that of David and of St. Peter.[1]

It would be impossible to enter here with any degree of fulness into the details of Grosseteste's relations with the monasteries, or even to attempt a complete list of those which he is recorded to have visited, as an account of what he did in one case would, for the most part, be merely a repetition of what he did in other cases, though it might be of interest to the local historian. It will be desirable, however, to group together in this place some of the salient features and incidents connected with this part of the subject, even though it be necessary, in so doing, to anticipate in some measure the subsequent course of events.

A letter of admonition addressed by Grosseteste to the prior of the convent of Newenham, a house of Austin Canons in Bedfordshire, probably belongs to the earliest portion of his episcopal career, as it was coupled, in the Cotton manuscript in which it used to be found, with an account of the archidiaconal visitation of the convent in 1232.[2] In a similar letter, written in 1240 to the Austin Canons of Missenden,[3] he urges them to exercise special care in the selection of their abbot. "When you have," he says, "to choose some one to look after your swine, you make diligent search for a person possessing the proper qualifications : you inquire whether he is physically capable, whether he has requisite knowledge, and whether he is willing to take them into fitting pastures in the morning, to see that they get their food during the day, to preserve them from

---

[1] *Hist. Anglorum*, ed. Madden, iii. p. 149.

[2] Cotton MSS. Otho, c. xv. 1, 2. Pegge refers to it (p. 140), but it is not included in Dr. Luard's collection. It is no longer among the Cotton MSS.

[3] Letter 85. The letter is written apparently in 1240. A former abbot of Missenden had been deposed by Grosseteste in 1236.

thieves and wild beasts, to bring them safely home in the evening, and to watch over them even by night. And are not your souls of more value than many swine?"

Simony was as odious to Grosseteste in the regulars as in the seculars. In 1239 he obtained from the Pope a mandate to transfer those who had been simoniacally received into monasteries situated in his diocese, to others of the same or of a stricter order, and to enjoin on them an adequate penance. If their entry into other monasteries was difficult, he was enabled to compel them to be received anew by way of dispensation, and the lowest places in the choir and the refectory were to be assigned to them, provided that the money simoniacally paid for their first entrance was given to the poor, or used for their sustentation, if it had already been transferred to other religious houses.[1] Another abuse was sternly and promptly repressed. It appeared that some married men, wearied of matrimony, had left their wives and betaken themselves to monasteries. Grosseteste thereupon obtained a faculty which enabled him to take proceedings, at the request of the wives themselves, against any husbands who without reasonable cause put away their wives and entered upon a monastic life.[2] The two incidents illustrate, on the one hand, the attractiveness of monasteries which induced men to compete with one another for the privilege of entering their walls, as well as to sacrifice, in some cases, domestic considerations, and, on the other hand, the Bishop's high sense of duty and inflexible tenacity of purpose.

One instance of Grosseteste's impulsiveness in his dealings with monasteries occurred in the case of the visit he paid to Hertford either in 1239 or in 1240. Before proceeding to that town for the purpose of carrying out his visitation, he had sent

---

[1] Bliss, *Calendar of the Papal Registers*, i. p. 178. Walter de Cantelupe, Bishop of Worcester, who was intimate with Grosseteste and followed his methods of dealing with the monasteries, enforced constitutions on the monks of his diocese, and resorted to a similar plan for banishing disobedient monks to other abbeys. *Ann. Monast.* (Tewkesbury), i. 146, 147, 150.

[2] Bliss, *Calendar of the Papal Registers*, i. p. 209 (1244).

in advance directions to the prior and convent asking for hospitality, not as a favour but as a right. The monks, in their desire to maintain intact their privileges, declined to admit him, whereupon, according to Matthew Paris,[1] he "suspended the churches of the secular clergy in the town, but, being reproved for so doing by the legate, at once withdrew the sentence so rashly pronounced by him, for he acted on evil counsel." The refusal of the monks in this case did not signify that they disputed the Bishop's right of visitation, which was unquestioned, but that they asserted the principle that their hospitality should be voluntary, and not compulsory. It was for precisely the same reason that, in 1253, the priory of Belvoir, connected with St. Albans, refused to entertain the Archbishop of Canterbury. Otho, the Papal legate, was in the habit of meeting the views of the monks in that respect by previously writing to the Abbot or Prior of the monastery in which he proposed to stay, intimating that he asked for hospitality as an act of charity.[2]

The bad management of the priory of Dunstable, which was a house of Austin Canons, excited on more than one occasion Grosseteste's indignation. In 1240 he insisted that each of the canons should take an oath to purge himself from complicity in any abuses, whereupon one of them, Walter de Gledley, preferred to leave the priory and to become a Cistercian monk at Woburn abbey.[3] A somewhat similar incident happened in 1249, when Grosseteste paid another visit to Dunstable, and when Henry de Bilenda, the cellarer, who had committed various abuses in connection with his office, left the priory in order to escape from the Bishop's jurisdiction, and took refuge in the Cistercian house of Merivale, where he henceforward enjoyed, in common with Walter de Gledley at Woburn, the Cistercian immunity from episcopal visitation.[4] In that same year the prior of Caldwell, against whom the monks brought charges of maladministration, took the advice of the Priors of

---

[1] *Hist. Maj.* v. 414. Cp. Luard's Introduction to the *Letters*, p. 48.

[2] *Ibid.* v. 411.

[3] *Ann. Monast.* (Dunstable), iii. 152.

[4] *Ibid.* iii. 178.

Dunstable, Newenham, Huntingdon, and Bushmead, and followed the example of Henry de Bilenda by betaking himself to Merivale.[1]

A dispute with the great Benedictine abbey of Bardney, situated at a distance of ten miles from his cathedral city, occupied a good deal of the Bishop's attention in 1243, involved him indirectly in a dispute with the monks of Canterbury, and resulted in other complications which throw an interesting light on the condition of the times. The abbey of Bardney was not, as has been inadvertently stated by one writer, exempt from episcopal visitation, although it enjoyed, by virtue of a grant of Henry the First, in whose reign it was re-endowed, the same privileges as were accorded by that sovereign to abbeys founded by himself.[2] It possessed, moreover, certain pontifical privileges which Thomas Wallensis, Archdeacon of Lincoln, a firm friend and staunch supporter of Grosseteste, was desirous of diminishing, as their continued existence had the effect of impairing the Bishop's control over the affairs of that part of his diocese.[3] An occasion for interference arose when a certain clerk, finding that he had difficulty in recovering from Walter de Beningworth, the Abbot, a debt due to him from his predecessor, brought the matter before the Archdeacon, who resolved, according to Matthew Paris, upon the adoption of strong measures " for the purpose of humiliating the monks," though it is more probable that he took that course from a sense of duty in order to protect the rights of the secular clergy. He accordingly summoned the Abbot to appear before him to answer to the law in respect of the clerk's complaint. The Abbot declined to appear, and pleaded privilege. Again he was summoned, and again he refused, " knowing," writes the historian, " that the Archdeacon was cunningly striving to bring the plaint before the Bishop, in which case it was inevitable that he would be in favour of the monks' subversion, as he was

---

[1] *Ann. Monast.* iii. 179.

[2] See Tanner's *Notitia Monastica,* s.v. Dugdale's *Monasticon,* i. p. 624.

[3] *Hist. Maj.* iv. 245 *sqq.*, 257, 258. Cp. the *Flores Historiarum,* ed. Luard, ii. 261, 265.

regarded as the general persecutor of religious recluses, especially of those who enjoyed privileges which he could oppose." The matter, however, was referred to Grosseteste, who cited the Abbot to answer for repeated acts of disobedience, and, on his refusal to obey the summons, excommunicated him for contumacy and rebellion, and, a few days later, sent to Bardney some inspectors, "secular priests, more ready to insult the monks than to correct abuses, if any could be found." The monks refused to admit them, caused the gate to be shut against them by the porters, and warned them that they had better depart quickly, as otherwise the exasperated villagers would make a rush upon them, and added: "Although it would be against our will, we could not check their violence."

The inspectors returned to the Bishop, gave what Matthew Paris describes as an exaggerated version of what had taken place, and alleged that they had been subjected to personal violence. The dispute now reached its height. The Abbot, having been informed that the convent of Christ Church, Canterbury, had the power of hearing appeals *sede vacante*—as the archiepiscopal see was then vacant, owing to the death of St. Edmund, and to the fact that Boniface of Savoy had not yet been consecrated—made his appeal to that body. Grosseteste, on the other hand, called together at Hertford three Benedictine abbots, one of whom, the Abbot of Warden, had recently been appointed Bishop of Connor, while the other two presided over the abbeys of Ramsey and of Peterborough, and with their concurrence deposed the Abbot of Bardney in his absence, and sent a notice to the monks that they need no longer obey his commands, as he had been both excommunicated and deposed. The Canterbury monks, in their turn, only too glad to have an opportunity of asserting their claim to the exercise of archiepiscopal powers *sede vacante*, convened fifty priests from the diocese of Lincoln, and, in full convocation, numbering fifty monks or more in priest's orders, proceeded to excommunicate Grosseteste with bell, book, and candle, much in the same way as they had previously passed a similar sentence on certain other prelates in the province of Canterbury, including the Bishop of Rochester,[1] who had declined to acknowledge their jurisdiction.

Grosseteste's indignation was unbounded. Only a few months before he had refused to admit the right of the Christ Church convent to interfere in the matter of the dispute with his own chapter, an account of which will be found in a subsequent part of this volume.[2] On receipt of the letter notifying to him the sentence of excommunication, he threw it on the ground and trod on it, to the astonishment of those who saw him, as the image of St. Thomas Becket was impressed upon the wax of its seal, and he was also heard to say, according to Matthew Paris, that "he did not desire the monks should otherwise pray for his soul as long as the world endured." The messenger who brought the letter was ignominiously sent away. To the sentence itself neither he nor any one connected with him appeared to pay any heed. He continued to officiate, to dedicate churches, and to exercise all episcopal functions as before.

The question, however, had attained to such dimensions that it had to be brought before the Pope. Special messengers and letters were sent by the Bishop, on the one hand, and by the Christ Church monks, on the other, to Anagni, where Innocent IV. had just been raised to the pontifical office, with the result that the new Pope despatched to the prior and convent of Christ Church, Canterbury, a letter, dated the 8th of August 1243, in which he ordered them to withdraw, within eight days after its receipt, the sentence of excommunication which they had pronounced against his venerable brother the Bishop of Lincoln, without prejudice to either side. If they failed to do so, the Archbishop of York and the Bishop of Durham were to relax the sentence and to restrain by ecclesiastical censure, without appeal, all gainsayers.[3] The Abbot of Bardney's deposition, therefore, remained uncancelled.

---

[1] *Ann. Monast.* (Dunstable), iii. 161.

[2] Pages 186 *sqq.*

[3] *Hist. Maj.* iv. 258. Letter 111 relates probably both to the Bardney

Neither the Canterbury monks, however, nor Grosseteste were satisfied with the Pope's decision, the former because it annulled their action, and the latter because it avoided dealing with the question of the right of the monks to exercise archiepiscopal jurisdiction at a time when there was no archbishop. He accordingly wrote a letter[1] to Cardinal Otho, formerly Papal legate in England, protesting with great logical force against the claim put forward by the Canterbury chapter. In his judgment it was impossible that the archiepiscopal jurisdiction and power should devolve, in the absence of an archbishop, upon any below the rank of the bishops who were his suffragans. As for monks, who, according to St. Jerome and other early Church authorities, were not equal in rank even to sub-deacons, it was monstrous that they should seek to usurp a position of superiority to the episcopal dignity, and, if their claim were not withstood, the consequence would be detrimental to the repute and the efficiency of the bishops all over England. It did not follow that, because the Archbishop of Canterbury was, as it were, an *archon* among Anglican prelates, any similar priority could be accorded to the Christ Church monks, who were separated from him by several intervening degrees. Even the Archdeacon of Canterbury, for instance, would have a prior claim to theirs. "Some of the monks," he continues, "are not even in priest's orders. How can they, then, be greater than the clergy so ordained, or *a fortiori* than the bishops? How can they even claim equality? To bishops and clergy have been handed the duty and the right of dispensing to the people the holy ministrations. To monks, according to the oldest traditions of the Christian Church, no such functions have been assigned, unless it be that some one of them, by a special gift of Providence, by the illumination of the wisdom arising out of the contemplation of truth, by the knowledge which proceeds out of charity, and by virtue of the honourable reputation he has earned through the saintliness of

dispute and to the dispute with the Dean and chapter of Lincoln. See also Letter 110, pp. 324, 325.

[1] Letter 110.

his conversation, is canonically raised from the penitential sub-
jection of the cloister's simple life to the highest position of
honour in the government of the Church." He concludes by
asking Otho to induce the Pope to examine the question not
only from the point of view of Grosseteste's own urgent necessities, but in the interest of the whole Anglican Church, and to
put an end to the humiliations and tribulations to which the
whole of the English episcopate is exposed, lest the collapse of
their authority should mean the destruction of the principal
column which supports a fabric already menaced by attack
from without and by sedition from within.

Grosseteste also states in his letter that his only reason for
appealing to the Pope is that otherwise the malignity of certain
persons might quote the sentence of excommunication against
him. It is not certain what further steps were taken by Innocent IV. in the matter, but it is probable that the indult which
he sent to the Bishop of Lincoln at the end of April 1244,[1] to
the effect that no one should issue against him any sentence of
suspension or excommunication, or any sentence of interdict
against his chapel, without special license from the Pope, has
reference to the action of the Canterbury chapter in connection
with the Bardney dispute. That some agreement was effected
after long discussions, and was publicly signed, is evident from
a letter addressed by Adam Marsh to Nicholas Sandwich, Prior
of Canterbury,[2] in which he expresses his regret that, after the
accommodation agreed upon between the chapter and the
Bishop of Lincoln, the prior still delays bringing the matter to
a termination, and relies upon legal objections. Adam Marsh
urges the need for peace within the Church, emphasises Grosseteste's anxiety for a speedy and satisfactory settlement, and
suggests that there are persons desirous of prolonging the strife
between them.[3] The arrival of Boniface of Savoy in England finally put an end to the struggle, by removing any

---

[1] Bliss, *Calendar of the Papal Regis-*
ters, i. p. 209.

[2] *Mon. Francis.* p. 211.

[3] *Ibid.* p. 219.

pretext for further interference on the part of the Canterbury chapter.

In addition to the embroilment with the Christ Church monks, the Bardney incident also involved Grosseteste in a correspondence with the King. On the deposition of the Abbot Henry III. had seized the temporalities, and was understood to have given to his official, William de Compton, who was sent to guard them, certain instructions which were likely to be construed as an encouragement to the deposed Abbot and his party. Grosseteste requests that the royal letter, if sent, may be re-called.[1] Even if the Abbot has justly rebelled, this must not be presumed until the question has been decided by the ecclesiastical jurisdiction upon which the civil power should not encroach. The King must beware lest he fall into the sin of Uzzah, who touched the ark, and reminds him of the etymological connection between the words *rex* and *rectum*, which ought to correspond with an inseparable relation between the two. If "a King can do no wrong," why does he encourage rebellion against duly constituted authority? Such were some of the developments which arose out of Grosseteste's endeavour to render Bardney abbey amenable to discipline, and it will be observed that he succeeded in spite of all opposition. His tenacity and strength of will had a way of overcoming the most formidable obstacles. Matthew Paris, in one place, speaks of "the Bishop of Lincoln, to whom quiet is an unknown thing; whose hand is against every man, as every man's hand is against him ; another Ishmael, ready to labour with any amount of toil, and to spend money in reckless profusion, that he may carry his point." There are, however, passages in Grosseteste's letters which indicate that he was not as harsh in his dealings with the monasteries as would appear from the foregoing statement of Matthew Paris, who, though broader in his views and deeper in his historical insight than the chroniclers of earlier generations, was naturally and necessarily prejudiced by his environment in

----

[1] Letter 102.

regard to all that concerned the rights and privileges of the monks. In one letter,[1] for instance, written to the Abbot of Leicester, he mentions that he intends to come in person in order to examine the case of a certain aged penitent, a canon of Dorchester, who wished to die amongst his brethren, and expresses the opinion that, if the Abbot's account be correct, he had better remain, as he will find more consolations for his infirmity and old age at Leicester than at Dorchester. In the same letter, with reference, apparently, to another matter, he adds: " You suggest to me that I have a heart of iron and that I am lacking in kindness. Would that, indeed, I had a heart as hard as iron, incapable of being softened by the blandishments of seducers, so strong that it could not be broken by the terrors of evil-doers, and so sharp that it could cut in pieces all vices and dislodge all opposing evils. In Ezekiel[2] all the house of Israel is said to have been of a hard heart, in the sense that it was full of the hardness of cruelty and malice, which may God avert! To the prophet, on the other hand, was accorded a countenance more powerful than their countenances, and a forehead harder than their foreheads, like unto adamant and flint. Of the latter hardness would that even a small share might be granted to me by Him who is the true Rock, concerning which the Apostle says, ' That rock was Christ.' If, indeed, I am hard as iron in cruelty and obstinate malice, pray ye the Lord for me, that He may be pleased to take away this hardness and grant me His gentleness ; but, if I am hard as iron after the manner of the prophet, pray ye the Lord that this hardness may ever, as long as I live, receive an increase." It may also be noted that Adam Marsh, one of the gentlest of men, on more than one occasion expresses the view that Grosseteste has shown more leniency than the circumstances require.[3]

The foregoing remarks must be borne in mind when we read

---

[1] Letter 55.

[2] Ezekiel iii. 7-9.

[3] E.g. *Mon. Francisc.* pp. 107. 148, 403.

the account given by Matthew Paris of Grosseteste's visitation
of the abbey of Ramsey in 1251,[1] illustrating the severity with
which he insisted upon a strict observance of the regulations
that monks should not possess private property, or any property
apart from that which belonged to them in their corporate
capacity, and that they should not indulge in luxuries. It is
there stated that, when he came to Ramsey, accompanied by
a body of secular clergy, he "personally examined the beds of
the monks in the dormitory, going round all, and turning every
thing upside down, and, if he chanced to find anything locked
up, he destroyed it, and dashed the casket to pieces, and any
cups which he found bound with rings or furnished with feet,
he trod under foot and broke to fragments, which, if he had
acted in a more temperate manner, he might at any rate have
given whole to the poor." It is necessary to make allowance
for the bias and the exaggerations of Matthew Paris's informants ;
and, having regard to the abuses existing in the monasteries in
respect of private property, as set forth, for example, by Jocelyn
of Brakelond at the close of the twelfth century, it cannot be
denied that Grosseteste had good grounds for insisting that the
monks should adhere to the vows which they had taken of
their own free will, and with full knowledge of what they
signified.

It is worthy of note, as has already been pointed out, that
in the whole of the great diocese over which he presided, and
with the large number of religious houses contained within its
borders, the only two instances in which he is known to have
had occasion to punish anything in the nature of flagrant
immorality on the part of monks were, first, in the case of the Prior
of St. Frideswyde's, and, secondly, in that of the small alien
priory of Minting, a cell of the abbey of Fleury.[2] The fact
speaks well for the moral tone which prevailed in the monasteries. Minting, however, was not the only alien priory which,
in other respects, was a cause of trouble to him. In the Papal

---

[1] Hist. Maj. v. 226.   [2] See p. 147.

registers is to be found a confirmation, addressed to Grosseteste, of a decision pronounced in his favour by William, Cardinal of St. Eustache, against the Abbot and convent of Marmoutier-les-Tours, who complained of his having excommunicated the monks of Tykeford,[1] and claimed that the priors instituted by the said Abbot had the right of administering without contradiction from the Bishop of the diocese. The incident formed part, apparently, of a scheme devised by the Cluniac monks for the purpose of securing immunities similar to those which the Cistercians enjoyed. Grosseteste's opposition to monks may, in fact, be summed up as having been occasioned by their lax interpretation and observance of the monastic rule, their attempts to avoid episcopal supervision, their reluctance to make proper provision for vicarages, and their disinclination to co-operate with the secular clergy and with the friars in the active work of the diocese. The monks were, in a certain measure, an aristocracy of intellect, and as such looked down upon the ignorance and low standard of the parish priests. They were also, to a considerable extent, an aristocracy of birth, and as such deemed the Franciscans and the Dominicans to be *novi homines*, intruders into a sphere which they regarded as already occupied. It was the existence of feelings and prejudices of that kind which angered Grosseteste. When, on the other hand, monks adhered strictly to their vows, and led lives of real usefulness, he was to be numbered among their champions and not among their opponents.

The condition of the nunneries, if it is permissible to draw an inference from the nature of the measures which Grosseteste is reported by Matthew Paris to have taken on the occasion of one of his visitations,[2] was not as satisfactory, from a moral point of view, as that of the monasteries. It is doubtful, too, whether the nunneries made, as a general rule, good use of their

---

[1] Bliss, *Calendar of the Papal Registers*, i. p. 257 (1248). The confirmation speaks of the monks of Newport Pagnell, but this must be an error for the monks of Tykeford, or Tickford, near Newport Pagnell. It was a Cluniac cell subordinate to Marmoutier-les-Tours. See Allen's *Alien Priories*, ii. p. 132, London, 1779.

[2] *Hist. Maj.* v. 227.

rights of patronage, or of the rectorial rights which they happened
to possess.[1] They cannot have had the opportunities for investigation and supervision which were within the power of
the monasteries. Adam Marsh writes to Grosseteste to warn
him against a priest of bad character who had been presented
by the Abbess of Godstow to the vicarage of Blokkesham,
and who had been ordained in Ireland in order to escape
undue inquiry into his antecedents.[2] On one occasion, in
1248, the Bishop found it necessary to depose the Abbess of
Godstow, Flandrina de Brewes, and Adam Marsh writes to
congratulate him on the beneficial results which are likely to
follow from his visitation of that abbey. And yet Godstow
must, on the whole, have been a well-managed nunnery, as is
shown by Adam Marsh's anxiety to obtain permission from
Grosseteste for Lady Eva de Tracy to remain there,[3] and for the
niece of Reginald de Bath to be admitted as a nun.[4] There is
also a probability that Grosseteste's own sister, Juetta, had
taken the veil there and had died within its walls, as it is
apparently from Oxford that Adam Marsh writes to inform him
first of her recovery from illness and, later on, of her death.[5]
It is possible that some of the difficulties which nunneries
encountered were due to the fact that they held lands and
churches just as if they were monasteries, and were expected to
discharge duties which were beyond their power. In 1251, for
instance, the Abbess of Shrewsbury was summoned to Chester
to take part in the military proceedings against Llewellyn,

---

[1] Richard Wyche, in the *Fasciculi
Zizaniorum*, ed. Shirley, p. 382, attributes to Grosseteste the saying :
Appropriatio ecclesiarum, potissime
feminis (that is, as the context
shows, to nuns), est contra Dei
ordinationem.

[2] *Monumenta Franciscana*, pp. 108,
117.

[3] *Ibid.* p. 99.

[4] *Ibid.* p. 122. On Archbishop

Peccham's measures with respect to
Godstow see his *Register*, ed. Martin,
Rolls Series, iii. 845 *sqq.* (1284).
Peccham was brought up under the in-
fluence of Adam Marsh, and therefore
indirectly of Grosseteste.

[5] *Ibid.* pp. 95, 164. In the latter
passage, however, Adam Marsh en-
quires whether masses for her are to
be celebrated "in oratorio suo de
Cofle."

exactly as if she were an abbot.[1]   In one respect, however, apart from the quiet and unostentatious work which they did in the neighbourhood of their nunneries, the nuns of Grosseteste's day are entitled to special commendation ; for, in addition to the time they devoted to study and to religious exercises, they brought the art of embroidery to a pitch of excellence to which it had not previously attained.   Matthew Paris[2] relates that when Innocent IV. saw the vestments worn in 1246 by the English prelates who were at Lyons, he inquired where they were made ; and on hearing that they came from England, he is reported to have exclaimed, "Truly England is our storehouse of delights, an inexhaustible well, and where so much abounds, much can be obtained from many" ; and he forthwith wrote to the Cistercian abbots in that country, ordering them to forward to him gold embroidery for the use of his chapel, "as though they could get it for nothing," but, adds the historian, "the order did not displease the mercenary Londoners, because they had them on sale, and sold them at their own prices."   It was in the nunneries that they were, for the most part, made.   It is not generally known, or always admitted, that some of the most famous embroidered vestments still preserved in Italy are the work of the English nuns of that period, such as the Lateran cope in Rome, the Piccolomini cope at Pienza, near Siena, and some at Anagni, Florence, and Bologna.[3]

It would be impossible to bring to a close a general survey of Grosseteste's relations with the religious houses without a reference to his own view of the ideal at which they ought to aim, as expressed in a letter which he addressed to the Abbot and convent of Peterborough,[4] in which he states that, having met,

---

[1] Taunton, *The Black Monks of St. Benedict*, i. p. 107.

[2] *Hist. Maj.* iv. 547.

[3] Middleton's *Illuminated MSS. in Classical and Mediaeval Times*, p. 112 ; Taunton, i. p. 113.

[4] Letter 57.   It is addressed "Abbati et Conventui de Burgo."   Dr. Luard thinks it was Peterborough, but Dr. Pauli (p. 52), with Luard's text before him, thinks it was Bury St. Edmunds. The former is the more probable supposition, as Peterborough was in Grosseteste's diocese, and he was frequently in communication with its Abbot, whose name happened to be

during a quiet week which he was able to snatch from his busy
and tumultuous life, with a Greek work on the monastic
state, he had spent a day in translating it for their benefit, and
now enclosed the condensed version he had made. The little
work, from which it is needless to quote at any length, contains
some etymological reflections on the origin of the word "monk,"
defines the adherents of a monastic rule as " viri philosophantes
circa regulas vitae in excellentia sanctitatis agendae," and
declares that "despite the frailty of their bodies, their conversation resembles that of the angel, they have deprived themselves
of worldly goods, they are crucified to the world, using the
necessaries of life solely for necessity and never for pleasure,
and preferring even in respect to them to mortify the flesh ; and,
as they have no possessions of their own, they labour with their
hands for the relief of the indigent." In communicating his
translation, Grosseteste adds : " These sentences I have extracted
from the treatise I have mentioned, and have placed them before
you, in order that you may see in them, as in a small mirror, a
miniature reflection of the form of monastic life. Just as young
maidens delight in a variety of mirrors, so do your virgin minds
find enjoyment in the contemplation of intellectual presentments
of their own state. In the Rule of St. Benedict you have been
able frequently to contemplate, as in the plane surface of a large
mirror, the beauty of the life you lead. You have also been
able to do so in the yet brighter mirror supplied by the rules of
St. Basil, and by the example and teaching of the lives of the
Fathers ; and if, therefore, you turn for a little while to look at
this small mirror brought from a foreign region of the earth, the
task ought not to be thought tedious by you. And if the
excellence of the monastic life be so great, who is there who
does not perceive how incongruous it is if the monastery itself,
the secure home of the monks, be not sanctified ? Who is there
who, if he were about to entertain an earthly king, would not

Walter of St Edmundsbury, about the
time when the letter was written. *E.g.*

Hist. Maj. iv. 247. Bury St. Edmunds,
however, is not impossible.

cleanse and purify in every way his abode, sparing neither labour nor expense, until the house was duly prepared with all adornment? But in your monastery the King of Heaven continually dwells, by virtue of His divine attributes, and also in the Sacrament of the Eucharist. The greatest beauty of this corporeal tabernacle is the glory and the holiness which it receives in its dedication to Him."

Words like these show that Grosseteste did not entertain the antipathy to monasticism which has sometimes been ascribed to him, and that he was hostile only to its laxity and to its failings. They also indicate how high was the ideal to which he was striving to attain, and help to explain what appeared at the time to be the undue severity of his visitations and the stringency of his reforms. His attitude towards the religious houses may also be illustrated by the fact that, although he was not himself the founder of any one of them,[1] the monastic writers, including even Matthew Paris, who so often criticises and condemns his policy, speak of him in terms of the utmost respect and reverence.

[1] The story that Grosseteste himself founded a small nunnery at Grimsby, and a priory for canons at Chetwoode, in Buckinghamshire, is disproved by Pegge, pp. 142, 143.

CHAPTER VIII

IT has been necessary, in some of the previous chapters, to anticipate in some measure the subsequent developments of Grosseteste's career, in order to be able to group together the salient features which characterised his dealings with the friars, the secular clergy, and the monks. It will now be possible to revert to the early period of his episcopate, and to adhere henceforward more strictly than has hitherto been desirable, to the chronological sequence of events.

The earnestness with which Grosseteste entered upon the first visitation of his diocese did not prevent him from commencing to take an increasing interest in the course of public affairs. It was, indeed, natural that such should be the case; for a bishop occupying as important a see as that of Lincoln was expected to be a statesman as well as a churchman. His sympathies in previous years had been, as has been shown, with the antagonists of Peter des Roches.[1] The death of Richard Marshall on the one hand, and the dismissal of Peter des Roches on the other, had modified and to some extent helped to clear the situation. A new set of questions, however, affecting

[1] See pp. 66, 93, 97, 110.

the relations of the ecclesiastical and of the civil powers, was
coming into prominence, and on two of these questions
Grosseteste took a leading part in 1236. The first of those
controversies had regard to the legitimation of bastards by the
subsequent marriage of their parents, and the second to the
action taken by the King in appointing certain abbots to be
justices itinerant.

The first of those questions is treated at some length by
Grosseteste in a long letter which he addressed, evidently some
weeks before the Council of Merton, to William de Raleigh, at
that time treasurer of Exeter, and afterwards Bishop, first of
Norwich and then of Winchester, with the object of convincing
him of the necessity for bringing the common law into harmony,
in that respect, with the provisions both of the canon law and
of the civil law.[1]   In so doing he was acting in harmony with
the declaration of the Lateran Council of 1179, that "such is the
efficacy of marriage that children previously born are to be held
legitimate after the marriage contract."   Grosseteste endeavours
to approach the question from every point of view, and brings
together a series of arguments, both forcible and ingenious,
derived from natural and divine law, as well as from the
analogies of Scripture, the analogies of nature, man's sense of
justice, the canon law and the civil law, and the ancient custom
of England, which he declares to be anterior even to the common
law.   William de Raleigh, who appears to have been somewhat
indifferent about the matter, replies in a light vein, which affords
a curious contrast to the Bishop's intense earnestness.   He
observes that Grosseteste's "brief" is wrongly so called, as it
is devoid of brevity, expresses surprise at the universality of
his legal acquirements, and suggests that he ought to be made
a judge.   Grosseteste retorts that, in view of the mass of available material and the importance of the subject, his letter did
not exceed reasonable limits, and adds that if William de Raleigh

---

[1] Letter 23. Dr. Luard, Introd. to   refers by a slip to the "civil law,"
the *Letters*, p. 29, lines 26 and 28,   when he means the "common law."

had as much acquaintance with the epistles of the early Fathers
as he had with his legal briefs, he would not bring those accusations of prolixity against his correspondent. He is, however,
quite willing to overlook the charge of undue length brought
against him, provided that his arguments are properly understood. As for "the universality of his legal knowledge," the
phrase must be ironical, as he had no practical legal experience ; [1]
and as for the suggestion that he should be made a judge, the
wish is hardly a filial one, for the pastoral office is as far
removed from the judicial as the east is from the west. "You
have," he continues, "a large pastoral care which has a claim
upon you for more labour than you could give to it, even if you
were free altogether from secular business." [2]

Grosseteste was summoned, together with other prelates, to
attend the Council, or Parliament, held at Merton shortly afterwards, and, although there is no record of the part he took on
that occasion, it is clear from the foregoing letters, as well as
from other indications, that he was one of the foremost in the
advocacy of the proposal to which that correspondence refers.
That Council, however, influenced in all likelihood by the
recollection of the misgovernment of Peter des Roches, and with
the apprehension of a similar condition of affairs arising out of
the influx of foreign favourites whom the marriage of the King
with Eleanor of Provence appeared likely to bring with it in its
train, resolved upon a manifestation of insular patriotism which
would have been more in place in connection with another
subject, took its stand upon the declaration : "Nolumus leges
Angliae mutari," and embodied the principle of the common
law in what is known as the statute 20 Henry III., chapter 9. [3]
The sustained interest which Grosseteste continued to take in
the question is shown by a letter which he addressed in the

[1] But see p. 13, and the letter of
Giraldus Cambrensis recommending
Grosseteste in 1199 to William de Vere,
Bp. of Hereford.

[2] Letter 24.

[3] See Bracton's *Note Book*, ed. Maitland (1887), pp. 104 *sqq.* The Council
of Merton met on the 23rd of January
1236. Grosseteste had been present,
earlier in the month, at the coronation
of Queen Eleanor. Hall's *Red Book of
the Exchequer* (Rolls Series), i. p. 755.

same year to Edmund, Archbishop of Canterbury,[1] in which he mentions that he has been summoned before the King's court for omitting to state, in the case of illegitimate children, whether they have been born before or after the matrimonial contract between the parents, and asks for his advice, as he wishes to offend neither God nor man. It would, indeed, have been better if the independence exhibited by the majority who opposed the prelates at Merton had been reserved for another occasion ; for it cannot be denied that the perpetuation of a law contrary to that which prevails on the subject in almost every European country, and which still differentiates Scotland from England by a broad, though unintelligible line of demarcation, has been open to grave objection on grounds of public convenience, apart from any inherent merits or demerits it may possess.

The immediate occasion for the second of the controversies in which Grosseteste was engaged in 1236, was the issue of a royal mandate to the Abbot of Ramsey, calling upon him to act as itinerant justice, together with certain others in Bedfordshire and Buckinghamshire. The explanation of the King's policy is to be found, probably, in his desire to obtain fresh funds, and may be taken in conjunction with his demand in 1237, for a tax of one-thirtieth on all movable property in the kingdom,[2] as well as with his appointment in 1240 of additional justiciaries, who were placed under the direction of Robert de Lexington for the northern counties, and of William of York for the southern, and who, according to Matthew Paris,[3] "under the pretext of administering justice, collected an immense sum of money for the use of the King, who squandered everything." What excited Grosseteste's indignation, however, was not so much the financial policy of the proposal, as the interference with the rights of the Church involved in the selection of ecclesiastical persons to perform certain duties as servants of the State. The royal letter to the Abbot of Ramsey was dated May 1236. Almost immediately afterwards Grosseteste wrote to the

---

[1] Letter 26, p. 104.   [2] *Hist. Maj.* iii. 381-383.   [3] *Ibid.* iv. 34.

Archbishop,[1] pointing out the objections, based on scriptural and canonical grounds, which might be urged against the course proposed, and asking him to induce Henry to recall the mandate, adding that otherwise, if the Abbot persisted in acting, it would be his duty to forbid him, even at some risk to himself. " If I do so," he writes, " the King's ministers will perhaps invade and confiscate my possessions, and, as opposition of the kind I have suggested has not previously been attempted in these parts, it will excite the scorn and derision of the worldly-wise. But, after all, what is called a temporal peril, as distinguished from one that is eternal, is of no account. There is compensation, more than sufficient, to one who is not forgetful of the past and who looks forward into the future." He ends by requesting the Archbishop's support. St. Edmund, who sympathised to some extent,[2] but who hesitated to take action, sent two replies to the effect that it would be best to wait until a Council had assembled and had reported upon the question. Grosseteste answers[3] that, if the King's mandate is wrong, and if it is contrary to Scripture and to the Canons to obey it, there is no need to wait for a council. It is a question of conscience. If it is a sin for men who have taken monastic vows to act as judges, and also for the clergy to submit themselves to secular tribunals in personal actions, surely it follows that it is a sin for the bishops, who exercise the pastoral care over them, to allow them to commit that sin even once. He concludes by calling on the Archbishop to come forward as " a leader in Israel," and to fight the fight of the Lord like Judas Maccabaeus.

Shortly afterwards, as may be gathered from internal evidence, he wrote what is called a letter " directed to " the Archbishop, but what might be more fittingly described as a mani-

---

[1] Letter 27.

[2] In his *Constitutions*, published in 1238, St. Edmund unites in the same condemnation priests who are " homicidae, advocati in causa sanguinis, simoniaci." It is probably owing to his knowledge of the Archbishop's views on that point that Grosseteste emphasises as an argument the possibility that justiciaries may be called upon, in the discharge of their functions, to inflict capital sentences.

[3] Letter 28.

festo on the grievances of the Church, dedicated to him, and sent to him for his approval previous to publication.[1] It is of considerable length, as well as of considerable importance in its bearing upon the history of the time, with special reference to the conflict which had arisen between the regal and the ecclesiastical authorities. Grosseteste's standpoint is not unlike that adopted by St. Thomas Becket in the previous century, though the particular questions at issue are no longer the same. The pamphlet begins, just as his earlier letter to the Archbishop had begun, by quoting the actual words of the King's mandate to the Abbot of Ramsey. It then enumerates six distinct forms of attack to which the Church has been subjected, deals with each of them in turn in an elaborate series of arguments, and, after a summary of the whole, concludes by citing the text of other rescripts issued by Henry the Third, the form and substance of which constitute also an infringement of ecclesiastical laws and liberties.

The six propositions are summed up thus : First, that abbots especially, and consequently other ecclesiastical persons, cannot, without grave fault, fill the office of justiciary or other posts which involve their rendering an account to the secular authorities. Secondly, that the clergy, whether regular or secular, err grievously in consenting to be tried by lay tribunals, and that the blame must attach not only to the King and the secular judges who compel them to do so, but also to the bishops who fail to oppose that encroachment on the liberties of the Church. Thirdly, that lay judges sin when they presume to determine in their courts whether a case is ecclesiastical or non-ecclesiastical, when there is doubt as to the tribunal to which it should be sent. In the fourth place, that the same judges have been known to decide in their own courts cases which are purely and unquestionably ecclesiastical. Fifthly, that the freedom of the Church is injuriously affected when the King prohibits or hinders the ecclesiastical judges from deciding ecclesiastical

----

[1] Letter 72, pp. 205 *sqq.*

causes. Lastly, that the King and the lay judges sin grievously when they compel bishops to render an account to them of the reasons why they refuse to institute certain persons presented to benefices.

The arguments by which those propositions are supported are illustrated by a serried array of quotations from the Scriptures, from the early Fathers, and from the decisions of General Councils. Grosseteste's previous study of the Canon Law is shown by his close acquaintance with the *Decretum* of Gratian. It is also evident that some of his references are to the *Decretals* of Gregory IX., published in 1234, two years previously, and sent by that Pope to Bologna and to Paris, with the command that they should be taught in the schools.[1] As the compiler of that work, the Dominican Raymund de Penaforte, who became general of the Order in 1238, and who was also the Pope's penitentiary, was an esteemed correspondent of Grosseteste,[2] it may be conjectured that a copy of Gregory's *Decretals* was sent to the Bishop either by the Pope himself or by Raymund, either out of courtesy or on account of his intimate connection with the University of Oxford, with a view to its introduction into the curriculum.[3] It is also, perhaps, worthy of note that the passages in the New Testament of which Grosseteste makes most use are, "If ye have judgments of things appertaining to this life ('secularia negotia' in the Vulgate), set them to judge who are least esteemed in the church,"[4] and "No man that warreth entangleth himself with the affairs of this life ('secularia negotia' quibus prohibet Apostolus 'militantes Deo implicari'),"[5] and that in both passages the force of the inference he draws depends largely upon the particular words to be found in

[1] Rashdall, i. p. 139.

[2] Letter 37.

[3] Bartholomew of Pisa, in his *Liber Conformitatum* (Milan, 1510), p. 79 b, quoted in the *Mon. Francisc.* p. 634, says that Agnellus sent ten pounds sterling to the Curia for a copy of the *Decretals.* Agnellus probably died in 1235. Little's *Grey Friars at Oxford,* p. 177. Although Gregory IX. approved the publication of Raymund de Penaforte's compilation in 1230, it was not actually published until 1234, and certainly cannot have been purchasable before that date.

[4] 1 Cor. vi. 4.   [5] 2 Tim. ii. 4.

the Latin version. The same does not apply, however, to the words, "He that is spiritual judgeth all things, yet he himself is judged of no man." [1]

Towards the close of the pamphlet the King is warned not to be guilty of the offence which led to the punishment of Uzziah, just as, in connection with the Bardney incident, he is warned to avoid the sin of Uzzah. [2] He is also reminded that in 1222 the Council of Oxford had excommunicated those who presumed to deprive the Church of her rights, and that by the Great Charter of 1215 the Church was to be free. [3] Grosseteste adds that "Stephen Langton, of cherished memory, and his suffragans had, with the consent of the King and the barons, excommunicated all who disobeyed the tenour of that Charter; from which excommunication the King and the barons had only recently been absolved at their own request, as they thought they had incurred it, by our venerable father Edmund, Archbishop of Canterbury, in the chapel of St. Catherine, Westminster; but the absolution had been given on condition that no further violations of the Charter should take place."

That Gregory the Ninth was in sympathy with Grosseteste's action is shown by the authorisation which he addressed to him in July 1236, to proceed against those clerks in his diocese who discharged the offices of justice or of sheriff. [4] The Archbishop, however, does not appear to have been moved, either by the merits of the case or by Grosseteste's earnest appeal to him to stand forth as leader, [5] to abandon his cautious and somewhat timid attitude. St. Edmund's saintliness of life and gentleness of disposition did not supply the place of the vigour and the energy which were chiefly needed at that juncture. The strength of Grosseteste's feelings on the subject may be inferred from the fact that in 1239, three years later, finding that the Archbishop would give him no assistance, he asked Cardinal

<hr>

[1] 1 Cor. ii. 15.
[2] Letter 102. See p. 160.
[3] Page 230 of the Letter.

[4] Bliss, *Calendar of the Papal Registers*, i. p. 155.
[5] Page 172.

Otho, the Papal legate, for his interference, in order to prevent Richard Bardney, Abbot of Croyland, from acting as itinerary justice ;[1] and that in 1245 he declined to institute Robert Passelew, who had been presented by Henry the Third to the living of St. Peter's, Northampton, and based his refusal on the ground that the presentee was a forest judge. In writing to the King he pointed out that his object was to secure that spiritual questions should be dealt with by ecclesiastics, and lay questions by laymen, just as military matters were managed by military men.[2] And when, on that occasion, Robert Passelew, after appealing against Grosseteste's decision, obtained a mandate for his institution from Boniface, Archbishop of Canterbury, the Bishop of Lincoln addressed to the latter words of indignant remonstrance.[3]

The indifference exhibited in 1236 by the Archbishop, and apparently by most of the English prelates, to Grosseteste's protests, accompanied by the fact that appointments of the kind he opposed had long been in vogue, seem to indicate that on that matter he was confronted with a powerful opposition, arising not only from the King's ministers, but from certain ecclesiastical vested interests which were anxious not to be disturbed. His own attitude with respect to the holding of civil appointments by the clergy, as well as to the cognate question of the competence of lay tribunals to try ecclesiastical causes, was doubtless influenced in no small measure by his profound regard for the Canon Law as well as by his conscientious feelings. In endeavouring to enter into the motives which guided him, it is necessary to bear in mind how great was the superiority of the canonical jurisprudence in that day to that which was administered by the civil courts. As Mr. Rashdall observes,[4] " We have to take ourselves back to a state of society in which a judicial trial was a tournament, and the ordeal an approved substitute for evidence, to realise what civilisation

<hr>

[1] Letter 82.

[2] Letter 124.

[3] Letter 126.

[4] Rashdall, i. pp. 140-143.

owes to the Canon Law and the canonists, with their elaborate system of written law, their judicial evidence, and their written procedure." It was in the main, in spite of its defects, one of the greatest among the civilising and humanising influences of the Middle Ages. It would be obviously impossible to discuss here the question how far the *Decretals* of 1234, and similar compilations, were regarded as having a binding force in England. It is manifest, however, apart from such facts as that the canons of the Provincial Council held at Oxford in 1222, and of the General Council of the English Church held in London in 1237, were largely based upon the canons of the Lateran Councils of 1179 and 1215, that the innumerable appeals made to the Roman Curia must have involved the recognition as well as the gradual adoption of the principles of jurisprudence accepted by that appellate tribunal, and also that the Roman jurisdiction must have extended far beyond the mere cognisance of appeals.[1]

In January 1237 Grosseteste's name appears in the list of witnesses to the confirmation of the Great Charter signed by the King on the occasion of the Council or Parliament held at Westminster, and attended by the archbishops, bishops, abbots, priors, earls, barons, citizens, and burgesses.[2] It was at that Council that a tax of one-thirtieth on all movable property, with the exception of houses and beasts of burden, was granted to the King. The Council of the Church, however, which was held in St. Paul's church, London, in November of that year, under the presidency of the Cardinal Legate Otho, was of even greater importance in connection with the march of events. The Legate had reached England towards the end of June at the King's request. As the promise made by Honorius III. in 1221, not to send another legate to England, only applied to the

---

[1] Bracton says that, just as the Pope "in spiritualibus super omnibus habeat ordinariam jurisdictionem," so also "habet rex in regno suo ordinariam in temporalibus, et pares non habet, neque superiores ; et sunt qui sub eis ordinariam habent in multis, sed non

ita meram sicut papa vel rex." Bracton, fol. 412, quoted by Maitland, *Eng. Historical Review*, October 1897, p. 629. See also Pollock and Maitland's *History of English Law*, pp. 94, 105 *sqq.*

[2] *Ann. Monast.* (Tewkesbury), i. p. 103.

lifetime of Stephen Langton, and that great Archbishop had died seven years later, there was no irregularity, as far as Gregory the Ninth was concerned, in Otho's mission; but it is not surprising that, as Matthew Paris relates, serious misgivings should have been aroused by the action of the King in summoning him, in opposition to the desire alleged to have been expressed in a contrary sense by the Archbishop of Canterbury, as well as to the declared wishes of the nobles.[1] The invitation to the Legate, coming as it did a few months after Henry the Third's marriage with Eleanor of Provence, was thought to open the door to yet further encroachments of foreign influence in the internal affairs of England. It is difficult, however, to agree with the view implied in Hook's *Lives of the Archbishops of Canterbury*, and emphasised by Archdeacon Perry, that it would have been possible at that time for Grosseteste to unite with St. Edmund in opposing the Legate's arrival.[2] As a matter of fact, even if St. Edmund actually protested — and Matthew Paris speaks with some doubt on the subject[3] — that protest was not followed up by any definite action. The bishops received Otho with great pomp and costly presents, the King met him at the seaside and paid to him every token of respect, and, when the Council met at St. Paul's, St. Edmund himself, together with the Archbishop of York, headed the procession; and the only question at issue, as far as he was concerned, was not whether he should or should not enter a formal protest against the Legate's presence, but merely whether he or the Archbishop of York should occupy the seat of honour on his right.[4] On the second day, it is true, a deputation arrived from Henry the Third with a formal message, on behalf of the King and his kingdom, prohibiting Otho or the Council from arriving at any determination contrary to the interests of the royal crown and dignity;[5] but no objection was taken at the Council, either

---

[1] *Hist. Maj.* iii. 395.

[2] Hook, vol. iii. ch. iii. ; Perry, pp. 107 *sqq.*

[3] *Hist. Maj.* iii. 395.

[4] *Ibid.* iii. 417.

[5] *Ibid.* iii. 418.

in words or in writing, to the Legate's presence. Indeed, as Matthew Paris, who was strongly averse to the Legate's mission, observes, he had conducted himself with such prudence and moderation, that he had succeeded in calming, to a considerable extent, the angry feelings conceived against him, both by the clergy and by the nobles.[1] It is also evident from the account given by the same historian, that the principal opposition with which Otho was threatened when he went to St. Paul's proceeded from "those who held several benefices, and especially the illegitimates."[2] Even the dignified speech of Walter de Cantelupe, Bishop of Worcester, which has often been praised for its independence, was delivered in the interest of the maintenance of pluralities, one of the abuses which it was sought to rectify. How could Grosseteste have been expected to identify himself with opposition of that sort to proposals which he himself favoured?

Grosseteste's attitude towards the Papacy at that period of his life was doubtless identical with that which he expressed in 1236, in letters addressed to Pope Gregory the Ninth and to Cardinal Egidius,[3] in the former of which he conveys the assurance of his profound devotedness to the Holy See, not only on account of the position assigned to it in the Christian hierarchy, but also by reason of the eminent qualifications of the existing pontiff, whilst in the latter he accentuates his respect for the College of Cardinals. At the same time, he had sufficient strength of character to consider questions on their own merits, and to exercise the right of private judgment, whatever might be his theory as to the nature of the obedience due to the earthly head of the Church. He did not hesitate, for instance, to resist, probably in that same year, the demand of Boetius, the Papal nuncio, accompanied though it was by threats, that he should give to one of his nominees free disposition of the church of Chalgrave, and replied that he feared not the threats of man.[4]

<hr>

[1] *Hist. Maj.* iii. 403 *sqq.*
[2] *Ibid.* iii. 415 *sqq.*
[3] Letters 35, 36.
[4] Letter 18, addressed to John Romanus. See p. 139.

In 1237, however, the main danger to which, in Grosseteste's opinion, the English Church was exposed, a danger to which he recurs again and again in his correspondence, was that which arose from the encroachments of the civil power, and from the confiscatory tendencies which had come to light in the reign of King John, and of which a recrudescence might again be discerned. Its power of resistance was impaired by the existence of internal causes of weakness which required the application of vigorous and stringent reforms. The ostensible, and to a great extent the real object of Otho's visit, was to promote, in harmony with the canons of the Lateran Council, the very reforms of which Grosseteste was the champion. Even if the latter entertained doubts as to the Legate's sincerity as an opponent of abuses, it must have been evident to him that to attack his mission at that juncture would have been to fight on ill-chosen ground and at an unseasonable opportunity. His efforts were concentrated against the enemies of reform within the Church and against its assailants from without. It is not surprising, therefore, that he should have been willing to avail himself of the Legate's assistance for the purpose of overcoming the widespread resistance to the introduction of certain definite and practical remedies which he deemed to be absolutely necessary.[1] It has been suggested that he was short-sighted in failing to perceive that Otho's aims were different from those which were avowedly put forward. It is more probable that he believed that those aims were capable of being rendered subservient to the great work of moral reconstruction which he had inaugurated in his own diocese, and of which he desired to witness the extension throughout the English Church. The main factor in Grosseteste's ecclesiastical career was his steadfast determination to uproot abuses. To secure that end he was willing, on the one hand, to welcome the co-operation of any allies, and on the other, to incur the hostility of any opponents, however

---

[1] On the relation of Grosseteste's *Constitutions* to the canons of the Council of London see p. 132.

powerful. He never swerved, moreover, from his reverence for
the Pope's authority, however vigorous in later years was his
opposition to particular instances of its exercise, as in the case
of the Papal provisions, and however vigorous were his denunciations of the abuses connected with the Curia. Just as he
resisted particular measures taken by the King, without dis-
puting the royal supremacy in matters of State, so he was able,
with an inconsistency which was apparent only, and not real, to
oppose specific measures taken by the Pope without denying
his supremacy in the ecclesiastical domain. In both cases,
however, he introduces an important limitation. Obedience, he
declares, is due to the King as long as he acts rightly,[1] and to
the Pope as long as his commands are in harmony with the
Scriptures.[2] If royal edicts are wrong they cease to be royal,
otherwise there would be a contradiction in terms. If apostolic
precepts are contrary to the teaching of the Apostles and of
Christ, who was Lord over the Apostles, they cease *ipso facto* to
be apostolic. It has been assumed by some that, during the
last few years of Grosseteste's career, a sudden change took
place in his attitude towards the Papacy. The traditional view
thus expressed will be discussed in the proper place.[3] Here it
will be sufficient to say that a careful perusal of his letters indicates that his theory of the Papal authority appears to have
remained absolutely unchanged, and that, as far as his opposition
to particular abuses of that authority was concerned, the ideas
which he expressed with so much vigour in and after 1250 with
respect to the Papal provisions had germinated in his mind
long before that date.[4] Times and seasons, however, required to
be taken into account ; and, in the words which he quotes from
St. Augustine in connection with another matter,[5] as a vindica-
tion of the wisdom of opportunism when no question of principle is at stake, "Cum mane surgit qui nocte quiescebat, vitae

---

[1] Letter 102. See also Letter 124.

[2] Letter 128. See also Letters 119,
35, and 127, p. 364.

[3] See chap. xiv.

[4] See, for instance, Letters 18, 49, 52,
106.

[5] Letter 3.

consilium non mutavit," "A man who rises up in the morning after resting during the night, cannot be said to have been inconsistent."

The belief in the unity of the Church, and in the consequent need for an earthly as well as a divine head, was, indeed, too widely spread and too profound to admit of any essential diversity of view in regard to the theory of the Papal supremacy in spiritual affairs, though it is probable that few defined it or explained it as Grosseteste did ; and, at a time when the civil power was identified, in the case of the Holy Roman Empire, with the cruelties, the eccentricities, and the reputed heterodoxy of Frederick II., and in that of England with the gross mis-government of King John and the combined weakness and rapacity of Henry III., the best minds were naturally impressed with the thought that the remedy for the ills from which the world was suffering was to be found in the exaltation and, at the same time, in the purification of the ecclesiastical system. The great merit of Grosseteste's point of view, as it gradually developed itself in the course of years, was that he clearly perceived that the exaltation of that system could only be justified by its intrinsic superiority, that its purification could only be effected by a determined destruction of abuses, and that neither the one nor the other could be brought about except by broadening the basis of its support, and identifying it with the forces within the nation which made for intellectual enlighten-ment and social progress.

It was not long after the date of the Council of London that an attempt was made upon Grosseteste's life, probably by some miscreant who had been, or expected to be, a victim of the severity of his visitations. Matthew Paris relates[1] that poison was the weapon employed in that, as in several other cases,[2] and that the cure was effected with great difficulty by John de St. Giles. In another passage he says that Roger de Campden was the physician to whose skill he owed his recovery.[3] Prob-

---

[1] *Hist. Maj.* iii. 394 ; v. 705.

[2] See Luard's Introduction to vol. vii. of the *Hist. Maj.* p. 34.

[3] *Hist. Anglorum,* ii. p. 398.

ably, in view of the gravity of his condition, the advice of both was called into requisition.   Grosseteste's constitution, according to his own account, was by no means strong, and he had never completely recovered from the effects of the severe illness from which he had suffered in 1232.[1]   It is permissible to imagine with what solicitude John de St. Giles must have watched over the Bishop's convalescence, and doubtless eased his hours of pain by talking over the numerous subjects of interest they had in common.   Perhaps he related anecdotes of the visit he had paid to Germany, when he accompanied the Princess Isabella to meet the Emperor Frederick at Cologne, and witnessed the Oriental magnificence of the marriage ceremonies at Mainz.[2] Perhaps, too, he had news to communicate to him concerning Friar Jordan of Saxony, with whom Grosseteste had enjoyed pleasant intercourse at Oxford, and with whom he renewed his acquaintance by letter in that very year;[3] and possibly, also, respecting a rising Dominican writer, known in later days as Albertus Magnus, whom John de St. Giles, as a leading member of that Order, and as one who had been connected with the three Universities of Montpellier, Paris, and Oxford, had doubtless visited on the occasion of his stay at Cologne, and to whom he had communicated, in all likelihood, some information as to progress achieved by Grosseteste in the principles of knowledge.

In 1238, however, the Bishop of Lincoln had sufficiently recovered to be able to publish his *Constitutions*, resume his visitations,[4] investigate the wretched condition of Minting priory,[5] and take part in the proceedings which followed the Oxford disturbances of ·that year, when a quarrel which had arisen between some of Cardinal Otho's Roman retainers and a couple of Irish and Welsh clerks, forming part of a deputation of students who had come to pay him a complimentary visit, ended in a general attack being made by the latter upon the

---

[1] See pp. 105, 319.
[2] *Hist. Maj.* iii. 319-327.
[3] Letter 40.

[4] *Ann. Monast.* (Dunstable), iii. 147.
[5] Letter 54.   See also Letter 108.

Papal legate in Osney abbey.   Matthew Paris [1] gives a spirited description of the incidents which led up to the attack, and tells how the Legate, in his panic, "betook himself to the tower of the church, clad in his canonical hood, and secured the door behind him," and how he was ultimately conveyed by dead of night to a place of safety, under the King's protection, by crossing the river on his best horse at a ford not far from the abbey.   Otho, in his resentment, put the University as a whole under an interdict, and excommunicated even the Chancellor, Simon de Boville, Prior of the Dominicans, with the result that the students threatened to leave Oxford in a body.   Several of the ringleaders were imprisoned in Wallingford Castle.   The Archbishop of York and several of the bishops were summoned to London with reference to the matter; but Grosseteste, as Bishop of the diocese in which Oxford was situated, and by virtue not only of his past connection with the University, but also of his existing official relations with that organisation, gave himself most trouble with the object of bringing about a settlement, and adopted an attitude distinctly favourable to the students, and which earned him a plentiful harvest of popularity in after years. He offered mainprise for the imprisoned ringleaders, and used every effort to bring about a reconciliation with the Legate. The latter, according to the *Dunstable Annals*,[2] towards the end of the year forgave the scholars the wrongs they had committed, gave them satisfaction for those they had suffered, and restored them, as though nothing had happened, to the benefices of which they had been deprived, and to the reputation they had forfeited.   To show his determination that the guilty parties on both sides should be punished, Grosseteste excommunicated, in the presence of the King and of the Legate, all, including the Legate's own servants, who had laid violent hands on the clerks.[3] That the offending clerks had been given up to him, and that

---

[1] *Hist. Maj.* iii. 481 *sqq.*   See also the *Annales Monastici*, almost all of which refer to the incident.

[2] *Ann. Monast.* (Dunstable). iii. 147.
[3] *Ibid.* (Tewkesbury, Burton) i. 107, 254.

he afterwards set them free, is clear from several of the monastic Annals.[1] It is strange, however, as Dr. Luard observes,[2] to find among those who owed their release to him the name of Odo de Kilkenny, who subsequently held a brief at the Roman Court for the Dean and Chapter of Lincoln in opposition to the Bishop to whom his liberty was due.

The *Dunstable Annals* give some particulars with respect to the visitation carried out by Grosseteste in 1238 :[3]—" He visited the monasteries, archdeaconries, and deaneries. In each of them he held a general chapter, preached a sermon, and promulgated his *Constitutions.* He suspended many rectors of churches, some of whom he allowed to clear themselves, whilst he bound others to enter into their own recognisances[4] to observe continency in future, on pain of losing their rank and their benefice. At that time we had great difficulty," continues the chronicler, " in obtaining from the Bishop the churches which we held at farm for a triennial period. And in the same year he dedicated many churches and monasteries." The abbey churches which he consecrated in September were those of Ramsey and of Sawtry, and the magnificent pile now known as Peterborough Cathedral.[5] The conscientiousness which he brought to the discharge of

---

[1] *Ann. Monast.* (Burton), i. 254, and (Osney, Wykes) iv. 91.

[2] Introd. to the *Letters*, p. 40 ; Wood, i. p. 90. One of Grosseteste's letters to Otho (Letter 76), on the subject of a certain clerk whom the Bishop had released from a sentence pronounced by the Cardinal, may, perhaps, refer to the Osney incident. Odo de Kilkenny was not the only distinguished Irish canonist in Grosseteste's diocese. William of Drogheda, who died in 1245 (*Hist. Maj.* iv. 423), was rector of Stratton Audley ; Bliss, *Calendar,* i. 214 ; Prof. Maitland's art. on " William of Drogheda and the Universal Ordinary," *Eng. Hist. Review,* October 1897, p. 631.

[3] *Ann. Monast.* (Dunstable), iii. 147.

[4] " Chartas obligatorias recepit."

[5] *Hist. Maj.* iii. 517 ; Letter 63. The editors of the *Cartularium Monasterii de Rameseia,* vol. iii. 180 (Rolls Series, 1893), say that the marginal note to the MS. of Letter 63 makes it apply to Ramsey abbey church, but that it must really relate to St. Ives on account of the coincidence in date, and because no mention of the consecration is contained in the records of the abbey. The former reason, however, is not conclusive ; and the Ramsey records are silent about a good many things relating to the abbey, for instance, about Grosseteste's severe visitation in 1251.—*Hist. Maj.* v. 226. It would be strange if both Matthew Paris and the marginal note were mistaken.

those duties is shown in the letter which he addressed to the Abbot and convent of Ramsey, to the effect that, before their church was consecrated, all furniture, other than fixtures, and all bodies were to be reverently removed, and to be replaced after consecration, as had been done when Archbishop Langton consecrated the conventual church of Holy Trinity in London.[1] Nor was his activity limited to his own diocese. On November 21 he assisted at the consecration of Richard de Wendover, Bishop of Rochester, at St. Gregory's, Canterbury,[2] and doubtless took the opportunity of holding personal intercourse with St. Edmund on the subjects on which he had previously addressed him in writing. It may also be supposed that he made inquiries into the progress of the dispute between the Archbishop and the monks of Christ Church, Canterbury, who formed his capitular body, with the object of gaining experience which might throw light upon the proper course to be pursued in regard to his own Dean and Chapter, with whom he had at that time, on the subject of the right of visitation, a serious misunderstanding which developed, in the following year, into a quarrel of long duration.

The Tewkesbury annalist[3] writes as if Grosseteste's quarrel with the Dean and Chapter of Lincoln dated back to a period almost immediately following his consecration in 1235. Matthew Paris, however,[4] and the chronicler of Dunstable,[5] both of whom were more likely to have correct information on that subject, state that it commenced in 1239. Some of the Bishop's letters, which seem to refer to the early stages of the dispute, appear to be addressed to his correspondents at Rome towards the end of 1238.[6] The dispute, which lasted six years and

---

[1] Letter 63.

[2] *Flores Historiarum*, ed. Luard, ii. pp. 226, 230 ; Wharton's *Anglia Sacra*, i. p. 349.

[3] *Ann. Monast.* (Tewkesbury), i. 97.

[4] *Hist. Maj.* iii. 528.

[5] *Ann. Monast.* (Dunstable), iii. 149.

[6] Letters 64 to 74. Gregory the

Ninth's license to Grosseteste to exercise his office in regard to the visitation of the Chapter of Lincoln, which has not hitherto been visited by himself or by his predecessors, is dated the 23rd of January 1239.—Bliss, *Calendar of the Papal Registers*, i. 178.

underwent many vicissitudes, until it was finally settled by the Pope at Lyons in 1245, excited an extraordinary amount of interest throughout the country, as it was felt that an important principle was at issue, and that the decision, whatever it might be, would create a precedent in other dioceses.   The consequence is that it occupies, in the pages of the chroniclers and of Grosseteste's own correspondence, more space, perhaps, than is strictly commensurate with its importance in relation to his career as a whole.   It involved, however, a considerable expenditure of time, money, and trouble, and interfered with much of the work in which he was engaged.   He found it necessary, on that account, to keep his proctor, S. de Arden, who had gone to Rome probably in 1237,[1] in continuous residence at the Papal court for several years, and to incur other outlays in connection with the question.

In a letter written in 1239,[2] Grosseteste appeals to the Dean and Chapter of Lincoln to explain wherein he has been wrong, instead of appealing to the Pope and indulging in vague denunciations.   He speaks of his weak health, of his paternal affection for them, and trusts that they reciprocate that feeling in filial fashion towards him.   If he can be shown to have committed any wrong against them, he is willing and anxious that it shall be redressed.   The letter breathes a thoroughly conciliatory spirit, which does not appear to have been shared by those to whom it was addressed, if it be true, as Matthew Paris asserts, that some of the canons were in the habit of reproaching their Bishop with the lowliness of his origin, and that, as Grosseteste was informed,[3] they had secretly despatched, as early as Whitsuntide of that year, an agent to Rome for the purpose of obtaining letters against him from certain judges whom he suspected.   Grosseteste's despatch of his own proctor to Rome in 1237 had been originally for the purpose of explaining to the Pope the nature of the reforms required in his

---

vast diocese,[1] and that proctor had remained there with the object of transacting any other business which might be necessary. The series of letters[2] written in 1238 to various correspondents at Rome, including Pope Gregory the Ninth himself, Cardinals Raymund, Egidius, Thomas, and Raynald, John de Ferentino, the Pope's chamberlain, and Ernulf his penitentiary, would also seem to refer to the general mission on which S. de Arden was sent in the first instance, that is, to the question of reforms, rather than to any specific question on which he was at variance with his Chapter. It is probable, however, that he anticipated, even in that correspondence, the resistance which was likely to be offered to his proposed visitation; though it is not clear that the reference in one of those letters[3] to his detractors, relates to the Dean and Chapter, as it may apply either to the abbots and monks who resented his severity, as well as the support he accorded to the friars, or else to the agents of Henry the Third, who were trying to undermine the Bishop's position and influence.

The fullest statement of Grosseteste's contention is contained in an important letter[4] which he addressed shortly afterwards to the Dean and Chapter on the right of a Bishop to visit the Chapter of his cathedral, and, as a necessary consequence, the prebends or churches attached to prebendal stalls, exactly in the same way as other churches. The letter, as is always the case with his longer writings, is full of scriptural quotations and analogies, sometimes far-fetched, but always woven with great skill into the texture of the argument. It is also of interest as an indication of his views on the government and organisation of the Church as a whole. He begins by recalling that Moses, whom he regards, in his administrative capacity, as the type of Christian prelates, in appointing assistants to help in his work, did not give up or diminish his power, but merely delegated it, and even then reserved to himself the most important cases.

---

[1] Letters 37, 64.
[2] Letters 64 to 70.
[3] Letter 66.

[4] Letter 127. See the analysis given by Luard on p. 114 of the Introduction.

The superior power naturally covers and includes the inferior, but the converse proposition does not hold good. Only individual cases are committed to the care of inferior judges, and, if a whole diocese or a whole chapter goes wrong, the duty of correcting what is amiss rests with the presiding prelate, and with him alone. To the prelates, therefore, is reserved the judgment of all cases, both universal and individual, within their cognisance ; but they may delegate to their coadjutors, who share their burden, any portion of their power, without thereby parting with it or impairing it. In the case of a mirror which reflects the sun's rays, the illumination produced is the work of those rays rather than of the mirror—nay, it is wholly their work. The Pope and the Bishops have power which corresponds to that possessed by Moses and his assistant judges. As the Pope is to the whole Church so is each Bishop to his own diocese. They may all take to themselves helpers in their task, who in their turn may delegate their duties to other helpers, and so on through all the various stages and gradations down to the lowest. Even the apparent exceptions serve to prove the rule. The rural deans, for instance, would seem at first sight to depend solely upon the archdeacons, but in reality the latter exercise an authority which they derive from the Bishop. The Cistercian houses, again, are exempt from episcopal visitation, but that is by virtue of a special dispensation granted to them by the Pope, and no such privilege has ever been conferred upon a dean and chapter. If the Pope, as Christ's vicar on earth, cannot diminish, and can only delegate his own powers, precisely the same principle applies to the Bishops, who themselves hold a delegated authority.

A Bishop's authority, moreover, is analogous to that of a father over his children. The father may delegate his power, but cannot part with it ; the law confers upon him a right which he cannot altogether waive, and upon him is imposed a moral obligation from which he cannot be released. Conversely, his children owe to him the filial obedience inculcated in the fifth Commandment, and the same kind of obedience is due to spiritual parents also. A Bishop is also bound to visit all in his diocese by reason of the pastoral character of his office, just as a shepherd has to tend the whole of his flock, and not a part only, and to observe the precept "Feed my sheep." There is, however, a difference between the pastoral methods employed by the clergy and those employed by the Bishop : the former may be described as *visores gregis*, because they have their flocks always before their eyes, whilst the Bishop, who can only view his sheep at intervals, on account of their multitude and the extent of the earth's surface which they cover, is their *visitator*, and has to take care that none of them are omitted from his visitation. The Dean, who always resides where the cathedral is, belongs to the former rather than to the latter category; but even if he could be its *visitator*, instead of its *visor*, that would be no reason why the Bishop should be excluded. The Benedictines and Augustinians are visited by superiors belonging to their respective orders, but the Bishops are not on that account deprived of their right of visitation over them. Even in the Cistercian Order, which is exempt from episcopal jurisdiction, the head of the whole Order is not prevented from visiting monasteries which are already subject to the visitation of the Abbot of their parent house. In the case of the Franciscans, the right of visiting the friars in each wardenship resides not only in the warden, but also in the provincial minister, the visitors appointed in the general chapters, and the minister general himself. In the Dominican Order similar arrangements prevail. It is largely due, he points out, to the fact that the superior visitor is able to supplement and to correct the defects, the want of power, the omission and the negligence of the inferior visitor, that the aforesaid Orders are kept in the continuous fulness of religious observance; and, far from diminishing the sense of responsibility felt by the inferior visitor, the knowledge that his work will be supervised by another has the practical effect of rendering him more zealous and more vigilant in his visitation.

Several other arguments are derived with considerable ingenuity from scriptural injunctions and analogies. Of Moses, for instance, it is written [1] that he "chose able men out of all Israel, and made them heads over the people, rulers of thousands, rulers of hundreds, rulers of fifties, and rulers of tens. And they judged the people at all seasons : the hard causes they brought unto Moses, but every small matter they judged themselves." David, again, defended his father's flock with his own hand against the lion and the bear,[2] and would not have been hindered in so doing by the shepherds under him. Of Samuel's circuit as a judge, it was said [3] that "he went from year to year in circuit to Beth-el, and Gilgal, and Mizpeh, and judged Israel in all those places. And his return was to Ramah ; for there was his house, and there he judged Israel." Why, then, should a Bishop, after visiting the rest of his diocese, be debarred from visiting his own cathedral ?

Grosseteste then proceeds to compare the Bishop, whose pastoral rule is the "art of arts," to an artificer in gold or brass, who ought to be able to know their difference and detect their impurities ; to the head watchman of a vineyard, having under him watchmen whose work he supervises, and whose help he welcomes, and to a physician with assistants for whose efficiency he is responsible. In view of what he deems the overwhelming force of the arguments from Scripture, he considers that neither civil law nor custom should interfere.[4] The fact that previous Bishops have not visited their chapters does not constitute a custom ; for a custom is not created by mere negation, but is a habit (in the Aristotelian sense) produced by a frequent repetition of positive acts, of a character agreeable to or not prohibited by law. Nor can it be said that absence of correction and reformation is liberty. True liberty consists in obedience

---

[1] Exodus xviii. 25.

[2] 1 Samuel xvii. 36.

[3] 1 Samuel vii. 15-17.

[4] Page 420.

to justice and to truth, and in serving Him of whom it was said, "If the Son shall make you free, ye shall be free indeed." To be subject to God, to the divine laws, and to the superior authorities constituted and ordained by God, is not, he maintains, servitude, but freedom. The absence of visitation, moreover, is in itself a positive evil.

In reply to the possible objection that the chapter consisted of persons too great to require visitation, Grosseteste says that the greatest men are always the humblest, and that it is their humility which constitutes their greatness. "Nescit praeesse qui non novit subesse." Even of Christ it was written that He was subject unto His parents. Surely the chapter cannot think themselves free from all need for a physician. "If they say that they have no sin, they deceive themselves, and the truth is not in them." "If we look through the whole of the Scripture," he adds, "we shall find that none have sinned more than priests, and especially chief priests." Even on the supposition that every member of the chapter is most honourable, and has not hitherto stood in the need of visitation, the necessity for prevention as well as for cure has to be considered. It is desirable, also, in the interest of the people themselves, that a Bishop should take a personal share in the work in connection with his cathedral, and that bells should be rung to give notice of his arrival, in order that the people may flock in, some to receive his blessing, others to have their children confirmed, the poor to receive alms, those who have been injured to make their complaint, the afflicted and the oppressed to obtain consolation, and the penitents—especially those who have most need for repentance—to make confession and to receive absolution. The more frequently he returns the better; no day passes on which some useful work cannot be found for him to perform, and he may sometimes succeed where others fail. Finally, Grosseteste reverts to the analogy of a father's rights, duties, and affection, and claims that a Bishop's paternal authority should be viewed in the same light. He is far more to the

Dean and Chapter than the Dean is to the canons. Let them beware of yielding to pride and of incurring its punishment!

Such is a brief summary of the letter in which Grosseteste states his case. Its interest is mainly due to the indication it affords of his views on the government of the Church as a whole, and especially his conception of the episcopal office. It will also be observed that his arguments are grounded throughout on the teaching and precepts of the Scriptures, however forced his illustrations may sometimes appear, and that he regards the Bible as the ultimate appeal in all controversies, just as, in earlier years, he wrote of the *auctoritas irrefragabilis Scripturae*. Some portions of the letter will also recall to the reader of the present day the purport and even the phraseology of modern discussions concerning the nature and inalienability of sovereignty. Other portions will suggest the thought that the dispute was an episode in the struggle between the *jus commune*, or law common to the Church as a whole, and the local *consuetudines*, or special customary observances of particular churches.[1]

The Dean and Chapter, on their part, appear to have taken their stand principally upon the ground that there was no precedent for any actual visitation, and that, moreover, no claim to visit them had been made from the earliest times. They had, it is stated, a court and a judge of their own, called the Dean of Christianity,[2] who decided matters of discipline affecting the parishes dependent upon them; but that can hardly have been considered a valid objection to episcopal visitation. They

---

[1] On the *jus commune* see Prof. Maitland's note on p. 76, part ii. of the *Lincoln Cathedral Statutes*, ed. by Bradshaw and Wordsworth. Also Pollock and Maitland's *Hist. of English Law*, p. 94.

[2] The Dean of Christianity must not, of course, be confused with the cathedral Dean. See Kennett's *Parochial Antiquities*, ii. pp. 341-345. The Dean of Christianity is mentioned in Grosseteste's Letter 84. The term denotes a *decanus foraneus*, a rural or urban dean as the case may be. See Ducange, *s.v.*, and the glossary at the end of Luard's edition of the *Letters*. The statement that the Dean of Christianity at Lincoln was appointed, unlike other rural or urban deans, by the Dean and Chapter, is made by Archdeacon Perry presumably on the authority of local records, which I have been unable, however, to verify.

also expressed the opinion that the Bishop had no power to judge causes or correct offences committed by canons or other persons connected with the cathedral, except by appeal or neglect of the Dean.[1]　In reply to the latter view Grosseteste pointed out the absurdity of the consequences which would follow from its adoption.　He also wrote to the Pope, expressing a hope that he would grant no letters to the Dean and Chapter against him to judges in England, until a special messenger whom he was sending with a statement of his position had arrived at Rome and explained how matters stood.[2]

The Dean and Chapter issued a mandate to the vicars and chaplains ministering in the prebends, and chaplains belonging to the chapter, ordering them to disobey the Bishop if he attempted to visit them.[3]　As they refused to revoke it, Grosseteste suspended the Dean, Precentor, and Sub-dean from entering the cathedral.　The account of what followed is given in a letter[4] which he addressed to his proctor, S. de Arden, for the purpose of giving him full information.　"On the eve of the Nativity of the Blessed Virgin," he writes, that is, on the 7th of September 1239, "I informed the said Dean and Chapter that I intended to visit the Chapter, armed not only with the ordinary authority, but also with that of the Apostolic See,[5] on the Thursday following St. Luke's day (the 18th of October).　I then began almost immediately to visit certain prebends; but all the canons having been summoned by the Dean and Chapter to meet on the day after St. Faith's (7th October) in the chapter-house at Lincoln, and having discussed the proceedings from the cathedral pulpit on the following Sunday,[6] they received publicly from the people permission to appeal to the Pope; and having entered an appeal against the injuries which, according to their own account, I was doing them, the Dean, Precentor,

---

[1] Letter 73.

[2] Letter 77.

[3] Letters 79, 80.

[4] Letter 80.

[5] The fact that he had received the authority from the Pope is also mentioned in Letter 82.　Cp. Bliss, *Calendar of the Papal Registers*, i. p. 178.

[6] That may possibly be the date of the occurrence mentioned on p. 124.

Chancellor, Treasurer, and several canons at once started for
Rome.   They also despatched letters and messengers to all the
cathedral chapters in England, and endeavoured to effect com-
binations against me, and to excite the multitude against me as
if I were a malefactor.   In spite of that, I came to Lincoln
church on the day fixed for holding the visitation of the
Chapter, but found there neither canon nor vicar, nor any of the
ministers of the cathedral, as they all purposely withdrew in
order to avoid meeting me.   I thereupon at once proceeded to
London, as I had been summoned by the Archbishop for the
3rd of November (the day after All Souls' day)[1] with reference
to difficult questions affecting his see.   When the Dean and
those with him heard that I was to be in London on that day,
they waited for me there, in order, as they said, to treat with
me concerning terms of peace, and many of the canons of
Lincoln came together to the meeting held for the purpose."
Grosseteste goes on to say that he was in doubt as to the right
course to pursue.   He might have taken the extreme step of
suspending and excommunicating them at once ; but that would
have aroused a general outcry, and have been unfair to the
older canons, who would thereby have been compelled to
undergo in person the fatigues, difficulties, and even dangers
of the journey to Rome.   On the other hand an important
principle was at stake.   On consideration he determined to
adopt a middle course, and to offer to submit the matter to
arbitration.   But at that stage a serious difficulty arose.   Where
was an impartial arbitrator to be found ?   Who was there who
would run the risk of offending all the capitular bodies in
England ?   "No one occupying a position inferior to that of a
Bishop would decide in favour of visitation, as everybody was
anxious not to be visited.   Few even among the bishops were
likely to pronounce in its favour, as they would probably think

---

[1] The 3rd of November 1239 happens
to have been the date on which the
Archbishop published throughout the
province of Canterbury the sentence of
excommunication he had passed on his
primatial Chapter ; but that may be a
mere coincidence.

that, in that case, they would be bound, on the same principle, to submit to archiepiscopal visitation ; and they hated the idea, as was shown by the dispute then pending between the Archbishop of Canterbury and the Bishop of London. Grosseteste, accordingly, put forward three consecutive proposals. The first was that the question should be referred to the Legate, the second that it should be referred to the Pope. These two proposals having been rejected, he substituted a third, which was accepted, to the effect that the Pope should be asked to appoint three commissioners, namely, Walter de Cantelupe, Bishop of Worcester ; William Scot, Archdeacon of Worcester ; and Alan de Beccles, Archdeacon of Sudbury, who should act as arbitrators ; and that, failing agreement on their part, the Pope should give the final decision, all action being suspended in the meantime. Two clerks were at once despatched to Rome to arrange for the appointment of the three arbitrators, and Grosseteste wrote to his proctor to inform him of the arrangement, and to tell him that he need not trouble himself about the matter, but might devote his attention to other business of a more edifying character affecting the Lincoln diocese.[1] He also wrote to Gregory IX., expressing the hope that he would assent to the proposal, and informed the Legate that, although he had previously been assured of the Pope's support, he had taken the course he had adopted in order to remove all occasion of scandal, and by the advice of many prudent persons.[2] From the *Papal Registers* it appears that the first important step taken by the Pope in regard to the dispute was to send a mandate to the Bishop of Worcester and the Abbot of Evesham, bidding them admonish the Dean and Chapter of Lincoln to obey their Bishop. Failing this they were to hear the case, if the parties were willing, and if not, to remit it to the Pope.[3] A few weeks later a similar mandate empowered the Bishop of Worcester and the Archdeacons of Worcester and Sudbury to decide the

---

[1] Letter 81.
[2] Letter 82.

[3] Bliss, *Calendar of the Papal Registers*, i. 185.

case between Grosseteste and the Dean and Chapter of Lincoln.
Failing consent or agreement the case was to be remitted to
the Pope by proctors within two years.[1] The former mandate
is dated on the 17th of January, and the latter on the 24th of
April 1240 ; but, if allowance be made for the length of time
occupied by the journey to Rome, and other inevitable delays,
they will be found to bear out the statements contained in
Grosseteste's letters written in or soon after November of the
previous year.

Hardly, however, had the Dean and Chapter agreed to
arbitration when they began to regret what they had done.
Matthew Paris, who entirely endorses their point of view, echoes
their dissatisfaction with the stipulation that no action should
be taken by either side pending a final decision; "for as the
Bishop," he writes,[2] "never did visit, he cannot cease who has
never commenced, any more than Diogenes can lose the horns
he never had ; whereas the Dean, by ceasing from his power to
visit, if only for an hour, would be deprived of an actual possession; whence murmurs were multiplied and a great scandal
arose. The canons did not allow the Bishop to enter the
chapter-house, and they regretted extremely that they had put
over themselves a Bishop of so lowly an origin, and this they
publicly expressed in his presence. After much trouble and
heavy expense on both sides an appeal was made to the Pope,
the Chapter appointing as their proctor Odo de Kilkenny," the
Oxford lawyer whose release had been procured by Grosseteste
after the Osney disturbance.[3] It is clear, both from Matthew
Paris's account and from that contained in the *Dunstable Annals*,
that the arbitration came to nothing, and that, under the terms
of the agreement, the question was referred to the Curia.[4] From
a letter written by Innocent IV. in December 1243, it appears
that, at some time before that date, the three arbitrators had

---

[1] Bliss, *Calendar of the Papal Registers*, i. 189.

[2] *Hist. Maj.* iii. 528, 529.

[3] See p. 185.

[4] *Ann. Monast.* (Dunstable), iii. 149, 160.

decided in Grosseteste's favour, and that the Dean and Chapter had appealed from them to the Pope.[1] The Priors of Ely and of Wartre, in the diocese of York, and the Archdeacon of Rochester, are there instructed to relax the sentences against the Chapter, and to fix a term of three months for appearance at Rome in the event of the Bishop renouncing the process since the appeal ; whilst, if he declines to renounce it, they are to proceed in accordance with the form sent to them.

It is evident, however, that recourse was had at one time—though the date is not clear—to a second arbitration, the arbitrators being Hugh de Northwold, Bishop of Ely, his official, Richard de Kirkham, and others whose names are not mentioned.[2] At one moment Grosseteste complains of the underhand intrigues which are being carried on against Richard de Kirkham by persons who are acting in the interest of the canons, and holds them responsible, " facitis enim illud fieri permittendo." [3] At one time the Chapter took what must have appeared the extraordinary step of obtaining from the King a prohibition forbidding the Bishop's judges from proceeding in any matter between himself and his capitular body.[4] Grosseteste thereupon wrote to remind them of the excommunications pronounced by the Council of Oxford in 1222 against " those who maliciously seek to break through or disturb the liberties of the Church," and points out that the question is one which can only be settled by an ecclesiastical, and not by a secular tribunal.[5] Before that incident—whatever the precise date may have been—the suspension of the Dean, William de Tournay, had become a deprivation, and he had been succeeded by one of Grosseteste's most intimate friends, Roger de Weseham, Archdeacon of Oxford, an East Anglian like himself, and one who had been his successor, with one interval, as lecturer to the Franciscans.[6] In

---

[1] Bliss, *Calendar of the Papal Registers*, i. p. 203.

[2] Letters 90, 96, 97.

[3] Letter 90.

[4] Probably in 1241-42. Addit. MSS. (British Museum), 21, 132, fol. 15.

[5] Letters 91, 92.

[6] Luard (Introd. to the *Letters*, p. 46, note) says that he has been unable to ascertain the date of Roger de Wese-

view of the fact that the election of the Dean was supposed to
rest with the Chapter, it is not clear how Roger de Weseham
was selected, in view of his close connection with the Bishop.
Possibly Pegge's hypothesis may be correct, that the Chapter refused to take part in the election, as they did not wish to acquiesce
in Dean Tournay's deprivation, and consequently that their
abstention " would produce a devolution to the Bishop, who
collated his friend and had him immediately installed." [1] If
that supposition be correct, it is difficult to understand on what
grounds Archdeacon Perry denounces Grosseteste's action as " an
arbitrary stretch of his authority." [2] It is doubtful also whether
the Chapter went so far as to excommunicate the newly-appointed
Dean,[3] though it is clear from a letter of Innocent IV., dated
November 1243, that the relations between Roger de Weseham
and the Chapter had at one time been strained, and that he had
endeavoured to effect an adjustment of the dispute without
previously obtaining from them procuratorial letters authorising
him to act on their behalf, with the result that they repudiated
his mediation. The Precentor, Chancellor, and Treasurer had
concurred in his effort, and had consequently shared the blame
imputed to him by the Chapter. Innocent IV. recalls
the fact that the dispute had been committed by his predecessor, Gregory IX., to the decision of the Bishop of

ham's appointment to the Deanery of
Lincoln. The date 1237 given in the
list quoted in Dugdale's *Monasticon*,
vol. vi. part iii. p. 1278, is obviously
a mistake ; 1240 may be regarded as
the probable date, though there is no
certainty about the matter. From
Addit. Charter 10, 639, which I have
consulted at the British Museum, it
is evident that Roger de Weseham
was still Archdeacon of Oxford in
1239.

[1] Pegge's *Grosseteste*, pp. 85, 86 ;
Pegge's *Wesham*, pp. 8, 9. Leland
says, " Capitonis beneficio ût Decanus
Lindianae ecclesiae."

[2] P. 127.

[3] Letter 94. " Injuste decanum nostrum in nullo vobis subjectum excom-
municare non erubuistis." As the letter
is addressed to the Dean and Chapter,
the words " decanum nostrum " can
hardly refer to Roger de Weseham.
There is no reference to any excommunication of the Dean in contemporary writers. If it does not relate to
a rural or an urban dean, it is possible
that the word " decanum " may have
been substituted by a transcriber for
" archidiaconum." It is by no means
unlikely that Thomas Wallensis, Archdeacon of Lincoln, and Grosseteste's
right-hand man, incurred the indignation of the Chapter.

Worcester and others, and implies that there should be no
interference with the course of procedure already arranged, but
recognises that the Dean and those who acted with him did
so not in malice, but in simplicity, and therefore rehabilitates
them.[1]

In spite of the obscurity of the dates it is manifest that, for
six years, from 1239 to 1245, the dispute dragged its weary
length, until it was finally settled at Lyons in Grosseteste's
favour. It will be necessary, at a later stage, to explain how
that settlement was effected in the last resort. Here it will be
sufficient to refer to two intervening incidents. In 1241 the
canons "were compelled" in Matthew Paris's quaint phrase,[2]
"to defend themselves" by exhibiting a document, purporting
to be authentic, which related how, in the reign of William
Rufus, a settlement had been made, under the authority of two
cardinal legates, eight archbishops, and sixteen bishops, by
virtue of which the Dean of Lincoln was to have disciplinary
powers over the canons, whilst, if he failed in his task, he might
call in the Bishop and after him the King. The document is a
tissue of palpable absurdities, and is a manifest forgery, which
does not throw a favourable light either on the conscientiousness of the Lincoln canons, or on their historic sense and
knowledge.[3] How, for instance, would it have been possible
for William Rufus to summon two legates and eight archbishops? Although the substance of the document, however,
does not require serious attention, it served its purpose for the
time being in complicating the issue, and in furnishing the
King with a pretext for being a party to the suit.[4] In 1242,
again, we are informed by the Dunstable annalist that Grosseteste was prevented by the Chapter from personally visiting the
prebends. It is not surprising to find that, on more than one

---

[1] Bliss, *Calendar of the Papal Regis-*
ters, i. 202.

[2] *Hist. Maj.* iv. 154-156.

[3] Pegge refutes it. Appendix 13.
Luard says (Introd. to the *Letters*, p.
51): "It gives a melancholy view of
the virulence of Matthew Paris's party
spirit that he could even pretend to
treat this document as genuine."

[4] See before, p. 198.

occasion, friends interposed with the object of bringing the quarrel to a close. The Dean and Chapter of Salisbury, with whom Grosseteste had formerly had relations as Rector of Calne and Archdeacon of Wilts, wrote to him in that sense. His reply was that he ardently desired peace, but that it must be a real, and not a sham peace.[1] Adam Marsh, too, conveys to him the deep regret with which many view the prolongation of the struggle.[2] It is pleasant to reflect that, after the settlement of 1245, to be described in a later page, complete peace and harmony prevailed between Grosseteste and his Dean and Chapter during the remainder of his life.

[1] Letter 93.

[2] *Mon. Francisc.* p. 146, " Aegre ferunt nonnulli, nec immerito, tam horrendam inter vos et subditos vestros dissensionem. Scitis quia distinguit divina praeceptio dominos ut multo amplius studeant a suis amari quam timeri ; et intelligant ecclesiasticae personae se plus patres pauperum quam principes populorum." The argument was one calculated to appeal to Grosseteste, who had apparently rejected a compromise previously suggested by Adam Marsh. It must be noted, however, that Grosseteste's letters to his Chapter are distinctly conciliatory.

CHAPTER IX

GROSSETESTE'S episcopal career was, indeed, one of "Sturm und Drang." During the six years which elapsed between the time when the dispute with the Dean and Chapter reached its height in 1239, until its settlement in 1245, Grosseteste found ample scope for his many-sided activity within his diocese. His visitations were carried on with strenuous vigour, and organised on a systematic footing. He was indefatigable in his attempts to raise the moral tone and to improve the efficiency of the clergy, in the encouragement he gave to the friars, and in the pertinacity with which he endeavoured to induce the monks to adhere more strictly to their rules, and at the same time to increase their usefulness, and to make satisfactory financial arrangements in respect of vicarages. The sphere of his interests, however, was by no means confined to his own diocese. Day by day it became broader and wider, and extended to the affairs of the Church and the nation as a whole, and even to the great struggle then in progress between the Pope and the Emperor.

The position occupied by Grosseteste, even in the early years of his episcopate, may be inferred from the fact that it was to him, as well as to the Archbishops of Canterbury and of York, that the Pope addressed in April 1238 letters requesting them and him to urge Richard, Earl of Cornwall, the King's brother, not to leave England at that juncture for the Holy Land, but also to ensure that, if he resolved upon that course, he should have full protection.[1] It was to the same three prelates that Gregory IX. wrote in November of the following year, asking them to secure that the Earl of Cornwall and his son Henry should not be molested, and also that the provisions of the former's will should be duly observed in the event of his death.[2] In September 1238 Grosseteste acted, in conjunction with the Archdeacon of Northampton and the Chancellor of St. Paul's, London, as arbitrator in regard to the disputed election to the See of Durham. He was empowered to annul the election of the Prior of Durham to that bishopric, if within two months Henry III. could prove the charges of simony and of hostility to the King which he had brought against the Prior, or if on examination he found the election to have been uncanonical. If, however, it was canonical, he and his coadjutors were to order the Archbishop of York to consecrate the Bishop-elect.[3] When St. Edmund desired to establish colleges of secular canons in certain of the churches of his diocese, which of right belonged to him, it was to the Bishops of Lincoln and of Norwich that a Papal mandate was sent requiring them to protect the Archbishop against molestation on account of the faculty which had been granted to him.[4] And in January 1239 the names of the Archbishop and of Grosseteste are coupled together in connection with certain proceedings which they were asked to take in connection with the diocese of Winchester.[5] With two Archbishops like St. Edmund and John de Gray, the former of whom, though of saintly life, was lacking in tenacity of purpose, while the latter was of feeble health and of undecided personality, Grosseteste was rapidly attaining, by reason of his great abilities and strength of character, to the position of virtual, though not nominal, head of the English Church, which he held during the

---

[1] Bliss, *Calendar of the Papal Registers*, i. 170. Cp. *Hist. Maj.* iii. 617.

[2] Bliss, *Calendar*, i. pp. 184, 185.

[3] *Ibid.* i. p. 176.

[4] *Ibid.* i. p. 189 (May 1240).

[5] *Ibid.* i. 179.

vacancy in the See of Canterbury created by St. Edmund's retirement in 1240, and retained in public estimation even after the consecration of Boniface in 1245.

It was owing to the exigencies of the great struggle with the Emperor that Gregory the Ninth adopted, in 1240, a measure which produced a strong feeling of irritation in England, and greatly increased his unpopularity. Frederick the Second was approaching Rome, and the Roman citizens were disposed to take his side. In order to retain their allegiance the Pope resorted, according to Matthew Paris,[1] to the plan of conferring upon as many of their friends and relatives as possible the emoluments derived from benefices situated in England, and despatched letters to St. Edmund, to Grosseteste, and to Robert de Bingham, Bishop of Salisbury, calling upon them to provide three hundred Romans with the first benefices which should become vacant, and prohibiting them from giving away any benefices until his requirements in that respect were satisfied. St. Edmund, who was wearied out by the protracted struggle with the Canterbury Chapter, and who had neither the perseverance nor the determination which enabled Grosseteste to carry his dispute with the Lincoln Chapter to a successful issue, was filled with despair at the sight of the troubles which afflicted the English Church, sailed from these shores, retired to the monastery of Pontigny, where St. Thomas Becket had dwelt in his exile, and died shortly afterwards at Soissy, receiving, after a remarkably brief interval, the meed of canonisation.[2] It is worthy of note that the two prelates who were ordered, not quite four years later, at the request of the monks of Pontigny, to inquire concerning St. Edmund's virtues and miracles, and to send the depositions of witnesses under seal to the Pope, were the Bishops of London and of Lincoln, Fulk Basset and Grosseteste, both of whom had been brought in contact with Edmund Rich in his Wiltshire days,[3] while the latter was also intimate with him at Oxford.

---

[1] *Hist. Maj.* iv. 31.

[2] January 24, 1244. Bliss, *Cal-endar*, i. 208. He died on the 16th

of November 1240.

[3] *Charters and Documents relating to Salisbury*, ed. by Jones and Mac-

It is not known what course was taken by Grosseteste himself on the receipt of the Papal letters in 1240. He had, however, previously obtained from the Pope a privilege by which he was exempted from providing for any one at his command, unless special mention was made of that privilege ;[1] and he therefore enjoyed a protection which stood him in good stead on at least one occasion,[2] and which probably enabled him to look with comparative equanimity on the message he had received. From a purely financial point of view it was clearly to the Pope's advantage that an increased number of alien holders of English benefices should be appointed, as it was easier to obtain subsidies from them ; six years later, for example, when Innocent IV. asked for one-third only from the resident clergy, he demanded one-half from those who did not belong to that category, and most of whom were Italians, whilst at the same time the exaction might be plausibly represented as a fine for non-residence.[3]

With regard, however, to the contribution of one-fifth which was demanded in 1240 by the Legate from the bishops, abbots, and rectors of churches, in order to assist the Pope in his struggle with the Emperor,[4] Grosseteste's attitude may, perhaps, be inferred from the resolutions passed by a meeting of bishops held at Northampton, in his diocese, in the presence of Cardinal Otho. "There," says Matthew Paris, "the bishops, being un-willing in a stiff-necked manner impudently to refuse their consent to the aforesaid exactions, preferred to oppose them in a moderate and cautious manner," and gave as reasons why they ought not to contribute, that the object was to " shed Christian

ray (Rolls Series, 1891), pp. 111-113. St. Edmund was rector of Calne after Grosseteste, who was also Archdeacon of Wilts. Fulk Basset was rector of Winterburn Basset, and had a dispute with Grosseteste respecting the tithes of Berwick Basset.

[1] Bliss, *Calendar*, i. 178 (Jan. 26, 1239).

[2] In the case of the Thame prebend, see p. 208, *Hist. Maj.* iv. 152.

[3] *Hist. Maj.* iv. 550. From Bliss, *Calendar*, i. 235, it appears, however, that Italian clerks in England were to give only one-fourth of their income if the value of their benefices amounted to 100 marks or less, and half their income if the value was greater (1247).

[4] *Hist. Maj.* iv. 10, 11. 38-43.

blood," and to conduct a crusade against one who was the King's brother-in-law and ally; that when the clergy had granted a tenth to the Pope in 1229, they had expressly protested against similar demands being made thereafter; that the country was impoverished by the King's requirements, and by the departure of many of the nobles for the Holy Land; and that it would be desirable to wait until a General Council had the opportunity of considering the matter.[1] Similar arguments, but couched in stronger language and developed at greater length, were addressed to the Legate by the rectors of Berkshire.[2] The King, in spite of his connection with Frederick the Second, appears to have supported the Legate, as is shown by his threat to imprison the Abbots of Bury St. Edmunds and Beaulieu, who objected to the exaction.[3] Matthew Paris adds that several of the bishops, whose names he does not mention, and also Alan de Beccles, were subsequently persuaded by the Legate of the desirability of the contribution.[4] As he states, however, elsewhere [5] that Alan de Beccles died in that year before the demand was actually put forward, the statement is obviously open to doubt. The fact that the Peterborough monks, upon whom a demand for a revenue of a hundred marks was made in 1241 on behalf of Gregory the Ninth, appealed through their Abbot to Henry III. and not to Grosseteste, their diocesan, was due probably to the consideration that the King was their founder and patron.[6] The Abbot, however, Walter of Edmundsbury, suffered a few years later for the independence of his attitude, as he was treated with great contumely at the Council of Lyons in 1245, and died of a broken heart.[7]

Whatever may have been Grosseteste's position with regard

---

[1] *Hist. Maj.* iv. 37.

[2] *Ibid.* iv. 39 *sqq.*

[3] *Ibid.* iv. 36.

[4] *Ibid.* iv. 43.

[5] *Hist. Anglorum,* ii. 432.

[6] *Hist. Maj.* iv. 102. In 1238 Grosseteste had been obliged to take strong measures to induce the Abbot and convent of Peterborough to provide for a certain clerk H., but that can hardly have affected their attitude in 1241. Bliss, *Calendar,* i. 168. It will be remembered that Letter 57, mentioned on p. 165, was, according to Luard, addressed to them.

[7] *Hist. Maj.* iv. 414.

to the demand for the fifth, the fearlessness by which his conduct was marked may be illustrated by some correspondence which passed, probably about the same time, between him and the Legate with reference to the collation, by the latter, of a certain Atto, or Acton, one of his clerks, to a Lincoln prebend, and also to a request that the Bishop should admit Thomas, son of Earl Ferrers, to the church of Randes in Lincolnshire, though he was under age and not yet in orders. In the former case, whilst admitting the Legate's right, Grosseteste urges strong reasons against the course proposed, and requests that the collation may be revoked; in the other, he declares that his conscience will not allow him to do what he is asked, and shows the impropriety of the act, adding that, if the Legate persists, the responsibility must rest on his shoulders, and even then a vicarage must be established with sufficient funds to secure the maintenance of a resident vicar.[1] Archdeacon Perry blames Grosseteste for not having given a decidedly negative reply in those two instances,[2] but it is manifest that the letters represent a polite way of saying No. In both instances the Bishop seems to have gained his point. As Pegge observes,[3] the name of Acton does not appear among the prebendaries of Lincoln, and Rand remains a rectory to this day, whereas, if the son of Earl Ferrers had been appointed, it would have been necessary, in accordance with Grosseteste's stipulation, to create a vicarage. Neither did he hesitate to summon before him William, Earl of Warren, for causing his chaplain to celebrate mass in his hall at Grantham, an unconsecrated place and in other respects unfit.[4]

It was also in 1240 that, according to the brief statement of

---

[1] Letters 49, 74, 52. The date of those letters is not quite clear. Luard thinks that the last two may have been written in 1239. The only certainty with regard to the period to which they belong is that they must have been written before Otho's departure in 1241. Letter 49, on the other hand, probably dates back to 1238, soon after his arrival.

[2] Page 110.

[3] Pp. 76, 77.

[4] Letter 56. It must have been written before the 27th of May 1240, the date of the Earl's death.—*Hist. Maj.* iv. 12.

the *Dunstable Annals*,[1] Grosseteste "honourably recovered the prebend of Thame, which John Mansel had occupied with the King's connivance." From the fuller account given by Matthew Paris, it appears that John Mansel, one of the King's clerks, was put in possession of the church at Thame, attached to a Lincoln prebend called by that designation, through the King's favour and by virtue of a Papal provision, in spite of the fact that Grosseteste had already appointed Simon of London, penitentiary to the Bishop of Durham.[2] When Grosseteste heard what had happened he was much annoyed, and at once sent word to Henry the Third, who was then in Wales, by William, Archdeacon of Huntingdon, and by John de Basingstoke, Archdeacon of Leicester, "to admonish him, out of gratitude for the unexpected victory granted to him over the Welsh, forthwith to make amends for his transgression, lest perchance God, in His anger, should convert his smiles into tears." The King replied that the matter was *sub judice*, as an appeal had been lodged, and that, moreover, he had acted in accordance with the Pope's authority. Thereupon one of the archdeacons, presumably John de Basingstoke, answered: "My Lord King, our master the Bishop of Lincoln holds a privilege granted to him by the Pope,[3] by which he is exempted from providing for any one at the command of the Apostolic See, unless special mention is made of that privilege; but in this Papal mandate, which the said John Mansel has obtained, and by dint of which he has forcibly thrust himself into this church, relying on your assistance, no mention is made of that privilege; wherefore the Bishop of Lincoln is not bound to reply to him in this case, particularly with respect to the giving away of the church at Thame, which he had previously, and with justice, given to another. And, even if he had no such privilege, it is absurd for any one to push himself into the possession of any church without consultation with, not to say

---

[1] *Ann. Monast.* (Dunstable), iii. 158.
[2] *Hist. Maj.* iv. 152, 153.
[3] See above, p. 205. Bliss, *Calendar*, i. 178.

against the will of the diocesan Bishop, even if he rely upon the Papal authority, inasmuch as the Pope wishes all things to be done in order." The Archdeacons then proceed to suggest, on Grosseteste's behalf, that he would be prepared, in view of John Mansel's circumspection and the sufficiency of his learning, to bestow upon him a better living, but that, if he persisted in remaining at Thame, he would be excommunicated. Henry the Third, leaving a German named Waleran in charge of the military defences in Wales, went shortly afterwards to London, and there was met by Grosseteste, "who had come fully prepared to pronounce anathemas on the disturbers of the Church in general, and on John Mansel in particular." The latter, however, justified his reputation for circumspection by resigning the prebend,[1] and was rewarded by the King with the living of Maidstone, to which Howden was afterwards added. In later years John Mansel played a prominent part on Henry's side during the civil war. Grosseteste, on the other hand, being thus pacified, complied with the King's request that he should preach a sermon in public, "as one in whose breast were stored the keys of knowledge, and commended the humility of both parties, amongst other things making a comparison between the rays of the sun, which are straight, and the King's justice, which ought to be straight."[2] Matthew Paris adds that Henry, seeing that Grosseteste was in a conciliatory frame of mind, took the opportunity of helping to settle a dispute of long standing between him and the abbey of Westminster respecting the church at Ashwell, or Heswell, with the result that the church in question fell into the possession of the Abbot of Westminster, whilst the right of presentation to the newly established vicarage was reserved to the Bishop of Lincoln.[3]

---

[1] Cp. Adam Marsh's letter to R. de Gravesend, Dean of Lincoln, written some months after Grosseteste's death. —*Mon. Franciscana*, pp. 185, 186.

[2] *Hist. Maj.* iv. 154.

[3] *Ibid.* iv. 151, 154. For the early stages of the dispute see Bliss, *Calendar of the Papal Registers*, i. 181 (April 1239). Grosseteste had, it appears, excommunicated at that time the Abbot of Westminster, and laid Ashwell church under an interdict.

The Thame incident is of importance in Grosseteste's life, partly because on that occasion he was obliged to take a decided line against the action both of the King and of the Pope, and partly because he was thereby brought, contrary to expectation, into personal and, to some extent, friendly intercourse with Henry the Third. His previous communications with that sovereign had been of a formal, and sometimes of a strained character. In 1236, for instance, a few months after his receipt of the customary present of bucks from the King,[1] he had, in what was apparently the first letter he wrote to him after his consecration as Bishop, made application for the release from prison of Richard Syward, the friend and ally of Hubert de Burgh and of Richard Marshall, on the ground that, having taken the Crusaders' vows, he was entitled to be released,[2] and that, even if that privilege were not recognised, there was a case for the royal clemency. He had also witnessed the confirmation of the chapters in 1237, and had repeatedly resisted, as has been seen, the King's attempted encroachments and his infringements of the rights of the Church. Nor can Grosseteste's intimacy with Richard Marshall, Earl of Pembroke, previous to his death in 1234, and with Simon de Montfort, who, although he had married Henry's sister, was now in disgrace, and had left England in 1240 for two years in order to take part in the Crusade, have been calculated to increase the Bishop's popularity with the King. Yet the latter appears to have accepted rebukes in no unbecoming spirit. Although rapacious for subsidies, which he spent as soon as they were within his grasp, and incapable of good government, he was of a mild disposition in private life, and his somewhat ostentatious piety saved him, on more than one occasion, from pushing matters to extremities in his struggle with the ecclesiastical powers.

The Priors of Rochester and of St. Augustine's, Canterbury, and the Archdeacon of Rochester, to whom the matter was referred, decided against Grosseteste.   [1] See p. 114.

[2] The question of the exemptions to be accorded to Crusaders was frequently discussed. See the Decretal of Innocent IV., dated August 3, 1245, given in the *Hist. Maj.* iv. 521.

> Vedete il re della semplice vita
> Seder là solo, Arrigo d' Inghilterra :
> Questi ha ne' rami suoi migliore uscita.[1]

Grosseteste might warn him in 1236 to beware of the example of Uzziah, and in 1243 to beware of that of Uzzah ; he might offer strenuous resistance to his attempts to use bribery and intimidation in ecclesiastical elections, especially in that to the bishopric of Hereford in 1240 ;[2] he might denounce at every turn his action in connection with the Winchester election, to which reference will be made later on ;[3]—in spite of all these denunciations, and notwithstanding his attitude of almost constant opposition, Grosseteste was able, during the remainder of his life, to preserve amicable relations, as far as private intercourse was concerned, with the King. At the same time he did not respond with much alacrity to Henry's advances when they appeared to be intended to diminish in any degree his independence. In one letter,[4] for example, written probably in 1242, he begins by thanking the King for the news he has given of himself, as well as of his Queen and family, and also for his inquiries after the writer's health. In reply, however, to Henry's complaint that Grosseteste rather neglected him and did not visit him in person, the Bishop refers to their relative positions, the King's prosperity, his own weak health, and the urgent character of his ecclesiastical work. About the same time Walter de Cantelupe, Bishop of Worcester, consulted Grosseteste as to the advisability of his accepting an invitation from Henry III. to accompany him abroad at the royal expense. Grosseteste replies[5] that his correspondent must necessarily be guided by the consideration of what is best for his flock in his own diocese, but promises to discuss the matter with Adam Marsh, if Walter de Cantelupe will give him his views on both sides of the question. The letter thus throws light on Grosseteste's own motives for not frequenting the court,

---

[1] Dante, *Purgatorio*, vii. 130.   [2] Letter 83.
[3] See p. 214.   [4] Letter 101.   [5] Letter 99.   ·

and also shows incidentally how his advice was sought and valued.

It is probable that the tact and judgment exhibited by Queen Eleanor, and also Grosseteste's friendship with the King's sister, the wife of Simon de Montfort, Earl of Leicester, helped to smooth over some of the difficulties which the Bishop encountered in his intercourse with the King. The character of the Queen appears in a highly favourable light in the correspondence both of Grosseteste and of Adam Marsh. When the appointment of her uncle, Boniface of Savoy, as Archbishop of Canterbury, was confirmed in 1243, Grosseteste wrote to him, asking him to induce the Queen, his niece, to intercede with the King for the purpose of preventing his entry into England from being disturbed by the discords he was fomenting in connection with the election to the bishopric of Winchester.[1] "Happy is the man," writes Grosseteste, "who has a good wife, as Wisdom testifies. He is often saved by her circumspection, and his heart is turned to a better purpose by her gentle and wholesome persuasiveness." He also wrote to the Queen herself the following letter full of good advice :[2]—

"It is written in the book of Wisdom, that 'as is the rising sun to the world, so is a good woman to her household.' The rising sun, that is to say, frees the world from the horror of darkness, brings in the pleasant and joyous light of the day, substitutes for the dangers and terrors of the night security and peace, and imparts, by the operation of natural forces, comfort, sustenance, life, light, and warmth to every plant, and to every creature on this earth. Even so should your kindness, goodness, and virtue introduce into your household, which consists in a special sense of the Church and kingdom of England, the brightness and the charm which the morning rays of the sun bestow upon the world. You may dispel the horrors of error

---

[1] Letter 86.

[2] Letter 103. From Bliss, *Calendar of the Papal Registers*, i. p. 209, it appears that in 1241 the Queen was placed, for certain purposes, under the special protection of the Archbishop of Canterbury and of Grosseteste.

by suggesting what is true, by favouring the cause of that peace and that tranquillity of which all stand in need in Church and State, and by affording to both of them, with all prudence, comfort, sustenance, life, light, and warmth.   For reasons which would be too long for me to explain, but which the bearer of this letter, a dear friend and clerk of mine, will lay before you if you are minded to hear him, the whole of the clergy and people of England have been plunged during these years in the darkness and terrors of a long and troubled night.   Now is the time, and here the place, for your bright presence to exhibit its usefulness, by persuading the King, if he is open to persuasion, to remove the new causes of disturbance which has arisen, a fitting task for his regal Majesty, and not to allow the recrudescence of other such causes ; but rather let him sit in the seat of judgment, as is written concerning the good King, and dissipate all that is evil by his glance ; and if he succeeds in so doing through your inspiration, yours will be the credit and yours, in truth, the act.   Following, therefore, the example of Esther, that excellent, holy, and prudent Queen, who freed her people from the sentence of death passed upon them by the King's decree, may you strive by instant influence with the King to set the people and the priesthood of this realm of England free from the unprecedented difficulties and dangers with which they are confronted.   I pray that your Majesty may ever fare well in the Lord."

In a letter written a few years later, Adam Marsh expresses his gratification that the Queen's good will to Grosseteste has opened the way to greater activity in the interests of the Church ;[1] and on another occasion he conveys to the Bishop of Lincoln an assurance that his confidence in the Queen's wisdom, diligence, and constancy has not been misplaced, and that she shows her sense of responsibility in scrutinising zealously the qualifications of those whom the King desires to present to benefices within his gift.[2]   It is evident, therefore, from that correspondence, as well as from various incidents which occurred in later years,

---

[1] *Mon. Francisc.* p. 102.   [2] *Ibid.* p. 116.

such as that in connection with the presentation to the church of Flamstead,[1] that Grosseteste's influence was not exerted in vain. Her want of popularity, to which Matthew Paris sometimes gives expression,[2] was doubtless due, in the main, to the action of her relatives rather than to her own.

The establishment of more friendly personal relations with the King was all the more desirable owing to the fact that, during the period now under review, Grosseteste was obliged to take a line of action opposed to his in connection with the elections to no fewer than three bishoprics—those of Hereford, Winchester, and Chichester, as well as, to some slight extent, that of Durham. In the case of Hereford, he had written to St. Edmund in 1240,[3] protesting against the possibility of bribery and intimidation on the part of royal agents, and insisting upon the urgent necessity for preserving the liberties granted to the Church by the Great Charter. In the case of the See of Winchester, which had become vacant as early as 1238, through the death of Peter des Roches, Grosseteste had addressed in that year two letters,[4] one of which was rather sharply worded, to Cardinal Otho, emphasising the importance of securing that a fit person should be chosen, and that the Chapter should enjoy perfect freedom of choice, and pointing to the fact that the King had been staying near that city, and had endeavoured by promises and threats to force the convent to elect his nominee, who was William of Provence, another uncle of the Queen, already elect of Valence. The Chapter began by electing Ralph Neville, Bishop of Chichester, but the election was, at the King's instance, disapproved by the Pope, and Grosseteste, when asked by Ralph Neville to use his influence on his behalf, replied[5] that the matter had better be left in the hands of Providence. After an interval the Chapter elected William de Raleigh, who, as Treasurer of Exeter and afterwards Bishop of

---

[1] With reference to that subject see *post*, p. 302. *Hist. Maj.* v. 209.

[2] *Hist. Maj.* iv. 510.

[3] Letter 83.

[4] Letters 60, 61.

[5] Letter 62.

Norwich, had always been on friendly terms with Grosseteste. In spite of the King's persistent opposition, the monks who formed the Chapter adhered to their choice, and in September 1243 William de Raleigh obtained the Papal confirmation.[1] Henry the Third, in his indignation, ordered the gates of Winchester to be closed, and the Bishop-elect to be denied admittance, and used other means of persecution, even cutting off the supply of provisions sent to him from Norwich by sea and land, after his arrival at Southwark, and prohibiting any one in the city of London from selling him even the neces- saries of life.[2]   Grosseteste thereupon, accompanied by Walter de Cantelupe, Bishop of Worcester, and Peter d'Aiguesblanche, Bishop of Hereford, hastened to Reading in order to rebuke the King.   The latter, informed of their coming, "took to flight, declining their salutary admonitions."   When at last they found him he broke into words of excuse and of hatred, and despatched to the Roman court messengers bearing a large sum of money, one of whom, however, instead of going to Rome, went to his home at Susa with the treasure, and, says Matthew Paris, "after the example of the raven which did not return to the ark, did not reappear in England."[3]   Grosseteste and the Bishops of Worcester and Hereford followed Henry to Westminster, rebuked him for his tyranny, and even threatened to lay his private chapel under an interdict.   The King, however, asked them to wait until he received news from Rome.   The three Bishops consented to the delay, and William de Raleigh, in despair, sailed secretly from the port of London, landed at St. Valery, and took refuge at Abbeville, where Louis IX. offered him protection.[4]   The French compared his sufferings with the treatment accorded, in different reigns, to St. Anselm, St. Thomas Becket, and St. Edmund.   The new Archbishop of Canterbury, Boniface, who was about to come over to England, and to whom Grosseteste wrote shortly afterwards on the subject,[5] perceived

---

[1] *Hist. Maj.* iv. 259.   [2] *Ibid.* iv. 285, 286.
[3] *Ibid.* iv. 286.   [4] *Ibid.* iv. 295.   [5] Letter 86.

the unpopularity Henry the Third was incurring through his obstinacy, and brought pressure to bear upon him. The Pope wrote in a similar sense, and at last the King gave way, and allowed William de Raleigh to enjoy his bishopric. The final reconciliation between them was effected a few years later, when Henry kept his court at Winchester in 1247, and accepted the Bishop's invitation to dine with him on Christmas Day.[1]

A more peaceful part was performed by Grosseteste in connection with the vacancy which arose in the See of Durham, and which the monks who formed the cathedral Chapter filled in 1241 by unanimously electing Nicholas of Farnham, a man of high character and wide knowledge, who had been a regent in arts at Paris for several years, had afterwards studied and practised medicine at Bologna, and, after attaining to great skill in physical science, had turned his attention to theology, and qualified himself to occupy the master's chair.[2] He seems to have been of an amiable disposition, in favour with the King and Queen and with all parties. He had shortly before refused the proffered See of Coventry and Lichfield, and was unwilling to accept that of Durham, on the ground that men might accuse him of declining a poor bishopric in order to obtain a rich one. Grosseteste, however, succeeded in overcoming his honourable scruples by pointing out that his presence was absolutely required, and that, if he did not consent, "the King, in his machinations, would place some foreign and untrustworthy, as well as ignorant, man in the office, to the subversion of the dignity of the Church and to the danger of the whole realm; for the bishopric of Durham is on the confines of the kingdoms of England and Scotland, and the castles within its borders, to wit, Durham and Norham, are in that part of the country the bulwarks against the assaults of all our enemies."[3] Nicholas of Farnham is stated by Matthew Paris to have replied, with a sigh : "I love the virtue of obedience : in your diocese I hold

<hr>

[1] *Hist. Maj.* iv. 590.　　　　[2] *Ibid.* iv. 86.　　　　[3] *Ibid.* iv. 86.

my benefices, which I have obtained through your favour, and I therefore obey your paternal commands."

In the case of the vacancy in the See of Chichester in 1244 the King, by intriguing with the canons, managed to secure the election of Robert Passelew, one of his clerks, a forest judge who, with the object of replenishing the royal coffers, was deemed to have "impoverished all, monks and seculars, noble and ignoble, to such an extent that many were ruined or imprisoned."[1] Boniface on that occasion sympathised with the indignation of the Bishops, who, with a certain sense of humour, arranged for the forest judge being examined in difficult questions of theology by Grosseteste, the most learned man of his day, and, as Robert Passelew was unable to satisfy his examiner as to his qualifications, the election was quashed.[2] The King was very angry at the outcome of the proceedings, but his anger was directed mainly against the newly elected Bishop of Chichester, Richard de la Wyche, who had been Chancellor of the University of Oxford, and was an intimate friend of Grosseteste. The Bishop of Lincoln was again brought in contact, probably in the following year, with Robert Passelew, whom he refused to institute when the King presented him to the living of St. Peter's, Northampton, partly because he was a forest judge, and partly on other grounds.[3]

The keen interest taken by Grosseteste in the European situation, during the period now under review, is reflected in an incident which took place in 1241. Several earnest though unsuccessful efforts were made in that year to bring about peace between the Pope and the Emperor, notably by Richard, Earl of Cornwall, on his way back from the Holy Land.[4] On the death of Gregory the Ninth, a few months later, followed by that of his successor, Celestine the Fourth, within seventeen days after his election, a meeting was held, under the presidency of the Archbishop of York, at which Grosseteste was present, together

---

[1] *Hist. Maj.* iv. 401.

[2] *Ibid.* iv. 509, 510.

[3] See above, p. 176. Letters 124, 126.

[4] *Hist. Maj.* iv. 145 *sqq.*

with his friend William de Raleigh, still Bishop of Norwich, and Walter Mauclerc, Bishop of Carlisle, whose sympathies with his views may be inferred from the fact that he had, in earlier years, been an active opponent of Peter des Roches and of the King's policy,[1] that he had helped to advance Nicholas of Farnham,[2] and that, towards the end of his career, he became a Dominican at Oxford.[3] The three Bishops, with the assistance of many other influential ecclesiastics, met together to deliberate on the manifold desolations of the Church, and resolved unanimously to send messengers to the Emperor for the purpose of urging him " to lay aside all feelings of rancour and indignation, to abandon all forms of tyranny, to allow the Church to breathe freely, and, in spite of the provocations to which he had previously been subjected, to promote its advancement."[4] Some difficulty arose, however, with regard to the choice of a messenger. In the unsettled state of Europe the roads were unsafe ; numerous prelates, sailing in Genoese galleys, had been captured by the Pisan fleet ; and Otho himself, the Cardinal Legate, had been made a prisoner by the Emperor. On the principle, therefore, that

" Cantabit vacuus coram latrone viator,"

they decided to send some of the mendicant friars on the errand, partly because they offered no inducement to robbers, and partly because they were wanderers and well acquainted with all countries. Grosseteste's hand may be discerned in the selection. The mission, however, was fruitless. Frederick II. was as unswerving in his determination to admit of no interference, as Gregory IX. had been in his answer to Richard of Cornwall. The Emperor, headstrong, restless, and versatile— " stupor mundi Fredericus," as Matthew Paris and other writers call him—was too intent upon his plans for recovering and consolidating his power in Italy to pay much heed to those

---

[1] *Hist. Maj.* iii. 148.

[2] *Ibid.* iv. 87.

[3] *Ibid.* iv. 564.

[4] *Ibid.* iv. 173.

who tried to restrain his course. In spite, or possibly in part because of his marriage with Henry the Third's sister, he does not appear to have been popular in England. The dominant feeling in this country, as far as can be gathered from contemporary records, was distinctly against him during his struggle with the Pope. Even his entry into Jerusalem had aroused no enthusiasm, in view of the fact that his recovery of the holy city was effected by connivance with the Saracens, not in open warfare, and was accompanied by what was deemed undue deference to Mussulman susceptibilities. Matthew Paris describes him as more of a Mohammedan than a Christian,[1] and his intimacy with the Sultan of Cairo and his reputed scepticism doubtless told against him in England. He made several attempts, however, especially in 1244, to conciliate English opinion;[2] and there can be no doubt that, although his marriage with Henry's sister may not have affected public opinion in any considerable degree, it helped to prevent the influence of the English Government from being thrown completely into the scale against him, just as the fact that Henry and St. Louis had married two sisters tended to mitigate the strain to which the relations between England and France were at that time subjected.[3] Grosseteste's antipathy to the Emperor was profound, and explains in a large measure the support he accorded, shortly after the Council of Lyons, to the collection of subsidies in aid of the Papal requirements necessitated by the continuance of the struggle.[4]

In the political and constitutional developments of those years Grosseteste played no inconspicuous part. In January 1242 he was present at the meeting of Parliament held in London, which refused the King's demands for funds to enable him to provoke war with France, and issued the first written

[1] *Hist. Maj.* iii. 521, iv. 435.
[2] *Ibid.* iv. 371, 372.
[3] Much in the same way the marriage of Richard, Earl of Cornwall, with Sanchia of Provence, another of the Queen's sisters, helped to detach him from the baronage with which his first marriage had closely connected him.—Stubbs, ii. p. 60.
[4] Letter 119.

protest known in parliamentary history.[1] Of greater importance was his action during the Parliament which met in Westminster Hall in 1244, when Henry, in order to meet the expenditure he had incurred in his indecisive expedition to Gascony, and with a view to a secretly contemplated attack on Scotland, asked for pecuniary assistance. The clergy and the nobility, after deliberating separately, met together, and appointed a Committee of twelve, of whom four represented the clergy, four the laity, two the barons, and two the abbots. The nominees of the clergy were the Archbishop-elect of Canterbury, Grosseteste, William de Raleigh, and Walter de Cantelupe; those of the laity were Richard, Earl of Cornwall, Earl Bigod, Simon de Montfort, Earl of Leicester, and Walter Marshall, Earl of Pembroke; those of the barons were Richard de Montfichet and John Baliol; and the abbots were represented by those of Bury St. Edmunds and Ramsey.[2] The twelve were chosen unanimously, and it was provided that they should draw up articles to be agreed to by the whole assembly, regulating the King's conduct and the nomination of his principal and responsible ministers. When the scheme of reform, framed by the Committee and approved by all, was presented to the King, he declined in the first instance to accede to it, but promised to amend spontaneously the matters of which they complained, and is said to have caused the proceedings of Parliament to be adjourned for three weeks until Candlemas, the 2nd of February.[3]

---

[1] *Hist. Maj.* iv. 185. Omnes episcopi, etc. The word "Parliament" came into vogue about this time, as applied to the Great Council of the nation. It is used in the *Dunstable Annals* (*Ann. Monast.* iii. 164) with reference to the Parliament which met at Windsor in Sept. 1244. Henry III. speaks in that year of the great assembly of 1215 as the *Parliamentum Runemede* (*Close Rolls*, 28 Henry III.) Matthew Paris first applies the term to the Parliament of 1246.

[2] *Hist. Maj.* iv. 362 *sqq.*

[3] Such is the statement of Matthew Paris. It is evident, however, that, as is shown by Stubbs, vol. ii. p. 61, he has confused incidents which took place in different Parliaments or Sessions held in 1244, and that the principal proceedings which he records must have occurred in the course of a Parliament held some time between the end of August and the middle of November of that year.

They next declared that they would be content to provide the king with the required funds on condition that he would agree to their demands as to the appointment of responsible ministers and the due observance of the laws of the land, and also provided that the money was expended by the aforesaid Committee of twelve as trustees for the King. Henry did all he could to influence the individual nobles and prelates, and exhibited a letter he had procured from Innocent IV., addressed to the clergy of England, urging them to give to the King the aid he required, and induced the Pope to write private letters in a similar sense to each of the bishops.

Matthew Paris, after referring to the vicissitudes of the six days' debate which ensued, describes how, on the last of those days, the King spent the whole of his time until the evening in trying to convince the prelates one by one. On the morrow they assembled in the infirmary of the chapel of St. John the Evangelist, and Henry sent to them by certain nobles, one of whom was Simon de Montfort, a message urging obedience, mainly on account of the Pope's request, but also with a view to the King's urgent necessities. Almost immediately afterwards, while the prelates were considering the Papal letter, the King suddenly appeared among them, protested with his usual oath that their honour was as dear to him as his own, and that the converse ought to hold true, and heaped entreaty on entreaty ; but as they persisted in their reply that they would take the question into consideration, he went away greatly perturbed. And, as some were anxious that they should give a milder answer to the King, Grosseteste rose and made a speech which persuaded the assembly, and in which he used the words : " Let us not separate ourselves from the general resolve ; for it is written, Divided we perish." Again the King endeavoured to influence them individually during the adjournment which took place ; again he failed ; and the decision of Parliament, to which he ultimately agreed, as recorded by the contemporary historian,[1] not only constitutes an important landmark in constitutional history, but may be regarded as a tribute, in a special sense, to the attitude adopted by Grosseteste. Whatever may have been, however, the importance of the principles of constitutional liberty and ministerial responsibility enunciated in that document, they were persistently disregarded by the King in the years which followed. The great merit of Grosseteste's policy in this respect—and it became even more conspicuous at a later stage—was that he attempted to identify the best interests of the ecclesiastical organism with the development of political freedom, and to pursue at one and the same time the reform of the Church and the reform of the State. The Committee of twelve of 1244 anticipates, in some measure, the Committee of twenty-four of 1258; and the emphasis laid in the former year upon the *communis sensus*, the *communitas regni*, and the *universitas*, is a forecast of the principles embodied in the song:

> Igitur communitas regni consulatur,
> Et quid universitas sentiat, sciatur,
> Cui leges propriae maxime sunt notae.[2]

---

[1] *Hist. Maj.* iv. 366 *sqq.*
[2] Wright, *Political Songs* (Camden Society), pp. 71 *sqq.*

CHAPTER X

IT might have been thought that Grosseteste's time, during the period which elapsed between 1239 and 1244, would have been so fully occupied with the reorganisation of religious work within his diocese, with the numerous disputes in which he was engaged, and with the active part he took in public affairs, that he would have found no opportunity either for literary occupations or for sustained interest in the fortunes of the University with which his career had been so closely interwoven. Such, however, was not the case. To the period in question must be assigned (1) his renewed effort to promote the revival of Greek studies; (2) his translation from Greek into Latin of the work known as the *Testament of the Twelve Patriarchs*, as well as of a treatise ascribed to Dionysius the Areopagite, and other writings;[1] (3) his contributions to the literature of rural and domestic economy; and (4) the action he took to obtain for the Chancellor and University of Oxford a royal privilege defining the extent of their jurisdiction.

---

[1] On the *Testament of the Twelve Patriarchs* see p. 227. Grosseteste's translation of the *Mystical Theology*, with a commentary, is the only one of his works relating to the author known as Dionysius the Areopagite which has been printed. The commentary is in the *Opera Dionysii Areopagitae*, Argent., 1503, pp. 264*b*-271*b*. He translated other works of that writer, and commented on them.—Tanner's *Bibliotheca*; Wharton's *Anglia Sacra*, ii. p. 347; Felten, p. 75.

Roger Bacon's assertion [1] that Grosseteste was not sufficiently acquainted with Greek to be able to translate out of that language until the latter portion of his life, taken in conjunction with other passages, merely means that he did not carry out actual and continuous translations until that period of his career, and that even then he required a certain amount of assistance. He had commenced the study of that language, as has been seen, whilst he was at the University, and had doubtless used, or at any rate consulted, the original text, in his lectures and commentaries on the *Posterior Analytics* and other writings of Aristotle. The importance, however, of his work as a pioneer of the study of Greek, lies rather in the impulse he gave to the efforts of others, than in the results he achieved himself. It was with that object that he summoned Greeks to England, and arranged for Greek manuscripts to be brought from Athens, Constantinople, and elsewhere.[2] Some of the Greek teachers thus invited by Grosseteste still remained in this country at the time when Roger Bacon wrote his *Compendium Studii Philosophiae* in 1271.[3] In the same work Bacon maintains that for seventy years no one but Grosseteste had enriched the Church by translations, as he had done in the case of Dionysius the Areopagite, St. John of Damascus, and some other sacred teachers.[4] Trivet mentions in terms of special commendation, in addition to his *Testament of the Twelve Patriarchs*, his *Commentary on the Books of Dionysius*, which he had "caused to be translated." It is to Grosseteste and his assistants that must also be attributed the Latin version of the letters of St. Ignatius, brought to light by Bishop Ussher in 1646, and of which the late Bishop Lightfoot has given a luminous account.[5] It is possible, too, that the renderings

<hr>

[1] *Opus Tertium*, ed. Brewer, p. 91. See p. 23.

[2] R. Bacon, *ibid.*

[3] *Ibid.* p. 434.

[4] *Ibid.* p. 474. Trivet, p. 243, etc.

[5] Lightfoot's *Apostolic Fathers*, part ii. vol. i. pp. 76 *sqq.* It is what is known as the Latin version of the Middle Recension of St. Ignatius' Epistles. Lightfoot thinks that the circulation of Grosseteste's translation was probably confined to the Franciscan convent at Oxford, to which he be-

from the Lexicon of Suidas ascribed to Grosseteste by Boston of Bury also belong to this period of his life.[1]

The difference between the translations which he effected, when unaided, and those which he carried out with the assistance of others, may, perhaps, be inferred from a comparison of the description he gives of his method of translating the Greek work on the monastic state which he sent to the Abbot and convent of Peterborough,[2] with the account given by various writers of the later versions connected with his name. In the former instance he says that he extracted as best he could the meaning of the words, and added what was necessary to elucidate their meaning. His later translations, such as those which belong to the greater part of the period now under review, which he effected with the aid of others working under him, are, on the other hand, extremely literal. Matthew Paris notes that the *Testament of the Twelve Patriarchs* was rendered " verbo ad verbum,"[3] and Bishop Lightfoot has given several instances of Grosseteste's close adherence to the original wording and even to the construction of the sentences.[4] For the efforts thus made he is deserving of the highest praise, and the difficulties and the defects inseparable from the initial stages of the study of a language are in themselves a tribute to the novelty as well as to the importance of the undertaking.

It was in 1242, according to Matthew Paris and most chroniclers,[5] that Grosseteste, assisted by Nicholas the Greek, trans-

---

queathed his books. John Tyssington and William Woodford, both of whom quote the Latin version of those Epistles, belonged to that convent in the thirteenth century. A MS. in the library at Tours, mentioned in Dorange's *Catalogue des Manuscrits de la Bibliothèque de Tours*, and examined by Canon Armitage Robinson on behalf of Bishop Lightfoot, distinctly ascribes the translation to Grosseteste, pp. 77, 274.

[1] The author of the above-named version of the Epistles of St. Ignatius shows acquaintance with Suidas. Lightfoot, *ibid.* p. 85.

[2] See p. 165; Letter 57, p. 173. " Extractum pro modulo meo verborum sensum, adjectis alicubi paucis ad dilucidationem in hanc paginam redigens, vobis destinare curavi."

[3] *Hist. Maj.* iv. 232.

[4] *Apostolic Fathers*, l.c. Cp. Felten, p. 86.

[5] *Hist. Maj.* iv. 232; R. Bacon, p. 474; Trivet, p. 243; Salimbene, *Chronicle of Parma* (Parma, 1856), p. 99; *Joh. de Oxenedes*, ed. Ellis, p.

lated the *Testament of the Twelve Patriarchs* into Latin. Nicholas, after being clerk to the Abbot of St. Albans, had become an inmate of the Bishop of Lincoln's household. It is probable, for reasons previously stated,[1] that Grosseteste had been acquainted with him during his university career at Oxford, and possibly at Paris. He appears to have resided at Oxford in 1238, as his name is to be found in the list of those who were bailed out by the Bishop after the attack on the Legate at Osney, and in the following year he had been presented to the living of Datchet by the Abbot and convent of St. Albans.[2] In view of the large number of Italians who held livings in England, though unacquainted with the English language, it is not remarkable that a Greek who had studied at Oxford, and spent apparently most of his life in this country, should have been made a rector ; and it must be borne in mind that the Latin Empire existing at that time at Constantinople formed an additional link between East and West, and rendered intercourse more easy.[3] Even Armenians came to England during that period : an Armenian archbishop, for example, visited St. Albans, one of their bishops died at St. Ives, others of that race travelled all the way to this country in 1250 to pay their respects at his tomb, and some found their way to St. Albans two years later, and related many things concerning Mount Ararat and the ark, as well as respecting the persecutions inflicted upon them by the Tartars.[4]

171, etc. Matthew Paris with his own hand transcribed a copy of the work for the use of the Benedictine monks at St. Albans. It is in the Royal MS. 4 D. vii. British Museum, together with a " tractatus quem episcopus Lincolniensis Robertus transtulit de Graeco in Latinum, de probatione virginitatis Beatae Mariae et sacerdotio Jesu." The colophon says : " Hoc quoque scriptum adquisivit frater Matthaeus Parisiensis ab episcopo memorato et ad usus claustralium manu sua scripsit ; cujus anima in pace requiescat. Amen." See Sir T. Duffus Hardy's *Descriptive Catalogue*, iii. p. 57, and plate 9 of the facsimiles at the commencement of the volume.

[1] See p. 21.

[2] For the evidence see Pegge, pp. 163, 164.

[3] It lasted from 1203 to 1261.

[4] *Hist. Maj.* iii. 163, 164 ; v. 116, 340, 341. Dean Stanley (*Eastern Church*, p. 8) states that the *Testament of the Twelve Patriarchs* forms part of the canon of the Armenian Church. If so, Grosseteste's belief in its authenticity may have been confirmed by one of the Armenian visitors

Grosseteste's principal English collaborator was his own Archdeacon of Leicester, John de Basingstoke, who is described as "a man of great experience in the 'trivium' and the 'quadrivium,' and fully educated in Greek and Latin literature."[1] He had studied at Athens, and it was through him that Grosseteste obtained a copy of the Greek original of the *Testament of the Twelve Patriarchs* for the purpose of translation. John de Basingstoke also introduced, according to Matthew Paris, Greek numerals into England, and instructed his intimate friends in their use and significance,[2] and composed a grammar called the *Greek Donatus*, based on a work written in that language. He was instrumental in bringing to England many valuable manuscripts.

Matthew Paris relates the following curious story which John de Basingstoke told to a friend of his with reference to his sojourn at Athens : "There was a certain damsel, daughter of the Archbishop of Athens,[3] Constantina by name, hardly twenty years of age, endowed with every virtue and well acquainted with the difficulties of the 'trivium' and 'quadrivium'; for which reason, on account of her eminence in knowledge, the said Master John used in jest to call her another Catherine. She it was who was the teacher of Master John, and all the good he acquired in the way of science, as he often asserted, he had obtained from her, although he had studied and read for a long time in Paris. This damsel was able to foretell, with unfailing foresight, pestilence, thunderstorms, eclipses, and, what was more remarkable, earthquakes."

Grosseteste's translation of the *Testament of the Twelve Patriarchs*, the sons of Jacob, produced a great sensation at the time, as is shown by the references in almost all the chronicles,

to this country. Malan, however, in his *Philosophy of Truth*, pp. 176 *sqq.*, disputes the statement. See note on p. 240 of the present work.

[1] *Hist. Maj.* v. 284 *sqq.*

[2] See Pegge's Appendix 11. The symbols are drawn by Matthew Paris, *Hist. Maj.* v. 285.

[3] Michael Acominatus. — Finlay's *History of Greece*, ed. Tozer, iv. 134. Luard also refers to the *Oriens Christianus*, ii. 174.

and was frequently printed in later ages.[1]   Of the English versions of his work, which subsequently appeared, nearly thirty editions are enumerated in Hazlitt's bibliographical collections. It is, perhaps, a matter for regret that he should have devoted so much care to what was unquestionably a spurious, though an early and highly interesting, work.[2]   The Greek original purported to be a version of one of the books of the Hebrew Scriptures, which had been suppressed or secreted by the Jews on account of its prophetic references to Christianity, and that is why Matthew Paris says that Grosseteste's desire was to confute the Jews, thus bringing his purpose into harmony with that of his *De Cessatione Legalium*.[3]   Grosseteste was certainly misled, in common with many others, into a belief in the authenticity of the work he was translating ; and in a letter to Henry the Third,[4] who had addressed to him the inquiry, What does anointing add to the royal dignity? he quotes as authoritative, in the course of his reply, a passage from the *Testament of the Twelve Patriarchs* on the superiority of the priesthood to

---

[1] *E.g.* at Haguenau in 1532 and Paris in 1539, and in Galland's *Bibliotheca Patrum*, i. 193 *sqq.*   An edition without printer's name, place, or date, black letter, was probably printed about 1520. Fabricius (ed. Mansi, Padua) mentions an edition printed at Vienna in 1483.

[2] On the *Testament of the Twelve Patriarchs*, see the works of the Rev. R. Sinker, D.D., who published the text in 1869, with notes, etc., an English translation in 1872, and a valuable appendix in 1879.   He regards it as one of the earliest monuments of Christian literature, written not later than the middle of the second century, and perhaps before the end of the first, and holds that it can hardly have had a Hebrew original, though intended primarily for Hebrew readers.   The Greek MS. which Grosseteste actually used, and which was sent to him at

his request by John de Basingstoke from Athens, is probably the one in the Library of the University of Cambridge, to which it was left by Archbishop Parker, numbered Ff. i. 24.

[3] *Hist. Maj.* iv. 232, 233 ; v. 285.

[4] Letter 124.   See Selden's *Titles of Honour*, part i. ch. 8.   Arthur Taylor's *Treatise of the Anointing and Crowning of the Kings and Queens of England.* Besides the Holy Roman Emperor, only four Kings received unction in addition to coronation : the Kings of Jerusalem, France, England, and Sicily. Dean Stanley suggests (*Memorials of Westminster*) that Henry the Third's recollection of his twofold coronation may have prompted the question he addressed by the "young king" to Grosseteste.   Letter 124 must, however, have been written after 1245, when at least twenty-nine years had elapsed since the King's accession.

the kingly office. However, as Dr. Pauli well remarks,[1] the revival of learning in the thirteenth century commenced, like that of the fifteenth, with what was least valuable and least profitable. It was, in fact, the impetus given to intellectual progress by the opening up of an access to new modes of thought and sources of information, which constituted the great step in advance, apart from the particular materials which were in the first instance brought into requisition.

Of a lighter but not less useful character were the attempts made by the Bishop during that period to spread sound notions respecting the management of landed estates and of domestic households. His interest in agriculture had doubtless been acquired in his early days at Stradbroke, and had never completely died out. Walter of Henley's *Treatise on Husbandry*, written at some time during the first half of the thirteenth century, was translated from French into English either by him or under his auspices.[2] The need for a translation shows that some of those for whose use the work was intended, whether lords or bailiffs, were unacquainted with, or at any rate imperfectly versed in the former language; though, perhaps, the object was to familiarise a wider circle with the contents. Nothing is known definitely with regard to the personality of Walter of Henley beyond the fact, which he mentions, that he had served the office of bailiff; but the title of one of the manuscripts of his treatise states that he became a friar preacher.[3] If it were not for that reference, it might be permissible to conjecture that he was identical with the W. de Hemingburgh, or Hemingberga, who was one of Grosseteste's clerks, and a correspondent of Adam Marsh, in view of his connection with the Bishop of Lincoln, and also seeing that Henley in Oxfordshire was sometimes called Henneburgh, or

---

[1] Page 41.

[2] "Walter of Henley, etc.," ed. for the Royal Historical Society by Miss Lamond, with introduction by Prof. Cunningham (London, 1890), contains Walter of Henley's *Husbandry*, the English translation of that work attributed to Grosseteste, an anonymous *Husbandry*, a *Seneschaucie*, and Grosseteste's *Rules* (*Les Reules Seynt Roberd*).

[3] Prof. Cunningham's Introduction, p. 21.

some other name of similar sound. Adam Marsh's letter to him,[1] recommending the messenger of the Archbishop of Canterbury to his good offices, implies, however, that he was a Franciscan and not a Dominican ; and the hypothesis must therefore be abandoned, unless it be assumed that on the above-mentioned title-page the words "Friar Preacher" were inserted by mistake for "Friar Minor." In any case, Walter of Henley's work, whoever the author may have been, was one of real importance, and was regarded for several centuries as being of considerable utility. Numerous manuscripts of it are still extant ; it was translated into Welsh and Latin, and the English version was printed by Wynkyn de Worde. The authority for the statement that the latter was due to the Bishop of Lincoln, is not the mere *ipse dixit* of Bale, in his *Scriptores Britanniae:* the title of a fifteenth-century manuscript[2] distinctly states that the work was written in French, and translated into English by Robert Grosseteste, and other manuscripts contain the same account of its origin.[3]

With greater certainty, however, can the Rules, written in French, which bear the name of *Les Reules Seynt Robert* be ascribed to him. They are described in the title as "The Rules that the good Bishop of Lincoln, Saint Robert Grosseteste, made for the Countess of Lincoln to guard and govern her Lands and Hostel : whoever will keep these Rules well, will be able to live on his means, and keep himself and those belonging to him." The Countess of Lincoln in question was Margaret, widow of John de Lacy, Earl of Lincoln, who died on the 22nd of June 1240.[4] Various manors were assigned by the King for her maintenance until her dowry out of her husband's lands should be set forth.[5] She afterwards married, in 1242, Walter Marshall, seventh Earl of Pembroke, the same who two years

---

[1] *Mon. Francisc.* p. 255.

[2] Sloane MSS. 686, f. 1 ; Cunningham, Introd. p. 31.

[3] Cunningham, Introduction, pp. 37, 39, 41. A copy of Wynkyn de Worde's extremely rare edition is in the Cambridge Library.

[4] *Hist. Maj.* iv. 34.

[5] Dugdale's *Baronage,* quoted by Pegge, p. 95.

later served with Grosseteste on the famous Committee of twelve.   If, therefore, the Bishop's rules were written for her guidance during her widowhood, as is most in accordance with probability, they must have been composed between 1240 and 1242.   Pegge points out[1] that Grosseteste's acquaintance with the de Lacys may have commenced at the time when he was Archdeacon, and John de Lacy, Constable of Chester.   The Countess' mother was also connected with Chester, as she was the sister of Ranulf, seventh earl of that name, with whom Grosseteste may possibly, too, have come in contact during his tenure of the archdeaconry of Leicester, as Ranulf held for several years the Montfort property in that district through a grant made by King John,[2] and is recorded to have kept Christmas of 1223 in the town of Leicester.[3]

Walter of Henley's Treatise and Grosseteste's Rules cover different ground.   The former deals with the two-field and the three-field system, and the practical details connected with the general management of an estate, on the supposition, as Professor Cunningham points out, that the lord or the bailiff would look into everything himself.   The Rules, on the other hand, were intended for the personal use of the Countess of Lincoln, who could not look into everything with her own eyes; and they deal not only with production, but with the consumption of products in the household, and explain the methods by which a large number of retainers can be directed to the best purpose.   Both treatises, however, have this in common, that they are concerned with a condition of things in which comparatively little was bought or sold, as the difficulties of communication rendered the interchange of heavy commodities expensive and often impossible, so that the object was to work the estate, as far as was feasible, on self-supporting principles. At the same time a change was gradually coming over the management of estates.   The great Benedictine monasteries

---

[1] Page 95.   and the authorities there quoted.
[2] Bémont, *Simon de Montfort*, p. 3,   [3] *Hist. Maj.* iii. 83.

were setting the example of improvements in tillage, the Cistercians were producing wool in large quantities for purposes of export, and the commercial activity encouraged by the Crusades was gradually affecting the methods of rural economy. Under the old state of things the villain worked, say, three days a week on the domain land, besides extra days at harvest-time, and performed sundry incidental duties, in return for which he had the benefit of his holding of about thirty acres, stocked with a yoke of oxen and half-a-dozen sheep.[1] Under the new order of things, the custom, on the part of the villains, of discharging their obligations in money, in lieu of labour or produce, was gradually spreading.   The twofold effect of the change was to allow them more time to look after their own holdings, and to introduce the necessity for the use of hired labour on the home farm or domain land, not, indeed, to such an extent as to supersede altogether the services of the villains, but in such a way as to diminish their importance, to concentrate the attention of the lord upon the requirements of the home farm, and to necessitate the keeping of accounts.   Walter of Henley and Grosseteste wrote during the transitional period, and their works must accordingly have been of the utmost practical value. The obligations of the villains were generally stated in terms of money : they might, however, be discharged wholly in service or in kind, or else be commuted in their entirety for a cash payment ; or, again, a middle course might be adopted, according as the special needs of the district or the will of the lord might direct.

Grosseteste's Rules show how a lord or lady shall know in each manor the rents, customs, usages, services, franchises, fees, and tenements, and tell the live and dead stock ; they indicate the best way of dealing with seneschals and bailiffs ; the method of making the various estates self-sufficing, leaving a certain surplus for sale ; when the granges should be shut and opened, and how the accounts should be examined.   Grosseteste then

---

deals, in a number of brief maxims, with the subject of household economy and the management of servants, hospitality, almsgiving, dress, and the service at table. In one rule he refers to the practice prevailing in his own palace, where "each quarter of wheat makes nine score loaves of white and brown bread, together of the weight of five marks each, and the hostel at meat is served with two meats, large and full, to increase the alms, and with two lighter dishes also full for all the freemen, and at supper with one dish not so substantial, and also light dishes followed by cheese ; and if strangers come to supper they shall be served with more according as they have need." After some further injunctions of that kind he reverts to the subject of agriculture, and touches upon the mode of threshing and selling corn, and the importance of keeping plenty of cows and sheep: the wool of a thousand sheep in good pasture ought, he says, to yield at least fifty marks a year, in scant pasture forty, and in coarse and poor pasture thirty ; and he observes that the return from cows and sheep in the way of cheese is in itself worth a considerable sum, without counting calves and lambs, and apart from the manure, all of which help the growth of corn and fruit. The minuteness with which he enters into questions likely to be of assistance to the Countess may be inferred from the fact that he even advises her when and where to make her purchases. " I recommend," he says, "that at two seasons of the year you make your principal purchases, that is to say, your wines and your wax and your wardrobe at the fair of St. Botolph, what you shall use in Lindsey and in Norfolk, in the vale of Belvoir, in the country of Caversham, in that of Southampton for Winchester, and in that of Somerset at Bristol; your robes purchase at St. Ive's." Grosseteste's Rules, being intended for private use, did not attain to the wide circulation enjoyed by the translation of Walter of Henley's Treatise with which he is credited. They were also translated at a later date into English, and a portion of them is printed in the *Monumenta Franciscana*.[1]

---

[1] *Mon. Francisc.* p. 582.

The translator was, however, under the impression that they were intended by the Bishop for the management of his own household and estates, whereas they were really addressed to the Countess of Lincoln, or Nicole, as the city was called in Norman French ; though it is possible, as Professor Cunningham points out,[1] that he composed separate sets of Rules, similar in character, for his own household and for her guidance. Apart from the light they throw on the condition of agriculture and of estate management at that time, and on Grosseteste's sustained interest in those questions, they reflect credit on the painstaking good nature with which he placed his experience at the disposal of those who had most need of it.

It has been seen how Grosseteste's thoughtfulness for the welfare of the University of Oxford continued unabated after his promotion to the See of Lincoln.[2] In 1238 he defended its liberties, and allayed the differences which had arisen in consequence of the attack upon Cardinal Otho at Osney.[3] In 1240, owing to a "town and gown" disturbance, a good many scholars migrated to Cambridge.[4] In 1244 he was called upon to take a step which may not, perhaps, have appeared of much importance at the time, but which produced a lasting effect on the constitution and the jurisdiction of the University. In that year a serious riot occurred, probably in connection with some question of usury. The clerks invaded the Jewry, broke into the houses, and sacked the contents, with the consequence that forty-five of them were sent to prison. They were, however, released by the king at the instance of Grosseteste, as no direct evidence could be brought against them showing that they had been guilty of felony.[5] A few weeks later a royal charter was

---

[1] Introduction, p. 43.

[2] Pages 132, 174, 184.

[3] Page 184.   [4] *Hist. Maj.* iv. 7.

[5] The *Chronicle of Osney* (*Ann. Monast.* i. 91) says : "Ad instantiam Sancti Roberti Lincolniensis episcopi jussu regis fuerunt liberati, eo quod nullus impeteret eos de pace regis fracta vel alio crimine." T. Wykes' *Chronicle*, on the same page, says : "Per dominum Robertum Lincolniensem episcopum liberati sunt omnes, quia nullus apparuit qui eos directe posset impetere de crimine feloniae." See also the *Chron. of Abingdon*, ed. Halliwell (Reading, 1844), p. 5.

procured, doubtless through Grosseteste's efforts, by which the Jews of Oxford were forbidden to take more than twopence in the pound per week as interest from the scholars, and a definite jurisdiction was granted to the Chancellor in all actions concerning debts, rents, and prices, transactions relating to horses, clothing, and provisions, and all other "contracts of movables" in which one party was a clerk.[1]   The charter involved the local recognition of a principle for which Grosseteste had often contended on wide and general grounds.   Although it did not include—as was the case with the charter of 1255, issued two years after Grosseteste's death—criminal jurisdiction over laymen for breach of the peace, its immediate effect was to confer upon the Chancellor a civil jurisdiction in addition to the spiritual jurisdiction which he already possessed by virtue of the ordinary ecclesiastical law as the Bishop's representative.[2] Its indirect effect was that, in course of time, the Chancellor became less and less of a Bishop's officer, and more and more a president of the University.   His authority was strengthened, and the self-governing power of the educational organisation correspondingly increased.   In Grosseteste's time matters constantly came before the Bishop of Lincoln, which in later years were left to the University authorities on the spot ; and, although the explanation is to be found partly in his commanding eminence as a man, and partly in the special character of his previous connection with Oxford, it must also be ascribed in some measure to the fact that the Chancellor's powers were merely delegated to him by the Bishop.

Thus it was that, on the occasion of some disputes which occurred seven years later in 1251, when Henry the Third and his Queen were on a visit to Oxford, two clerks happened to

---

[1] *Patent Rolls*, 28 Henry III. m. 6, a. 7 ; Rashdall, vol. ii. pp. 393, 394. The deed of acknowledgment was executed at Reading, and signed and sealed on behalf of the University by the Prior of the Friars Preachers, the Minister of the Friars Minors, the Chancellor of the University, the Archdeacons of Lincoln and Cornwall, and Friar Robert Bacon.—Little's *Grey Friars in Oxford*, p. 8.

[2] Rashdall, *l.c.*

have been imprisoned for certain offences, whereupon the
"whole body of scholars"[3] requested that all clerks, whatever
might be the offence of which they were accused, should be
surrendered out of the royal prison into the hands of the
Chancellor; "for," writes Adam Marsh to Grosseteste, "the
King has granted to them that it should be done in the case of
offences which the Chancellor, as the Bishop's delegate, is able
to visit with condign punishment; but in the case of serious
crimes, requiring either deposition or degradation, the King has
only consented that incarcerated clerks should be handed over
to the Bishop, or his official, or a vicar specially appointed for
the purpose. . . . The King has in this instance released the two
clerks aforesaid unconditionally at the request of the scholars.
The masters, however, had ceased their lectures for several days,
and they have not yet resumed them." Mr. Rashdall notes
that "so long as the See of Lincoln was filled by Robert Grosseteste, the most distinguished son that the University has yet
produced, almost unbroken harmony prevailed between the
University and the Diocesan," and that it was not until the
accession of his successor, Henry de Lexington, that the first
disagreements of any consequence broke out. Doubtless,
as he also points out, the distance of Lincoln from Oxford
tended to render the University gradually and at last wholly
independent of episcopal control, and differentiated it in that
respect from many of the mediæval universities of continental
Europe.

Grosseteste's correspondence with Adam Marsh shows the
continuous interest he felt in the organisation of the Oxford
curriculum, and the management of the affairs of the University. He was frequently asked to help individual scholars by
letters of recommendation or by pecuniary assistance, and
appeals to his generosity were never made in vain. Memorials
forwarded by the masters and scholars were often transmitted
to the Bishop through Adam Marsh, and it was through him

---

[1] "Universitas scholarium," *Mon. Francisc.* p. 115.

that Grosseteste communicated to them his wishes with respect
to certain articles which they were to draw up for the government of the University.[1] It was on that occasion, in all
likelihood, that a committee of seven was appointed to frame
what is known as the first statute of the University, enacted in
1252 or 1253, which provided that no one should be admitted to
inception or theology who had not previously been a regent in
arts, and read one book of the Canon or the Sentences, and
preached publicly in the University.[2] Questions relating to the
use of a University seal were also transmitted to Grosseteste :
Ralph de Sempingham, for instance, the Chancellor, " to whom
he had committed the duty of governing the congregation of the
scholars of Oxford," is rebuked by him for making use of that
symbol.[3] In 1248 Grosseteste writes to Robert Marsh, his
official,[4] with reference to the murder of a scholar who was
passing by St. Martin's Church, Oxford, and orders the murderers
to be excommunicated, and to be punished in accordance with
the agreement which had been made between the University
and the town, under the auspices of Nicholas of Tusculum, the
Papal legate, in 1214.[5]

Of greater interest is the fact that Grosseteste was the first
who instituted the loan chests, which were the nearest approach
presented at that time to the scholarships and exhibitions of a
later date. It was by an ordinance of his that the annual fine
imposed upon the town of Oxford by the Legate Nicholas in
1214,[6] and which in 1219 had been transferred by arrangement to the Abbot and convent of Eynsham,[7] was applied
in 1240 to the establishment of a University chest at St.

---

[1] *Mon. Francisc.* pp. 99, 346.

[2] *Ibid.* p. 346 ; Anstey's *Munimenta Academica*, p. 25. Most writers
have assigned the discussions to 1251,
and the statute to 1252 : but Mr.
Little (*Grey Friars at Oxford*, p. 38,
note) gives strong reasons for preferring 1252 as the date of the former,
and 1253 as the date of the latter.

[3] *Mon. Francisc.* p. 100.

[4] Letter 129.

[5] See p. 28. *Munimenta Academica*,
pp. 1 *sqq.*

[6] *Munimenta Academica*, p. 1.

[7] *Ibid.* p. 4. Cp. *Lincoln Cathedral Statutes*, ed. Bradshaw and Wordsworth, part ii. introduction p. 67.

Frideswyde's, where Christ Church now stands.[1] The immediate object was to enable poor scholars to borrow without interest for a reasonable period of time, and to keep them from falling into the hands of the Jewish and other usurers. The plan was that would-be borrowers should deposit some pledge, such as an article of clothing, or a cup, or a book, exceeding in value the amount of the loan, and liable to be sold by auction if the pledge was not redeemed within the year. The strictness of the rule appears to have been relaxed in specially deserving cases. The idea gained ground rapidly, and not only was the St. Frideswyde's chest increased by private donations and bequests, but numerous other chests were founded at Oxford in subsequent years. It is to the University chest thus established that Adam Marsh refers in the letter[2] in which he asks R. de St. Agatha, who was Chancellor in 1256, to allow a certain Symon de Valentinis to borrow forty pounds from the funds of the University of Oxford, deposited through the benefaction of Master William of Durham. As that scholar and patron of learning had died in 1249, the reference shows that, within nine years of Grosseteste's institution of the University chest, it had already begun to be augmented by bequests, which may, perhaps, in certain cases have been ear-marked for special purposes.

It was Grosseteste, again, who obtained from Innocent IV., in May 1246, a bull to prevent any of the scholars at Oxford from teaching in any Faculty unless they had been examined as at Paris, and approved by the Bishop or his deputies.[3] In the same year, in all likelihood,[4] he wrote his celebrated letter[5] to the Regents of Theology at Oxford, exhibiting at one and the same time the deep interest he took in the course of studies, and the predominant importance he attached to a thorough

---

[1] *Munimenta Academica,* p. 8 ; Rashdall, ii. p. 350.

[2] *Mon. Francisc.* p. 257.

[3] Bliss, *Calendar of the Papal Registers,* i. p. 225 ; Wood (i. p. 236) was under the impression that the bull only applied to degrees in arts.

[4] Luard, Introd. to the *Letters,* p. 129. Wood attributes the letter to 1240.

[5] Letter 123.

knowledge of the Scriptures. In that letter he holds up to them as an example worthy of imitation the system of teaching adopted at Paris, and insists upon the need for ensuring that the foundation-stones of learning should be truly such, and not merely called by that name, and that non-fundamentals should not be mistaken for fundamentals. Hence he argues that, as the Scriptures must be the basis of all their teaching, and as they can best be inculcated at the morning hour, presumably because the mind is then freshest and most receptive, the subjects of all their lectures at that time should be taken from the New Testament or from the Old, in order, he says, that, "like the scribe who is instructed into the kingdom of heaven, you may be like unto a man that is an householder, which bringeth forth out of his treasure things new and old." For other matters, such as aids to Biblical study, and the study of the Fathers, other opportunities should be selected. Grosseteste here emphasises the importance of Biblical study above other departments of theology, and takes his stand, as on other occasions, on the 'auctoritas irrefragabilis Scripturæ.' Although the letter, however, relates mainly to the order and relative importance of the studies, and must be interpreted, not as an attempt to eliminate any branches of knowledge, but merely as an effect to subordinate them to what he deemed the primary object to be pursued, it appears at the same time to differentiate Grosseteste's attitude from that of the new scholasticism which endeavoured to combine theology with philosophy. When Roger Bacon wrote in 1267, that new scholasticism had completely captured the Paris theological schools, the methods of which Grosseteste had approved some twenty-one, or it may be some twenty-seven years earlier. In Grosseteste's estimation, as in that of the Fathers of the Western Church, and of the pre-scholastic writers, the two streams of theology and of philosophy flowed in separate channels, and were not to be intermingled. It is true that, in his teaching, he finds himself unable to adhere rigidly to that doctrine, and

his influence is to be discerned in the writings of the schoolmen, as well as in those of the men whose methods are most
akin to his own; and it must be borne in mind that both
Albertus Magnus and Thomas Aquinas eliminate the essential
mysteries of Christian dogma from the domain of metaphysical
discussion, assigning to them the province of faith. In the
main, Grosseteste may be said to represent a conservative force
in theology, whilst in other departments of thought and learning, as well as in the political sphere, he represents a pro-
gressive force. In the former case he acknowledges the reason
of authority, in the latter he bows to the authority of reason.[1]

---

[1] Since the present chapter has been in the press, the Rev. Dr. Sukius Baronian, whom I have consulted with regard to the hypothesis suggested in note 4, page 226, has informed me that Mr. Malan's view that the *Testament of the Twelve Patriarchs* never formed part of the canon of the Armenian Church, is correct. This is shown (1) by the statement of Moses of Khorene in the fifth century (*Hist. of Armenia*, iii. 53) that the number of books of the Old Testament then translated into Armenian amounted to twenty-two, the same as now, a figure which does not admit of the inclusion of the work in question, and (2) by the fact that it has never been authorised to be read at the services of the Church, and has not been made the subject of a commentary. At the same time Dean Stanley's view was undoubtedly based upon the occurrence of the *Testament of the Twelve Patriarchs* in some Armenian copies of the Scriptures of comparatively late date, and it is quite possible that some of the Armenian visitors to England in the thirteenth century may have been guided by those copies.

CHAPTER XI

It was in 1244, the very year in which Grosseteste played so conspicuous a part in the Parliament of Westminster, and was appointed a member of the Committee of twelve, that Martin, one of the Pope's chamberlains, was sent as a nuncio to England with more than legatine powers,[1] for the purpose of obtaining fresh supplies to assist him in his struggle with the Emperor. His clumsy proceedings and exorbitant demands excited widespread indignation. According to Matthew Paris, Martin asked for no less than thirty thousand marks, seized benefices with more than thirty marks a year, and conferred them upon Italians without regard to rights of patronage, and resorted freely to the weapons of excommunication and interdict when his proposals were resisted. Shortly after his arrival, before the opposition to him had taken the definite shape which it afterwards assumed, it happened that at Pinchbeck, in Lincolnshire, the Prior of Spalding, with whom rested the right of presentation to the benefice in that parish, opposed the nuncio's claim, and some of the agents sent by the latter were attacked and ill-treated by people belonging to the locality. To Grosseteste, as Diocesan, Martin at once appealed, requesting him to call upon the Prior to answer to the nuncio for his refusal, and asking for advice. The Bishop, in courteous

---

[1] *Hist. Maj.* iv. 363.

R

terms,[1] declined to accede to the request relating to the Prior of Spalding, stating that the parish of Pinchbeck was a large one and required the presence of a resident vicar, but permitting the nuncio to reserve a living without cure of souls in the gift of the Prior, to which the Pope might collate by virtue of his existing powers, and also allowing him to excommunicate those who had laid violent hands on his agents. The letter also contains a threefold warning to him : first, always to give his authority for his actions ; secondly, to use tact and discretion in the exercise of his authority, and not to act up to it where it is unreasonable ; and, thirdly, if he finds that his commands are opposed when they are within the bounds of reason, to argue with the opponents in the first instance instead of taking strong measures. It is evident that Grosseteste was much annoyed by what occurred, and afterwards expressed his opinion on the subject to the Pope.[2]

It is not a matter of surprise that the abbots complained that " with the exactions of King and Pope, they were between the hammer and the anvil, and between the upper and the nether millstone,"[3] and that the prelates, of whom Grosseteste was one, refused to agree to the demands in view of the fact that the Archbishop-elect of Canterbury and the Archbishop of York were absent, and that the Sees of Coventry and of Chichester were vacant.[4] A second time the question was brought before the prelates in February 1245, but at that time Grosseteste was not in England ; and the reason which they then gave for their refusal was that they were not present in full numbers, that the Archbishop-elect of Canterbury and the Bishops of Lincoln and of Durham had left the country for the purpose of

---

[1] Letter 106.

[2] Cp. *Hist. Maj.* iv. 519. The indult granted to Grosseteste in April 1245, though not bearing upon the Pinchbeck case, has probably some reference to Martin's proceedings in the previous year.—Bliss, *Calendar*, i. 216. Otherwise it would be a mere repetition of the one of January 1239. —Bliss, *Calendar*, i. 178. It declares that Grosseteste shall not be compelled to bestow pensions, prebends, or other benefices on any one without special Papal mandate.

[3] *Hist. Maj.* iv. 371.

[4] *Ibid.* iv. 374-376.

attending the great Council at Lyons, and that, in the absence of those three, they could not be expected to arrive at a decision. The questions arising out of the nuncio's presence were, however, solved in a rough-and-ready way, described with gusto by Matthew Paris,[1] by a number of leading men in the country, who met in the neighbourhood of Luton and Dunstable, ostensibly for the purpose of attending a tournament, which was, however, prohibited by the King, as he suspected a hidden danger. They despatched Fulk Fitz Warren, one of their number, to Martin, who was staying in London at the New Temple. Fulk, on entering into the nuncio's presence, said to him with a stern look, "Leave England without delay"; and when asked in whose name he spoke, "In the name of the whole body of men entitled to bear arms, who have met at Luton and Dunstable; and unless you take sound advice, and depart within three days, you will be cut to pieces." Breathless and trembling, Martin made his way to the King, who had previously supported him, and asked whether it was his doing. "No," replied the King, "but my barons can hardly restrain themselves from rising against me, on the ground that I have tolerated the depredations and injuries you have committed, and I have great difficulty in preventing them from putting you to death." Martin asked for a safe-conduct to enable him to leave England, whereupon the mild King, losing his patience, exclaimed, "To hell with you!"[2] and was with difficulty quieted by those who sat around him. He gave orders, however, that Martin should be escorted as far as the seaside, and the nuncio sailed from Dover, not without fear of his life whilst on the journey. It is clear, both from Grosseteste's letter and from Matthew Paris's account, that Martin was understood to have exceeded his instructions, and that the responsibility for his

---

[1] *Hist. Maj.* iv. 420. It is strange that the *Dunstable Annals* should make no reference to an incident which is stated to have taken place near Dunstable.

[2] "Diabolus te ad inferos inducat et perducat."—*Hist. Maj.* iv. 421. This can hardly have been Henry's "usual oath" mentioned in *Hist. Maj.* iv. 365.

extortions was attributed rather to the rapacity of the Roman Court than to the Pope himself, as is shown by the fact that it was to Innocent IV. that the English nobles sent a deputation, headed by Roger Bigod, to complain in the name of the " universitas regni " of the exactions.[1]

The occasion of the great Council of Lyons, which now engrossed universal attention, was as follows:—Gregory the Ninth had intended to summon a General Council, and had issued invitations addressed, in these islands, to the Archbishops of Canterbury, York, and Dublin, the Bishops of Exeter, Carlisle, Chichester, Worcester, Norwich, Lincoln, Ely, Glasgow, and St. Andrews, as well as to the Kings of England and Scotland, the Earl Marshal, five earls, and certain others.[2] A delay arose, however, first owing to the capture of the Genoese galleys which conveyed many of the prelates, including the Cardinal legate Otho, on their way to Rome; and, secondly, in consequence of Gregory's own death, the fortnight's reign of his successor, and the subsequent interregnum.[3] It has been seen how the Archbishop of York and three of the English bishops, including Grosseteste, endeavoured in 1241 to induce the Emperor to give breathing-time to the Church in order to allow of an election to the pontifical office,[4] and how one of the first acts of Innocent IV., after his election in 1243, was to order the Canterbury monks to relax the sentence of excommunication which they had pronounced against the Bishop of Lincoln in connection with the Bardney dispute,[5] an act which he followed up in the following year, possibly in connection with the quarrel with the Dean and Chapter, by an indult that no one should issue against Grosseteste any sentence of suspension or excommunication, or against his chapel sentence of interdict, without special license from the Pope.[6] In 1243 Grosseteste had written to Innocent, expressing the gratification he felt that the Church,

[1] *Hist. Maj.* iv. 419, 420, 431.
[2] Bliss, *Calendar*, i. 195.
[3] Milman's *Latin Christianity*, book ix. ch. 15, p. 423 ; Dr. Felten, p. 44.
[4] Page 218.
[5] Page 156.
[6] Bliss, *Calendar*, i. 209.

sorely oppressed and in deep tribulation, had at last found a head,[1] and the Emperor himself had sent warm congratulations and overtures of peace.[2] The negotiations, however, led to no practical results beyond a paper treaty,[3] and on the 28th of June 1244, the Pope, in order to procure his independence, fled on a swift horse to Civita Vecchia,[4] avoiding a force of cavalry which the Emperor had sent to intercept him, and took refuge on board a Genoese fleet which conveyed him to Genoa, where he remained for a few months, afterwards reaching Lyons in December.

There he was in safety; for although Lyons, as a portion of the old kingdom of Burgundy, nominally formed part of the Empire, it was in reality a free city, with an Archbishop, Primate of all the Gauls, who enjoyed the protection of the King of France. It must be noted, however, that it was not French territory,[5] and Matthew Paris relates that both St. Louis of France and James I. of Arragon preferred not to receive Innocent within their borders, whilst Henry the Third's Council, when a suggestion was made by one of the cardinals that he should invite the Pope to England, put forward, as a pretext for refusing, the indignation which had been aroused by the proceedings of the nuncio Martin and by previous exactions, although the King himself was favourable to the proposal.[6] St. Louis, who had promised his aid to Innocent, and was a devoted son of the Church, may have been influenced by motives similar to those which guided Henry the Third's Council in their refusal; for he also had grievances of a like nature, and complained that Innocent had given away more benefices in France than all his predecessors.[7]

A few weeks after his arrival at Lyons Innocent IV. resumed the plans of Gregory IX. at the point at which they had been

---

[1] Letter 111.

[2] Milman, book ix. chap. 15 (iv. 419 sqq.)

[3] Hist. Maj. iv. 332.

[4] Ibid. iv. 355 sqq.

[5] It was not annexed to France until 1310.

[6] Hist. Maj. iv. 392, 409, 410, 422.

[7] Ibid. Additamenta, vi. 99, 105.

interrupted, but with the difference that the questions now at issue were of a more definite and more urgent nature, and summoned a General Council to meet at Lyons in June 1245. His action was criticised by some on the ground that a previous General Council had been held in 1215, and that thirty years did not constitute a sufficiently long interval. The conflict with the Emperor was, of course, the principal object for which the Council was called together, but other matters, such as the irruption of the Tartars or Mongols, who had overrun Friesland, Gothland, Hungary, and Poland, and now threatened the rest of Europe, the Greek schism, the deplorable condition of the Holy Land, and the internal wounds of the Church, also claimed attention.

Grosseteste's visit to Lyons has been attributed mainly to his desire to obtain from the Pope a definite settlement of his dispute with the Dean and Chapter of Lincoln, which had now lasted nearly six years.[1]   It is evident, however, that the dispute was only one out of many questions affecting Church government which took him there.   He would probably in any case have been present at the Council, in spite of the fact that he had declined the invitation in 1241 on the ground of ill-health;[2] and, moreover, most of the English prelates attended, except those who were prevented by illness or old age, even the excuses of the Archbishop of York, conveyed through Henry III., not being accepted.[3]   At the same time, it was doubtless on account of the Lincoln dispute that Grosseteste left England earlier than would otherwise have been necessary.   Although the Council was only to meet on the 26th of June 1245, he started on the 18th of November of the previous year,[4] and was followed soon after by Roger de Wescham, the Dean, and some of the canons of Lincoln.   Before his departure he addressed a

---

[1] As late as the 31st of August 1244, as indicated in a document belonging to Wells Cathedral, the Lincoln Chapter had been making inquiry as to precedents from other sources. *Lincoln* *Cathedral Statutes*, ed. Bradshaw and Wordsworth, part i. p. 61.

[2] Letter 105.

[3] *Hist. Maj.* iv. 390, 391.

[4] *Ibid.* iv. 390, 391.

long and earnest letter[1] to his archdeacons, instructing them as to their duties during his absence, urging upon them increase of zeal in the discharge of their pastoral office, and bidding them "occupy till I come." After his arrival at Lyons he wrote[2] to his intimate friends, Walter de Cantelupe, Bishop of Worcester, and William de Raleigh, Bishop of Winchester, who had been the last to bid him farewell as he left England, to announce to them the completion of his journey, and the courteous reception accorded to him by the Pope and Cardinals. He was accompanied on his journey by Adam Marsh, who writes[3] to the Minister of the Franciscans in England to the effect that Grosseteste has reached Lyons in better health than usual, and has been welcomed with special honours, that the Pope will shortly give his decision about the dispute, but that the issues of war are proverbially doubtful, and that intrigues are rife. Grosseteste intends to remain at Lyons for the meeting of the Council, but will take up his abode in some suitable place outside the Papal court as soon as he is able to move. Adam Marsh mentions that some of the leading Franciscans will be asked to attend, and that missions have been first proposed, and then abandoned, to the Holy Land, to the Tartars, and to the Saracens; he apprehends, however, that the bishops will show antagonism to the friars at the Council. How Grosseteste and he proposed to occupy themselves until the meeting of the Council, when not engaged with other business, may be inferred from the request that the *Morals* of St. Gregory, Rabanus on the *Nature of Things*, and the chapters of the *First Prophecy*,[4] belonging to the late Thomas of York, may be forwarded from Reading, packed with great care. It is possible, too, that Grosseteste was engaged about that time in his Commentary on the *Nicomachean Ethics* of Aristotle.[5]

---

[1] Letter 112.

[2] Letter 113.

[3] *Mon. Francisc.* p. 376.

[4] Possibly one of Abbot Joachim's works. See pp. 80, 300.

[5] The grounds for the supposition are : (1) In the letter to Martin, written shortly before his departure in 1244 (Letter 106), he quotes from the *Nicomachean Ethics*, whereas in previous

The settlement of the dispute with the Dean and Chapter was preceded by an incident which smoothed the way for a reconciliation. On the 19th of February Roger de Weseham, the Dean of Lincoln, was consecrated Bishop of Coventry and Lichfield at the instance of Grosseteste, who took the opportunity of alienating the church of Aylesbury from the deanery of Lincoln, for the purpose, according to Matthew Paris, of impairing the power of subsequent deans.[1] Dr. Luard, remarking on the fact that almost immediately after Roger de Weseham's consecration the suit between Grosseteste and the Chapter of Lincoln was determined almost wholly in the Bishop's favour, says:[2] "However much one might wish to think differently, it is difficult not to suspect unfair dealings between the Bishop and the Dean. In the first place, the Dean is Grosseteste's intimate friend; he is sent by the Chapter to represent them and plead their cause. He has not been at Lyons more than a few weeks, when, by Grosseteste's influence, he is elected Bishop of Lichfield, and immediately afterwards Grosseteste gains from the Pope a bull giving him all he asks for against the Chapter. It is difficult not to suspect that a bargain was struck between these two." It may be observed that Matthew Paris, who would have been the first to call attention to such a bargain if it had really existed, as he was distinctly against the Bishop of Lincoln in the dispute, goes out of his way to point to Roger de Weseham's eminent qualifications for the post.[3] There is more to be said for Dr. Felten's hypothesis,[4] that Grosseteste helped to bring about Roger de Weseham's election

<hr>

letters he quotes from the *Eudemian Ethics* (Letters 94, 101); (2) he must have had a copy transcribed before 1251 (*Mon. Francisc.* p. 114); and (3) St. Gregory's *Morals* would help to elucidate the subject. A translation of, and commentary on, the *Nicomachean Ethics*, ascribed to Grosseteste, used to be in the Bibliothèque des Jacobins, Rue St. Honoré, Paris. Hauréau, ii. p. 175.

[1] *Hist. Maj.* iv. 424, 426; *Ann. Monast.* (Dunstable), iii. 168. Matthew Paris states that Grosseteste conferred the living of Aylesbury immediately on Robert Marsh, though according to Le Neve's *Fasti*, ii. 95, it was first conferred upon William of Shirewood, the writer on logic.

[2] Introd. to the *Letters*, p. 62.

[3] *Hist. Maj.* iv. 425.

[4] Felten, p. 46.

in order thereby to make a slight concession to the Chapter itself, and thus to facilitate a settlement; for it must be remembered that de Wescham had not been appointed dean by the Chapter, but had been collated by the Bishop after the deprivation of William de Tournay, presumably owing to the refusal of the Chapter, in those circumstances, to recognise that deprivation by any act of their own.[1] Through the elevation of Roger de Wescham to the See of Coventry and Lichfield, the Chapter were enabled to fill the vacancy with a nominee of their own choice, who would necessarily be more of a *persona grata* to them than one who had been placed over them by another. Grosseteste, therefore, by the action he took, secured the appointment of a really able man to a post for which he was in every way fitted, and at the same time took a step calculated to bring about more friendly relations with his Chapter without prejudice to the question at issue. It may also be noted that Roger de Wescham's consecration took place in February, and the final settlement with the Chapter was not effected until the 25th of August of that year.[2]

The Papal bull relating to the dispute provided that the Bishop was to have power, as ordinary, to visit the Dean and Chapter, the canons, clerks choral and ministers, the vicars of the churches of the chaplains, and their parishioners, and to correct abuses. The right of visitation extended to the prebendal churches, the churches of the dignitaries, and those belonging to the corporate body, the power of the Dean in any of those respects being taken away. Secondly, the power of correcting irregularities in the cathedral was allowed to the Chapter, and, if they failed in their duty, to the Bishop. In the third place, the canons were to pay canonical obedience to the Bishop, but need not take an oath to that effect, which would be unprecedented and unnecessary. Fourthly, the privileges of the Chapter, except in so far as they were over-ridden by the

---

[1] See pp. 198, 199.
[2] *Hist. Maj.* iv. 497 *sqq.* ; Bliss, *Calendar*, i. 219.

previous decisions, were to remain unimpaired. The general purport, therefore, of the decision was strongly in Grosseteste's favour, without unnecessarily wounding the susceptibilities of the Chapter.[1]

The proceedings at the Council of Lyons must have been of the deepest interest to Grosseteste, but it is unnecessary to deal with them here. A long account of them is to be found in the *Historia Major* of Matthew Paris.[2] The impassioned address of Innocent on the one hand, and the eloquent pleas of Thaddeus of Suessa on the other, excited the attention of all Europe, and must have produced a profound impression on all who were present. The sentence of deprivation pronounced by the Pope against the Emperor was signed by all the prelates who were there, and consequently, it may be assumed, by Grosseteste.[3] The regulations relating to the Crusaders must have come home to him, in view of the fact that he had once offered to preach to the Saracens,[4] that he had taken a keen interest in the maintenance of the privileges granted to Crusaders,[5] that in after years he organised, as will be seen,[6] the collection of funds in England in aid of the Crusade, and that, later on, he was kept specially informed of the progress and disasters of the expedition to Egypt, and of the unfortunate capture of St. Louis near Damietta.[7] The English grievances, too, relating to the exactions of Martin and the intrusion of Italians into English livings, were stated by the proctors who represented the "universitas Angliae," and a letter was also presented by them explaining in detail the specific grounds of complaint.[8] They estimated that more than sixty thousand marks, a sum exceeding

---

[1] *Hist. Maj.* iv. 497-500 ; Pegge, pp. 136-138 ; Perry, p. 170 ; Bliss, *Calendar,* i. 219. A copy of the bull is among the documents belonging to Lincoln Cathedral.—*Twelfth Report of the Hist. MSS. Commission* (1891), appendix 9, p. 567. *Lincoln Cathedral Statutes,* part i. p. 315, part ii. p. 232.

[2] *Hist. Maj.* iv. 430 *sqq.*, 456-473, 479, 519-522, 527 *sqq.*

[3] *Ibid.* iv. 479.

[4] Letter 49.

[5] Letter 29.

[6] See p. 261.

[7] *Mon. Francisc.* p. 109. See p. 299.

[8] *Hist. Maj.* iv. 431, 441-444, 527-529, 557.

the amount of the King's annual revenue, passed out of the country into the hands of Italian beneficiaries. The Pope took some time to consider the questions thus submitted to him, and which were doubtless discussed with him by the leading English bishops. The outcome of his consideration was the issue by him, on the 3rd of August 1245, of a series of "privileges," by virtue of which certain suspensions inflicted by Martin were removed, the Pope agreed to give away only twelve more benefices, promotion was promised to English clerks proficient in their studies and of good conduct, and the existing rights of presentation appertaining to bishops and other patrons of benefices were fully confirmed.[1] Matthew Paris complains that the concessions were vitiated by the presence of a *non obstante* clause, which allowed of exceptions. It was probably felt, however, by the English prelates that the advantages which they and the other representatives of England, acting from various standpoints, had gained, were sufficient for the purpose, and that it would be unchivalrous to bring too much pressure to bear upon a Pope in exile. That explains why they, or some of them, agreed to renew, or confirm by their signatures the annual tribute to the Pope promised by King John,—a tribute which, though humiliating in its inception and recalling some of the darkest days in the history of the country, had gradually lost its original character and significance, and had become practically a voluntary contribution, inasmuch as it was given not of necessity, but as a free-will offering.[2] The laity, however, including the King, are said to have taken a different view of the matter, and to have been strongly opposed to a renewal of the pledge. It may be gathered from the pages of Matthew Paris that many of the clergy must have sympathised with them, without, however, exhibiting the same determination. He also states that the proctors left the

<hr>

[1] *Hist. Maj.* iv. 519-522 ; Rymer's *Foedera*, i. 262.

[2] *Hist. Maj.* iv. 478, 479. But the date of Innocent's bull on the subject is 5th or 6th October of that year, after Grosseteste and most of the prelates had left Lyons.

Council "swearing terribly" that they would not pay the tribute. Henry III., however, was of so weak and yielding a disposition that the opponents of the contribution must have been aware that it would be useless to rely upon his consistent support of their views, or of any action they might take, as he was easily persuaded to pass from one opinion to another. As Matthew Paris says, "Many of the prelates, fearing the King's instability in his determination and the pusillanimity of the royal counsellors, favoured the Pope's cause, although they must have seen that by such expenses the Church could not gain, but must incur heavy loss."

Grosseteste's attitude, as well as that of the other English prelates who shared his views, must be judged with reference to the European situation as a whole. In the struggle between Innocent and Frederick he sided, on general grounds, with the former, and, in view of the exiled Pope's necessities, he exercised his own judgment as to the pecuniary subventions which might properly be sent to assist him. Consequently he occupied an intermediate position between such prelates as Boniface (who had been consecrated Archbishop of Canterbury at Lyons in January) and Peter d'Aigueblanche, Bishop of Hereford, on the one hand, who were favourable to the Pope's demands in their entirety, and, on the other hand, the representatives of the laity and monks of the type of Matthew Paris, whose opinions, however, were stronger on the subject than those of other contemporary writers. In common with most men of independent opinions and action, Grosseteste incurred the hostility, as he has since been subjected to the criticism of extremists on both sides of the controversy. His position was that he considered most of the Pope's requests for funds to be necessitated and justified by the circumstances of the case, and did his best, whilst he was at Lyons and also on his return to England, to secure the removal of the abuses incident to their collection. To the Papal Provisions, on the other hand, he continued to offer an opposition which increased in force as time advanced, and,

in the course of a few years, when the Pope's imminent peril
had disappeared, he did not hesitate to meet with unflinching
resistance the whole system of encroachments and exactions
which impaired, instead of strengthening the spiritual authority
of the head of the Church, and to denounce in the strongest
terms the corruptions of the Roman Court.

The foregoing considerations explain, to some extent, the
apparent inconsistency between Grosseteste's attitude, when at
Lyons, in regard to the new Archbishop of Canterbury's
endeavour to obtain from the whole of his province, with
Innocent's sanction, a grant of a subsidy to the See of Canterbury, and his subsequent acquiescence in that proposal on the
27th of August of the same year. At first he informed
Boniface[1] that if he affixed his seal to the suggested letters
enforcing the Pope's grant of a subsidy to the See of Canterbury,
he would "render himself odious to the whole clergy of the
province, who might publicly proclaim that he had to the
utmost of his power concurred in imposing upon them an
intolerable burden, especially as the Pope, and the King with
the Pope's authority, were asking from the same clergy at the
same time subventions to no moderate amount." On the 27th
of August, however, Grosseteste forwarded,[2] together with a
statement that he had inspected it, a letter from Innocent IV.
granting to the See of Canterbury the first year's revenue of
vacant benefices in the province for seven years, until the sum
reached ten thousand marks. The ostensible object of the
demand was to clear off the accumulated debts of the See, but
Matthew Paris hints that Boniface wished partly to support the
cause of his own relatives in Provence,[3] and partly to promote
the Pope's interests.[4] Grosseteste's reluctance was probably due
to some such apprehension, and may have been removed,
perhaps, by the Pope's willingness to consent to the reforms

---

[1] Letter 89. Luard's Introd. p. 127.
It was written between the 15th of
January and the 5th of March 1245.

[2] *Hist. Maj.* iv. 506-508.
[3] *Ibid.* iv. 405.
[4] *Ibid.* iv. 403, v. 5, 36, 37.

previously mentioned, and by assurances given by Boniface
himself. His letter, however, is dated two days after the Pope's
definite decision in his favour in the dispute with the Chapter
of Lincoln, and it is in accordance with human nature that his
intense gratification at the result may have rendered him more
willing to agree to requests made in that moment of his
triumph. A litigant who had just won a case which has lasted
six years is not in a mood for saying No. At the same time
Grosseteste was fully aware of Boniface's shortcomings as an
archbishop, and it was on that account that he wrote at the
same time to Cardinal Hugo,[1] pointing out the importance of
the place occupied by the See of Canterbury in the English
Church, and the necessity that Boniface "should have the
'lateral' assistance of friars belonging to both Orders, acquainted
not only with the laws of England and with the canon and
civil law, but also with the laws of God, that is to say, the
sacred Scriptures, and keeping the wisdom which they derive
from that source inscribed in their hearts and expressed in their
works."

The mode in which the Pope's concessions were carried into
effect does not appear to have given satisfaction even to the
bishops. Early in the following year—to anticipate by a few
months the course of events—it was found, when Parliament
met on the 18th of March,[2] that more than twelve benefices had
been conferred by Innocent since the 3rd of August, that the
exactions continued, that one Italian had succeeded another,
and that patrons had consequently been unable to present.
Strong letters of protest were thereupon addressed to the Pope
by the bishops in the province of Canterbury, of whom
Grosseteste must have been one, by the abbots and priors, by
the nobles, clergy, and people, and also by the King himself.
The protest led to some modifications of an unimportant
character.[3] A confirmation of the explanation given in the

<hr>

[1] Letter 115.　　　　　[2] *Hist. Maj.* iv. 526 *sqq.*
[3] *Ibid.* iv. 550.

previous paragraphs with regard to Grosseteste's attitude at the time of the Council of Lyons and during the ensuing months, is afforded by his reply to the King,[1] who expressed his astonishment that after his return to England he should propose personally to assess and collect the tallage in aid of the Pope from monks and seculars. Grosseteste, after referring to the fact that all the other bishops shared his views on that point, and had adopted precisely the same course in obedience to the Pope's authority, goes on to say: "There is no reason for surprise at the action of my fellow-bishops and myself in this matter, but there would be good grounds for surprise, and also for indignation, if we should not be ready, even without being asked or commanded, to do a thing of this sort or even a greater thing. We behold our spiritual father and mother, to whom we owe honour, reverence, obedience, and help—we behold them suffering affliction, exile, persecutions, and tribulations without number,—we see them robbed of their patrimony and without the wherewithal to sustain their existence. If we were to fail in our duty of rendering help to them in this sad hour of their fortunes it would be a violation of the spirit of the fifth commandment. Your sense of generosity and of kindness will not, I trust, stand in the way of the filial services we are seeking to perform, but will rather commend and encourage our efforts." It was, indeed, a feeling of deep compassion and chivalrous consideration for the weakness and sorrows of the head of the Church which influenced Grosseteste's action during that period; he preferred to support the moral and spiritual forces represented, however imperfectly, by Innocent, than to increase the power of the man of "blood and iron," the reputed heretic Frederick II., the author of many acts of wholesale cruelty, by withdrawing from his antagonist the means of support which would enable him to restore his fallen fortunes and to resume his place in the eternal city. At the same time, the close contact in which he was brought with the Curia

[1] Letter 119.

removed some illusions he may have entertained, and nerved him for the fight in which he was prepared to engage, in a more convenient season, against the Papal Provisions and other abuses of a similar character.

Such, then, was Grosseteste's first visit to Lyons, when he was privileged to witness one of the most stirring scenes in European history, and brought back with him vivid impressions of the strength and weakness of the Papacy, of its grandeur in misfortune, and of the vivality it displayed in spite of its corruptions. His homeward journey is described in a letter[1] which he wrote to William de Nottingham, Minister of the Franciscans in England, and which is of special interest, among other reasons, on account of its reference to the death of the great Franciscan teacher, Alexander de Hales. "It has come to pass," he writes, "in God's providence that Friar John,[2] the companion of Friar Adam Marsh, is suffering from a quartan fever which he caught at Beanne on our way back. We brought him, with frequent rests, as far as Nogent, and then sent him by the Seine in advance of us to Paris; and as it did not appear safe either to Friar Adam or to myself that he should follow us from there to the sea-coast, or that he should remain at Paris in view of the unhealthy condition of that city, we decided that he should proceed by water to Rouen, and Adam accompanied him, as he was unwilling to leave him until he had left him in the keeping of some friars whom he knew, and who lived in a healthy spot. We also agreed that he should go on from there and meet me at the seaside. However, when they reached a town called Mantes, Friar John became much weaker, and Friar Adam found it impossible either to take him farther or to leave him alone. Both of them have accordingly remained at Mantes, and I earnestly entreat you to send to that town Peter

---

[1] Letter 114.

[2] This was Friar John of Stamford, afterwards custodian of Oxford, and Peter of Tewkesbury's successor as provincial Minister. — Little's *Grey Friars at Oxford*, p. 128, and the authorities there quoted. He was the "socius" of Adam Marsh in the technical Franciscan sense of the term.

of Tewkesbury,[1] with some brethren who can stop with Friar John, while Peter himself returns with Adam Marsh. They are both anxious that you should do this. Besides, it is not safe that Friar Adam should linger in these parts, for there are many who wish to secure him for Paris, now that Alexander de Hales and John de Rupellis are dead; but if that were to happen, both you and I would be robbed of our greatest comfort. Let it be so arranged that the said Peter may see me before he sails. I hope, God willing, to reach the Isle of Wight by the 14th of October, the Saturday after the feast of St. Dionysius. With regard to the cause of the visitation, thanks be to God, there has been a clear decision in my favour and consequently in that of all the bishops."

Shortly after his return to England Grosseteste happened to meet the King who was on his way back from Wales, and had with him a private interview, in the course of which he appears to have placed before Henry his impressions respecting the special consideration which the Pope required in view of the difficulties and the dangers by which he was surrounded, and recalled the services rendered to the English crown in the early part of the reign by the Papal influence. It was, indeed, the moral weight of the assistance given to Henry in his youth, immediately after the death of King John, by Honorius III. through the Legate Gualo, which had been mainly instrumental in recovering to him the allegiance of the kingdom, and in arousing public opinion against Louis and thereby preventing the success of the French arms. Nor was the King unmindful of his obligations in that respect. "My Lord Bishop," he replied to Grosseteste,[2] "what relates to our crown and regal office we intend to preserve unimpaired in accordance with our

---

[1] He afterwards became the 5th Minister of the Franciscans in England. He was intimate with Grosseteste, and probably skilled as a physician.— *Mon. Francisc.* 10, 65, etc. For his biography see Mr. Little's *Grey*

Friars at Oxford, p. 127. In 1245 he was probably custodian of the Franciscan convent at Oxford.

[2] Letter 117, in which Grosseteste relates the interview to Innocent IV.

duty, and our hope is that the Pope and the Church will help us in this; and you may be assured that always and in all respects we shall show obedience, fidelity, and devotion to the Pope as our spiritual father, and to the holy Roman Church as our spiritual mother, and will adhere to them stedfastly, in adversity as well as in prosperity. On the day on which I cease to do this, may I lose an eye, or rather let my head be cut off! God forbid that anything should separate me from the devotion I owe to my spiritual father and mother. For, besides all the reasons which affect me in common with other Christian princes, I am bound to the Church on special grounds, inasmuch as, just after my father's death, when I was still a minor, and the kingdom was not only alienated from me but actually in arms against me, our mother the Roman Church through Cardinal Gualo, then Legate in England, recalled this realm to peace and submission, anointed and crowned me King, and raised me to the throne."

CHAPTER XII

REFERENCE has already been made, by anticipation, to the proceedings of the Parliament which met early in 1246.[1] In the case of the Parliament which assembled at Oxford in April of the following year, we are told by Matthew Paris that some of the prelates had intended to oppose the Papal request for additional contributions, but that, when the time came, they all agreed to vote eleven thousand marks, to be collected through the Bishops of Winchester and Norwich.[2] What part Grosseteste took in the preliminary conferences on that occasion is unknown. The following anecdote, however, which relates apparently to the period which preceded the meeting of that Parliament, seems to indicate that he was one of those who felt some hesitation on the subject. Innocent had commenced the practice of employing Franciscans and Dominicans for the purpose of collecting subscriptions towards the Crusades, the Latin Empire at Constantinople, and a variety of other objects, including his own requirements, and also in order to secure the property of clerks who died intestate.[3] Two of these Franciscans, named John and Alexander, Englishmen by birth, were sent by the Pope with that intention, received a special license from the King, and rode about the country, spurred, booted, and wearing fine apparel, and without adhering to their simple rule.[4] They

---

[1] Page 255.
[2] *Hist. Maj.* iv. 622, 623.
[3] *Ibid.* iv. 552, 565.
[4] *Ibid.* iv. 599.

are said to have asked for procurations exactly as if they were legates, and not to have hesitated to use threats. "When they came," writes Matthew Paris, "to the Bishop of Lincoln, who was conspicuous for the love he felt for their Order, and who at one time of his life had thought of joining them, he was greatly startled at the sight of so monstrous a transformation in the garb, bearing, and office of the Friars Minors; for it was not easy to understand to what Order they belonged, or what was their calling. Exhibiting the Papal mandate, they demanded a contribution of six thousand marks from his See. In language of pained surprise the Bishop replied: 'Friars, this exaction, saving the authority of the Pope, is unprecedented, dishonest, and impracticable. It does not affect me alone as an individual, but it concerns the whole body of the clergy and people, aye, all the estates of the realm. It would be absurd on my part to give you a hasty answer on this matter without consulting the commonalty of the realm.' The two friars thereupon left Grosseteste's presence. Matthew Paris goes on to relate how they proceeded afterwards to St. Albans, and, instead of being satisfied with the accommodation with which Friars Preachers and Friars Minors were content, in a building specially erected for their use, they insisted that they should be entertained in the principal guest-rooms, 'where, forsooth, bishops and noblemen are lodged.'"

The foregoing anecdote appears to indicate opposition to the methods of collection and to the amount asked for, as well as to the general procedure adopted, rather than to the character of the requirement itself; and there is no reason for thinking that, either then or at any other time, Grosseteste opposed a well-considered and *bona-fide* demand by the Pope for his own necessities, however vigorously he may have resisted both the abuse of the system of Provisions, and the demands put forward by the Pope on behalf of others, as, for instance, in the interest of the King in 1252.[1] On the subject of the Crusades he felt, as

---

[1] Prof. Prothero sees this clearly.—*Simon de Montfort*, p. 142.

has been seen,[1] so strongly, that it is not a matter of surprise that, between 1247 and 1250, he took a leading part in this country in obtaining funds towards that object. A generation which has failed to be aroused by the Armenian massacres of 1895 can hardly be expected to enter into the feelings which prompted men in "the dark ages" to attempt the rescue of the Christian East from its Moslem conquerors. Badly organised as those expeditions were, as well as based upon a miscalculation of forces, and intermingled with lower motives, they represent, nevertheless, in their inception and in the inspiration of religious duty and self-sacrificing altruism to which they owe their origin, one of the redeeming features in the history of mankind. Little light is thrown by the narrative of Matthew Paris upon the part taken by Grosseteste in that respect, though he includes in his *Additamenta*[2] the text of Innocent's letter respecting the collection for the Crusade, which was forwarded by the Bishop of Lincoln. From the *Papal Registers*, however, it is clear that Grosseteste's exertions in that cause were continuous for several years.

As early as June 1247, he and Walter de Cantelupe, Bishop of Worcester, had begun their task. Grosseteste had by that time collected directly a thousand pounds in his diocese towards the Crusade, and another thousand, also in his diocese, from the redemption of vows of those who found themselves unable to take ship to the Holy Land, after expressing their willingness to do so.[3] Both sums were handed over, later on, to William Longespée, called by courtesy Earl of Salisbury, who afterwards became the English leader in the Crusade, was killed at Mansourah after exhibiting great prowess, earned the admiration even of the Soldan, and was buried at Acre.[4]

---

[1] Page 250.

[2] *Hist. Maj.* vi. 134.

[3] Bliss, *Calendar*, i. 224 ; see also i. 242.

[4] He was the son of the third Earl of Salisbury, who is said to have been deprived of his earldom.—Kennett's *Parochial Antiquities*, i. 315. According to Matthew Paris, William Longespée himself had been deprived of the title of Earl.—*Hist. Maj.* iv. 630. In Grosseteste's Rolls he is called Earl of Salisbury out of compliment.—Kennett, *l.c.* ; *Hist. Maj.* 152 *sqq.*, 342. But see Mr. Hunt's art. in the *Dict. of Nat. Biography*.

Grosseteste and Walter de Cantelupe were empowered in the same month to collect legacies, sums promised, and redemptions of vows for the Holy Land, and to distribute them among the Crusaders, notwithstanding the inhibition of the Bishop of Tusculum, Papal legate, or any other.[1] In August [2] Innocent wrote to Henry the Third to the effect that, as the moneys for the Crusade had been granted, at the instance of his ambassadors and of the prelates, to the Bishops of Lincoln and Worcester, to be distributed to needy Crusaders and inhabitants of the realm at the time of the general passage, they could not be handed over to the King. The Pope was willing, however, that they should transmit to the King such sums as they could spare for objects connected with the Crusade, but not to the injury of the people of the realm. In January of the following year [3] the Bishops of Lincoln and Worcester were instructed to deposit in certain places, in the name of the Roman Church, all sums collected for the Holy Land, with the exception of those assigned to Richard, Earl of Cornwall. In April 1248 two thousand marks were paid over to William Longespée.[4] In 1250, shortly before Grosseteste's second journey to Lyons, he appears to have found it necessary to be relieved of his duties as trustee of the fund, and to have left its management in the hands of Walter de Cantelupe, in conjunction with John Anglicus, a Franciscan, probably the same to whom the anecdote narrated by Matthew Paris refers.[5] The Bishop of Worcester also retired soon after from the management, and his place was taken by Richard de la Wyche, Bishop of Chichester, who, with the Archdeacon of Essex and the said John Anglicus, was responsible thenceforward for the sums in question.[6] Walter de Cantelupe's reason for retiring was probably identical

---

[1] Bliss, *Calendar*, 234 ; Nicholas of Tusculum had been Legate in the time of King John.

[2] Bliss, *Calendar*, i. 248, 249.

[3] *Ibid.* i. 249.

[4] *Ibid.* i. 255. These two thousand "marks" are clearly in addition to the two thousand "pounds" previously mentioned.

[5] See pp. 85, 260.

[6] Bliss, *Calendar*, i. 263, 264.

with Grosseteste's, as it is known that he also was at Lyons in the year 1250.[1]

A remarkable incident occurred in 1247, illustrating the religious feeling of the age, the keen international competition for sacred relics, and also the manner in which people naturally turned to Grosseteste for the solution of difficult problems in theology. St. Louis, King of France, had become possessed of what were deemed to be the fragments of the true cross. On the day preceding the feast of the translation of St. Edward the Confessor, October 13, 1247,[2] Henry III. invited all the magnates of the kingdom to meet him at Westminster, in order that they might hear tidings of joyous import, as well as celebrate the feast of that king, and be present at the knighting of William of Valence, Henry's uterine brother.[3] On their arrival they were informed that a well-known Templar had brought from Palestine a crystal vase, of exquisite workmanship, containing some of the drops of blood that flowed from Christ's wounds, certified by the seals of the Masters of the Templars and of the Hospitallers, by the Patriarch of Jerusalem, and by many archbishops, bishops, and abbots. Henry, as a "most Christian King," received it with the deepest veneration, following the example set on similar occasions by the Emperor Heraclius and by St. Louis, and carried it himself in the procession from St. Paul's to the new church which he had built in connection with Westminster Abbey. Walter de Suffield, Bishop of Norwich, preached a sermon, in which he exalted the treasure of which England had become possessed above that which had passed into the hands of the King of

---

[1] Bliss, *Calendar*, i. 264.

[2] *Hist. Maj.* iv. 640 *sqq.* Some confusion has arisen owing to the fact that the translation of St. Edmund of Canterbury took place in June of the same year, at Pontigny. —*Hist. Maj.* iv. 631 ; v. 76, 192. Archdeacon Perry, p. 192, probably by a slip, confuses the two.

[3] It is interesting to note that Henry, in order to secure full publicity for the proceedings. and to ensure that a faithful record should be kept, asked Matthew Paris to write an account, and invited him to dinner with three of his brother monks. —*Hist. Maj.* iv. 644, 645.

France. There were some, however, who entertained and expressed doubts on the subject, and inquired " how it came to pass that, as Christ had risen with His body perfect, His blood could be there in a separate state." The question was submitted to Grosseteste as the most learned theologian of the day. Without committing himself to the genuineness of the particular relic, except in so far as persons of authority had vouched for it, he demonstrated its possibility by an elaborate argument, which Matthew Paris took down in writing from the Bishop's own lips, and included in the *Additamenta* to his history.[1] The subject is treated with great reverence, but at the same time with what may appear to some to be excessive refinement of ingenuity. He draws a distinction between two kinds of blood, of which the first is generated of the aliments we take, and is frequently lost during lifetime by bleeding and other processes, whilst the second is of the substance, or essence of every animated body. Of the first kind some must have been left, and probably preserved on earth ; and it may be assumed that what had been sent in this vessel belongs to that category. " Of the second kind of Christ's blood, however, we have, perhaps, none upon earth ; I say ' perhaps,' because with God all things are possible." He then proceeds to deal with the nature of the resurrection. It is evident that Grosseteste is not discussing, as might perhaps be supposed, any question connected with the mystery of the Eucharist,[2] but is merely replying to the specific question put to him, namely, how the presence of a portion of Christ's blood contained in the vessel which has been sent to the King, assuming its genuineness, is consistent with the Scriptural statement. It must be remembered, however, when we read the account of the incident and the expression of Grosseteste's opinion, as recorded by Matthew Paris, and especially his reference to Joseph of Arimathæa, that the legend of the Holy Grail had, within a comparatively recent number of years, been made widely

---

[1] *Hist. Maj.* iv. 643 ; vi. 138-144. [2] Cp. p. 335.

known through the writings of Walter de Mapes and others in the latter half of the twelfth century.[1]

In spite of the King's display of piety on that and on other occasions, he was in frequent, and, indeed, in almost constant conflict with the Church and with his own subjects during the period now under consideration. At one moment he opposed the Papal demands, was threatened by his brother Richard, Earl of Cornwall, for so doing, and withdrew his opposition.[2] Innocent's phrase that Henry was " Fredericizing " was sufficient to suggest serious possibilities. At another moment he incurred the public indignation for allowing the Pope to interfere with the rights of patrons.[3] His exactions and general misgovernment increased, and his monetary difficulties, largely due to the favours he conferred on his own and his wife's relatives, were such as to earn him the nickname of "the beggar kinglet," "regulus mendicans," which Matthew Paris gives him in one passage, afterwards, however, trying, though ineffectually, to erase the words.[4] The Parliament which met in London in February 1248, and which was attended by nine prelates, including Grosseteste, nine earls, and a large number of barons, knights, abbots, priors, and clerks, took the opportunity, afforded by Henry's demand for a subsidy, of taking him to task for his misrule.[5] He was reminded that on the last occasion on which he had made a similar exaction, he had promised not to inflict any further injuries upon the realm. And yet he had summoned into the kingdom an increasing number of foreigners, and lavished English funds upon them : he was accused of obtaining from traders the meat, drink, and clothing for his court by force, and without paying for them, with the result that native dealers withdrew and foreign dealers refused to come, thus dealing a serious blow to " that commerce

---

[1] See especially Mapes' *Quest du Saint Graal*, edited by Furnivall for the Roxburghe Club.

[2] *Hist. Maj.* iv. 560.

[3] *Ibid.* iv. 655.

[4] *Ibid.* v. 52 ; Luard's note, as well as his Introduction to that volume, p. 12.

[5] *Hist. Maj.* v. 5 *sqq.*

by which nations are strengthened and enriched."[1] He was
charged with seizing silks and other materials, for the purpose
of giving alms to the poor and candles to churches, thus
snatching a reputation for benevolence and piety out of other
people's pockets; even the poor fishermen were subjected to
such extortions that they found it more profitable to trust
themselves to the high seas, and to sell their herrings and
other fish on distant shores; bishoprics and abbacies were kept
vacant, and their revenues turned to the King's own use; and,
to crown all, he never appointed responsible ministers, such as
a justiciary, a chancellor, or a treasurer, in accordance with the
advice of the kingdom as a whole, but merely officials who
yielded implicit obedience to his personal rule, and only sought
their own advantage. Henry at first promised amendment, but
adjourned a definite reply until the month of June, but Parliament was then dissolved without having received a satisfactory
answer, whilst the King failed in obtaining the subsidy for which
he asked,[2] and resorted to the process of selling the royal plate
to citizens of London, and afterwards exacting large contributions from them over and above the price they had paid.[3]
He also extorted from the monasteries considerable sums,
amounting, in the case of Bury St. Edmunds alone, to 1200
marks.

It is not surprising, therefore, that, in view of the general
maladministration of the kingdom, Grosseteste should, in at
least two instances, have overstepped his legal rights and have
come into conflict with the royal authority. One instance
occurred towards the end of 1249 or the beginning of 1250 in
the county of Rutland, which formed part of the diocese of
Lincoln. Grosseteste had passed a sentence of deprivation and
excommunication on a certain beneficed clerk guilty of incon-
tinence. As the latter remained in possession for more than
forty days, the Bishop instructed the Sheriff of Rutland to
imprison him, and, as the Sheriff, who was a friend of the

<hr>

[1] *Hist. Maj.* l.c.   [2] *Ibid.* v. 21.   [3] *Ibid.* v. 22, 47.

clerk, refused to act, he excommunicated him also. Henry the Third thereupon appealed to the Pope, and obtained from Innocent a letter forbidding the King's bailiffs to be summoned before ecclesiastical courts in secular matters.[1] The other instance is to be found in the course of one of Grosseteste's visitations of his diocese, apparently in 1246, when, at the suggestion of the Franciscans and Dominicans, he endeavoured to extend his inquiries and his reforming energy to the task of effecting an improvement in the morals of the laity, as well as in those of the clergy, and gave instructions to that effect to his archdeacons and rural deans.[2] As grave complaints arose, the King addressed a letter to the Sheriff of Hertfordshire, requiring him not to allow any laymen to appear before the Bishop or his delegates for the purpose of answering inquiries on oath or of making attestations in other than matrimonial and testamentary causes. Although Matthew Paris speaks as if the Bishop's instructions were of a general character, the King's letter, addressed as it was to the Sheriff of Hertfordshire alone, would seem to indicate that it related to some exceptional incidents which had occurred in that county. Although Grosseteste exceeded his powers in both cases, the inability of the civil authority to check wrongdoing and the King's misgovernment may have supplied valid reasons, with which we are unacquainted, for the course he thought fit to adopt. That he was as intent as in the early days of his episcopate upon the necessity for preventing the clergy from holding secular appointments, may be inferred from the Papal mandate, which he obtained in February 1247,[3] authorising him to exercise his office without fear against the rectors of churches in his diocese who took the offices of justice, sheriff, bailiff, or notary in the secular courts. Various ecclesiastical disputes of a minor character, apart from the work connected with his annual visitations, also occupied some of his time. A dispute, for instance, between John de

---

[1] *Hist. Maj.* v. 109, 110.   [2] *Ibid.* iv. 579, 580.
[3] Bliss, *Calendar*, i. 230.

Vercelli, Papal subdeacon and prebendary of Walton in Lincoln cathedral, who was a Buckinghamshire rector, and the Archdeacon of Buckingham, appears to have commenced in 1239, and only to have been settled in 1251 in favour of the former, and the correspondence with the Pope on the subject was carried on by Grosseteste.[1] The excommunication of one Roger Gray of Buckingham necessitated in 1246 a communication to the King.[2] The Papal Provisions in his diocese, though his resistance to them did not reach the stage to which it attained after 1250, were such as to cause him much concern, and were productive of serious difficulties. During Grosseteste's first visit to Lyons he was informed in October 1245, that in February of that year a mandate had been sent to John Sarraceni, Dean of Wells and Papal chaplain, to give to John de Romania, Papal chaplain, or his proctor, corporal possession of the church of Coleby in the diocese of Lincoln, which the Bishop had conferred upon Master Simon, now deceased.[3] In 1247 a dispute occurred between an Englishman, Alan de St. Faith, and an Italian, Bartholomew de Rovata, both of whom had been presented to the same church of Ledenham in Lincolnshire, with the result that in January of the following year Grosseteste found himself compelled to sequestrate the church pending a decision of the rival claims.[4] In 1248 Grosseteste had to procure a revocation of whatever had been attempted to his prejudice by certain executors, who had suspended him from the collation of prebends, and who had apparently received Papal authority for so doing.[5] He was also called upon in the same year to take steps to secure Nicholas of Farnham, sometime Bishop of Durham, who had resigned his See, against any molestation to which he might be subjected on account of the provision of certain manors made to him by the Archbishop of York under Innocent's orders.[6] It was probably on account of

---

[1] Bliss, *Calendar*, i. 181, 266.

[2] Roberts, *Calendarium Genealogicum*, i. 19.

[3] Bliss, *Calendar*, i. 214.

[4] *Ibid.* i. 239, 241.

[5] *Ibid.* i. 244.

[6] *Ibid.* i. 255.

applications of a similar character on other occasions that
he found it necessary to apply to the Pope for an indult,
which he obtained in June 1247, granting him the privilege
that he should not be summoned more than one day's journey
from his diocese, which is there stated to have been five days'
journey in length, unless special mention was made of this
indult in the apostolic letter, and also that he need not take
cognisance of the suits of litigants committed to him by the
Pope.[1] It may be noted that a similar privilege was conferred
upon his successor, Henry de Lexington, in 1255,[2] and the
reason is doubtless to be found in the vast extent of the
bishopric.

One of the most important features during this part of
Grosseteste's life was the quickening of the bonds of friendship
which united him with Simon de Montfort, Earl of Leicester,
and his increased interest in the party of political reform, an
interest which he had commenced to show, as has been seen,
some years before he became a bishop, and which he had
exhibited in a conspicuous degree in the Parliaments in which
he took part, as well as in connection with the Committee of
twelve in 1244. The first reference to Simon de Montfort
in Grosseteste's correspondence is to be found in the letter
which he addressed in 1231, whilst Archdeacon of Leicester, to
the Countess of Winchester, with regard to the Jews who had
been expelled from the domain of the new Lord of Leicester.[3]
In a letter written to Earl Simon himself in 1238, Grosseteste
warns him against the injustice of over-severity, and urges him
not to punish a certain burgess of the town of Leicester,
probably Simon de Curlevache, above the measure of his fault.[4]
The letter is couched in affectionate terms, which imply a
friendship of long standing. In 1239 we find Grosseteste
exhorting him to bear with patience the trouble which had come

---

[1] Bliss, *Calendar*. i. 234.
[2] *Ibid*. i. 309.
[3] See p. 100, and note. Letter 5.
[4] Letter 48. Luard's Introduction, p. 109. *Hist. Maj.* iii. 479. Simon de Curlevache was an alderman of Leicester. See Miss Bateson's *Records of the Borough of Leicester*, pp. 26, etc.

over him in consequence of the King's hostility, and offering to plead his cause with Henry.[1] The letter was probably written shortly after he had gone into exile. A reconciliation with the King took place a few months later, but it is not known how far Grosseteste's suggested mediation contributed to that result. From 1240 until 1243 he was, with one brief interval, out of England, first in connection with the Crusade in Palestine, and then with the campaign against Louis IX. In the Parliament of 1244 he and Grosseteste were both placed on the Committee of twelve, and, as has been shown, the Bishop was on that occasion more thorough in his views and more opposed to the King's exactions than the Earl. For the next few years the latter appears to have spent most of his time in Leicestershire without taking an active part in political affairs, and to have been in frequent communication with Grosseteste, and more especially with Adam Marsh. Rishanger[2] says that it was in accordance with Grosseteste's advice that he handled what was difficult, attempted what was doubtful, and completed what he had begun, in regard to all things by which he hoped that his merits would be increased. There can be no doubt that it was the influence of the Bishop, who discerned the sterling worth and true greatness of his character, in spite of his impulsive nature and occasional harshness of temper,[3] contributed greatly towards the formation and development of the Earl's opinions. It was for his benefit that Grosseteste wrote a short treatise, entitled *The Principles of Kingship and of Tyranny*,[4] in which a distinction was doubtless drawn between the methods of responsible government under a constitutional monarchy and

---

[1] Letter 75.

[2] Rishanger, ed. Riley, Rolls Series, p. 36.

[3] M. Bémont (pp. 61, 62) is probably right in his view that Letter 143, from Grosseteste to Simon de Montfort in 1250, and Letters 18 and 25 (*Mon. Francisc.* pp. 103 and 110) from Adam Marsh to the Bishop, relating to

acts of the Earl's agents, imply that Grosseteste is disposed to blame his friend's somewhat hasty and inconsiderate proceedings.

[4] *Mon. Francisc.* p. 110. The date of the letter is uncertain. It was written either immediately before the Earl's return to Gascony in 1248, or immediately before his return there in 1252. The former is more likely.

those of personal rule under a despotism. In his turn Simon de Montfort was highly pleased with the Bishop's plans of ecclesiastical reform, and was ready to further them with the utmost enthusiasm. "The Earl of Leicester," writes Adam Marsh to Grosseteste,[1] "has spoken with me about the most salutary and splendid project with which Heaven has inspired your heart for the liberation of souls from bondage; he approves of it, extols it, and embraces it with all his ardent devotion to great ideas, and is ready to put it into execution at once with his partisans, if any are found. But in his anxiety for your bodily weakness he says that he does not see how you can face such difficulties and dangers in person." The precise meaning of the passage is obscure, but it relates in all likelihood to Grosseteste's views on the need for combining in one and the same effort the struggle for the liberties of the State and the struggle for the liberties of the Church, and for co-operation between the friends of progress in the one and the friends of progress in the other, in view of the fact that they were confronted by similar encroachments and similar perils. Frequent communications passed between him and the Bishop through the medium of Adam Marsh, and they often held personal intercourse with one another.[2] In 1248 Simon de Montfort was appointed Lieutenant of Gascony, and for the next five years, except from November of 1251 to June of 1252, he was continuously absent from England. It was probably in that year, therefore, that he entrusted to Grosseteste's charge[3] his son Henry, who must at that time have been ten years of age, and who is described as being of tender years, but old enough to be taught the rudiments of literature and to be trained in the way he should go. His youngest son, Almeric, was also placed under the Bishop's care not long afterwards.[4] No mention is made by name of the Earl's other sons, and it may therefore be assumed that the eldest and the youngest were the only two who were sent to Grosseteste.

---

[1] *Mon. Francisc.* p. 111.
[2] *Ibid.* pp. 107, 111, 262, etc.
[3] *Ibid.* p. 110.
[4] *Ibid.* p. 163.

Adam Marsh writes frequently to the Earl, stating how they are progressing. In one letter he says :[1] "Thanks to God, the Lord Bishop of Lincoln is well, and so are your children, who are showing remarkable capacity and are full of promise, making advance from day to day in all that is good." Rishanger relates that Grosseteste, when nearing his end, laid his hand upon the eldest son's head, and foretold that he and his father would both sacrifice their lives one day in the cause of truth and justice,[2] a prediction which was fulfilled when, on the 4th of August 1265, they fell on the field of Evesham, and were honoured as the martyrs of liberty by the people of England.

Simon de Montfort, who was a man of varied literary tastes, took a special interest, for instance, in John de Basingstoke's researches,[3] and was well read in the Scriptures and in the writings of some of the Fathers, found intellectual delight as well as spiritual comfort in Grosseteste's conversation. The Countess of Leicester, too, must have served as an additional link between them. She was the sister of Henry the Third, and the widow of William Marshall, Earl of Pembroke, with whose brother Grosseteste had been on terms of special intimacy, and to whom he had addressed his letters on the glory and riches of heaven, and on the two kinds of wisdom.[4] The Countess was devoted to her husband, accompanied him into exile when he was driven from England by her brother, the King, and inspired him with wise counsels when his rashness was apt to lead him astray.[5] She had, however, her weaknesses. Adam Marsh, for instance, does not hesitate to tell her on one occasion that she spends too much money on dress, and is not sufficiently guarded in her language or in her temper.[6] How pleasant, however, were the relations between Grosseteste and the family may be inferred from one little incident. The Bishop's cook having

---

[1] *Mon. Francisc.* p. 268.

[2] Rishanger's *Chronicle* (Rolls Series), p. 36.

[3] *Hist. Maj.* v. 284.

[4] Letters 6, 7.

[5] *Mon. Francisc.* pp. 298, 299.

[6] *Ibid.* pp. 294, 295.

died, he borrowed from the Countess a certain John of Leicester, who held the same office in her household. As he was a good cook, and probably Simon de Montfort had already started for Gascony, so that he no longer required to dispense hospitality, Grosseteste thought it advisable to retain the said John's services, and asked Adam Marsh, in a letter which excited in his correspondent both laughter and tears, to convey his excuses to the Countess. Her reply was that, even if she had the best of servants, she would rejoice at the opportunity of being able to place all or any of them at Grosseteste's disposal.[1] Her gratitude to the Bishop for his support of her husband during his trial in 1252 was unbounded.[2]

The most important part of Simon de Montfort's life belongs, no doubt, to the period which followed Grosseteste's death; but the inspiration which led him to seek his triumph at Lewes and his fall at Evesham was due, in no small measure, to the principles with which he had been imbued by his friend. In the early part of his career there was little, beyond his ancestral connection with this country and his marriage with the King's sister, to distinguish him from the numerous foreign adventurers who came to these shores during the reign of Henry the Third, but his great qualities of heart and mind gradually asserted themselves above his defects; and it was Grosseteste's object to induce him to seek a broader basis of support than was to be found by the mere assertion of the rights and privileges of his own order, and to include the advocacy of such reforms as were in harmony with the needs of the Church and of the nation as a whole. When from May 9 to June 11, 1252, Earl Simon had to answer the accusations brought against him by the nobles of Gascony and the Archbishop of Bordeaux, in a trial of which a vivid description is given in a letter written by Adam Marsh

---

[1] *Mon. Francisc.* p. 170.

[2] *Ibid.* p. 130. For further details respecting Eleanor, Countess of Leicester, see the introduction to her *Household Roll* of 1265, edited by Turner for the Bannatyne Club in 1841, and also her biography in Mrs. Green's *Lives of the Princesses of England*, vol. ii.

to Grosseteste,[1] the testimony of the representatives of the whole community of Bordeaux was used to discredit his adversaries, and to show that it was his strictness in the administration of justice which had aroused their enmity, and that his horizon was not bounded by the interests of his own class. It was Grosseteste who, when nearing his end in 1253, asked the Earl to return good for evil, to forget the insults which Henry the Third had addressed to him, and to come to the rescue of his dominions in Gascony against the attacks of the King of Castile and a new insurrection of the Gascon nobles; and Simon de Montfort, " who regarded," says Matthew Paris, " the Bishop in the light of a father confessor, and was on terms of most intimate friendship with him, inclined his ear and his heart in obedience to his request."[2]   And when, in the memorable year 1265, the Earl summoned by separate writs representatives of the towns in addition to those of the counties for the purposes of Parliament, and independently of the machinery of the Sheriff's Court, he was acting in accordance with the spirit of Grosseteste's maxim, laid down on a different occasion, that " unless we all stand together we shall all utterly perish," and was guided by that regard for " truth and justice " which he had derived from his great teacher.

How closely Grosseteste and de Montfort were associated in the popular imagination is indicated in the story, given by Rishanger,[3] that, on the Sunday before the battle of Evesham, a lad was brought to Grosseteste's tomb to be healed. After a long sleep he woke and told his parents that it was needless to wait longer, for the Bishop was not present; he was gone to Evesham " to help Earl Simon, his brother, who was to die

---

[1] *Mon. Francisc.* pp. 122-130. The letter is translated in Mrs. Green's *Lives of the Princesses*, vol. ii. pp. 447 *sqq.*

[2] *Hist. Maj.* iv. 415, 416.

[3] *Chronicle*, ed. Camden Society, p. 71, quoted in Prof. Prothero's *Simon de Montfort*, p. 144.   For songs relating to Simon de Montfort see Prof. Prothero's fourth Appendix, the Appendix to Rishanger's *Chronicle*, published by the Camden Society, M. Bémont's Introduction, pp. 15-19, and Prof. Maitland's edition of one of the songs in the *English Historical Review* for April 1896.

there." And in a song relating to the death of Simon de Montfort,[1] written shortly after that battle, occur the lines :—

> Hic Robertum sequebatur
> Cujus vita commendatur
> Certa per miracula.
> Dictis ejus vir obedit ;
> Fert Robertus, Symon credit
> De statutis talia :
> Si verum confitearis
> Et pro dictis moriaris
> Magna feres praemia.

It is clear, however, from the anecdote related by Matthew Paris, that Grosseteste was able not only to direct the Earl's policy in a forward direction, and to broaden the range of his sympathies, but also to exercise over him a moderating influence when the needs of the case required it ; and there can be no doubt that, had he lived a few years longer, he would have used every effort to avert a civil war, whilst upholding Simon de Montfort's efforts to redress misgovernment, and to establish the constitution of the realm on a wider foundation.

It has been necessary in previous chapters to deal by anticipation with much of the work in which Grosseteste was engaged after his return from Lyons in 1245, in connection with the visitation of his diocese, his endeavours to make satisfactory arrangements with religious houses for the establishment of vicarages, and his renewed attempt to improve the condition, and at the same time the standard of conduct and of learning of the clergy.[2] As far as the Chapter of Lincoln was concerned, the Pope's decision had brought about a reconciliation, and one of the first duties to which he turned his attention after his arrival in England was that of visiting the cathedral and the prebendal churches.[3] In spite of the settlement of the dispute a few minor questions still remained in abeyance. The new dean, for instance, Henry de Lexington, asked Grosseteste

---

[1] Edited by Prof. Maitland from Caius College MS. No. 85, *English Historical Review*, April 1896, p. 317.

[2] See pp. 144-146, 154, 162, 163.

[3] *Ann. Monast.* (Dunstable), iii. 171 ; (T. Wykes), iv. 94.

to alter the order in which he proposed to carry out his visitations, and to leave the cathedral to the last, and, when the Bishop changed his plan at his request, and began with the prebends in the archdeaconry of Stow, turned round and accused him of inconsistency.[1] Grosseteste also noted that the looks of the canons expressed the annoyance they felt in their hearts at the decision, and appealed both to them and to the Dean not to be influenced by petty considerations, but to co-operate with him loyally in future in the great work in which they were all engaged.[2] The letter appears to have been successful, for from that time forward no unpleasantness marred the relations between him and them; and although Matthew Paris asserts that Thomas Wallensis, Archdeacon of Lincoln, accepted the bishopric of St. David's, which was offered to him at the end of 1247 or the beginning of 1248, because he was annoyed at the humiliation to which the Dean and Chapter had been exposed, it is hardly likely either that, as Grosseteste's right-hand man, he would have been affected by that reason, or that, as a Welshman, he would have declined a promotion which took him back into his native land, to a See which Giraldus Cambrensis in his day had ardently coveted, however barren and stony St David's may have been at that time.[3] Moreover, in a letter [4] in which he offers the archdeaconry of Huntingdon with the prebend of Buckden to a friend who had previously refused the offer of the prebend of Gretton on the ground of the prolongation of the dispute, he expresses his thankfulness that peace now reigns between himself and the Chapter; and in any case his visitation of the Chapter and of all the prebends without exception met with no opposition from any quarter.[5]

Into the story of his visitations during these years it is

---

[1] Letter 121.

[2] Letter 122.

[3] *Hist. Maj.* iv. 647 ; Giraldus Cambrensis, *Itinerarium Cambriae*, ii. 1 ; Felten, p. 50. On the other hand a passage in one of Adam Marsh's letters, *Mon. Francisc.* p. 150, rather suggests that some coolness had arisen between Grosseteste and Thomas Wallensis.

[4] Letter 118.

[5] *Annales Monastici*, l.c.

needless to enter here. Suffice it to say that to the year
1249, in which he appears to have paid special attention to
the monasteries, belong his visits to the priories of Dunstable
and Caldwell, with the results previously mentioned,[1] and his
deposition of the Abbess of Godstow.[2] His action in regard to
the abbey of Peterborough shows the confidence felt in him
by the monks in spite of his severity ; for it was the convent
itself which appealed to Grosseteste against its Abbot, on
account of the inordinate expenditure incurred by the latter for
the enrichment of his own relatives ; and the Bishop of Lincoln,
who, says Matthew Paris in that passage,[3] "was always ready
to punish those who strayed from the right path," was only
prevented from taking strong measures by the spontaneous
resignation of the Abbot ; whereupon "one of the manors
connected with the abbacy was assigned to him, although he
did not deserve it, in order that he might live more honestly
and more honourably, like a hermit, during the rest of his
life." The King, who had benefited by the Abbot's liberality,
was greatly annoyed by the proceedings.

It was towards the close of 1249 or the beginning of 1250
that Grosseteste, in his anxiety to place the vicarages on a
definite and satisfactory footing, summoned all the beneficed
monks in his diocese to meet him, first at Stamford, then at
Leicester, and then at Oxford, for the purpose of showing him
their founders' charters, episcopal confirmations, and Papal
privileges,[4] of which he kept a copy, with the intention of consulting the Pope on the general question involved. Matthew
Paris, who refers only to the Leicester meeting, which took
place on the 13th of January 1250,[5] states that Grosseteste
was able to communicate a privilege which he had already

---

[1] See p. 154.

[2] See p. 164. Grosseteste *Roll* of
that date, under the head of the Archdeaconry of Oxford ; Luard's Introd.
to the *Letters*, p. 69.

[3] *Hist. Maj.* v. 84.

[4] See p. 144. *Ann. Monast.* (Dunstable), iii. 180.

[5] *Hist. Maj.* v. 96 ; *Hist. Anglorum*, iii. 68, 69 ; Luard's Introd.
to the *Letters*, p. 71 ; Pegge, p.
171.

obtained from Innocent IV., and which is given in the *Addita-menta*,[1] by sending to the Roman Court a certain Master Leonard, his clerk, at great expense to himself. The Pope's letter, dated the 17th of May 1249, authorises Grosseteste, in cases in which monks have appropriated churches or tithes to their own use without the consent of the Chapter of Lincoln, to annul their action, and to forbid similar proceedings in future, through the operation of ecclesiastical censure and without appeal. The course advocated was one which Grosseteste had long been pursuing, but the letter was intended to strengthen his hands and to help him to overcome the obstacles which stood in his way. How great was the resistance he encountered from the wealth, the *vis inertiae*, and the *esprit de corps* of the monastic bodies, may be gathered from the strenuous opposition offered to his efforts in the pages of Matthew Paris. Appeals against the Bishop's decisions were made to the Pope on the part of the Templars, the Hospitallers, the exempt abbots and priors, mainly Cistercians,[2] the Premonstratentian Abbot of Newhouse,[3] and also by others, who, with large sums of money, purchased peace for themselves from Innocent, much to the sorrow of Grosseteste, who thus found his action thwarted, and much of his work undone.[4]

---

[1] *Hist. Maj.* vi. 152.

[2] *Ibid.* v. 97.

[3] *Hist. Anglorum*, iii. 70.

[4] The manner in which the attempts to undo Grosseteste's work with regard to vicarages continued after his death may be inferred from the following entry under the year 1254, *Ann. Monast.* (Dunstable), iii. 195 : " Eodem anno obtinuimus in causa contra Walterum vicarium nostrum de Stodham (Studham), quia retractata fuit augmentatio vicariae suae facta per dominum Robertum Grosteste Lincolniae episcopum. Et per abbatem Westmonasterii, judicem nostrum delegatum, redacta fuit ad statum pristinum."

CHAPTER XIII

IT was under the conditions described in the latter part of the previous chapter that Grosseteste, in order to defeat the efforts to undermine his establishment of vicarages, decided to proceed in person to Lyons. Other questions also took him there, one of which was the question of the conduct of Boniface, Archbishop of Canterbury. Grosseteste had anticipated, some years before,[1] that the other bishops would not be over anxious to see him triumph over his Chapter, as the outcome of that decision might be that the Archbishop of Canterbury would claim similar rights over them, though the cases were by no means parallel. And, indeed, it so happened that Boniface cited Grosseteste's example as a precedent for visiting not only the prebends connected with his own Cathedral, but also the canons of St. Paul's, in defiance of the Bishop of London.[2] The Archbishop, however, was one of the most singular persons ever raised to high ecclesiastical office, and Grosseteste's eyes had long been open to his incapacity. It was mainly on that account that he had urged, some years earlier, that Boniface should be assisted by friars of both Orders possessing the qualifications previously mentioned.[3] In the affairs of Robert de Passelew the Archbishop had acted merely as the King's tool.[4] The request for a subsidy

---

[1] Letter 80, p. 257.
[2] *Hist. Maj.* v. 119-121.
[3] P. 254, Letter 115.
[4] Letter 126.

from the whole province had only been granted after much hesitation,[1] and, as years went on, Boniface's attitude gave rise to strong opposition on the part of the English prelates. Some anecdotes related by Matthew Paris[2] exhibit him in the light rather of a condottière than of an ecclesiastic, and his appointment had certainly been due originally to the King's weakness and to the fact that he was the Queen's uncle. His visitations were intended, says the St. Albans historian, "not for the advancement of religion or the reform of morals, but to satisfy his usual greed for filthy lucre."[3] The officials sent as his representatives extorted large sums of money from the dioceses to which they went, and aroused the indignation of the bishops. The connection between the action of the Archbishop and Grosseteste's visit to Lyons may be inferred from the fact that his companions on his journey were the Bishops of London and of Worcester,[4] both of whom had grievances to urge against Boniface, and both of whom subsequently took part with Grosseteste and certain other prelates in the meeting held at Dunstable, in 1251, to protest against his claims and exactions. The Bishop of Lincoln was also accompanied by Robert Marsh, Archdeacon of Oxford, and by John de Crackale, Archdeacon of Bedford,[5] and several of his clerks. The companion of his previous journey to Lyons, Adam Marsh, was unable to go with him: he writes to Grosseteste that he wept as he stood on the shore of Dover, earnestly desiring that he might, in filial

---

[1] Letter 85.

[2] *Hist. Maj.* v. 123. Adam Marsh, however, points out (*Mon. Francisc.* p. 163) that a good many exaggerated and mendacious stories concerning Boniface's proceedings were current among the clergy and the people, and it is possible that some of them may have been repeated by Matthew Paris.

[3] *Hist. Maj.* v. 187.

[4] *Ibid.* v. 96, 97 ; cp. *Hist. Anglorum*, iii. 562. Sir F. Madden suggests that *Wigorniensis* may be a mistake for *Wintoniensis.* It is improbable, however, that the mistake would occur in both passages. It is true that the Bishop of Winchester was also in France in 1250 for about eleven months before his death at Tours on the 21st of Sept. 1250. The point, however, is settled by the document cited in Bliss, *Calendar of the Papal Registers*, i. 264, showing that the Bishop of Worcester was at Lyons in 1250.

[5] See p. 324.

obedience to the Bishop, follow his directions in works of piety; but that this could not be done without leave, which he was desirous of obtaining, from the Pope or from the Minister-General, and serious obstacles had been placed in the way of the suggestion by the King, the Queen, and the Franciscan Order itself, and could only be removed by Grosseteste's strenuous exertions.[1] What was the precise object at which Grosseteste and Adam Marsh both aimed is not quite clear from the letter in question: possibly the Bishop may have wished him to give up his connection with the Court and with the Archbishop, which occupied much of his time, in order to devote himself to spiritual and other work; or, possibly, he may have wanted Adam Marsh to accompany him, as before, to Lyons, for the purpose of supporting his statement as to the evils from which the Church was suffering. In a letter[2] written almost immediately afterwards to William de Nottingham, the Provincial Minister in England, Friar Adam expresses his deep regret that he was unable to go with Grosseteste, refers in terms of gloomy pessimism to the religious outlook in England, and says that his feelings of annoyance are increased owing to the fact that he has to be constantly in the Archbishop's company.[3]

Grosseteste's second visit to Lyons presents some important differences as compared with his first visit to that city. In 1245 the principal objects of his journey were to secure an authoritative decision in the dispute with the Dean and Chapter, and to take part in the proceedings of the General Council. In 1250 his main objects were, first, to overcome the resistance of the monastic orders, especially such as were exempt, to the establishment of vicarages and of proper financial arrangements for the maintenance of vicars; secondly, to explain to the Pope the evils from which the Church in England was exposed, with special reference to the encroachments of the King, the exactions

---

[1] *Mon. Francisc.* p. 156.
[2] *Ibid.* p. 312.

[3] "Domini Cantuariae contubernio aggravatus."

and claims of the Archbishop of Canterbury, and the state of the clergy; and, thirdly, to state the objections entertained to the Papal Provisions, and to point out the abuses which did most to injure the reputation and efficiency of the Roman Court. It is possible, also, that he may have been desirous of holding some personal intercourse with Simon de Montfort, who was at Lyons for a few months that year;[1] but no record of their interviews has been preserved.

It is natural that Matthew Paris, as the avowed champion of monastic rights and privileges, should devote most space to the first of the three objects above named, and should endeavour to make it appear as though Grosseteste only turned his attention to the second and the third after he had failed in the first, in order that he might be thought not to have been utterly defeated in his purpose.[2] As a matter of fact, however, he was not entirely unsuccessful in the first of those objects. Adam Marsh writes to William de Nottingham that he has received a letter from the venerable Bishop of Lincoln, dated from the Roman Court, in which he states that he is returning in good health and has prospered in his business.[3] And Matthew Paris himself cites,[4] though under the year 1252, the text of a letter addressed by Innocent on 25th September 1250, to Grosseteste, practically agreeing to his principal suggestions on the subject of vicarages. The reason why the publication of that letter was delayed is not stated. The letter runs thus:— "Whereas in your city and diocese certain monks and others forming communities hold possession, for their own benefit, of the parochial churches, in which the vicarages are either too small or non-existent: we, by this apostolic mandate, authorise you to institute vicarages in the said churches out of their revenues, or, if need be, to augment them from the same source in order to make them less poor, in accordance with the will of

---

[1] See M. Bémont, *Simon de Mont-fort,* p. 89.

[2] *Hist. Maj.* v. 98.

[3] *Mon. Francisc.* pp. 308, 309.

[4] *Hist. Maj.* v. 300.

God and the custom of the country, notwithstanding that the aforesaid persons may be exempted or otherwise protected by any apostolic privileges or indulgences, by which the mandate may be impeded or deferred, and of which special mention ought to be made in these presents; and we empower you to postpone all appeal and to restrain all opponents by ecclesiastical censure."

It is evident, therefore, that the conversation stated by Matthew Paris [1] to have taken place between the Pope and Grosseteste cannot represent an accurate report of what actually occurred, in so far as it rests upon the supposition that the Bishop did not succeed in the first of the three objects for which he went to Lyons. Grosseteste is reported, after saying that he blushed to have failed in his purpose, to have used the words, "O money, money, how much power you have, especially at the Roman Court!" whereupon the Pope, overhearing what he said, retorted, "O ye English, most wretched of men are you. Each of you is trying to impoverish his neighbour. How many monks, subject to you like sheep, your own countrymen and servants, intent upon prayers and hospitality, you are wearing out, in order that you may satisfy your tyranny and cupidity, and enrich others who may be foreigners!" Grosseteste's words, if any such were spoken, are more likely to have formed part of his general indictment of the abuses of the Roman Court, than to have been applied in a special sense to the appeal made by the Templars, Hospitallers, Cistercians, and others; the reference to money paid to foreigners is not one which is likely to have proceeded out of Innocent's mouth; and Grosseteste was the last man in the world to whom the accusation of "cupidity" could have been applicable. In all probability the conversation was written down in the scriptorium at St. Albans on the strength of some tenth-rate hearsay evidence. If, as Matthew Paris states, the Bishop departed "amid the insulting cries of all present," [2] and returned to England "with

---

[1] *Hist. Maj.* v. 97, 98.   [2] *Ibid.* v. 98.

empty hands and a sad countenance,"[1] the cause of the former incident must have been due, not to any failure with respect to the question of vicarages, but to the odium which his plain-spoken denunciation of abuses aroused among those who winced under his attack, while the cause of the latter must be sought in the apparent hopelessness of the task of redressing the griev-ances of the Church.

It is possible that some of Grosseteste's dissatisfaction may have arisen from the support accorded to Boniface at the Roman Court.[2] On that subject he despatched to his brother bishops in England reports, on the strength of which they decided to collect funds for the purpose of opposing the Archbishop's demands, and neutralising his influence at Lyons; for, observes Matthew Paris, the Curia was apt to be turned now one way, now another, by the intervention of money, like a reed shaken by the wind. It must be remembered, however, that Innocent was under peculiar obligations to Boniface, whose brother Philip was Archbishop-elect of Lyons as well as Bishop-elect of Valence, and also head of the Papal military forces ;[3] indeed, the two militant archbishops on one occasion undertook to protect the Pope by main force not only against the Emperor but also, if necessary, against the King of France.[4] It may also be surmised from one passage that Innocent was practi-cally in Philip's hands at Lyons, and was obliged to submit to his will.[5]

The main cause, however, of Grosseteste's despondency—a despondency so intense that it nearly induced him to resign his See, and actually led him to commit for a time the administra-tion of the affairs of his diocese to Robert Marsh[6]—is to be found in the failure of his attempt to secure adequate recognition of the abuses he denounced with a view to their removal. It was on 13th May 1250 that, standing in the presence of the

<hr>

1 *Hist. Maj.* v. 186.
2 *Ibid.*
3 *Ibid.* iv. 426.

4 *Ibid.* v. 175.
5 *Ibid.* v. 226.
6 *Ibid.* v. 186.

Pope and the College of Cardinals, and with no one at his side save Robert[1] Marsh, Archdeacon of Oxford, Grosseteste first asked permission to call attention to a matter of grave importance, and produced four copies of an elaborate memorandum, or sermon, as it is sometimes called, which he had prepared on the evils prevailing in the Church. One copy he handed to the Pope himself, a second to Cardinal bishop William de Sabina, a third to Cardinal priest Hugh de Sabina, and a fourth to Cardinal deacon John de St. Nicholas, the last of whom read it aloud, with scarcely any interruption, in the presence of the assembled Pope and cardinals.[2] No stronger denunciation of ecclesiastical abuses has ever been penned, and the vigour of its invective is rarely surpassed even in the writings of the sixteenth century; but it is obvious that it must have been composed with the object of placing before the Pope, without extenuation or palliation, the worst evils connected with the existing system, in the hope of convincing him and those who shared with him the responsibility for the central government of the Church, of the imperative necessity for taking the most drastic measures to destroy the corruption which was eating into its heart. The unflinching courage displayed by Grosseteste in placing the facts before such an assembly is hardly equalled in history; and it must be recognised that Innocent showed no small degree of toleration and breadth of view in allowing such a document to be read aloud.

The early part of the memorandum deals with the general question of the form of the Christian Church and the nature of the pastoral power, somewhat on the lines laid down in Grosseteste's letter of 1239, on the subject of the right of a bishop to visit his chapter.[3] After referring to the humility

---

[1] "Richard" in the text is a mistake for "Robert."

[2] The memorandum is printed in the Appendix to Brown's *Fasciculus*, ii. 250-258, with an introductory note by Robert Marsh, who was present.

It is partly translated, partly paraphrased by Archdeacon Perry, pp. 207-223. Portions are quoted by Wycliffe in his *De civili dominio*, i. chap. xliii. pp. 385-394.

[3] Letter 127. See pp. 188-193.

of Christ, and the purity and simplicity of the early Church,
he points out that the spread of Christianity and the necessities of proper organisation led the first planters of the faith
to ordain and constitute fellow-labourers, men of power, fearing God, hating covetousness, elders not so much in years as
in wisdom and virtue, to assist them in their work, and to hand
on unimpaired the truths they had received, in holy deeds and
the endurance of tribulations and martyrdoms. Out of those
beginnings grew an elaborate system, and necessarily so, inasmuch as the methods of government applicable to a very small
number of persons were not adapted to the requirements of
large numbers, but the type and principle of the organisation
remained the same. And "although all pastors in common are
but one in the first pastor Christ, and all represent Him and
occupy His place, yet, by a special prerogative, those who preside
in this most holy See are peculiarly the representatives and
vicars of Christ, as the cardinals represent the apostles, and
other pastors those first fathers." All these ought incessantly
to labour for the coming of God's kingdom. Such is the theory,
but what are the facts? Part of the world is in a state of
unbelief, part has been severed by schism,[1] and of the remainder
a considerable portion is a prey to heresy[2] and vice; and the
cause is to be found in the lack of good pastors, the multiplication of bad pastors, and the restrictions placed upon the pastoral
power. Then follows a fierce denunciation of the covetousness,
the avarice, and the immorality of the clergy. "As the life of
the pastors is the book of the laity, it is manifest that such as
these are the preachers of all errors and wickednesses. They are
in truth teachers of heresy, inasmuch as the word of action is
stronger than the word of speech: they are worse than those
who practise abominations, for they defile the soul."

"But what," he continues, "is the first cause and origin of

[1] The Greek Church. See *Hist.
Maj.* iii. 470, v. 191, vi. 336.

[2] The term had no application to
England, where the thing may be said
to have been absolutely unknown at
that time. See p. 61 for the probable
reference.

these great evils? I fear to speak it, but yet I dare not be silent, lest I should merit the reproach of the prophet, 'Woe is me, because I have held my peace!' The cause, the fountain, the origin of all this, is this Roman Court, not only because it does not put to flight these evils and purge away these abominations, when it alone has the power to do so, and is pledged most fully in that sense; but still more because by its dispensations, provisions, and collations to the pastoral care, it appoints in the full light of the sun men such as I have described, not pastors, but destroyers of men; and, that it may provide for the likelihood of some one person, it hands over to the jaws of death many thousands of souls, for the life of each one of which the Son of God was willing to be condemned to a most shameful death. He who does not hinder this when he can is involved in the same crime; and the crime is greater in proportion as he who commits it is more highly placed, and the cause of evil is worse than its effect. Nor let any one say that this Court acts thus for the common advantage of the Church. This common advantage was studied by the holy fathers who endured suffering on this account; it can never be advanced by that which is unlawful or evil. Woe to those who say, Let us do evil that good may come! The work of the pastoral cure does not consist alone in administering the sacraments, repeating the canonical hours, and celebrating masses—and even these offices are seldom performed by mercenaries — but in the teaching of the living truth, the condemnation of vice, the punishment of it when necessary, and this but rarely can the mercenaries dare to do. It consists also in feeding the hungry, giving drink to the thirsty, clothing the naked, receiving guests, visiting the sick and those in prison, especially those who belong to the parish and have a claim on the endowment of the Church. These duties cannot be performed by deputies or hirelings, especially as they scarce receive out of the goods of the Church enough to support their own lives. This bad use of their office is greatly to be lamented in the case of the seculars, but in their case, at any rate, there is always the possibility that others of a better mind may follow them. When, however, parish churches are appropriated to religious houses, these evils are made permanent. Those who preside in this See are in a special degree the representatives of Christ, and in that character are bound to exhibit the works of Christ, and to that extent are entitled to be obeyed in all things. If, however, through favouritism or on other grounds they command what is opposed to the precepts and will of Christ, they separate themselves from Christ and from the conception of what a Pope should be; they are guilty of apostasy themselves and a cause of apostasy in others. God forbid that such should be the case in this See! Let its occupants, therefore, take heed lest they do or enjoin anything which is at variance with the will of Christ."

Grosseteste then passes to the subject of the difficulties with which the bishops are confronted in the discharge of their pastoral duties, especially in England, owing to various restrictions, both ecclesiastical and secular. The exempt monasteries are a source of grave scandal, the secular arm intervenes to prevent inquiry into the morals of the laity, and the appeals to the Roman Court and to the archiepiscopal See enable offenders to secure the postponement of their punishment for a year or for ever, with the result that they continue to wallow in their vices. Those difficulties are disheartening to bishops who have a sense of the importance of their task and are earnestly devoted to its performance. "If a bishop out of zeal for souls removes from the cure of souls unfit persons, he is at once subjected to intolerable vexation, particularly if those whom he has rejected happen to be related to persons holding offices or dignities in the State. Each art is best carried out in accordance with its own laws: the highest art, which is that of providing for the salvation of souls, ought to be carried out in accordance with the laws which God has appointed for it, namely, by the Gospels, which constitute the standard and measure of its right performance. Let this holy See, therefore, be bound by these precepts. As it is, the Curia has filled the world with lies, and has even taken away confidence in documents. By disobeying the precept given to St. Peter, 'Put up thy sword into thy sheath,' it invites the woe denounced, 'All they that smite with the sword shall perish with the sword.' Moses and Samuel, the types and figures of this Court, received no gifts; they oppressed and afflicted no one; but the whole people and clergy of England murmur against this Court for having conceded to the Archbishop of Canterbury the first-fruits of all the benefices in the province for a year, which were levied with the utmost violence and oppression, although the church of Canterbury had sufficient for the payment of its own debts. In proportion as the days are more evil ought we the more diligently to keep ourselves from evil actions and to cling to those things which are good. Where the battle rages most fiercely, there ought sloth and cowardice to be most avoided, and most resolution to be displayed. It is much to be feared, nay, it is certain that the calamities under which this holy See is now labouring have been brought upon it because it has done such evil things that good might come of them. Unless it corrects itself in this without delay the time will soon come when it will be deprived of all good things, and when it shall say 'Peace and safety,' then shall sudden destruction come upon it. These few considerations, with fear and trembling, I hand to your fatherhood, being impelled by a vehement dread of that woe which terrified Isaiah, and by a desire to obtain the correction of the evils which I have described. Think it not, most humbly, earnestly, with anxious heart and abundance of tears— think it not, in your paternal kindness, an act of presumption that, urged on by this fear and this earnest desire, I, a grievous sinner, have ventured upon this exhortation."

It will be observed that by far the greater part of the foregoing memorandum represents ideas, and is even clothed in language familiar to the readers of Grosseteste's letters. His view as to the nature of Church government, and the relative position of Pope and cardinals, bishops and pastors, is worked out in a similar way in his letter of 1239 to the Dean and Chapter of Lincoln.[1]   The high standard of conduct and attainments which he requires of the clergy is explained, in almost the same words, in the rebuke he addressed in 1235 to the monk who wished him to institute to the cure of souls a deacon who was illiterate and in other respects unfit,[2] as well as in the numerous letters in which he declines to admit improper presentations.   His high sense of the responsibilities and importance of the episcopal office, and his aversion to restrictions which militate against its efficiency, are again and again reflected in his writings.   What is new, therefore, is that he traces the evils to their source, and asks for a reform of the abuses connected with the central administration of the Church as an essential condition of improvement in the Church as a whole.   The germ of the idea is no doubt to be found in some of Grosseteste's earlier letters, for example in those addressed to Cardinal Otho,[3] but it had not developed fully, or even assumed a definite form until personal experience had brought him in close contact with the proceedings of the Papal Court.   In 1245 his chivalrous desire not to add to the difficulties of an exiled Pope, and his sympathy with Innocent in his struggle with Frederick, had induced Grosseteste to hold his peace, and, while protesting against particular acts, such as the grant of a subsidy to Boniface, to refrain from any action calculated to embarrass the Pope.   In 1250, although Innocent was still at Lyons, he was no longer faced by the great dangers which had confronted him five years earlier ; he felt more secure in his position ; he could afford to alienate sympathy by refusing twice within a few months to agree to the Emperor's overtures ;[4] and his unyielding and aggressive attitude must have inspired Grosseteste, as well as many other loyal sons of the Church, with the conviction that it constituted at that time

---

[1] Letter 127.

[2] Letter 11.

[3] Letters 49, 74, 76.

[4] *Hist. Maj.* v. 78, 99.

the principal obstacle to the peace and to the best interests of
Christendom. St. Louis himself, his brothers, and subsequently
the Duke of Burgundy, used every effort to induce Innocent to
come to an arrangement with the Emperor, as he was the only
person who could give effective aid in the Crusade;[1] and
Frederick's sudden death in December 1250 is said to have
destroyed the French hopes of assistance towards the rescue of
St. Louis from his perilous position.[2] It was possible, therefore,
for Grosseteste, in May of that year, to utter his thoughts
without being affected by the consideration that he was thereby
weakening the Pope's influence for good. On the contrary,
his object was to strengthen the Pope's hands by inducing him
to reform the abuses which prevailed in connection with his
Court, and to address himself seriously to the task of removing the corruptions of the Church. The memorandum must,
therefore, be regarded as antagonistic not to the existence
or to the exercise of the Papal power, which Grosseteste continued to uphold as before, but to the neglect and misuse
of that power. It will be observed later on that, after the
Emperor's death, Grosseteste spoke and wrote with even less
restraint. To ascribe to him, however, the ideas and the
motives which influenced the reformers of the sixteenth
century, or even those of the fourteenth and fifteenth, is to
misunderstand his point of view, and to lose sight of the value
and importance of the action he took at that juncture. His
object was not to subvert the existing edifice in order to raise
another in its place, but to strengthen its foundations. He
desired to consolidate the Church by eliminating its corruptions
and abuses ; not to weaken the hierarchy, but to purify it and
render it more effective for good, by insisting upon the rigid
adherence on the part of all who held the pastoral office, from
the highest to the lowest, to the Christian rule of faith and of
conduct.

It is not surprising that Grosseteste's exhortation should

---

[1] *Hist. Maj.* v. 70, 175.　　　　　[2] *Ibid.* v. 190 ; vi. 197.

have been received with mixed feelings by those who heard it. Innocent himself does not appear to have been greatly, if at all disconcerted: it did not prevent him from acceding to Grosseteste's request in the matter of vicarages; and, as it can hardly be supposed that he would have allowed so severe an indictment to be read in the presence of himself and the College of Cardinals unless he had some previous notion of its general purport, it may, perhaps, be assumed that he was not altogether unwilling that his hands should be strengthened by the moral authority of so eminent a man as the Bishop of Lincoln, with a view to overcoming the reactionary and corrupt influence exercised by the majority of his advisers. Even in that case it is easy to understand that the scowling looks and the contumely with which Matthew Paris says[1] that Grosseteste was met at the Roman Court, proceeded from those who thought themselves designated and attacked in the memorandum, rather than, as the chronicler supposes, from the special champions of the monks against the seculars. The clearest view of the impression produced is to be obtained from a letter written by Adam Marsh, on the 15th of August 1250,[2] to Grosseteste, in reply to a letter from the Bishop communicating the news of his protest. Friar Adam expresses his deep concern and surprise at hearing that things are in so deplorable a condition, and that no signs for the better can be discerned. Were the words of the text applicable, that "they would not hear him, because the Lord would slay them"? He compares the firm stand taken by Grosseteste on behalf of right and truth with the attitude of Elias, John the Baptist, St. Paul, St. Stephen, Hilary of Poitou, St. Athanasius of Alexandria, St. Augustine of Hippo, who at sundry times and in divers places withstood the tyranny of the oppressor, and who had striven against "principalities and powers, against the rulers of the darkness of this world, against spiritual wickedness in high places." Personally he takes comfort in the words, "If the

---

[1] *Hist. Maj.* v. 98.   [2] *Mon. Francisc.* pp. 153-157.

Lord be for us, who can be against us?"   He rejoices to read Grosseteste's determination not to yield, but to proceed along the path which he has marked out for himself with the help of God, and that he has no intention of resigning his See.   There is so much in Grosseteste's diocese that still requires correction, there are so many evils to be uprooted, that he earnestly trusts that no consideration will induce him to leave his post, whatever may be the anxiety of the times, and however weak his bodily strength.   In a subsequent letter,[1] written from Buckden on the 15th of September, Adam Marsh expresses his joy at the prospect of Grosseteste's speedy return to England, and asks where he shall meet him.   He refers to the Bishop's work at Lyons as affording an example of apostolic holiness and prophetic inspiration, and then bursts into a pæan of ardent thanksgiving for the fruit of his labour, "which for a brief time, at least, breaks the power of those sins which cumber the world, and for all time to come gives encouragement and strength to the defenders of the Lord's camp."   It is clear, therefore, that in the course of the month intervening between those two dates Adam Marsh must have received from Grosseteste a letter giving a less gloomy account of the outlook, and anticipating some change for the better.

When the Bishop, however, returned to his diocese, he was still, according to Matthew Paris,[2] in an extremely depressed frame of mind.   "Perceiving that confusion was threatening the universal Church, and desiring to find time for contemplation, prayer, and study, he divested himself of the worldly cares in which he had been entangled to no purpose, handed over to the charge of Robert Marsh all business matters connected with the See, and conceived the intention of bidding farewell to a world which was about to perish, and of resigning his bishopric. In so doing he was following the example of Nicholas of Farnham, Bishop of Durham.   But, fearing the King's rapacity, which was in the habit of impoverishing vacant Sees, and to

---

[1] *Mon. Francisc.* pp. 157, 158.   [2] *Hist. Maj.* v. 180.

impose upon them unfit persons in an underhand way, he decided to postpone his secret resolve, and waited anxiously, not knowing what the turmoil of events would bring forth." The letter of Adam Marsh, previously quoted, would appear to indicate that reports of the Bishop's proposed resignation were current, and also that they were without foundation. Still less is there any reason for thinking that the Lanercost *Chronicle* is correct in its assertion that Grosseteste offered to resign his See whilst at the Roman Court.[1] One passage, indeed, in the letter[2] he addressed to his archdeacons and clergy soon after his return, has been interpreted to mean that Grosseteste contemplated resignation, but was prevented by an authority which he could not disobey. As Archdeacon Perry, however, points out,[3] the words do not refer to any intention of resigning, but merely to the fact that he was unable to be amongst them at that moment; and what is probably the correct explanation is supplied by Dr. Felten,[4] who suggests that the reference is simply to the physician's orders not to endanger his life at that moment by a personal visitation. Matthew Paris is correct in his statement that Robert Marsh was entrusted by the Bishop with the management of business matters connected with the See, but he would appear to have acted in some such capacity for some years before the second visit to Lyons, for in a letter of the year 1248[5] Robert Marsh is addressed as the Bishop's *officiarius*, though it is possible that the term may there be applied to him with reference solely to his official position at Oxford as Grosseteste's representative for certain purposes. It was he, however, who was instructed by Grosseteste to draw up a list of the privileges of the clergy,[6] and the position he occupied may be inferred from the fact that when, after Grosseteste's death, a

---

[1] *Chron. de Lanercost*, p. 43. See Luard's Introd. to the *Letters*, p. 74.

[2] Letter 130. Luard's Introduction, p. 74.

[3] Page 220. The words are: "Intervenit auctoritas, cui non parere nefas censetur, quae nos ad tempus subtrahit vestrae praesentiae et a concepto salubri proposito nos retardat."

[4] Page 57.

[5] Letter 129.

[6] *Ann. Monast.* (Burton), i. 425.

question arose between the Archbishop of Canterbury and the Chapter of Lincoln with regard to the right of jurisdiction during the vacancy of the See, it was he who was selected to act as joint arbitrator.[1]

Grosseteste's letter to his archdeacons and clergy[2] recapitulates in a practical form his previous denunciations of the incapacity, the slothfulness, and even the vices of the seculars, and of the bad example they set to the laity. He declares that the sight of all those evils drives him to despair, and implores those to whom he writes to redeem the time they have lost, and in future to watch over themselves and their flocks, and to feed them with the word, the example, and the sacrament of life. "As my testament," he says, "I leave to you zeal for souls, zeal which, because it is lukewarm and slight in me, I pray you to increase by your prayers. Let us pray in common that from the truth of the gospel and from the love of our flock no human fear may ever tear us." The letter was to be published by the archdeacons and their officials in all their synods and chapters, and to be brought to the knowledge of all rectors and vicars of what condition soever, in order that they might have no excuse, and that he might escape the charge of silence.

Grosseteste's illness, indicated in the foregoing letter as well as in Adam Marsh's correspondence, cannot have been of long duration; for early in the following year he had resumed his usual activity, and was engaged in his visitations, in the course of which he visited Dunstable on February 24, and met there Fulk Basset, Bishop of London, the Bishops of Salisbury, Norwich, Ely, and Worcester,[3] and the proctors of the other bishops who did not appear in person. The object of the meeting was to protest against the Archbishop's claim to visit their dioceses. They signed and sealed an agreement binding them to joint resistance, and made arrangements to collect

---

[1] *Ann. Monast.* (Dunstable), iii. 190; *Hist. Maj.* vi. 264; *Mon. Francisc.* p. 324.

[2] Letter 130.

[3] *Ann. Monast.* (Dunstable), iii. 181; *Hist. Maj.* v. 225. The Bishops of Ely and Worcester are mentioned by Matthew Paris alone.

funds for the purpose of defraying the necessary expenses. In March they sent representatives to the Pope, empowering them to use every effort to oppose Boniface's attack, even if it cost four thousand marks to do so; and he was also informed that the Archbishop had already collected more than the eleven thousand marks previously assigned to him. Innocent had left Lyons, now that the Emperor's death had removed the peril which kept him away from Italy, and arrived at Perugia, after a short stay at Genoa.[1] It was to Perugia that not only the proctors sent by the bishops, but also Boniface himself hastened in order to fight out their respective cases. The Pope's decision[2] limits the Archbishop's right of visitation to the officers of the province and the heads of conventual establishments, and even in those cases stipulates that he shall not receive for each day a procuration of more than four marks. It exempts the parish churches of the several dioceses altogether from archiepiscopal visitation and from procurations, pronounces his censures to be null and void, and especially absolves the Dean and Chapter of St. Paul's, who had been excommunicated by Boniface for their opposition. As a reason for exemption the letters state that the province of Canterbury contains abundance of prelates who are diligent in the performance of their duties. The Pope also rehearses the canon of the third Lateran Council, limiting the retinue of an archbishop to less than fifty horsemen, that of a bishop to less than thirty, that of an archdeacon to five or seven, and that of a rural dean to two, and providing that none of them are to hunt with hounds or hawks, or indulge in sumptuous repasts, but to remember the sacred duties in which they are engaged. The Bishops of Lincoln, London, and Bath are

---

[1] It was from Genoa that, on the 7th of June 1251, Innocent dated a license to Manuel, son of Henry "Pictavinus," citizen of Genoa, to hold the rectory of St. Mary Ludeborch (? Lutterworth), in the diocese of Lincoln, and to receive other benefices, without any obligation to reside or to receive orders. —Bliss, *Calendar*, i. 271.

[2] *Hist. Maj.* v. 346; vi. 228; *Ann. Monast.* (Burton), i. 300-304, where the Pope's letters are given most fully. They are dated 1252, but some of them may have been written in the previous year, and then all dated together.

appointed " conservators," to see that the conditions as to visitation are duly observed. The Burton annalist says that the Papal letters cost as much as was anticipated, namely, four thousand marks, and that two thousand marks were paid to the proctors who were sent from England out of the funds collected from various quarters.[1]

The severity of Grosseteste's visitation continues in 1251 to excite the indignation of Matthew Paris, who recognises, however, the excellence of its motives, and unconsciously admits its necessity. It is to that year that his rigorous proceedings in regard to the abbey of Ramsey and several of the nunneries, to which reference has already been made in connection with his relation to the monastic orders,[2] are to be assigned. He also carried out a careful scrutiny of his whole diocese, with special regard to the morals of the clergy, punishing offenders by deprivation, and endeavouring to purify the whole of his bishopric from all taint of vice. By gentle entreaties, as well as by severe modes of persuasion, he tried to induce all holders of benefices to take priest's orders. He frequently preached to the people, and convened the priests who lived in various districts, compelling them to listen to his words.[3] It had been his practice in the earlier years of his episcopate to preach to the clergy in Latin, and to employ others to preach to the people in English ; but the foregoing passage helps to confirm the tradition that he was in the habit also, at any rate during his later years, of using the latter language also in his sermons. The reason why many of his Latin sermons are still extant, while none of the English ones have been preserved, is doubtless due to the fact that the former were committed to writing, whilst the latter were extemporary.[4] It is strange that strenuous opposition should have

---

[1] It is not quite clear whether the sum of 2000 marks which the Pope demanded, on the 5th of June 1252, of the Bishops of Lincoln, London, and Worcester, as payment to the proctor of the province of Canterbury (*Hist. Maj. Addit.* vi. 213-217), was in addition to, or included in, the foregoing sums.

[2] See p. 162, 163 ; *Hist. Maj.* v. 227.

[3] *Hist. Maj.* v. 256, 257.

[4] See p. 32. Wharton, in his *Anglia Sacra*, refers to some, but no trace of them can be found. On Grosseteste's

been aroused by his attempt to induce all beneficed persons to be ordained priests, and still stranger that it should have been partly successful. Matthew Paris relates that many of them united together, collected a considerable sum of money, which they sent to the Roman Court, and obtained special license to frequent schools[1] for some years (*scholas exercere*) without being properly ordained, whilst retaining their benefices. The incident illustrates the difficulty of carrying out reforms. Grosseteste himself had frequently permitted incumbents to resort for a time to a course of theological training for the purpose of improving their qualifications for the post, proper provision being made in the meantime for a deputy to take their place;[2] nor was he averse to the introduction of the lay element into religious work, as he had shown by his active support of the friars, a large majority of whom, at any rate in their early days, especially in the case of the Franciscans, were laymen, in the sense that they were not in holy orders; but he was consistent throughout his life in denouncing the holding of a cure of souls by any but properly ordained priests, and in repeatedly refusing on that ground to institute deacons.

A letter from Adam Marsh, written in 1251,[3] shows that, in spite of Grosseteste's ill-health and the strain of his personal visitations, as well as of his activity as a preacher and a reformer of abuses, he had time to think of the interests of the University of Oxford and of the advancement of learning, Three questions of urgency had arisen at the University. The first was that of the extension of the Chancellor's jurisdiction

use of the English language see Eccleston, *De Adventu Minorum, Mon. Francisc.* p. 64, "surrexit et confessus est Anglice," etc.

[1] Archdeacon Perry, p. 240, translates *exercere scholas* "to teach"; but see Pegge, p. 312, who quotes other instances from Matthew Paris of the use of *exercere* in the sense of "to frequent." *Hist. Maj.* v. 279.

[2] See p. 146.

[3] *Mon. Francisc.* pp. 113-116, cp. p. 107. The date of Letter 22 (p. 107) is fixed by the reference to the approaching marriage of the King of Scots to Margaret, daughter of Henry III., which took place at Christmas, 1251. Letter 26 cannot have been written much later. But see p. 237, and Mr. Little's *Grey Friars at Oxford*, p. 38, note.

raised by the incarceration of two clerks, and brought before the King's attention on the occasion of one of his visits to Oxford, when a compromise was effected after a cessation of lectures and a general strike of scholars.[1] The second related to a dispute between the Northerners and the Irish, which was settled in the following year by the establishment of a tribunal of arbitration.[2] The third was connected with the discussions which led up to Oxford's first statute of 1252 or 1253, requiring graduation in arts on the part of those who desired to be admitted to a license in theology.[3] The last of those questions must have been of special interest to Grosseteste, on account of the support he had always given to the Franciscans. A similar step had been taken in 1250 by the University of Paris, with the avowed object of checking the multiplication of friar doctors.[4] It was probably due to the influence of Grosseteste that the Oxford statute, instead of being, like its Paris prototype, a mere measure of protection designed by the Theological Faculty for the purpose of guarding the secular theologians against the competition of their rivals of the Dominican and Franciscan schools, was passed by the University itself with the object of securing its control over regular graduates, and in the interest of the studies within the purview of the Faculty of Arts. A dispensing power was, however, preserved to the Chancellor and regents. If, as is probable, Adam Marsh's letter[5] to Grosseteste relating to the use of the University seal and other matters, belongs to the early part of 1252, it would appear that the form of the statute was based upon the Bishop's own recommendations. Such was the advance which had been effected in the University of Oxford since the days when Grosseteste had first become connected with it, that in 1252 Matthew Paris could rank it without fear of contradiction on a par with that of Paris.[6]

---

[1] See above, p. 235.

[2] Anstey's *Munimenta Academica*, pp. 20 *sqq.*

[3] See above, pp. 237, 298.

[4] Rashdall, i. 373, 374; ii. 378, 379.

[5] *Mon. Francisc.* pp. 99-102.

[6] *Hist. Maj.* v. 353.

The Bishop was still engaged, in his leisure moments, in his work connected with Aristotle's *Ethics*.[1] Adam Marsh asks [2] that the copy which the Bishop has caused to be transcribed for his own use may be sent to the house of the Grey Friars in London, in order that it may be recopied by a certain Hugh de Berions. He adds that Master Peter de Alpibus,[3] rector of the church at Wimbledon, the Queen's physician and a man well versed in literature and of high integrity, will vouch for the safe transmission and return of the valuable manuscript. The variety of Grosseteste's interests at this time is also indicated by the fact that Adam Marsh sends him a collection of the prophetic writings of the mystical Abbot Joachim de Floris, to whom Richard the First had given an interview at Messina in 1190, and who had foretold for the year 1260 the coming of "the new era of the Spirit," and asks his opinion on the subject. What the reply was is not known ; but in the depressed condition of his mind with regard to the future of Church and State,[4] Grosseteste may have been in a mood for examining with sympathy works of that description. All news relating to the vicissitudes of the Crusade was eagerly welcomed by him, as well as information relating to such matters as the excesses of the Pastoureaux in France, and a volcanic eruption which took place in the island of Guernsey.[5] Hardly any question of high ecclesiastical or political importance at that time is left untouched in the correspondence of Adam Marsh's letters with Grosseteste, and it is a matter for deep regret that none of the letters written by the Bishop to his friend at that period of his life should have been preserved. There can be no doubt that he was taxing his strength to the uttermost with the

[1] See above, p. 247, note.

[2] *Mon. Francisc.* p. 114 ; Pauli, p. 17.

[3] Presumably a Savoyard.

[4] Cp. *Hist. Maj.* v. 186 ; "proponens mundo perituro vale dicere," and his letter to the archdeacons, both, however, relating to 1250, not 1251 or 1252. Joachim was not the author of *The Eternal Gospel*, but that work was largely based upon his writings ; see Rashdall, ii. pp. 737 *sqq.*, and the authorities mentioned there ; Sabatier, *Vie de St. François d'Assise*, p. 55. Cp. p. 247.

[5] *Mon. Francisc.* pp. 109, 121, 151.

large number of duties which he had imposed upon himself, in spite of his advanced years, and which he discharged with unfailing conscientiousness. It is on that account that Adam Marsh urges him to be more careful about his health, and especially to relax his ardent devotion to literary studies.[1]

In spite of his continued and increasing opposition to the King's encroachments and to the exactions of Boniface, his relations with the royal family were on a friendly footing. Soon after his return from Lyons he appears, in accordance with Adam Marsh's advice,[2] to have written conciliatory letters to the King, the Queen, and Richard, Earl of Cornwall. In 1251 he is assured by Friar Adam[3] that the Queen is resolved, as far as in her lies, to present none but suitable clergymen, a determination which harmonises with his earlier conception of the promise of her character. Adhemar, the King's brother, at one time conveys to Grosseteste his desire to have a conference with him concerning his own spiritual welfare.[4] In November 1251, the Bishop of Lincoln was present at the dedication of the church and monastery of Hayles, erected by the Earl of Cornwall at a cost of ten thousand marks, in fulfilment of a vow make by him when in danger of shipwreck. The King and Queen were present, and almost all the nobles and prelates of England, and more than three hundred knights. Although thirteen bishops were there, Grosseteste took precedence over them all, and celebrated mass at the high altar.[5] About the same time Adam Marsh suggests to the Bishop the propriety of sending a suitable wedding present to the Princess Margaret, who was to be married at Christmas to the King of Scots at York.[6] The magnificence of the ceremonies and the lavish expenditure incurred on that occasion have been fully described by Matthew Paris, who, perhaps by way of contrast,

---

[1] *Mon. Francisc.* p. 143.

[2] *Ibid.* p. 153.

[3] *Ibid.* p. 115.

[4] *Ibid.* p. 175. Not to be con-fused with Æthelmar, Bishop-elect of Winchester, the King's uterine brother.

[5] *Hist. Maj.* v. 262.

[6] *Mon. Francisc.* v. 107.

relates a few pages farther on how the Franciscans refused to accept from Henry III. a present of woollen garments, on the ground that they were not his to give, as he had extorted them from the plunder of the poor.[1]

On one occasion the King's misuse of patronage led to a difference of opinion between himself and the Queen, with the result that Grosseteste took decided action on behalf of the latter. On the death, early in 1252, of Richard de Thiony, treasurer of Anjou, who held many revenues in France, England, and Scotland, his churches fell vacant, and, amongst others, that of Flamstead, not far from St. Albans. The Queen, as guardian of Richard's son, bestowed the living on the chaplain William, a clerk of St. Albans, and there appears to have been no fault to find with the choice, or any dispute as to her right. Henry, however, when he heard what had happened, exclaimed against the insolence and self-assertion of women, cancelled the Queen's act, and conferred the church on a Burgundian clerk of his own, named Hurtold, who promptly ejected the Queen's nominee. Grosseteste thereupon excommunicated Hurtold, laid an interdict on the church, and seems to have succeeded, though the sequel is not told, in securing the reinstation of the original presentee.[2]

In October 1252, Grosseteste took an active part in resisting the King's demand for a tenth from the whole kingdom, equivalent to a whole of the revenues of the Church, for the space of three years, in aid of his proposed Crusade, although the demand was supported and emphasised by a Papal mandate.[3] A meeting of all the prelates, with the exception of the two archbishops, who were unavoidably absent, and the Bishop of Chester,[4] who was ill, took place for the purpose of considering the King's message. The objections urged were directed not against the ostensible object for which

---

[1] *Hist. Maj.* v. 275.

[2] *Ibid.* v. 299.

[3] *Ibid.* v. 325 *sqq.*

[4] Roger de Wescham, Bishop of Coventry and Lichfield, sometimes styled Bishop of Chester.

the money was asked, but against the amount of the sum and the mode of its collection; for it was to be estimated not according to the old computation of the value of the churches, but according to the judgment and discretion of the royal agents. Moreover, ever since the loss of Normandy in the days of King John, the English nation had consolidated its unity and its strength, and the national instinct was at that time opposed, and rightly so, to expeditions on the mainland, which had the effect of frittering away the country's strength and impoverishing its resources.[1] Grosseteste's antagonism cannot have been directed against the Crusade itself, in view of the prominent part which he, the Bishop of Worcester, and the Bishop of Chichester had taken, between 1247 and 1250, towards the promotion of its objects.[2] The King, however, desired to receive the money in advance of the expedition, and it was evidently suspected that he intended to use it for other purposes, such as the payment of his own debts, or perhaps an attempt to recover Normandy.[3] Matthew Paris, who has preserved some record of the debate, says that, when Grosseteste heard how the sum was to be levied, he exclaimed : " By our Lady, what is this ? You are proceeding on the strength of alleged concessions which have not been made to you. Do you suppose that we shall consent to this accursed contribution ? Let us not bend the knee to Baal." Æthelmar de Lusignan, Bishop-elect of Winchester, and uterine brother of Henry III., replied : " My father, how shall we be able to oppose the will both of the Pope and of the King ? The one pushes us on, and the other draws us. In a similar case the French agreed to a similar contribution in aid of their King when he was about to depart on his Crusade. They are stronger than we are, and have been more accustomed to resistance ; but what

---

[1] The offer of the Sicilian crown to Richard, Earl of Cornwall, in 1250 and again in 1252, also excited apprehensions of a similar character, cp. Stubbs, ii. p. 69.

[2] See above, pp. 260-263. The latest letter written to them on the subject is dated September 1250.—*Hist. Maj. Additamenta*, vi. 200.

[3] *Hist. Maj.* v. 280 *sqq.*

means have we of resisting ?" Grosseteste retorted : " It is precisely because the French contributed that we ought to oppose ; for two acts create a custom ; and, besides we now see clearly what has been the result of this tyrannical extortion by the King of France. Let us be warned by past examples. That neither the King nor we may incur the divine wrath, for my own part I declare without hesitation that I oppose his injurious contribution." His argument convinced even the Bishop-elect of Winchester, who had suggested the difficulties of the course he proposed. That Fulk Basset, Bishop of London, and Walter de Cantelupe, Bishop of Worcester, should have sided with him, is not surprising, as they were usually found on his side ; and it is also worthy of note that Richard de la Wyche, Bishop of Chichester, who was specially favourable to the Crusade, was among Grosseteste's supporters on that occasion, as were almost all the rest, with the exception of the Bishop of Salisbury, who wavered in his views.[1]

The King at first was filled with indignation, but, being appeased by his courtiers, altered his tone and changed his demand into a request, which he made as a suppliant, and by virtue of the Papal injunction. The bishops replied that if the Pope had been truly aware of the oppressions and exactions with which the English Church was burdened, the King would never have obtained such a concession from the Roman Court, and that if he were to be informed of the real state of affairs he would doubtless revoke his mandate. After rehearsing some of Henry's injuries to the kingdom, they proceed to state that they will grant the subsidy, provided that he undertakes to observe the Great Charter, so often violated, to refrain from similar exactions in the future, to collect the money on the usual basis, and not at the good pleasure of the royal agents, and to provide adequate guarantees that the money shall be expended for the purposes for which it is asked.[2] Henry declined to accept the conditions named, and the bishops declined to take

---

[1] *Hist. Maj.* v. 324-326.   [2] *Ibid.* v. 326-328.

further steps in the absence of the two archbishops, one of whom was on the Continent, and the other in the far north.[1]

In the great Parliament held in London in April of the following year, Grosseteste again played a conspicuous part. After debates which lasted more than fifteen days, it was agreed that the King should receive from the Church one-tenth of its annual revenues for three years, and from the knights a scutage of three marks for one year, with a view to his pilgrimage and Crusade, on certain conditions, one of which was that he should observe the provisions of the Great Charter. On the 3rd of May, in the presence of Henry and the nobles, the prelates assembled in the great hall at Westminster, clad in their pontifical robes, and with candles lighted, solemnly pronounced sentence of excommunication on "all violators of the liberties of the Church, and of the liberties or free customs of the kingdom of England, especially those contained in the Charter of the liberties of England, and in the Charter of the forests." The King, too, swore to maintain the Charter inviolate. It was, however, noted that, at the commencement of the solemn proceedings, when lighted candles were given to all present, Henry alone of all in the assembly refused to take one, on the ground that he was not a priest. Grosseteste revolving the matter in his heart, and reflecting on the King's previous violations of his promises, and fearing lest he should withdraw from his engagements, "caused on his return to his See a sentence of excommunication to be solemnly pronounced in every parish church in his diocese, which for their great number it would be difficult to reckon, against all violators of the Charter, and especially against priests, so that this sentence tingled in the ears and awed the hearts of all who heard it."[2]

<hr>

[1] *Hist. Maj.* v. 328.　　　　　　[2] *Ibid.* v. 377, 378.

CHAPTER XIV

IN the meantime, in addition to his opposition to the King's demands and encroachments, Grosseteste was engaged more and more in a struggle against the Papal Provisions. Matthew Paris, in one passage, declares that the Bishop of Lincoln "hated like poison the dishonest Romans who had the Pope's precept for obtaining a provision. He was in the habit of saying that, if he were to hand the cure of souls over to them, he would be acting Satan's part. Consequently he often threw away letters sealed with the Papal bulls, and acted directly in contravention of such commands."[1] There is no doubt that Grosseteste had refused, almost from the commencement of his episcopate, to appoint or institute foreigners to English benefices save in exceptional cases in which they had special qualifications, just as he scrutinised and rejected all improper presentations, whatever might be the nationality of the presentee. It is equally certain that, particularly after his second visit to Lyons, his feelings revolted even more strongly against the system. The language, however, of Matthew Paris, who is apt to ascribe to others his own opinions and motives, conveys, in this and in other passages, a somewhat exaggerated and in

---

[1] *Hist. Maj.* v. 257. Eccleston (*Mon. Francisc.* p. 64) gives a reason for thinking that Grosseteste's main ground for refusing "eos quos Papa instituit et nepotes cardinalium" was not so much their ignorance of the English language, as the fact that "non quaerebant nisi temporalia." He had sometimes availed himself in his diocese of the services of friars who were unacquainted with English, in order that they might teach by their example.

other respects inaccurate notion of the nature of the Bishop's opposition.

On at least four occasions during the last three years of his life, apart from his general denunciations of the system, is Grosseteste recorded to have taken definite action in antagonism to " Provisions." The first was when he refused to institute an Italian, who was ignorant of the English language, to a certain benefice in his diocese, and is said to have been suspended in consequence of his refusal.[1] It is not quite certain whether the incident occurred in Lent 1251, or in Lent of the following year.[2] In neither case can the suspension have been of long duration; for in November of the former year he celebrated mass at the dedication of the church at Hayles, and in the latter year he performed all his episcopal duties as if nothing had occurred, and was, as has been seen, appointed " conservator " for certain purposes by the Pope. Nor is there any other mention of his suspension.[3] The second instance is to be found in a letter of 1252, sent by the Pope to Archbishop Boniface, and by his official to Grosseteste, ordering him to provide for Robert, a mere boy,[4] son of John de Salins, who styled himself Count of Burgundy, with one benefice or more of the value of three hundred marks.[5] Grosseteste appears to have declined to do so, as is indicated by the fact that the Pope asked the King to give Robert de Salins a living of five hundred marks, as a return for

---

[1] *Hist. Maj.* v. 227.

[2] " In quadragesima sequente." See Luard's note, Introd. to the *Letters*, p. 77.

[3] It is remarkable, however, that the *Calendar of the Papal Registers* (ed. Bliss) should make no reference to any letter addressed by Innocent to Grosseteste, between the end of January 1251, p. 266, and the middle of March 1253, p. 284. Numerous dispensations, etc., were in the meantime granted direct to clerks in his diocese.

[4] " Puerulo."

[5] Cotton MSS. *Nero* d. 1, an addition to the *Additamenta* of Matthew Paris. Luard (Introd. to vol. v. of the *Hist. Maj.* p. 19) says that as the Vatican MS. of the Papal Letters speaks of only one benefice, and this of the value of 200 marks, he inferred at first that Archbishop Boniface tampered with the letter in the interest of the nominee, who was a relative of his own. He ascertained afterwards, however, that two other MS. copies of the letter in the *Vatican Register* give the higher figure, so that the supposition fell to the ground.

supporting the election of Æthelmar of Valence to the See of Winchester.[1] The third instance is to be found in the inquiries which Grosseteste caused to be made throughout his diocese and elsewhere in 1252, with the object of arriving at a correct estimate of the revenues of foreign beneficiaries. In the words of Matthew Paris,[2] "it was ascertained that the present Pope, Innocent IV., had impoverished the universal Church more than all his predecessors had done from the time of the establishment of the Papacy; and the incomes of the foreign clerks appointed by him in England, whom the Roman Church had enriched, amounted to more than seventy thousand marks. The clear revenue of the King did not amount to one-third of this."

The fourth, and most celebrated instance, is that of the letter which he sent on the occasion of the one written by Pope Innocent IV., on the 26th of January 1253, to Hugh Mortimer, Archdeacon of Canterbury, and "Master Innocent, our writer, sojourning in England," requiring that a vacant canonry at Lincoln should be conferred upon his nephew, Frederick de Lavagna.[3] Hugh Mortimer was the Archbishop of Canterbury's official, and was the usual intermediary in transactions of that character. His name occurs in that capacity in the letter forwarded by Boniface to Grosseteste in 1249, enclosing the Pope's recommendation in favour of Albert, the rural dean[4] of Campilio, a relative of the Queen. The letter respecting Frederick de Lavagna is couched in remarkably dictatorial language. The Pope begins by stating that William, Cardinal deacon of St. Eustache, "has canonically conferred, at our special command, a canonry of Lincoln on Frederick de Lavagna, a clerk in holy orders, our nephew, and by his ring has

---

[1] *Hist. Maj.* v. 224.

[2] *Ibid.* v. 355; *Hist. Anglorum*, iii. 128, 129.

[3] For the Pope's letter to the Archdeacon of Canterbury and Master Innocent, and for Grosseteste's letter to them, see *Hist. Maj.* v. 389-392; vi. 229-231; *Ann. Monastici* (Burton), i. 311-313, 436-438; Grosseteste's Letter 128; *Mon. Francisc.* pp. 382-385.

[4] "Plebano." *Hist. Maj.* vi. 186, cp. Bliss, *Calendar*, i. 249. Mr. Bliss renders the word "curate." The usual meaning of *plebanus*, however, is "an urban or rural dean," *qui plebem regit.* See Ducange, *s.v.*

corporally invested him in the same, so that from that time forward he became a canon of Lincoln, and had the full name and right of a canon, and a title to any prebend which should become vacant after our venerable brother the Bishop of Lincoln had been informed by those letters as to receiving and providing for him in the same church, or which he shall have reserved according to the apostolical donation to be conferred upon its vacancy." The letter proceeds to threaten with excommunication all who oppose Frederick's installation, and adds that they are to be cited peremptorily to appear at the Roman Court within two months, "notwithstanding any privileges or indulgences granted by the said See to the inhabitants of the kingdom of England generally, or to any person, dignity, or place in particular." The tone of the letter, which is of an unusual character, plainly indicates that opposition has already been threatened, or possibly offered, by Grosseteste to the appointment, and its intention is to overawe his resistance.

That intention, however, failed in its effect. Grosseteste's reply, addressed, not as some, including Dr. Luard,[1] have supposed, to the Pope himself, but to "Master Innocent," his representative in England, refuses in firm and resolute, though respectful terms, to carry out the mandate. "It is well known to your wisdom," he writes, "that I am ready to obey apostolical commands with filial affection, and with all devotion and reverence; but to those things which are opposed to apostolical commands I, in my zeal for the honour of my parent, am also opposed. By apostolical commands are meant those which are agreeable to the teaching of the Apostles and of Christ Himself, the Lord and Master of the Apostles, whose type and representation is specially borne in the ecclesiastical hierarchy by the Pope. The letter above mentioned is not consonant with apostolical sanctity, but on the contrary utterly at variance and at discord with it."

[1] Dr. Luard, however, states the fact correctly in his index to the *Flores Historiarum.* This is the letter described by Higden and by Trevisa (Higden's *Polychronicon*, ed. Lumby, viii. pp. 240, 242) as a "sharpe pistle," "epistolam satis tonantem."

He proceeds to argue, first, that the innumerable exemptions granted under *non obstante* clauses lead to the worst results, disturbing and confusing the purity of the Christian religion and the quiet of social intercourse among men; and, secondly, that no sin can so resemble that of Lucifer and of Antichrist, or can be so distinctive to the highest interests of the human race, as that which consists in defrauding and slaying souls which need to be quickened and saved by the pastoral office and ministry, by robbing them of those means of grace; and this sin is shown by the clearest testimonies of Scripture to be committed by those who, being constituted shepherds, provide for their own carnal and temporal desires and necessities from the milk and wool of Christ's sheep, and fail to administer the duties of the pastoral office with a view to the eternal salvation of their flocks; for the neglect to perform those duties brings loss and destruction to the sheep. And, inasmuch as the cause of evil is worse than the particular effect which it produces, those who are responsible for the introduction of such slayers of the divine image and handiwork are worse even than those murderers, and are nearer to Lucifer and Antichrist; and in this gradation of wickedness those excel most who, from a greater and a diviner power given to them from on high for edification and not for destruction, are more especially bound to exclude and root out from the Church of God those destroyers. It is not possible, therefore, that the apostolic See, to which has been handed down from Christ Himself power for edification and not for destruction, can issue a precept so hateful and so injurious to the human race as this; for to do so would constitute a falling off, a corruption and abuse of its most holy and plenary power. No one who is subject and faithful to the said See in immaculate and sincere obedience, and is not cut off from the body of Christ and the said holy See by schism, can obey commands or precepts such as this, even if it emanated from the highest order of angels; but he must of necessity, and with his whole strength, contradict and rebel against them."

Grosseteste goes on to say that it is owing to his obedience and fidelity to the Christian Church and the apostolic See, and because the precept issued is contrary to the unity of the former and the sanctity of the latter, as well as opposed to the spirit of Christ and the welfare of the human race, that he takes the stand which he has done. "It is out of filial reverence and obedience that I disobey, resist, and rebel."[1] "To sum up," he concludes, "the holiness of the apostolic See can only tend to edification and not to destruction; for the plenitude of its power consists in being able to do all things for edification. These provisions, however, as they are called, are not for edification, but for manifest destruction. They are not, therefore, within the power of the apostolic See: they owe their inspiration to 'flesh and blood' which 'shall not inherit the kingdom of God,' and not to the Father of our Lord Jesus Christ who is in heaven."

It will be observed that the letter is an attack, not upon the authority of the Papal See, to which, indeed, Grosseteste repeatedly expresses his devotion, but upon specific abuses and corruptions connected with its exercise. The Bishop's desire is to purify and strengthen the Church, by eliminating from it all causes of offence and occasions for falling. Just as at various periods of his life he has been engaged in struggles against the King's encroachments and exactions, against the resistance offered by the monastic bodies to the establishment of vicarages, against the failings and inefficiency of the clergy, against the opposition of his Dean and Chapter to episcopal visitation, and against the defects and errors in the existing system of ecclesiastical administration, so, on this occasion, he concentrates his efforts upon the removal of one of the gravest blots on that system. His method of controversy is, it may be noted, the same as it was in the days when he resisted the King's appointment of abbots as itinerant justices: he begins, that is to

---

[1] "Filialiter et obedienter non obedio, contradico et rebello."—Letter 128, p. 436.

say, by citing the exact text, in the one case, of the royal mandate to the Abbot of Ramsey, and, in the other case, of the Pope's letter to the Archdeacon of Canterbury and Master Innocent, and from these particular instances he deduces, on the strength mainly of arguments derived from Scripture, conclusions applicable, in the former instance, to the general question of the invasion of the liberties of the Church by secular interference, and, in the latter, to the general question of the use and abuse of Papal Provisions, with special reference to the absolute necessity for securing the appointment of properly qualified persons to cures of souls. Although the language of the letter is full of vigour, the sequence of the thoughts is less logical than when Grosseteste's faculties were in their prime. His position, in fact, was one of great difficulty. As an upholder of the prerogatives of the Roman See, and at the same time as an unflinching adversary of abuses, he tries to uproot the latter without assailing the former. The formula that a Pope can only act apostolically, and that for him to act otherwise is a contradiction in terms, enables Grosseteste to reconcile those two lines of action, just as the constitutional formula that the King can do no wrong had enabled him to resist Henry's encroachments and exactions without attacking the kingly office.[1]

The effect produced by the issue of a letter of that kind by the most learned man of his time produced a great sensation. In a letter addressed shortly after Grosseteste's death to the Minister of the Franciscans in England,[2] Adam Marsh speaks in terms of admiration of "that fearless answer, written with so much prudence, eloquence, and vigour, which will with the aid of God benefit all ages to come." Although Grosseteste's letter was not addressed to Innocent IV., its purport must have been

---

[1] See Stubbs, ii. pp. 300 *sqq.*

[2] *Mon. Francisc.* p. 325. This can hardly have been written to William of Nottingham, who probably died in 1251. See Mr. Little's art. in the *English Historical Review* for October 1891, and his *Grey Friars at Oxford*, p. 184. It must, in that case, have been addressed to Peter of Tewkesbury, his successor, and the "W." have been inserted by mistake in the heading.

communicated to him almost immediately.[1] Matthew Paris, who
sometimes assigns appropriate conversations, much in the same
way as Thucydides attributes fitting speeches, to the personages
about whom he writes, relates[2] that the Pope, who had removed
from Perugia to Rome, exclaimed in an outburst of indignation,
" Who is this raving old man, this deaf and foolish dotard, who
in his audacity and temerity judges my actions ? " adding that,
if it were not for the mildness of his disposition, he would hurl
him to headlong ruin, and suggesting that the King of England,
as vassal of the holy See, might be ordered to imprison the bold
prelate.   Thereupon the Spanish Cardinal Egidius, Giles de
Torres, Archbishop of Toledo, who was a friend of Grosseteste,
and to whom four of his letters are addressed,[3] took the Bishop's
part, and urged that it was impossible to take proceedings
against him, as what he said was true. " We cannot condemn
him : he is a Catholic, yea, and most holy, even stricter in his
religious observances than we are, and, indeed, he is believed
to have no equal, still less a superior, among all prelates.   This
is known to the whole clergy of France and of England, and our
opposition to him would be of no avail.   The truth of such a
letter, which has by this time, perhaps, become known to many,
will have the power of stirring up many against us ; for he is
held a great philosopher, fully learned in Latin and Greek
literature, a zealous champion of justice, a reader of theology in
the schools, a preacher to the people, and a persecutor of
simoniacal offenders."[4]   The other cardinals took a similar line,
and advised that the Pope should pass the matter over and
pretend not to notice it, lest a tumult should be excited,
especially as it was known that Grosseteste's death could not
be far distant.[5]   Although the actual words spoken may not

---

[1] The *Burton Annalist* states that
the Archdeacon of Canterbury and
Master Innocent forwarded Grosseteste's letter to Innocent IV.—*Ann.
Monast.* (Burton) i. 313.

[2] *Hist. Maj.* v. 392.

[3] Letters 36, 45, 46, 67.

[4] *Hist. Maj.* v. 393.

[5] The words " quia scitur, quod
quandoque discessio est ventura " have
been rendered " because it is known
that there will be a schism " ; but the
other is the more likely interpretation.

have been those which Matthew Paris records, there is nothing intrinsically improbable in the supposition that Innocent, who was of an impulsive and often dictatorial temperament, may have expressed indignation, and possibly have used threatening language with regard to Grosseteste, and that Cardinal Egidius, who had enjoyed better opportunities than most of those present for personal intercourse with the Bishop, and who was able to appreciate his great qualities, exercised a restraining influence.

A legend, however, grew up in the course of years, and was embodied in the Lanercost *Chronicle*, as well as in those of Capgrave, Knyghton, and others, and in Richard of Bardney's metrical life, to the effect that Grosseteste was excommunicated by the Pope;[1] but there is no contemporary evidence for the statement, and the foregoing passage from Matthew Paris is directly opposed to the supposition. " In his last days," says the Lanercost *Chronicle*, " he was excommunicated, which sentence he, being himself tenacious of justice, bore patiently and accepted, and also appealed to the tribunal of the Highest Judge." The others speak as if the Bishop had been summoned to Rome. The whole story, however, is a legend, based probably upon a confusion between the suspension which would seem to have been pronounced on Grosseteste in 1251 or 1252,[2] and the incident arising out of the letter concerning Frederick de Lavagna in 1253. The only sentence of excommunication known to have been ever directed against the Bishop of Lincoln was that which was passed against him by the monks of Christ Church, Canterbury, in connection with the dispute relating to Bardney Abbey,[3] and he was expressly protected by a Papal indult of April 1244 against similar proceedings in the future without special license from the Pope.[4] Perhaps, too, the error may have been due to a misunderstanding of the sentence in

<hr>

[1] See Luard's Introduction to the *Letters*, p. 81, note.

[2] See above, p. 307.

[3] *Ibid.* p. 156.

[4] Bliss, *Calendar*, i. 209.

which Matthew Paris relates that Sewal, Archbishop of York, who was excommunicated by Pope Alexander IV. in 1257, was comforted and strengthened by the example of St. Thomas Becket, by the example and teaching of St. Edmund, and by the faithfulness of St. Robert of Lincoln.[1] Certainly Grosseteste could not have himself excommunicated the violators of the Great Charter in May 1253, and again subsequently throughout his diocese, as well as carried out his usual episcopal functions during that year, if he had himself been subject to that sentence. It may also be noted that on the 16th of July Grosseteste was appointed by the Pope "conservator" in connection with a certain indult granted to the Bishop-elect of Winchester.[2] It may be added that the terms in which all contemporary, or nearly contemporary, chroniclers speak of his last days and of his death are absolutely inconsistent with the notion.[3]

Grosseteste's letter on the subject of Frederick de Lavagna is as well authenticated as any document of that period can possibly be. It occurs not only in the *Historia Major*, but in the Annals of Burton, and in numerous independent manuscripts. The same certainty does not apply, however, to an address to " the nobles of England, the citizens of London, and the commons of the whole kingdom " against the Papal Provisions and the exactions of foreign clerks in England, which has been printed among his letters.[4] The style differs in many respects from the Bishop's, and it is hardly likely that, with his strong views against secular interference in questions of ecclesiastical administration, he would have appealed to those to whom the letter is addressed to " arm effectively the secular power in order that, by excluding altogether provisions of this sort, the priesthood of the kingdom may increase in the Lord, and the treasure of the English may be kept for its support."[5] Never-

---

[1] *Hist. Maj.* v. 653.

[2] Bliss, *Calendar*, i. 289.

[3] *E.g.* T. Wykes (*Ann. Monastici*, iv. 104): "Obiit venerabilis Robertus Grosseteste Lincolniae episcopus, in catalogo sanctorum merito connumerandus." See also p. 327.

[4] Letter 131.

[5] Letter 131, p. 444.

theless, although the letter cannot well have been written by Grosseteste himself, it contains much that is in harmony with his known views, and its general purport may have been inspired by him with the object of enlisting public sympathy on behalf of his protests, but he must not be held responsible either for the wording or for the form of the appeal.[1]

An important point, however, which is left out of sight by Matthew Paris in his History, though it is indicated in the documents contained in his *Additamenta*, is that Grosseteste's struggle was, after all, successful, at any rate for a time, inasmuch as it helped to secure from the Pope a recognition of the principle for which he was striving. Just as in 1250 Matthew Paris speaks of his failure and ignores his success, so on this occasion he conveys the impression that no result was achieved. As a matter of fact Innocent IV. addressed in 1252 and 1253 two letters to the English bishops on the subject of the Papal Provisions of English benefices. The first is dated from Perugia on the 23rd of May of the former year, and is a reply to the complaints of the bishops with regard to the amount of money which goes out of the country into the hands of alien beneficiaries, to the detriment of the best interests of the Church and of the nation.[2] The Pope expresses regret at the amount, and mentions that he has frequently been compelled by the force of circumstances to assent to measures of which in a period of less difficulty he

---

[1] M. Charles Jourdain, in an article in the *Académie des Inscriptions et Belles Lettres* for 1868, reprinted in his *Excursions Historiques*, published posthumously in 1888, pp. 147 *sqq.*, disputes the authenticity of certain utterances against the Roman Court attributed to Grosseteste. They are (1) the memorandum read in 1250 in the presence of the Pope and Cardinals; (2) the letter to "Master Innocent" concerning Frederick de Lavagna; (3) the address to the nobles, citizens of London, and commons of the realm (Letter 131); and (4) the deathbed conversations recorded by Matthew Paris. Dr. Felten, who examines the criticisms carefully, pp. 109-112, comes to the conclusion that the authenticity of (1) and (2) is absolutely unshaken by M. Jourdain's attack, but that (3) was not written by Grosseteste, and that (4) is entitled to slender credence. I agree with Dr. Felten's view as to (1), (2), and (3), but only with certain reservations as to (4). See farther on, pp. 320, 321, 323.

[2] Rymer, i. 166; *Hist. Maj.* vi. 210; Rapin's *Acta Regia*.

would not have been able to approve. At the same time he
maintains that, in the majority of cases, the system of Provisions
has been not only a means of recompensing individuals who
deserved well of the Church, but also has been of advantage to
the particular parishes. He ends by suggesting that, in view
of the serious grievances put forward by the English bishops,
they might, by way of compromise, be satisfied with a limitation
of the total amount paid to foreign clerks to a sum of eight
thousand marks a year. As the suggested compromise does not
appear to have given satisfaction, Innocent issued, on the 3rd
of November 1253, about one month after Grosseteste's death, a
bull dealing with the whole subject of the Papal Provisions.[1]
The Burton annalist distinctly states[2] that it was written in
consequence of the Bishop of Lincoln's letter, after the Pope
had read and understood its purport. It is addressed to the
archbishops, bishops, abbots, priors, and other ecclesiastical
authorities of the Church in England, as well as to chapters,
convents, and colleges, and to all patrons, both clerical and lay,
and removes all hindrances and impediments to the free exercise
of the rights of collation, election, presentation, and institution
on the part of those who are thereunto entitled. Grosseteste's
efforts, therefore, were crowned with success, as far as concerned
the recognition of the principle for which he had contended:
but in practice the question remained unsolved, and, indeed,
gave rise to serious difficulties within a few years after that
date. Sewal, Archbishop of York, found it necessary to write
to Pope Alexander IV. in the sense of Grosseteste's letter.[3] In
1266 a bull of Clement IV. specially reserved for Papal nomination all benefices of which the possessors died at Rome; in
1268, or the following year, the abuse was the immediate cause

---

[1] *Ann. Monastici* (Burton), i. 314-
317 ; *Hist. Maj. Additamenta*, vi.
260-264.

[2] P. 314.

[3] *Hist. Maj.* v. 692. It was to
Archbishop Sewal that Adam Marsh
addressed, apparently in 1256, a long
letter or pamphlet, divided into 47
chapters, based largely upon Grosseteste's views, and referring especially
to his sanctity, courage, and perseverance.—*Mon. Francisc.* pp. 438-489,
particularly p. 466.

of the somewhat doubtful Pragmatic Sanction of St. Louis, the charter of the liberties of the Gallican Church; in 1298 Boniface VIII., and subsequently other Popes, reasserted the principle; and, as far as England was affected, it led in the fourteenth century to the passing of the Statute of Provisors.[1]

[1] 25 Edward III. chap. 4.

CHAPTER XV

GROSSETESTE'S bodily health, never strong at any time, showed increasing signs of decay. It will be remembered how in 1232, during a severe illness, he resigned his preferments with the exception of his Lincoln prebends,[1] and how, five years later, he was indebted to John de St. Giles and another for the preservation of his life, after an attempt had been made to poison him.[2] In 1238 he offered, though feeble and infirm in body, to go to preach the gospel to the Saracens if ordered by the Pope and Cardinals to do so.[3] In writing to his Dean and Chapter in 1239,[4] and to the King a few years later,[5] he refers to his weak constitution, and in 1242 he asks Cardinal Otho to explain to Gregory IX. that his infirmities will not permit him to attend the proposed General Council. In 1245, however, Adam Marsh writes that he has reached Lyons in better health than usual. At a later date, especially after his return from his second visit to Lyons in 1250, his increasing weakness aroused the keenest anxiety both of Simon de Montfort[6] and of Adam Marsh. The latter urged him not to overwork himself by combining too intense a devotion to literary pursuits with his multifarious

---

[1] See p. 105, Letter 8.
[2] Page 182.
[3] Letter 49.

[4] Letter 71.
[5] Letter 101.
[6] *Mon. Francisc.* p. 110.

activity in other spheres,[1] and recommended to him two physicians, John de Stokes, who became a member of his household,[2] and Adam de Hekesover.[3] Both his hearing and his eyesight appear to have been affected; the former may be inferred from the remark attributed to Innocent by Matthew Paris,[4] and the latter seems to be mentioned in a letter from Adam Marsh.[5] The pressure of work during the last few years of his life, and the anxiety arising out of the strenuous conflicts in which he was engaged, had taxed his strength to the uttermost. He must have reached the age of seventy-eight when, in the summer of 1253,[6] he was attacked by his last illness at his residence at Buckden, and summoned to his side his friend John de St. Giles, the learned Dominican theologian and physician who had cured him twenty-six years earlier, in order that he might act in the twofold capacity of medical adviser and of spiritual comforter. Matthew Paris devotes several pages to Grosseteste's conversations during that last illness. How far the account given by Matthew Paris is founded upon a correct version of what the Bishop actually said, is a question which cannot be solved authoritatively in the absence of either corroborative or contradictory evidence. Some portions, however, are evidently highly coloured by the St. Albans historian's prepossessions, who, however accurate may be his statement of ascertained facts, may have, on this as on other occasions, built up elaborate discourses on the slender foundation of hearsay evidence.[7] It is certainly curious that some of his alleged denunciations, such as that of the Caursins, are almost identical, alike in thought and in language, with the

---

[1] *Mon. Francisc.* p. 143.

[2] *Ibid.* p. 113.

[3] *Ibid.* p. 137.

[4] See above, p. 313. *Hist. Maj.* v. 372.

[5] *Mon. Francisc.* p. 348: "Profectus sum Tyngehyrst ad dominum Lincolniae multis ex causis valetudinem satis molestam sustinens oculorum." Luard, Introd. to Grosseteste's *Letters*, p. 82, interprets these words to refer to the Bishop's eyesight, and not, as might naturally be supposed, to that of Adam Marsh. This species of *constructio ad sensum*, due to hasty writing, is not uncommon in Adam Marsh's letters.

[6] *Hist. Maj.* v. 400.

[7] *Ibid.* v. 400 *sqq.* Cp. the revised and abbreviated account given in the *Historia Anglorum*, iii. 145.

views expressed with regard to them by Matthew Paris himself
in several passages of his History. The special praise, too,
accorded to the rule of St. Benedict,[1] and the complaint with
regard to a letter addressed by the Pope to the Abbot of St.
Albans, are not likely to have proceeded at that time out of
Grosseteste's mouth, but come naturally from the pen of the
St. Albans monk. The conversations must be received, therefore, with considerable caution, and it must be remembered that
they represent at best a second-hand report in which particular
phrases may have been taken out of their context, and understood in a somewhat different sense from that in which they
were actually employed.[2]

In speaking of the two orders of friars, whom he had so
consistently and so strenuously supported, Grosseteste is stated
to have rebuked them on the ground that, although they had
taken the vows of poverty, and consequently enjoyed greater
freedom of action and speech than those who were shackled
by the possession of riches, on Juvenal's principle that

> " Cantabit vacuus coram latrone viator,"

they did not sufficiently use that freedom for the purpose of
reproving the errors of those in power. " As for you, Friar
John, and the rest of you preachers, I regard you as downright
heretics for not boldly reprobating the sins of the nobles and
unveiling their offences. What, by the way, is heresy ? Give
me a definition." And, as John de St. Giles hesitated for a
reply, the Bishop, referring to the Greek etymology of the
word, said : " Heresy is an opinion chosen by human sense,
contrary to the Holy Scripture, openly taught, and obstinately
defended." He then proceeded to apply that definition to the
failure of the friars to oppose the Papal Provisions, and to the
Pope's own action in regard to them, arguing that to give the
cure of souls to a child or other unfit person might be described

---

[1] *Hist. Maj.* v. 403.

[2] On the respective views of M.

Jourdain and of Dr. Felten see above,
p. 316.

as a prelate's "opinion, chosen by human sense, contrary to
Holy Scripture," which forbids those to be pastors who cannot
keep off the wolves, as well as "openly taught" in characters
bearing the seal and the bull, and "obstinately defended" by
the weapons of suspension and excommunication. As, then, in
the words of St. Gregory, he who does not oppose a manifest
crime is a participator in it, it follows that the Pope himself,
unless he ceases from this course, and the friars, both Minors
and Preachers, unless they show themselves anxious to resist
it, come under the definition of heresy and deserve its punishment. There is, moreover, he is reported to have added, a
decree in existence which says that, for such an offence, namely
heresy, the Pope himself can be called to account. The
reference in the last sentence appears to be to a decree of Pope
Hadrian II. in the Roman Council of 868, cited in the seventh
Act of the Fourth Council of Constantinople held in the
following year, and included in the *Decretum* of Gratian.[1]
Whatever may have been the attitude of the English Dominicans with regard to the Papal Provisions, it is clear from the
correspondence between Adam Marsh and the Provincial
Minister of the Franciscans, that the leading Minorites, at any
rate, in this country shared Grosseteste's view of the controversy, and it is strange, therefore, that he should have included
them in his rebuke, unless it be that he merely meant that
they did not openly give utterance to their feelings on the
subject. His reference to the Pope seems rather to be of the
nature of a hypothetical instance adduced to illustrate a
definition, and the point of the remarks is that moral delin-
quency falls in certain cases into the category of heresy, as well
as error of opinion.

It is quite possible, and indeed probable, that, in his love
for the friars, he warned them against the dangers to which
they were exposed, and that, in his earnest desire for the
removal of all abuses and corruptions in the administration of

---

[1] See Luard's note to *Hist. Maj.* v. 402.

the Church, he repeated, in a different form, the warning he
had addressed in 1250 to the Pope and the assembled cardinals.
It is impossible, however, to read carefully the long discourse
which he is said to have pronounced on the 7th of October [1]
in the presence of some of his clergy, when " worn down with
illness, oppressed with weariness, and uttering his words with
difficulty, and amid sighs and tears," without coming to the
conclusion that, for the reasons already mentioned, more of that
utterance is due to the pen of Matthew Paris than to the lips of
Grosseteste.   All due allowance being made, however, for the
alterations and additions introduced by the chronicler, there still
remains much that must have been uttered by the Bishop, and
much that is in harmony with views previously expressed by him
with regard to the rapacity of those connected with the Roman
Court and the exactions and oppressions to which the Church
was exposed.   The concluding sentences indicate, perhaps, what
was uppermost in Grosseteste's thoughts.   He, whose last great
public act had been to join in securing from the King, on the 3rd
of May in that year, the renewed confirmation of Magna Carta,
and to cause the sentence of excommunication pronounced upon
the violators of the liberties granted by that instrument to be repeated throughout the length and breadth of his vast diocese, was
filled with apprehension lest the liberties thus obtained should
be placed in jeopardy by the combination of Pope and King
against the wishes and against the rights of the united clergy
and laity.   As one who, in the last letter he is known to have
written, expressed his devotion to the head of the Church,
whilst deploring and strenuously attacking the abuses which
he failed to correct, and as one who, whilst opposing the King's
encroachments, nevertheless strove on his deathbed to reconcile
to him his greatest enemy, Simon de Montfort,[2] Grosseteste desired reform and not revolution in the Church, and the advent
of freedom by peaceful means, and not by civil war, in the

<hr>

[1] *Hist. Maj.* v. 402-407.
[2] *Ibid.* v. 415 ; see above, p. 274.

State. It was, therefore, with the deepest anxiety that he looked to the troubled conditions of the times, and to the signs of coming strife. With prophetic insight he is said to have breathed the words : "The Church will not be freed from her Egyptian bondage except at the point of the blood-stained sword. These evils of which I have spoken are but slight as compared with those which will come in a short time, perhaps within three years." Hardly had he uttered those words when his voice faltered and was hushed, and in a few hours that mighty heart had ceased to beat. His prophecy found its fulfilment not indeed within three years, but within a brief period, on the fields of Lewes and of Evesham.

The 9th of October was, in all likelihood, the date of Grosseteste's death.[1] Mediæval legends often afford a clue to the place held by the deceased in the hearts and minds of the nation. Matthew Paris relates that on that night, as was mentioned to him by John de Crackale, the Bishop's confidential clerk and a man who enjoyed the high esteem of all who knew him,[2] it so happened that Fulk Basset, Bishop of London, who was in the neighbourhood of Buckden, though far from any convent, heard as it were the melodious music of a great convent bell resounding from the sky. "On the same night also certain Minorites, who were journeying in haste towards

---

[1] That is the date mentioned by Matthew Paris and those who follow him. The Winchester *Annals* mention the 4th, those of Burton the 7th, and those of Dunstable the 14th of that month. Other dates assigned are the 8th of October and the 8th of November, the latter being obviously a mistake of the Lanercost *Chronicle*. John de Schalby (App. to *Giraldus Cambrensis*, vii. p. 205) mentions the 10th of October. See Dimock's note to that passage, and also Luard's note, p. 83 of the Introduction to the *Letters*, and Dr. Felten, p. 101. Stubbs, in his *Registrum Sacrum Anglicanum*,

adopts the 10th of October as the date. From an ordinance of 1321 respecting the tombs of St. Hugh and of St. Robert, it seems that the anniversary of his death was celebrated in that year on the 8th of October, St. Pelagia. —*Lincoln Cathedral Statutes*, ed. Bradshaw and Wordsworth, i. pp. 335, 337.

[2] John de Crackale was Canon of Lincoln as far back as 1242. Addit. Charter (British Museum) 21, 881. He accompanied Grosseteste to Lyons in 1250 whilst Archdeacon of Bedford. His name frequently occurs in the correspondence both of Grosseteste and of Adam Marsh. See p. 280.

Buckden, where Robert, Bishop of Lincoln, then was,—for he was a comforter and father to the Franciscans and Dominicans,—lost their way in the royal forest of Wauberge, and, while wandering about, heard in the air a sound as of bells, amongst which they clearly distinguished one bell of sweeter note than any they had heard before. When the dawn appeared they met some foresters, of whom, after obtaining directions to enable them to regain the right road, they inquired what meant that solemn peal of bells which they had heard in the direction of Buckden; to which the foresters replied that they had not heard, and did not then hear anything, though the sound still greatly filled the air. Greatly wondering, the brethren made their way to Buckden, and were there told that at the very time of night when they had heard those melodious sounds the Bishop of Lincoln had breathed forth his happy spirit." [1]   Of a different character is the legend mentioned also by Matthew Paris and by later chroniclers, that Innocent IV. wrote to the King of England, asking that Grosseteste's bones should be disinterred and placed outside the church, but that, on the following night, the deceased Bishop of Lincoln appeared to him in a vision, smote him with his pastoral staff, and rebuked his pride. [2]   The Pope is also said to have exclaimed, when he heard of the death of Conrad, King of Sicily, that in him and Grosseteste he had lost his two worst enemies. [3] Those stories are of value in so far as they throw light upon the popular estimation of his character and attitude. There are, however, as has been shown, no reasons whatsoever for believing that he was ever excommunicated by Innocent, and the requests for canonisation addressed to successive Popes make no mention of any such sentence.

Boniface, Archbishop of Canterbury, happened to be at Lincoln on the 7th of October, for purposes connected with the visitation of the province, but had left that city almost

---

[1] *Hist. Maj.* v. 408.　　　[2] *Ibid.* v. 429, 470.
[3] *Ibid.* v. 460.

immediately, and had arrived at Newark.[1] On hearing the news of Grosseteste's death he retraced his steps in order to attend his funeral. Although often opposed by Grosseteste of late years, Boniface was not blind to his great qualities, and must, indeed, have felt that he was indebted to him, when he first came to England, for friendly counsels which might, if followed, have kept him from many errors. Among those present were also Fulk Basset, Bishop of London, who had known Grosseteste in his Wiltshire days,[2] and Walter de Cantelupe, Bishop of Worcester, who had stood by him in many a fight, and who, in days yet to come, was to receive the dying confession of Simon de Montfort at the battle of Evesham. Many abbots and priors were also there, as well as an innumerable concourse of clergy and people.[3] Grosseteste was interred in the upper south transept of the cathedral. His tomb is described by Leland, who saw it, as a goodly one of marble, with an image of brass over it.[4] It shared the fate of many other tombs when, in the middle of the seventeenth century, the Parliamentary forces commanded by the Earl of Manchester inflicted upon the interior of Lincoln Cathedral injuries similar to those which it had suffered at the hands of royalist troops more than four centuries earlier in 1217.[5] In 1782 the coffin was opened, and it was found that with the great Bishop had been buried part of his crosier-head, on which was carved the inscription—

> Per baculi formam
> Praelati discito normam,

and also his seal-ring engraved with his name, and a chalice and paten.[6] Close to him, as the Lancercost *Chronicle* declares, was

---

[1] On Boniface's subsequent dispute with the Dean and Chapter of Lincoln, who should exercise the right of giving away the prebends and revenues of the bishopric *sede vacante*, see p. 295. *Hist. Maj.* v. 412, 413 ; *Ann. Monastici* (Dunstable) iii. 190 ; *Mon. Francisc.* p. 324.

[2] See p. 26.

[3] *Ann. Monast.* (Burton), i. 314.

[4] Leland, *Itinerary*, viii. pt. 2, p. 4.

[5] *Ann. Monast.* (Waverley), ii. 287.

[6] They are described by Pegge, pp. 215-217. What is supposed to be a representation of the slab is given in

buried a few years later, between his grave and the southern wall, his faithful friend Adam Marsh, in order that, as they were lovely and pleasant in their lives, in death they should not be divided.[1] It was found that in his will Grosseteste had bequeathed to the Franciscan library at Oxford the books which he had collected with such assiduous care from various parts of the world.[2]

There is nothing surprising in the fact that, even without formal canonisation, he should have been described almost immediately after his death as a saint. The Tewkesbury *Annals* assert erroneously that the title was actually bestowed upon him by the Pope in 1257,[3] and almost all the chroniclers confer upon him that designation. Roger Bacon constantly speaks of him as Saint Robert, and the rules which he composed for the guidance of the Countess of Lincoln were called the "Reules Seynt Roberd." In the public estimation those who stood forth as the champions of the liberties of the Church and of the people were by an almost unconscious and automatic process added to the catalogue of the saints. It was thus that Simon de Montfort, a few years later, in spite of all the efforts of those in authority, was hailed as the "blessed martyr."[4] In the case of Grosseteste even the royalist chronicler Wykes asserts without hesitation his claim to the title.[5] As early as 1255 Richard, Earl of Cornwall, the King's brother, made a pilgrimage

---

Gough's *Sepulchral Monuments of Great Britain*, vol. i. plate 16, and reproduced in Pegge's *Grosseteste*, p. 114. See also Browne Willis' *Cathedrals* (London, 1742), ii. p. 7. Gough, i. p. 48, quotes from Camden's *Remains* an epitaph which Grosseteste is said to have composed for himself, and another which was written after his death ; but both are of doubtful authenticity.

[1] *Chron. de Lanercost*, p. 58. Adam Marsh, however, died not in 1253, but a few years later, probably in November 1258. — Little's *Grey Friars at Oxford*, p. 138. The boy, St. Hugh of Lincoln, not to be confused with St. Hugh, the Bishop of Lincoln, was also buried near Grosseteste's tomb a few years later. — *Ann. Monast.* (Burton), i. 344.

[2] See p. 86.

[3] *Ann. Monast.* (Tewkesbury), i. 159.

[4] See M. Bémont's *Simon de Montfort*, Introd. pp. 15-19. See above, p. 274.

[5] *Ann. Monast.* (T. Wykes), iv. 103.

to the Bishop's tomb at Lincoln,[1] and miracles are reported by
Matthew Paris,[2] as well as by the Burton and Tewkesbury
annalists, to have occurred there. In 1300 a special guardian
had to be appointed for his tomb under the name of " Custos
Tumbe Santi Roberti," and in 1314 Bishop Dalderby granted a
forty days' indulgence to pilgrims who visited it.[3]

That particular kind of homage, though indicating
Grosseteste's firm hold on the imagination, as well as on the
affections of the English people, was not such as to bring out
the real greatness of his life and character, and would probably
have been out of harmony with the feelings of humility which
animated him. The efforts made to secure his canonisation are,
however, of considerable importance, as the grounds on which
they were attempted are clearly shown. One such effort was
made in 1286, when letters advocating the adoption of that
course were written by John Romanus, Archbishop of York,
and the Bishops of Worcester and St. David's, as well as by
the Abbots and convents of Grimsby, Newhouse, Thornton,
Hagnaby, Osney, St. James, Northampton, Revesby, Peterborough, Louth, and Bardney, and by several prominent laymen.[4]
Similar letters were written in 1288 by Oliver Sutton, Bishop
of Lincoln, and the Dean and Chapter of that cathedral, and
also by the Bishops of Durham and Ely.[5] In 1307 a general
application was made to Clement V. for the purpose by the
Dean and Chapter of Lincoln, who sent one of their number,
Robert de Killingworth, to Rome with that object,[6] and also by

---

[1] *Ann. Monast.* (Burton), i. 344.

[2] *Hist. Maj.* v. 491.

[3] Pegge, pp. 213, 214. *Giraldus
Cambrensis,* Appendix, vii. (ed. Dimock),
p. 206.

[4] *Twelfth Report of the Historical
MSS. Commission* (1891), Appendix
ix. pp. 566, 567. The letter from
Archbishop John Romanus is given in
Raine's *Letters from Northern Registers*
(Roll Series, 1873), p. 87, with the
date 1287.

[5] *Historical MSS. Commission Reports,* l.c.

[6] Register quoted by Pegge, p. 218.
See also *Giraldus Cambrensis,* vii. (ed.
Dimock), Appendix, p. 206, where
John de Schalby states that steps were
repeatedly taken in that sense by the
Dean and Chapter. From Chapter
Acts of the 10th of May 1307, it
appears that Robert de Killingworth,
or Kivelingworth, was allowed his ex-
penses of travel and residence, whilst

the Dean and Chapter of St. Paul's, London,[1] the Abbot and
convent of Osney, King Edward the First, Greenfield, Archbishop of York, and the University of Oxford.[2] The letter
from the Dean and Chapter of St. Paul's states that Grosseteste
" far surpassed all the philosophers of his time, and outstripped
all theologians in divine knowledge and doctrine. His most
famous works remain to testify this to scholars of our day, and
by virtue of his genius, which was wonderfully strengthened by
divine grace, he might say 'I have more understanding than all
my teachers.' But most of all did he excel in humility,
simplicity, and sanctity, so that he passed his life in innocency,
chastity, and purity." Edward I. wrote twice, once himself and
once through the Chancellor. He speaks of the Bishop as " excelling in merits, illustrious for holiness of life, like the morning
star discerned through a gap in the clouds, like a candle not
put under a bushel, but on a candlestick, that all may see the
light." He adds that what he asks for is in accordance with
the views of the English Church, the pontifical testimony, the
recollection of the aged, and in harmony with the wishes of the
clergy, the knighthood, and the people, and that the whole
population of England of both sexes reveres his tradition. The
most interesting testimony, however, is that from the University
of Oxford, which says that he never did anything connected
with the office he held or his pastoral care through fear of any
man, and that he was ready, if need be, to suffer martyrdom for
what he believed to be right. It also speaks of his magnificent
services to the cause of science, and of the admirable character
of his " regency " at Oxford. What was the precise influence
which prevented his canonisation is unknown, though his
attitude of sturdy independence may have contributed to the

---

engaged at Rome in furthering the
canonisation " beati Roberti."—*Lincoln Cathedral Statutes*, ed. Bradshaw
and Wordsworth, i. p. 82.

[1] Wharton's *Anglia Sacra*, ii. p.
343.

[2] Wood's *Antiquities of the University
of Oxford*, i. p. 105 (=249); Prynne,
Collect. pp. 1135-1184 ; Pegge,
Appendix 9, pp. 369, 370; Raine's
Letters from Northern Registers, pp.
182, 183 ; Luard, Introd. p. 84.

result.   Higden, in his *Polychronicon*, attributes it to the
"sharpe pistle" he wrote on the subject of the Papal Provisions.[1]
John de Schalby, Canon of Lincoln, who wrote in or about
1330, declares that he is absolutely ignorant as to the grounds on
which the canonisation has failed to take place.   "The efforts,"
he says, "have not been successful previous to the writing of
the present treatise—for what reason God only knows."[2]

It would be impossible in this place to collect all the lauda-
tory references to Grosseteste contained in the Chronicles of
his own and of succeeding generations, and there is hardly one
of them which fails to bear witness to the reverence in which he
was held.[3]   The special testimony, however, of three of his contemporaries deserves to be accentuated and emphasised.   The first is
contained in the letter written by Adam Marsh to the Minister
of the Franciscans in England shortly after Grosseteste's death,[4]
and in a subsequent letter addressed to Sewal, Archbishop of
York, probably in 1256.[5]   To both passages some reference has
already been made, but it may be added that in both the writer
finds a parallel for the fearless character of Grosseteste in that
of Elijah.   The second consists in Roger Bacon's previously
quoted tribute to the universality of the Bishop's attainments
and the marvellous profundity of his intellect.[6]   The third is to
be found in the pages of Matthew Paris, who had so often been

---

[1] Higden's *Polychronicon*, Trevisa,
etc., ed. Lumby, ii. pp. 240-242.
"Epistolam satis tonantem."

[2] *Giraldus Cambrensis*, vii. (ed.
Dimock), Appendix, p. 206. Wycliffe,
Select English Works, ed. Arnold, iii.
p. 467, with regard to the failure to
secure his canonisation, says : "How
gloriouse a cause he had, ande pleyne
treuthe, and comyne profite of holy
Chirche, and what gloriouse bokis he
wrote, more than any other grete
seintis of his londe, to comyne profite
of all Christendome." Even in the
early part of the seventeenth century his canonisation by the popular

voice had not been forgotten. Michael
Drayton writes in his *Polyolbion*, bk.
xix. p. 91 (London, 1622) :—

As Lincolne to the Saints our Robert Grosteste lent,
A perfect godly man, most learn'd and eloquent,
Than whom no bishop yet walkt in more
upright wayes,
Who durst reproue proud Rome, in her most
prosperous dayes, etc.

[3] Some of them have been collected
by Sir Thomas Pope Blount in his
Censura, London, 1690.

[4] *Mon. Francisc.* p. 325 ; see p.
312.

[5] *Ibid.* pp. 466, 487 ; see p. 317.

[6] See pp. 51 *sqq.*

an adverse critic of the severity of his visitations, whilst approving of his resistance to the King's exactions and to the Pope's Provisions. " He was an open confuter," writes the Benedictine historian,[1] " of both Pope and King, the corrector of monks, the director of priests, the instructor of clerks, the supporter of scholars, a preacher to the people, a persecutor of the incontinent, the unwearied student of the Scriptures, a hammer and despiser of the Romans. At the table of bodily refreshment he was hospitable, eloquent, courteous, pleasant, and affable; at the spiritual table devout, tearful, and contrite. In the episcopal office he was sedulous, dignified, and indefatigable." Here, then, are contemporary testimonies from three writers, each of whom approaches the question from a different point of view: first, from Adam Marsh, a scholar and Franciscan, heart and soul, who, in addition to his interest in the advancement of learning and the necessities of spiritual work, is in agreement with most of Grosseteste's views as to general policy; secondly, from Roger Bacon, a scholar like Adam Marsh, though on different lines and of more penetrating insight, a Franciscan, though without much vocation for that calling, and a royalist, whose hereditary sympathies are opposed to the frame of mind which enables Grosseteste to reckon among his warmest friends Richard Marshall and Simon de Montfort; and, thirdly, from one who, whilst primarily a defender of monastic rights and privileges, is at the same time a patriotic Englishman and a friend of the liberties of the nation. And yet those three, from their various standpoints, are able to concur in their estimate of the value and greatness of Grosseteste's place in the life and thought of his country and of his generation. And the reason, apart from his personal influence, is plain. Each of the forces represented, to a greater or less extent, by those three names received from Grosseteste a most powerful impulse, the effect of which endured long after he had left the scene: the revival of religion, the revival of learning, and the revival of the national

---

[1] *Hist. Maj.* v. 407.

spirit owed to him, in no small degree, their strength, their inspiration, and their support.

It must not be supposed, as might be inferred from a perusal of his letters, all of which are couched in language of deep and often extreme earnestness, that Grosseteste's austere severity of demeanour was never relaxed. In order to realise the truth of Matthew Paris's statement that he was "as a host hospitable, eloquent, courteous, pleasant, and affable," it is necessary to turn rather to the letters of Adam Marsh, which throw light upon the friendliness of his intercourse with all sorts and conditions of men, from members of the King's family, cardinals, prelates, and nobles, to the poorest scholar who needed his assistance and the humblest friar who desired his counsel. The incident of the Countess of Leicester's cook affords an instance of the lighter side of his nature,[1] the Lanercost *Chronicle* mentions the pleasure which the charm and refinement of his hospitality gave to the Earl of Gloucester,[2] and Trivet tells how he found his chief delight in the society of friars of both orders, and in talks with them on scriptural subjects.[3] They were, indeed, kindred spirits, and their interest in scientific studies, and their acquaintance with foreign countries, must have given an additional inducement to his intercourse with them.[4] The pages of Eccleston's narrative of the coming of the Minorites contain several anecdotes concerning him and his relations with the Franciscans both as a teacher and as a friend. At Oxford he encouraged students to think questions out for themselves, and thus stimulated their intellectual faculties. One story told by Eccleston[5] can best be understood when it is remembered that the lecture of that day was not, as a rule, a monologue delivered by a professor *ex cathedra*, but consisted largely of the to-and-fro toss of disputation between the lecturer and the students,[6] with the object of developing their mental alertness.

<hr>

[1] See p. 272.

[2] See p. 7 ; *Chron. de Lanercost*, p. 44.

[3] *Trivet*, ed. Hog, p. 243.

[4] See Brewer's Introd. to the *Mon. Francisc.* p. 45.

[5] *Mon. Francisc.* p. 39.

[6] See Brewer's Introduction, p. 49.

They also made notes, and reproduced them afterwards as a lecture. On one occasion Grosseteste told a promising pupil that "he had not known that the lecture he had given was his own," meaning that as much had been elicited by the remarks and suggestions of the listener as by that which he had previously prepared. He attached, however, great importance to due preparation for lectures.[1] He used to tell the friars that, unless they studied, and were assiduous in the knowledge of the Scriptures, they would be like certain monks who walked in the darkness of ignorance.[2] He told Peter of Tewkesbury[3] that he could not help loving him and members of his brotherhood, though he had sometimes to reprove them.[4] It was their practice to settle in the lowest parts of the suburbs of the towns amid the dregs of the population. Grosseteste used to advise them, on sanitary grounds, not to build their houses too near the water's edge, but at a higher level.[5] He liked to see their friars' robes patched, implying thereby, it would seem, that the vow of poverty was no reason why they should not look neat. Of excessive austerity he did not approve. Three things, he once said to a Dominican, are necessary for temporal salvation, —food, sleep, and good humour.[6] To another friar who was of a very melancholy temperament he suggested, as a penance, that he should drink a cup of the best wine, and, after it had been drunk with great reluctance, said to him : " Dear friar, if you frequently underwent such a penance, you would have a better ordered conscience."[7] Anything that savoured of bribery was utterly abhorrent to him. Soon after his elevation to the See

---

[1] *Mon. Francisc.* p. 66.

[2] *Ibid.* p. 64.   [3] See p. 257.

[4] *Mon. Francisc.* p. 65.

[5] *Ibid.* p. 66.   [6] *Ibid.* p. 64.

[7] *Ibid.* He once expressed the opinion (*ib.* p. 66) that a little pepper gave more flavour to sauce than ginger. In the Countess of Leicester's *Household Roll* for 1265 (Bannatyne Club, 1841) the following spices are named : aniseed, cinnamon, cloves, galingal, ginger, and pepper. It will be remembered that Grosseteste had borrowed her cook probably seventeen years earlier. In the same connection it is curious to note that in the Countess's accounts, April 7, 1265, occurs the following entry : "For spicery, three pounds of pepper, ginger, cinnamon, and galingale, and one pound of cloves ; thirteen pounds of rice ; saffron, thirty-eight pounds ; three frails of figs, and one of raisins for Lent."

of Lincoln, when he was in need of horses, his seneschal came, whilst he was sitting at his books, and told him that two white monks, who presumably hoped for some favour to come, had brought him as a present two splendid palfreys.[1] The Bishop refused to admit the monks or to receive the horses, and said, " Were I to take them, they would drag me down by their tails into the infernal regions." On another occasion (though it is not quite clear whether the story is told of him or of St. Edmund of Canterbury), when friends offered him some precious jewels and entreated him to accept the gift, he replied, " Si prenderem, penderem : between ' prendere ' and ' pendere ' there is only one letter."[2] Other anecdotes repeated by Eccleston also convey an impression of his good-natured common sense.

Grosseteste's fondness for music is mentioned in the English version by Robert Mannyng (Robert de Brunne) of William de Wadington's *Manuel des Péchés*, which has sometimes been wrongly attributed to the Bishop himself :[3]

> " Y shall you tell as I have herd
> Of the bysshop seynt Roberd ;
> His toname is Grosteste,
> Of Lyncolne, so seyth the geste.
> He lovede moche to here the harpe,
> For mans witte it makyth sharpe ;
> Next hys chamber, besyde his study,
> Hys harpers chamber was fast the by.
> Many tymes, by nightes and dayes,
> He hadd solace of notes and layes.
> One askede hem the resun why
> He hadde delyte in mynstrelsy :
> He answerde hym on thys manere
> Why he helde the harpe so dere :
> ' The virtu of the harpe, thurgh style and ryght
> Wyll destrye the fendys myght ;
> And to the cros by gode skeyl
> Ys the harpe lykened weyl.'
> Thirefore, gode men, ye shall lere,

---

[1] On the care taken by the Cistercians in the breeding of horses see *Giraldus Cambrensis, Speculum Ecclesiae,* iv. 130, and Brewer's preface to vol. iv. of his works, p. 24.

[2] *Mon. Francisc.* p. 65 ; Luard's Introd. to the *Letters,* p. 89.

[3] See pp. 39, 40.

> When ye any gleman here,
> To worshepe God at your power,
> And David in the sauter,
> Yn harpe and tabour and symphon glee,
> Worship God in trumpes and sautre :
> Yn cordes, yn organes, and bells ringyng,
> Yn all these worship the hevene King." [1]

Dr. Luard remarks that "probably no one has had a greater influence than Grosseteste upon English thought and English literature for the two centuries which followed his time ; few books will be found that do not contain some quotations from *Lincolniensis, The great clerk Grostest.*" [2] It is worthy of note that both Wycliffe and Tyssington, engaged on opposite sides in the great theological controversies which raged after a period of more than a century after the date of his death, are equally in the habit of appealing to his authority. Wycliffe ranks Grosseteste above Aristotle,[3] and frequently cites his writings in terms of approval.[4] Tyssington says that " to compare Grosseteste with modern doctors is like comparing the sun to the moon, when the latter is eclipsed," [5] and repeatedly quotes the Bishop of Lincoln in favour of his views, and in antagonism to those put forward by Wycliffe with

---

[1] *Handlyng Synne,* by Robert Mannyng de Brunne, has been edited by Furnivall for the Roxburghe Club in 1862. The passage is quoted by Warton, *Hist. of English Poetry,* i. p. 61 ; by Pegge, pp. 362, 363, and most of it by Dr. Luard and Archdeacon Perry.

[2] Luard's Introd. to the *Letters,* p. 1.

[3] Wycliffe, *Trial,* iv. chap. 3. He mentions Democritus, Plato, St. Augustine, and 'Lincolniensis" as being "longe clariores philosophi, et in multis metaphysicis scientiis plus splendentes." See p. 330.

[4] Shirley's pref. to the *Fasciculi Zizaniorum,* p. 49. Mr. G. M. Trevelyan, *England in the Age of Wycliffe,* London, 1899, p. 172, gives the following references : *De Civili Dominio,* ed. Lane-Poole, i. pp. 385-394 ; *De Officio Regis,* p. 85 ; *Select English Works,* ed.

Arnold, iii. pp. 467, 469, 489 ; and *Opus Evangelicum,* i. p. 117. To these may be added the tract entitled *Lincolniensis, Select Works,* iii. 230-232 ; and vol. ii. p. 58 of the *De Civili Dominio,* ed. Loserth, Lane-Poole, and Matthew. See especially chapter 43 of the *De Civili Dominio,* where Wycliffe quotes largely from Grosseteste's "sermon" of 1250 before Innocent IV. John Huss, *De Ecclesia,* chap. 18, also quotes at some length from it. The MSS. which Huss probably used are contained in thirteen volumes in the Royal (formerly the University) Library at Prag, described by Mr. Sheppard, travelling Bachelor of the University of Cambridge, in the Cambridge University Library MS. Oo. vi. 97, § 49.

[5] *Fasciculi Zizaniorum,* p. 135.

regard to the nature and meaning of the Eucharist.[1] The question has been asked, What would Grosseteste's attitude have been towards the Reformation, had he been born during that period of the world's history? The question is one which does not admit of a definite answer, and it is an unprofitable speculation to consider what the views of men who lived in the thirteenth century would have been had they lived in the sixteenth. On the one hand his opposition to the Papal Provisions, his denunciation of the abuses and corruptions connected with the existing system of ecclesiastical administration, and his constant appeals to the authority of the Scriptures as the paramount authority in matters of faith, mark him out as a pioneer and precursor of the movement which led to the Reformation, much in the same way as he may be said to occupy a similar position in regard to the Renaissance. On the other hand, he never wavered in his adherence to the accepted doctrines of the Catholic Church, in his belief in the unity of Christendom, in his recognition of the obedience due to the authority of the Pope, in so far as his commands were in accord with apostolic teaching, or in his conception of the inherent value and dignity of the episcopal office; and, moreover, the resistance he offered to encroachments on the part of the civil power, and the fact that his object in denouncing abuses was to strengthen and not to weaken the Church, suggest a different hypothesis. It is possible that he might have chosen the part of Cranmer, Ridley, and Latimer. It is equally possible that he might have chosen that of Sir Thomas More. It is possible, again, that his great intellect might have conceived and carried into execution a settlement other than that which was actually effected. It is fruitless to attempt the solution of such a problem: it is a mystery, not perhaps unknowable, but which to us must remain unknown. One thing alone is certain: in the language in which the University of Oxford spoke of

---

[1] *Fasciculi Zizaniorum*, pp. 152, 161, 162, 166, 175.

him after his death, he would have been ready, if need be, to suffer martyrdom for what he believed to be right.

Grosseteste, then, may be regarded in a threefold aspect: first, as a reformer who sought to reform the Church from within and not from without, by the removal of existing abuses, by the encouragement he gave to the great religious revival of the early part of the thirteenth century, and by the example of unflinching fearlessness and rectitude which he set in his performance of the episcopal office; secondly, as the teacher who guided the rising fortunes of the University of Oxford, gave a powerful impulse to almost every department of intellectual activity, revived the study of neglected languages, and grasped the central idea of the unity of knowledge, with which he was the first to inspire the encyclopædic writers and thinkers of that century; and, thirdly, as the statesman who, applying to new conditions the policy associated with the name of Stephen Langton, endeavoured to combine into one effort the struggle of the clergy for the liberties of the Church with the struggle of the laity for the liberties of the nation, imbued Simon de Montfort with principles of " truth and justice " which went far beyond the mere maintenance of the privileges of his own order, and at the same time, by his effort to reconcile him with his sovereign and by the whole tenour of his actions, showed that, had he lived a few years longer, his influence would have been directed to the task of achieving by peaceful means the constitutional advance brought about by those who, taking the sword, perished by the sword. The services rendered by Grosseteste in each of those capacities, taken singly, are such as to entitle him to lasting gratitude; taken in conjunction, they exhibit the true greatness of his life and work, and render his name imperishable.

Additional Note to pages 5 and 6.—Canon Raven, as an additional argument in favour of his hypothesis that Grosseteste may in his youth have been brought in contact with John of Oxford, Bishop of Norwich, refers to the incident described in Lord Campbell's *Lives of the Chief Justices* on the authority of Ralph de Diceto (i. p. 435, ed. Stubbs, *sub anno* 1179) and others, as indicating that the experience gained by that prelate as to the objections which might be urged against the tenure of secular offices by ecclesiastics may have been subsequently imparted by him to Grosseteste, and have had some influence upon the line of action he adopted in later years. See Chapter VIII.——Davy, in his MS. notes, transcribes all the older inscriptions in the church and churchyard of Stradbroke, but they throw no light on the subject of this biography. Canon Raven is of opinion that certain stones of the coffin-lid order, devoid of inscription, are coeval with Grosseteste. There is a faint possibility that the contents, if unearthed, might convey some information bearing upon his relatives. However, *requiescant in pace.*

INDEX

[This Index is not intended to include either the names of the authorities, or the
titles of the works cited in the text and in the notes. In exceptional cases,
however, references to the former are inserted ; for example, under the head
of Matthew Paris mention is made of the pages on which his credibility is
discussed, but not of the numerous passages in which his writings are
quoted or otherwise used.]

THE END